An Isla

SAM SELVON was born in Trinidad, where he completed his first novel, *A Brighter Sun*, which brought him instant recognition. Later he moved to UK, where he spent more than twenty years and wrote most of his major works. He is widely recognized as one of the major Caribbean writers to have emerged in the post-War era and has been awarded the Guggenheim fellowship. He lives in Calgary, Alberta.

Other Books By Sam Selvon

A BRIGHTER SUN
THOSE WHO EAT THE CASCADURA (TSAR Book)
WAYS OF SUNLIGHT
TURN AGAIN TIGER
I HEAR THUNDER
THE HOUSING LARK
THE PLAINS OF CARONI
THE LONELY LONDONERS (TSAR Book, Canada)
MOSES ASCENDING

An Island Is a World

Sam Selvon

TSAR

Toronto

1993

The publishers acknowledge generous assistance
from the Ontario Arts Council and the Canada Council.

TSAR Publications
P.O. Box 6996, Station A
Toronto, Ontario
M5W 1X7 Canada

First published in 1955 by Allan Wingate (UK).

Canadian Cataloguing in Publication Data

Selvon, Samuel
    An island is a world

ISBN 0-920661-34-3

I. Title.

PS8587.E44717 1993   C813'.54   C93-094971-4
PR9199.3.S4517 1993

cover art: Natasha Ksonzek
author photograph courtesy *Calgary Herald*

Printed and bound in Canada

Introduction

... my most ambitious novel in scope and theme, which does not
mean to say the object was accomplished. It falls short, but of all
the books I've ever written it is the only one in which I set out
consciously to express or try out some of my beliefs ...

Sam Selvon, in a personal communication

An Island Is a World is Sam Selvon's second novel. It was first
published in 1955. It was not reviewed enthusiastically, and it
has received little critical attention over the years. It is not
taught at secondary schools or at the University. It is almost
unknown among ordinary readers, either in Trinidad where the
author was born, or in other parts of the West Indies, or
anywhere else in the world. It has never been reprinted.

But this is the Selvon novel that lies behind all the other
Selvon novels; the one that draws most directly and identifiably
upon the life of the author and the lives of people he knew in
the 1930s and 1940s, so much so that it is tempting to make the
mistake of calling it autobiographical. The issues it agonises over
are the issues that are dramatised in all his other fictions, and
they are issues that are more urgent today than they were in
1955. Finally, *An Island Is a World* is the novel in which we
encounter most fully, the philosophical Selvon of the poetry and
of the early journalism recently collected in *Foreday Morning:
Selected Prose 1946-1986* (1989). If its discussions of social issues
seem relevant nearly forty years after the book first appeared,
it is because the perspective of the philosophical Selvon pene-
trates the forms to examine the sources of social and political
problems. If there is tragedy "behind the ballad and the
episode," and a brooding seriousness "under the kiff-kiff laughter" of the later work, it is because the submerged but not erased
Selvon of *An Island Is a World* is there giving muscle to the comedy.

Although *An Island Is a World* was not generally appreciated, its
troubled main character did attract the attention of those who

v

noticed the book. An English reviewer ignored the Prologue and the closing pages of the novel and patronisingly declared that Selvon's central figure is "a vaguely disturbed, spoilt, talented young man at odds with life till he finds the right girl." (*Spectator*, April 15, 1955.) A West Indian, G A Holder, writing in *Bim* (Vol 6, No 23) picked out Foster as a man who is "at once fascinated and frightened by the depths and uncertainties of life." And in his BBC *Caribbean Voices* broadcast, V S Naipaul was quick to recognise that Foster is "a symptom of the intellectual malaise that is eating away at Trinidad and the rest of the West Indies."

The main character of *An Island Is a World* is introduced in the Prologue as a man who wakes up each morning with the world spinning in his brain. Sometimes he is big, the globe is small, and he can reach out and shatter it with his fist. More often, the globe is huge, his island is a dot, and he is lying on the dot, transmitting thoughts from his random brain out into the immensity, "like how RKO introduce their films with a radio station broadcasting into space." The original intention of this advertisment is reversed in Selvon's novel. Foster chafes at his inability to give coherence to the thoughts that fly off in different directions from his brain. The broken lines in the RKO logo flow endlessly into a void signifying lack of communication. Over the course of the novel, the phrase "the spinning world" is used again and again, and it takes on for the reader some of the numbing connotations that it has for Foster: the things that confuse his mind and paralyse his will; all the activity going on outside of and beyond himself; any order in which he does not have a place; his own aimless movement; the whirring in his brain; and a sense of things going round and round in repeating cycles.

On the surface, Foster is different from Tiger, the Indian peasant hero of *A Brighter Sun* (1952), and Moses, the Afro-Trinidadian centre of consciousness in *The Lonely Londoners* (1956). Yet each of them has a capacity for wonder, a longing for clarity, and a penchant for asking awkward and literal questions. Each of them takes on the burden of consciousness and attempts to think originally (however homespun the terms) about what it is to be a person in the world, what it is that people live for, and what principle, creed, or belief should give direction to a life. In *A Brighter Sun* (1952) and *The Lonely Londoners* (1956) these philosophical matters are contained within the engrossing life stories of the main characters, and are worked in as parts of a convincingly realised imaginative construct, a vividly rendered society in which there are other interesting and distracting phenomena. In *An Island Is a World* the philosophical substance dominates the character of the characters. It doesn't only go into the conception of the characters, it affects or determines the way they are disposed over the stretch of the novel. We find in addition that the division of the book into three parts, its language, and its devices are all determined by the author's aim "to express or try out some of my beliefs."

The great changes in the world and in Trinidad society after the War of 1939-1945 occasioned much soul-searching and a desperate feelng about "the modern condition." Some of this is reflected in the differences between *An Island Is a World* and the work that preceded it. Selvon's first novel, *A Brighter Sun,* was essentially the story of Tiger, a young peasant awakening to the wider society beyond the confines of his village, and becoming conscious of the immensity of the Universe in which human beings find themselves. But he is too solidly based in a defined community to be described as placeless, and too involved in the tangible social process of becoming an adult and responsible member to be confusing his brain with the metaphysics behind or above it all. In the second novel, the setting is no longer sugar-cane and market-gardening country, and the previous book's community of Indian characters, intimate with the land and bound to it by their work in the fields, is succeeded by urban and semi-urban denizens whose outlook, attitudes, and lifestyle indicate a considerable creolisation the most obvious aspect of which is an adoption of the lifestyle and attitudes of the more urbanised Africans. (In an early episode, for example, we notice a husband and wife of Indian origin about to have a roti-less breakfast of salted cod and avocado with bread; and later, a newly married Indian woman who has spent her life in the city expects her brother-in-law to agree with her that it would be a backward step to set up house in an expanding suburban development just a few miles from Port of Spain: " 'Boy, Foster,' she said, 'your brother wants me to go and live in the bush. All my friends living in Port of Spain, I don't believe I can live anywhere else.' ")
    The tragic alternative to this form of mimicry is given

expression in the later pages of the novel when a shipload of Indians leave the island for Mother India. They are observed by Andrews, and Foster (whose Indianness is now mentioned in the novel for the first time). Foster understands their anxiety to have something to belong to, and he manages to see the old departing Indians as more fortunate than island-born Indians like himself:

> Foster looked about him, a strange emotion in his heart. He was one of them, and yet he couldn't feel the way they did, nor share in the kinship they knew. They were going back home. They had a home. It was far away, but they hadn't forgotten. When they had come to Trinidad they kept some of India hidden in their hearts. They had tried to live in Trinidad as they had lived in India, with their own customs and religion, shutting out the influences of the West. They had built their temples and taught their children the language of the motherland. They had something to return to, they had a country.
>
> He had nothing. He had been brought up as a Trinidadian—a member of a cosmopolitan community who recognised no creed or race, a creature born of all the races in the world, in a small island that no one knew anything about. (211)

This capacious novel wants to be about everything: the movement from which the quotation comes makes a necessary distinction between Indians who were born in India, and their island-born descendants; the last paragraph is a description of a condition that forms the basis of Selvon's later theory of the unique constitution of the Trinidadian person. But the main reason for citing the passage here is to emphasise the differences between the stability of the characters in *A Brighter Sun* and the lack of a sense of belonging of characters in the novel of 1955.

So, while the characters in the first novel have a sustaining relationship with their natural environment, the key figures in *An Island Is a World* have no ties that bind them: no sense of belonging to a community, no strong commitment to persons, no fixed place of abode, and no relationship with the work they do. This is exhibited in the lives of the two main groups of characters introduced in Part I of the novel. The first group consists of Johnny, a post-indentureship immigrant from India, who lives with his wife Mary and their two island-born daughters in the city of Port of Spain. His workshop is wedged between a rumshop and a cinema in a poor and slummy part of the city, and Johnny, tagged by the author as "an Indian, a jeweller and a drunkard," has more appetite for drinking rum than for practising his craft. The girls are "modern" young women who have no intention of being as deprived of a life as their mother has been. Jennifer "would go with any sort of man, just to live in New York or London, and see snow and travel in an underground train." The older daughter Rena is a law unto herself, making the rounds of the dance halls and the good time places, and ending up living with an American in Venezuela.

The same restlessness or instability is to be seen in the novel's second group of characters who live in San Fernando, in the South of the island. Rufus upbraids his younger brother Foster who hasn't had a steady job for more than two years and who wanders around from here to there as if he can't make up his mind about anything. Rufus himself has made up his mind to go to Port of Spain to work on the American base, and he assures Foster that when he gets the chance he will leave for America (41). Selvon's plot links the two unrelated groups by a marriage made necessary after a casual affair in the city between Rufus and the jeweller's party-loving daughter. But the meeting with the jeweller's family only makes for a pause in a movement that takes the driven Rufus to America, and, two years later, lands his drifting brother in London. The brothers have no contact with each other for five years, but Selvon organises Part II of the novel to plot the parallel courses that lead to their return to the island at almost exactly the same time, Rufus to divorce Rena and forsake Trinidad forever, Foster to stay in Trinidad and marry Rena's sister Jennifer.

The relationship between Rufus and Foster is based upon Selvon's relationship with his brother Dennis who died in 1978, and who had once taken the same backdoor route to America that we see Selvon giving to Rufus in the novel. But Selvon alters the facts to suit a fiction designed to discover and test ways of dealing with the centrifugal forces of an unstable world. In a discussion with Andrews, Foster notices the lethal peacefulness of the household of Regald and Muriel, pretends to be attracted to it, but takes the view that "marriage is a resigned state of life" (61). Nevertheless, Selvon uses Foster and his brother to examine the possibility of love as a solace in a world without solace or centre. In London, Foster falls desperately in love with an Englishwoman "because it seemed to him then that there was little else in the world and he wanted to make a big thing of it" (132). This love dies down. For Rufus, on the other hand, love is a viable solution: it gives meaning and purpose to his life. He must return to the island to effect a divorce from Rena, but his mind is fixed upon Sylvia and the child she is bearing. All the way to Trinidad, "it was as if the ship were travelling backwards." After the divorce, and in spite of having been refused a visa to re-enter the United States, Rufus packs his suitcase, passes through Venezuela, and enters Mexico: "He had been through a lot, and whatever the future held he would go through with it together with Sylvia. There was to be no more looking back, no regrets" (201). Rufus can be imagined to be living happily ever after. Foster is too complicated to settle so early and so easily. The first complication comes from Foster's resemblance to a living person, his author.

Like Selvon, Foster grew up in San Fernando, and like Selvon who served as a wireless operator in the Royal Naval Reserve between 1940 and 1945, Foster serves in the British navy. After demobilisation, Foster works for a while in the city of Port of Spain and then emigrates to England, a course the author himself followed. From London, Foster writes to his friend Andrews that he is enmeshed in the struggle to find himself (105). Towards the end of his two-year stay, his plaint is formulated thus: "If only there were some creed to hold on to, some culture, some doctrine that offered hope, something worth dying for" (152). Shortly before his disillusioned return to Trinidad, he tells his lover, Julia, that he had been hoping to find in England "a way of living that has a purpose" and "something to offer hope for the future" (154).

A fictional character is not a living person. But there are indeed intimate connections between the author and this character who is searching for something to believe in. It comes as no surprise that Foster is writing in his spare time. Since the novel was deliberately not projected as a portrait of a young artist trying to write his first book, Foster's efforts are not presented directly or at length. They are referred to from time to time by his friend Andrews who is watching his progress. His sister Muriel talks to him about his bad habit: "When are you going to look for a job? . . . You only idling your time away writing." The character himself confides to his friend that he is now trying his hand at verse (69). And at the end of the novel, the priest, Father Hope, suggests that the peaceful valley in which the Church has been built is just the place for Foster to finish the book he is writing.

These references lose some of their casual character when they are read in conjunction with an intense movement in Part II that deals with the creative process (128-130). In these pages are described the efforts of a young writer to find a beginning, his struggle to reconcile the act of writing with the "the actuality of life, the exact moments of existence," and his determination to capture the moment live:

> "This will never do," he told himself time and time again, and hurried off to write down a few thoughts. "I shall call my work 'Ha-Ha,' " he said, "or 'Skiff-skiff' or 'Hello How Are You This Morning,' " and he would sprawl over the typewriter with all his life pressing down on him, wondering which of the brilliant beginnings to use. Oh, he had the shape of it in his mind, there was no doubt about that. It would be a slow, painstaking effort, hesitation and memory, each sentence capable of standing on its own feet away from the others. The greatest compliment would be to hear someone say, "Ah, that's life for you." (130)

(It is relevant to notice that some of the ideas in this passage recur in the essay "Little Drops of Water" in *Bim* (XI, 44, 1967) where Selvon is speaking directly.)

The motif of the artist's attempt to give shape and coherence to the life pressing down on him has strong autobiographical backing. It is introduced, however, as part of Selvon's portrayal of Foster as a character enmeshed in the struggle to find himself. As the argument develops we can make out that Foster is interested in a number of spheres: the world of his immediate social relations; the larger world understood in the phrase the brotherhood of men and nations; the inner world of the individual; and the nebulous universe whose eternity and space make man's life seem so slight. These four spheres are not separate from one another, and Foster does not want them to be. He is looking for nothing less than a meaning that will reconcile all these worlds, and integrate all the levels of his existence. He knows instinctively that the personal and metaphysical questions cannot be left to be sorted out at one's convenience after the social and political issues are resolved. This makes life difficult for the reader who keeps being shifted from one kind of consideration to another without warning. But of one thing we can be sure: from the care with which Selvon lays out Foster's quest for meaning it is more than apparent that *An Island Is a World* is not a modernist cry of despair. As we shall see, it is less a response to the decline of the West than an anguished New World exploration of the task of giving things a name.

"Why bother with whys and wherefores? You could spend the rest of your life trying to reason out why the world is as it is, and be no nearer a conclusion at the end. I thought we were both agreed on that? Are you going on in this frustrative manner? Are you nearer the truth now?" (213) Andrews's exasperation in no way deters Foster from his meanderings. After two years in England, and only dusty answers for soul, he returns to the island where he continues to drift and search.

In Part III, the novel's argument about belief is conducted towards a climax. Father Hope has always been impressed by the ardour of Foster's search for meaning, and now that he is about to withdraw he invites the younger man to take over the Church and live among the people of the Caura Valley: "You are pursuing truth. You want a faith, a hope, a destination that will make your life worthwhile. Here in this valley you could live and learn and get to understand the things you believe in" (218). At first Foster merely demurs. Then he positively resists. For, as Father Hope's follow-up remark indicates, what is really at issue is whether a secular belief can take the place of belief in God: "No man formulates a theory of life to which he could adhere all the time. But in God you have a lasting belief. A remote Goodness, an almost forlorn hope that there's purpose behind it all" (218). The damaging concession in the suspect last sentence is in keeping with an earlier argument by the unorthodox priest: "If even religion proves imperfect, you will find it the least imperfect of all beliefs in the world, and the only one from which you could get any lasting consolation" (76). As far as Foster is concerned, however, these concessions weaken the case. He is more logocentric than the priest. He wants a belief that can produce human happiness. He wants a belief that is absolute, perfect and everlasting. He wants a belief that can answer unanswerable questions.

Nothing the priest says can divert Foster from wondering about the fact of death, and what happens to all the people in the world who have died ("quaffing milk and honey or shoving coal?"). Neither is he moved by Father Hope's Jesuitical reproach that the young man wants to give his best years to worldly pursuits and turn to God only when he has nothing more to offer but "creaking joints and crinkled skin, and a mind tired with evanescent joys and fearful of the thought of death." According to Foster, people were born "to be happy and to make the most of these miserly years on earth," and a man who loves "the heartbeat, the pulse, the kiss, wine and the nearness of women" should not be told to give this up just because he wants to save his skin. But because human beings are not given a long enough life-span to work out their beliefs, they play safe towards the end of the normal span and take up religion. It is by default, then, that man opts for God: "God is forced upon man, making mock of all his efforts to attain happiness."

So Foster doesn't allow the priest's offer to seduce him. He resists the priest because taking over the Church will commit him to religious belief and put an end to his search for other possible beliefs; he is reluctant to embrace religious belief because religious belief privileges spirit above flesh when both should be served equally: "To hell with Father Hope. It was all well and good to talk about the spirit, but one had a body of flesh and bone to contend with too. And the world, spinning off there in space, the indifferent world, the millions of people utterly unconcerned." To escape the trap that Father Hope has prepared for him, an anguished Foster proposes marriage to Jenny, and pleads with her not to make him want anything but her and their happiness together. (226) The novel ends with this marriage still to take place. But that is not all.

Father Hope dies. And the manner of the death of this supposedly unshakeable man disturbs Foster profoundly. Foster does not want to believe that Father Hope has jumped off the edge of a cliff, and he tries to fool himself and others. But the evidence of suicide is strong. Whether Father Hope has taken his own life because he cannot face being arrested, or because he cannot accept being let off by the English detective who has by chance discovered him in the retreat of the Caura Valley so many years after the alleged killing makes no difference to Foster. Father Hope had said: "I accept my fate, because I have something to hold on to, a belief that I am close to God." Father Hope had lost faith. Although Foster was not ready to believe in what Father Hope believed, the existence of someone holding an absolute belief was encouraging. The novel ends with a despondent Foster looking through the windscreen wipers towards the spinning world in the rain and distance:

> Looking through the windscreen, he tried to shake off the despondency he felt. He could see the world spinning ahead of them. It was as if they were going towards it, but it kept its distance, they were never nearer. Somehow it didn't seem to matter anymore. (237)

So the Prologue that introduces Foster is more an epilogue than a prologue. In it, the marriage has taken place, domesticity has set in, and Foster's mind is still not settled. The transforming logos has not been found. The routine of having breakfast and getting dressed for work, and the sorrowful fellowship of other people going through the same motions help to insulate Foster from his fears. Unlike Naipaul's Mr Biswas, he gains confidence, shares in the confidence of the unthinking when he goes out into the world. But Foster is still prey to his awkward thoughts. He still finds it necessary to school himself to accept the accepted, and he continues to live with the unrelieved sense of a random universe in which human affairs have no authoritative or authorising centre:

> He went out to the main road, and he caught a bus going to Port of Spain. He sat down, feeling sorry for all the passengers. It was a humble sorrow, like if he had said, "We are all in the same boat, I am sorry."
> On the journey he diagnosed this sorrow: the result of too much aimlessness and hopelessness (as if I didn't know).
> And in the bus he felt the old fear coming on him, the fear of nothing, the fear of man and crossword puzzles and the cow jumping over the moon and the bus fare is six cents

. . .
    To hell with it, he thought, to hell with it. Because: so
what? Everyone in this bus is more or less happy, thinking
about small pasts and presents and futures. It is the way
of life (as if I didn't know). Alternatively, oblivion. (4)

We can read the novel straightforwardly as being about a
world-weary hero unable to find meaning in the world. But this
might make *An Island Is a World* sound like grist to be theorised
into a modernist or post-modernist text by people who don't read
literature but like to re-write it. It is necessary therefore to make
a timely discrimination about the nature of West Indian societies, and West Indian cultural practice.

The similarities are obvious enough between modern Euro-
American deconstruction and the process of decolonisation evi-
dent both in the themes of West Indian literature, and in its
attitude to the language of the coloniser. But it is worth pointing
out that a great deal of the energy and creativity of West Indian
societies comes from the fact that they are still logocentric. They
still believe in the existence of the Absolute and the Eternal. At
the popular level this commitment manifests itself in the rich
animism of the region's cultural and religious practices. West
Indian artists and intellectuals often regret a weakening of this
capacity in themselves but they still celebrate it in their work.
Unlike the majority of intellectuals in Europe and America, they
are at one with ordinary people in believing in the possibility of
belief. The dismantling or deconstruction that is sometimes
proposed in West Indian thought and writing is not a denial of
the possibility and desirability of belief. It is, rather, an attempt
to replace what has been colonially imposed by something less
authoritarian and inflexible than the European monolith, but
something authoritative because it has evolved or has been
arrived at from within.

The attempt to find meaning and truth in this novel is an
affirmation of the author's belief in their existence, and in the
possibility of reconciling seeming contraries. The ground covered
during the search includes politics, education, music, writing,
art and art criticism, the need to belong, love, philosophy,
religion, and the nature of thinking itself. The discourse is

dialectical—one point of view being placed beside or against another with the implication that no one opinion is the right one. There is a lot of talking: lengthy face-to-face discussions in Parts I and III between the unorthodox priest, Father Hope, the questioning Foster, and the painter Andrews; and in Part II, letters passing between Andrews and Foster during the latter's two-year sojourn in England.

A sympathetic early reviewer (G A Holder, referred to above) found that *An Island Is a World* did not quite grip, and suggested that this was because "Selvon gets under the skulls but not quite into the skins of his characters, as he does in *A Brighter Sun*: he is reporting rather than creating. He adopts the detached attitude which, though it can be very effective, is yet difficult to handle." Compared with *A Brighter Sun*, the new novel seemed to be less natural, its characters not as spontaneous, its descriptive language more flat and restrictive, its letters and conversations too bookish, and its philosophical discussions too removed from the problems of ordinary living.

The publication in 1956 of Selvon's third book did not help the fortunes of *An Island Is a World*. The disturbing comedy and the memorable episodes of *The Lonely Londoners* had instant appeal. Its truimphant experimentation with dialect made it exciting, and its large cast of outrageous, ebullient, and resourceful creatures ("smart men," "saga boys" and "samfie artists"), shape-shifters who remain obstinately themselves as they extract a precarious living from a hostile environment made it entertaining as well as sociologically topical. There is comedy in *An Island Is a World*: the pretentious mimicry of law graduate Ranjit (22-26); the botched attempt to manufacture evidence to obtain a divorce (192-199); and the comic character Johnny working out a scheme to harness gravity, and carrying out the first insure-and-burn (insuranburn) scam in West Indian literature. But it cannot compete with the brew in *The Lonely Londoners* that came to be regarded as "typical Selvon." *An Island Is a World*, which had already failed to be like *A Brighter Sun* would soon be confirmed as not being "typical Selvon."

But if *An Island Is a World* did not have the very different attractions of the works that preceded and followed it, it was recognised at once as an ambitious and complex attempt at something different. The germ of the novel, a piece published in *Bim* in 1952, first appeared, fittingly, under the title "Talk," which coincides almost word for word with pp. 62-65 of the novel. It provides a sample of the characteristic mode of the novel, it expresses the character's existential angst, and it puts in place the metaphysical dimension of *An Island Is a World*. The subject of this conversation is fear of life:

"It's everything and nothing. It's sun shining, man eating, wind blowing, the sound of gurgling water. It's an ant and a giant, and a telephone conversation and the cow that jumped over the moon. It's poetry and music and the smell of dirty drains and the flight of birds over the sea." [first speaker]
"And all these things, when you think of them, make you afraid?" [second speaker]
"All these things, and all manner of things, action and inaction, animation and inanimation, the spin of the world on its axis, a woman's underwear, saxophones and gramophones, and how some words sound, like macabre slip gristle crispy." (*Bim* Vol IV No 15, 1952 p.153).

In the *Bim* version, the second speaker is Foster, and the first speaker is Andrews. Andrews is suffering from fear of life. In the finished novel, however, Selvon has worked out what he wants his characters to do and be. He switches things around, makes Foster suffer from fear of life, and develops Andrews as a painter and art education officer. (Andrews is portrayed as a person of African origin, but it is interesting to note that the prototype is a Trinidadian painter and friend of Selvon, the late M P Alladin, a man of Indian origin—an indication of Selvon's interest in projecting the Trinidadian person as someone not defined by race or colour.) The characters still think alike on social questions and are on intimate terms, but Selvon makes Andrews into the stable figure of an artist whose commitment to the business of ordinary living draws him into politics. This is in contrast to Foster who is in ruthless pursuit of an absolute. It is necessary to digress a little at this point, and notice in passing that Andrews's passion and Selvon's sense of the speaking voice allow us to glimpse, in Andrews's reproof of his friend's course, the stirring of an author who is to fabricate the language of *The Lonely Londoners*:

You have hauled your tail off "to see the world" and left

Marleen with child, depending on your good friend Andrews to see that all goes well with her. You are one son of a bitch, you know. Do you think you could just push your head in the clouds (and murky clouds at that, God knows) and leave your relationships and responsibilities to take care of themselves?

Do you think, when Marleen's mother threw her tail out when she discovered she was having a child, that Marleen could have said, Art is long life is fleeting?

And you think it was easy for me to explain to my mother and sister, that I want them to take she in because I promise you to take care of she? You think while my mother was 'busing me for interfering in people business, that I had time to think of the universal kiss? You think when my mother say: "I don't want to have anything to do with this business," that I could have said, "Adopt a philosophical attitude to the problem, mother?" (112)

The relationship between Andrews and Foster is the most prominent thread in a web of relationships connecting Foster at the centre to a number of characters who are skilfully introduced by the end of Part I. All but one of these relationships have an autobiographical basis, and with the exception of Father Hope, it is possible to identify the persons in real life from whom the fictional characters are derived. What stands out if we do the necessary research is the degree of remodelling that has taken place, and the distancing of the fictional characters from their prototypes—the clearest of indications that for Selvon, the patterning was crucial: Foster and these characters seem to make up one self or consciousness. It is easier for us at this stage to think of them as different aspects of Foster.

The initial contrast between Rufus's positiveness and Foster's hesitancy, between Rufus's pursuit of love and achievement and Foster's entanglement in thought and speculation does not prevent us from recognising the parallels between the two brothers' lives, and projecting Rufus as a personification of one aspect of Foster. The same pattern exists in Foster's shadow relationships with the family of the Port of Spain jeweller (modelled upon but radically different from the relatives of another Trinidadian novelist): the young girl Jennifer (bewildered, held in, and full of yearning) is an echo of Foster and a portent of the spreading malaise; her father Johnny (a character like Sookdeo in *A Brighter Sun*) is a figure of the dereliction Foster senses and wishes to beat off. Johnny's lifelong ambition to harness gravity is a comic version of Foster's attempt to lead the facts of existence into manageable order. The sense of the characters being aspects of a single self is even stronger in Foster's relationships with Andrews, and with Father Hope. Father Hope and Foster are at one on the need for an Absolute belief, but argue, as we have seen, over which belief is the best. Andrews and Foster are best friends, but they take two different attitudes to being in the world: Selvon uses Andrews to try out a practice of commitment to the business of life, and involvement in "the immediate problems of existence in this colony."

It is true that there are differences on the surface between *An Island Is a World* and Selvon's better-known writings. It is true that in Selvon's abstract configuration, the characters participate in a dialogue of a Self with its selves, the various verbal exchanges, the debates and discussions being part of an elaborate scheme to create something new and satisfying out of the play of alternatives and opposites. But this does not mean that Selvon's novel is not responsive to the great public issues of its time. On the contrary, it is more responsive than most because it deals with those issues out of a wider and deeper perspective than that of the moment.

This neglected novel can be read as anticipating the continued peripheralisation or the reperipheralisation of colonies that became new nations in the two decades after the Second World War. It raises issues specific to its time, but its sense of underlying causes helps us to understand how these countries pursued "progress" without cultivating self-knowledge and self-respect; how the developmental paths they followed in this fashion after independence led them to act as if they possessed nothing and were nothing in the wide wide world; and how they came to surrender national sovereignty, and many of the personal freedoms and choices of their powerless citizens to adjustment programs dictated by the World economic order. It helps us to understand, not because it has groundings in economics or in political science, but because it is a philosophical novel asking radical questions about the foundations upon which individual lives are built and societies constructed.

xix

An Island Is a World was written in the early 1950s, a time when the imminent West Indian Federation held out an inspiring prospect to artists, intellectuals, and other thinking people in the region that the cultural nationalism they felt uniting them was about to be recognised and nourished by a new political disposition; and the title, *An Island Is a World*, might suggest that the novel was in tune with the optimism of the 1950s. But it wasn't. The book interrogates the whole political process. Like Walcott's poem "Allegre" it saw the beauty and the danger of an elation that could overlook the basic truth that for the individual as for the nation, "to find the true self is still arduous." It pointed to a public discourse that relegated doubts, objections and awkward questions to the closet. Remarkably for a West Indian novel of the 1950s, it warned of the heresy of seeking first the political kingdom. At its centre is the character Foster through whose desperate personal quest Selvon explores not the separation of the private and personal from the public and social, but the necessity for the one to be involved in the other.

The characters are aware of the coming thing, and it is their hearts' desire to see the islands united into a West Indian nation. But Selvon does not let them get carried away by the public practices and professings in the air. They are only too aware of differences and difficulties: "Over here things are moving slowly as usual. Federation, the move to put us on the map, is treated with suspicion and mistrust: each island is waiting to see what the other does, and no one does anything." (147) In this letter to his friend Foster, the painter Andrews goes on to give one of the accounts of how the Federal movement of the 1950s was activated. The colonies clamoured one by one for self-government, and the British Government countered by proposing that they should form a Federation. Though the islands had not been too sure what self-government entailed, the move was felt to be a move in the right direction. But the British proposal threw them into confusion: "What shall we do, what is federation, what is this all about, what have we put ourselves into?" (147) The Federation was inaugurated with drums and colours in 1959. Its lack of life was recognised by formal dissolution in 1962.

The lack of self-knowledge and inner direction that crash the Federal programme also bedevil the politics of each island. In his letter to Foster, Andrews delivers a most despairing report on the politics of Trinidad, an account we can take as being more or less true of each of the twelve territories forming the Federation. Andrews is convinced that in spite of all the talk, there is "no honour here, no ideal, no great sincerity or desire to make conditions any better." (147-148) The island administration is corrupt and dishonest, and individuals are selfishly seeking their own ends. Those ends, however, are not clear: "Hard as I am trying, I can't seem to get a clear picture in my mind of what it is we're after." (147) Twenty years after the publication of *An Island Is a World*, and dealing with the same phenomenon gone mad, Vidia Naipaul invented this epigraph for one of his novels: "When everybody wants to fight there is nothing to fight for. Everybody wants to fight his own little war, everybody is a guerrilla."

The novel criticises those who perpetrate social evils and then turns on those who do nothing about it: "All over this island, little knots of intelligent men get together and talk as we are talking now, deploring the systems and methods of education, labour, politics, social service. . . .There is a lot of fury and indignation on the surface, but no one does anything" (72). These little knots that Selvon's novel has picked up are today's verbal guerrilla cliques that refuse to unite for the common good because there might not be enough credit to go around. Through Andrews, Selvon criticises an even more basic feeling in them: "[T]he conditions that exist offer excuse for all our failings, so why should we bother to make things better?" (148)

But Andrews can still intone a political "I believe" ("I have faith in Trinidad, and in the destiny of the West Indies") and is developed as the artist drawn by his sympathies into a political career. This is because the novel's criticism of current political practice is not a repudiation of politics itself. These criticisms of the emptiness of pre-Independence politics are criticisms of societies that do not allow the philosophies that animate them in their religious and cultural practices to enter into spheres subject to the play of power. The critique materialises as part of a larger investigation of what it is that makes people come together as a society, and what the individuals in any society live for. The model it proposes and seeks to demonstrate through its main character is to begin with the thinking and feeling self as centre, to work from the inside, and to see freshly through the islands' clouds of unknowing. This was not a recipe for parochialism but a preparation to ensure that it would be possible to reach out to the desirable world not as centre that reduces but as periphery that can be made to enrich our self-fulfilling projects. This gives special interest to Selvon's treatment of his characters' exile in America and London.

An Island Is a World runs from the late 1930's to around 1950, registering the Second World War, and the presence of American soldiers based at Chaguaramus, Docksite, and Wallerfield as forces intensifying change in the economy and society of Trinidad. Then came the movies whose images completed the lodging of America in the consciousness of English-speaking West Indians as a source of fantasy and longing and as a destination for oppressed and ambitious migrants. So even while the great exodus to the Mother Country ("colonisation in reverse") was taking place in the 1950s, America was shaping to displace England and become the powerful cultural and economic reality to West Indians that it is today. Many of the features of this period are reflected in calypsoes, short stories and in the daily newspapers. *An Island Is a World* is the West Indian novel that marks the historical moment when the shifting of the balance decisively began. The novel accompanies this with a doctrinal rejection of the Mother Country.

The account of Foster's sojourn in England carries more weight than that of Rufus's working and studying in America. In addition to a comprehensive critique of English culture and civilisation, it contains tantalising glimpses of the West Indians who are to be the subjects of *The Lonely Londoners* (153-154), and a moving evocation of a writer's dialogue with himself—about ever being able to represent experience, and about the guilt of the hand that betrays the poetry of the moment as it strives to capture it in writing (128-134). In this part of the novel, Foster experiences the loneliness of the exile ("But sometimes a man feels as if he hasn't got a country, and it's a lonely feeling, as if you don't really belong nowhere"). But he also learns some bitter truths about the political nature of the world, and about the innocent beliefs his colonial upbringing has encouraged him to hold. The first of these is that a Trinidadian person, mixing with so many nationalities, belonged to the whole world, not to any small part of it:

I used to think of this philosophy as being the broadest,

the most universal, that if it ever came to making a decision on an issue involving humanity itself, we'd have an advantage with this disadvantage as it were, that we'd be able to see the way clearer, unbounded by any ties to a country or even a race or a creed. (106)

This belief takes some blows now that he is meeting other peoples. Like Trumper before him (*In the Castle of My Skin*), but in a different spirit, Foster discovers that the world is a world of camps:

Other people belong. They are not human beings, they are Englishmen and Frenchmen, and Americans, and you've got to have something to fall back on too . . . So I feel now that all those idealistic arguments we used to have at home don't mean a thing. You can't belong to the world, because the world won't have you. The world is made up of different nations, and you've got to belong to one of them, and to hell with the others. (106)

This is a hard lesson to learn, a sad loss of the dream of universal understanding and tolerance. Earlier, the novel had opened up and left open the question as to whether an island is a world, with Foster's view that an island restricts one's horizons being balanced by Father Hope's persuasion that an island is a sufficient world. (65, 73-74) Now, Foster recognises the necessity for cultural nationalism:

We have a task to build up a national feeling, living as we are in scattered islands with our petty differences. Hitherto I have always been a little proud that in Trinidad we never felt strongly about belonging to the island . . . We never sort of visualised Trinidad as part of the world, a place to build a history, a young country which could reap the benefit of the bitter experiences of older countries. (106)

In his letters to Andrews, Selvon uses Foster the cultural nationalist to deliver a comprehensive critique of English culture and civilisation. In one of these letters, the critique reflects his discovery and his disappointment that the English people are even more lost than he is because they hardly know what is happening to them:

> You could feel a tensity and a crazy anxiety for movement in the people, as if they felt that to stop and take stock would be to court disaster. One day of any day, if you stand still in Oxford Street or lean against a wall in Piccadilly Circus, you would see the English people rushing about madly. You would say to yourself: This is a great country and a great people, but if they are like this, what hope for us? You will see them full of no purpose, sure of no destination, streaming in the streets of London, going to the theatre, to the cinema, going to the security of jobs. But always they are going. (118)

In an earlier letter, Foster is stung by the condescension of people whose tastes, feelings, and ideas are so programmed that they cannot be said to taste, think or feel:

> These fools feel they know the answer to everything, because they are full of knowledge. The pure mind, uncluttered with false ideas and theories (if you could find such a one these days) is called naive. Such a mind giving expression is laughed at and debunked . . . It is a crime to be simple, to be astonished, to be sentimental. See how people disguise their natural feelings, as if they were ashamed to be moved or touched by anything, quickly brushing away a tear, as if they have succumbed to a weakness by crying. . . .The fundamental things of life aren't fundamental anymore. (108)

This mounting critique of those who substitute an accumulation of dead knowledge for the capacity to think and feel for themselves is, of course, a debunking of the world and the ways of the coloniser. But this is not the Empire writing back in terms set down by the coloniser. It is more positive and unconditioned than that. Before Walcott had fine-tuned the perception, *An Island Is a World* knew that Joyce was afraid of thunder, and it was proclaiming this awe to be the enabling condition of the person in the West Indies, a condition that held the possibility of self-determined and exciting growth.

Kenneth Ramchand
Dept. of English
Colgate University
Hamilton, NY 13346

Prologue

Every morning when Foster awoke, it was the same thing. The world spun in his brain.

The world spun in his brain, and he imagined the island of Trinidad, eleven and a half degrees north of the equator. He saw it on a globe, with the Americas sprawled like giant shadows above and below, and the endless Atlantic lapping the coastlines of the continents and the green islands of the Caribbean. The globe spun and he saw Great Britain and Europe, and Africa. The eastern countries, Australia. Foster imagined Trinidad as it was, a mere dot on the globe. But he saw himself in the dot.

He saw himself in the dot, and he transmitted thoughts into the universe. He was lying down on the dot and thoughts radiated from him like how RKO introduce their films with a radio station broadcasting into space.

Lying there on the double bed after his wife had got up to prepare breakfast, Foster was big and the globe was small, spinning off there in space. Sometimes he gave the globe a blow with his fist and he shattered it. And sometimes he put out a finger and he stopped it spinning.

Because the thoughts kept recurring during the day, Foster was never tempted to make an effort to marshal them and thrust them all at once at the sky. If they came, they came—and went up. But he sometimes felt it would be a good idea if he could put them side by side (at such times he remembered the story about the man who broke one stick, but couldn't break three or four put together) and see if something wouldn't happen. Like, say, a hundred questions forcing one answer.

Whenever Foster tried to pursue one thought to the end (at the same time thinking, what end?) the end never came. And becoming more involved—like he imagined a man with an uncontrolled mind would be, my God—he would quickly change the topic, saying to himself, "It's no different if I think merry-go-round or left-wing footballer or ha-ha-ha instead."

After a while Foster would get up: as he got up this morning, clapping a mosquito to death against the net and staining it with blood. Whose blood? Jennifer's or his? He had a feeling the holes in the net were too large, that a blood-thirsty mosquito, bent on sucking red and white corpuscles (as he thought of blood) could easily squirm through one of the holes. Nearly every morning when he got up he saw one or two resting on the inside of the net, their bellies swelling with blood. But the people who made mosquito nets knew their business, they wouldn't make one with holes too large, would they?

The mosquito net could be the start of a chain of thoughts. He ignored it and opened the window, and the genial warmth of the morning sun came through.

Anywhere he turned, it was so easy. He could speculate on the sun and sunlight, and the zinnias in the garden before him.

It wasn't really a garden, it was just a small piece of land in front of the house which he and Jennifer had beautified by planting roses and zinnias. The roses were difficult because of the ants, but last week they had grown four buds which Jennifer picked and put in a vase on the table in the drawing-room. They lasted four days.

Abruptly, he turned from the window. He took off his drawers—he never slept in pyjamas because of the heat. Jennifer often argued about this. What would happen if they went to spend a few days from home? Or had to stay overnight at friends? Would he sleep in his drawers then? But Foster said that people didn't see you when you slept.

On Sundays, and even after work on evenings, if he was at home he walked about the house in his drawers. He sometimes wondered why someone didn't introduce a nudist colony in Trinidad. He had heard that there was once a group of people who used to go by boat to one of the tiny islands in the Gulf of Paria and gambol in the sunlight and the water. Wind and sun and sea on bare flesh; rolling in the sand, in direct contact with earth. But nasty rumours soon killed that venture. Nudism wasn't for him, anyway. The thought of a beautiful woman standing completely naked next to him made the hairs on his body rise.

Foster wrapped a towel around his waist and went into the bathroom and turned on the shower. This morning the water was flowing. Often the pressure in the pipes was too low, and he had to go out in the yard where there was a low sink, and fill a

2

bucket. The cool water sent exhilaration through his body, and when he came out he was whistling softly.

Foster dressed slowly. He never wore a tie, because he couldn't see the necessity for it. In Trinidad the tie is a badge of the middle-class society, it is a sign of aspiration to better things. Foster was never "well-dressed," because he never wore a tie. When he was getting married Andrews, his friend, got a plain blue one and painted a coconut palm in gold on it, and Foster wore it for the occasion, because everyone insisted, and he was too tired to argue.

He watched himself in the mirror as he combed his hair. He broke the neck of his shirt, pressing the V to make two seams. He was not fastidious, but he liked to be neat—no sense in appearing dirty, hair dishevelled, shirt baggy.

Jennifer called him to breakfast. She had made "buljol"—a West Indian dish of salted codfish, one of the poor man's staple items of diet. The fish is soaked until it loses its hardness, and broken up into small pieces. Or roasted and treated the same way. It is served with olive oil and fresh tomatoes and onions, and avocado pears, if they are in season. There is a kind of bread called "hops" and the "buljol" is most enjoyable with it.

This morning Jennifer had bought an avocado pear from a passing Indian vendor. The pear had come from Grenada, an island about one hundred miles from Trinidad, which could be seen from the Chachachacre lighthouse on a clear day, looking through a telescope. The pear had been boxed with scores of others, and shipped on a schooner.

It was a large pear, purple. It glistened. Jennifer said: "You know how much I pay for the zaboca (pear)? A shilling!"

"Things still going up," Foster replied abstractedly, looking at the zaboca. He began to cut it.

"You know saltfish gone up too," Jennifer said, "everything going up. The *Guardian* say cost of living rise three points again."

"I don't know what that means." Foster tasted the zaboca. "I don't understand how they reckon it by points. Must have something to do with economics. Anyway what it boils down to is that one has to spend more money. I wonder why they don't say things out plain—like if you used to spend one dollar before, now you'll have to spend ten cents more. Instead it is points. Nobody knows what the hell that means."

3

Foster spoke proper English when he felt like it, using local dialect for contrast and emphasis.

A typical conversation habit in Trinidad is the abrupt changing of the subject.

Jennifer said, "You have to pay the rent to-day, don't forget. Bring some rabbit home for dinner when you coming back."

"What o'clock now?"

"About twenty to ten."

"Jeez, I didn't know was so late. I have to hustle."

Foster sometimes found a uselessness in talking.

He went out to the main road and he caught a bus going to Port of Spain. He sat down, feeling sorry for all the passengers. It was a humble sorrow, like if he had said, "We are all in the same boat, I am sorry."

On the journey, he diagnosed this sorrow: the result of too much aimlessness and hopelessness (as if I didn't know).

And in the bus he felt the old fear coming on him, the fear of nothing, the fear of man and crossword puzzles and the cow jumping over the moon and the bus fare is six cents. . .

To hell with it, he thought, to hell with it. Because: so what? Everyone in this bus is more or less happy, thinking about small pasts and presents and futures. It is the way of life (as if I didn't know it). Alternatively, oblivion.

He got himself interested in the news by glancing at the newspaper a man was reading in the seat before him. New York, London, the Middle East. Things happening all over the world. And he, in a dilapidated bus travelling from Petite Bourg to Port of Spain—a city with emotion and life and radios and a modern sewerage system, but unknown to the billions of people on the earth—with the world spinning in his mind, and fearful of everything and nothing. He was a fool.

He began to whistle a calypso softly, watching the traffic and the houses at the side of the road.

By the time the bus got to the city his mind was comparatively at ease.

Always it was like this. To go out in the world was to regain his confidence. Mornings would begin fearfully, alone in bed with the world on your mind, but get dressed, have breakfast and go out and meet people, and suddenly you are just a part of it as everyone else, and you could snatch consolation from every face. I am going here, I am going there. I am going to see Mavis. I

4

going to work. I have to meet a fellar down Frederick Street. I just going to town to fix up some business. Purpose. That was it. Something to do to let an hour go by. Things to do, eat, sleep, talk, work, and before you know it another day goes by. Work was a routine millions indulged in: he was always aware of it as such, and used to wonder what people would do if all the offices and factories in the world were shut down. However, that was not the important thing, what was important was that Time wouldn't stand still because of it, the day would pass, and a thousand other days. He thought how securely a man could look forward to the future, in the sense that nothing could stop the future from coming. A man could say, "In 1960 I shall build a house," and he may die and the idea may be forgotten, but 1960 would come.

The thought had possibilities, he sensed that as he walked slowly down Marine Square, oblivious of the blind beggar who sat cross-legged on the cold pavement. The thought had security, it was a safe thing. Providing, of course, there was intelligence to appreciate it. What if by the time 1960 came there was no more intelligence in the world? Supposing the world was dead by that time? Well, what of it? Time was outside, eternal . . .

He stopped suddenly in front of a grocery and watched his dim reflection in the glass.

"My God," he whispered to himself, pretending to look at the tins of potted meat and bottles of rum on display, "is it possible for a man to think as I have been thinking since I got up this morning?"

And instantly another thought came to him, how he was stupid to ask that, when it *had* been possible, and here he was at it again, by God, here he was having another go . . .

PART ONE

Chapter One

Every morning when Johnny awoke in the largest room of his house, he used to feel for his wife, though he knew she had risen long ago to prepare breakfast. But he did it all the same, out of habit, because Mary was a big ball of soft flesh, and he liked when he could throw his legs over her, and his arms. It was like laying down on feather pillows, and it was the only physical comfort he could get from her now.

Johnny was an Indian, a jeweller and a drunkard. Johnny had come to Trinidad from India, and set up a small jeweller's shop. And when he prospered he bought a house and married Mary. Mary bore Johnny two girls and fattened quickly.

Johnny was a short man with bloodshot eyes and a small moustache. When war broke out he trained the moustache like Hitler's for fun. The stubby hair lay on top of a surprisingly beautiful curved upper lip. This was a physical attribute which his two daughters had inherited. Jennifer had it. And when Rena smiled the inheritance was obvious. On Johnny, this bit of beauty was lost in a flabby, forty-five year old face and partly hidden by the Hitler moustache.

For Johnny, the days of hangover were done. In earlier days it used to happen that he woke with a splitting head and cotton wool in his mouth after a night of drinking, and gave Mary a world of trouble, saying he was sure he was going to die. And Mary would bring ice from the refrigerator and put it on his head, and after the fire died away a little he asked: "What I do last night?" And Mary said: "As if you was fighting, you only throwing your legs and arms out, and cuffing me, and grinding your teeth, and groaning."

All he did now was grind his teeth. He couldn't help for that: after all, it was such a small thing in comparison with those hellish nights when his whole body was on fire and his brain was like an engine gone crazy.

After he felt for Mary's body and it wasn't there, Johnny would allow his body to go limp again on the bed, as if he were just going to sleep, and light a cigarette. Johnny rarely smoked; he allowed the cigarette to burn, and he watched the smoke. The ash would fall on the sheets, and he would brush it off. He used to wet the end before putting it in his mouth, because he liked the taste of the nicotine. Sometimes Johnny forgot he had a cigarette in his mouth, and it burned right down until it scorched his lips. He would spit it out and light another. He was always forgetting his lighted cigarettes about the house, putting them down thoughtlessly here and there, so that the house was marked in all odd places with burnt scars, and on tables and ledges. Mary placed innumerable ashtrays about, and yet Johnny seemed always to miss them when he had to put down a cigarette. Mary urged Johnny to get the house insured against fire, pointing out the danger. Johnny was no fool, he realised that one night in his drunkenness he himself might set the place on fire. So he insured his house, and the insurance company gave him sort of a plaque which he nailed up near the doorstep in the front of the house. The plaque was green, and it had a red flame painted on it, and the name of the insurance company.

It was a big wooden house, with a galvanised roof. There were six large rooms, and at the back of the house there was a small spare room next to the kitchen and the bathroom.

When Johnny was on a spree he came home well-lit and Mary made haste to hide all the rum there was in the house. Johnny would wander about in a sort of drunken cunning, as if to find the rum would be proof that he was not out of his senses. When he didn't find it he would begin cursing. He cursed so much that Mary stopped having friends home because of the way he behaved. If he didn't like a visitor he said so bluntly. He embarrassed and insulted. If it was a regular visitor who knew his ways, like Mary's numerous cousins and relatives, Johnny would pull one of them aside and ask him to go and buy a bottle of rum. Mary would say: "No no, don't go, he drunk enough already." Johnny would say: "Don't listen to that damn woman, go and bring the rum, man."

But there was no telling what form his drunkenness would take. If he did a good business deal, like if he bought a shipment of raw gold from British Guiana and sold it quickly at a profit, he came home in high spirits. He would then begin distributing money to the family left and right, pulling the dollar bills from his pocket. Or he might just collapse in a chair, and Mary would have to leave him snoring there for hours, and take embarrassed visitors to the bedroom or dining room. Or he might come in and try to pick a quarrel with everyone. When they kept a discreet silence and edged out of his way, he jeered and taunted. Another time he would be like a maniac, threatening to kill them all. He would rush into the kitchen looking for a cutlass with which Mary cut the firewood, and seizing it walk about the house swinging the blade to and fro. "I cut off somebody head tonight," he grunted. Everybody kept the doors locked until he calmed down.

Whenever Johnny's body broke down under the strain the family doctor came to see him. "It's the same old trouble again, I am warning you for the last time to lay off drinking. It will kill you." But there had been so many "last times" Johnny remembered, and nothing had happened to him. Johnny had long given up losing sleep that he might be killed with rum. But he always gave the doctor the impression that he was anxious to cooperate, nodding his head vigorously, and shaking the doctor's hand before he left.

And for a day or two, even a week, Johnny was sober, and a restless sort of peace lay on the house. Johnny moved about in a white merino, his trousers held up with an old necktie, just waiting for the day. When it came he dressed slowly and went to work like a reformed character.

One night Johnny fell off the bed and broke his ankle. The doctor ordered him to stay home and rest for two weeks. Mary did her best to enforce the habitual warning about keeping away from the bottle. But two weeks was a long time: Johnny managed to hide a small bottle under the mattress.

When Jennifer came in the morning to make the bed, Johnny drove her away.

Jennifer went to Mary. "I don't know what happened to Pa, all the bed clothes dirty, but he don't want to get up for me to change them."

Mary investigated, found the bottle (as she had suspected) and forced Johnny out of bed. But though she was in the house more than Johnny, she couldn't know all the nooks and crannies as he did. Half hour later he was stealing a drink from a bottle he had cached in a jacket pocket in the wardrobe.

On some Sundays Johnny stayed sober to catch up on his correspondence. He had a pair of thick, horn-rimmed glasses which he wore low down on his nose as he read the letters from all the firms abroad. Johnny got a lot of pleasure out of this; it was pleasing to know that you could write to these people all over the world and receive replies. He wrote for catalogues and samples of new types of jewellery. If they came during the week, they were put on his desk to receive his attention on Sunday.

Johnny took great pains when he was writing a letter, and the waste paper basket was filled with torn sheets before he was ever satisfied.

Johnny knew that people thought he was a good-for-nothing old rascal, but in his own mind he had a secret which was his defence against the world. He thought about it often, especially in the mornings when he felt too lazy to get up and go and open his shop. About the Big Invention. Since he was a boy, the idea had obsessed him, and Johnny had kept it in the back of his mind. Because it was his own idea. There may have been other scientific minds that thought the same way, but to hell with it, the idea had come to him of its own accord, he hadn't read about it in no book, or heard people talking. About how one day he was going to harness the great force of Gravity.

He had been working on it for years, secretly, slyly, chuckling that he had this great scheme in the back of his head while everyone thought he was only an old drunkard. He had stacks and stacks of diagrams locked up in a drawer in his desk. It never occurred to him to seek assistance from someone with more knowledge; Johnny felt that if he thought about it sufficiently, one day the answer would come, and he would be a rich and powerful man.

No one knew about Johnny's invention, even when he was drunk he kept his mouth shut about it. It was his secret, it was what he would throw in their faces one day when he discovered the formula. Johnny had wanted a son badly, so he could hand over the work he had done on the formula. That was why he had taken to drinking so badly.

Before he went to work he put two dollars on the dining-room table every morning. This was for Mary to run the house for the day. Johnny liked good food: he had a messenger boy who came every midday to collect his lunch put away in food carriers in a basket, and Johnny would sit on the stool in his shop and eat. The amount of money never varied, was never more or less, despite the rise in the cost of living. If Mary wanted anything for herself she had to steal the money from his pockets.

This was no trouble, as Johnny was always complaining of losing money when he was drunk.

Sometimes when a stranger brought him home he would say, when he sobered up in the morning, "Jesus Christ, that man rob me of twenty dollars I had in my pocket!"

And Mary would say: "Is the money you studying? You should be glad you still alive, and not dead in some canal! The man was good to bring you home."

Johnny shook a little silver remaining in his pocket and swore again. "These bitches, always robbing a man when he drunk."

Smart taxi-drivers called at Johnny's shop some mornings.

"Morning Mr. Johnny, was I who take you home last night, you know. You did forget to pay me, so I come now to collect."

"Man, I had twenty dollars in my pocket last night, this morning I only find a few shillings."

"Anyway Mr. Johnny I don't know about that. My fare was one dollar."

And Johnny would have to pay the driver, because he couldn't remember anything.

Johnny had a distant relative called Maraj living in British Guiana. Maraj negotiated for the raw gold and silver from the mines, and sent the minerals to Johnny to be either sold in bulk or made into trinkets and ornaments. They shared the profits between them: Maraj was always accusing Johnny of being unfair and threatening to take an aeroplane right away and fly to Trinidad, "to see which part all the money was going."

Once, after a particularly successful business deal in which he sold five pounds of raw gold, Johnny decided to go to British Guiana to allay Maraj's fears that he was holding out on him (especially as he was, in fact, doing just that).

There was another reason for the trip. Mary was behind him day after day to take her somewhere for a holiday, she said she hadn't been anywhere from the day she got married. So Johnny decided to kill two birds with one stone; he didn't tell Mary he had to go on business, he said he was taking her for a holiday in BG.

Mary didn't stop to reason what had come over her husband. She bought some new saris in Frederick Street and spread the news among all her relatives and friends. It wasn't everyone who could afford to take a holiday trip to BG., and in spreading the news Mary raised the social status of the family considerably in

12

the neighbourhood.

"Not that we won't have gone long time," she said, as if holidays for them happened every day, "but is just that Johnny so lazy to go any place, he always putting the shop in front."

The rum in British Guiana is darker than in Trinidad. When you pour it, it glows a kind of ruby colour, a deep amber; a "novice" might easily think he is drinking a potent wine. Not that the colour of the rum made any difference to Johnny. While Mary visited all the friends they knew, he and Maraj wrangled over the price of gold, and the condition of the market in Trinidad. All this talking being done with a bottle or two between them.

A few days before he left, Maraj told Johnny he had a good bit of raw gold in hand, but they would have to pay a hell of a lot to get it through the Customs. There was one way he might get away with it—if he made an elaborate ornament, Mary could wear it as part of her personal jewellery. Then later, in Trinidad, he could melt the ornament and sell the gold.

Johnny thought it was a brilliant idea; he praised Maraj for thinking of it and for the next few days spent the time in Maraj's shop making a long kind of chain for Mary to wear around the neck. The thing was thick and heavy, with little knobs of gold all the way round.

When Mary put it on it fell almost to her stomach. She had to double it so that it went down to her bosom and was hidden by her great breasts.

It did not matter to Johnny where he was as long as he could get rum. The idea of going around from place to place to see the country had no appeal; it was Mary who did the social calls on all the people they knew.

And it was Mary, the day before they left, who brought Patrick along to see Johnny. She said he was a relative's relative, he had finished school and was just idling about the place, couldn't Johnny give him a job in the shop in Trinidad, and keep him out of mischief?

Patrick had just turned twenty. He had large eyes and thick eyebrows and when he laughed spittle flew from his mouth though he had big, firm teeth and there wasn't any space between them. He was training a moustache.

When he had left school he was automatically apprenticed to a jeweller's shop (not Maraj's) where he learned the trade.

13

Patrick was ambitious. He had big ideas, but he lacked push. He was too easily satisfied. He told friends how he could make five dollars into ten, how he could buy and sell stuff at a profit. "If I only had the money to make a start," he used to say.

The idea of going to Trinidad was one of his secret ambitions. In that part of the world Trinidad was the irresistible mecca of the colonies, where one could make money quickly and life was on a higher level. So great was the inflow of the West Indians from the other islands that the colony had to introduce special laws to control the situation.

Johnny wasn't keen on having someone else in the shop, he had the feeling that Mary was arranging the whole thing so Patrick could spy on him and report his activities. But on the other hand he saw where Patrick could be very useful, and after a bit of grumbling and display of a reluctance he didn't feel, he agreed to the proposal.

One month after Johnny returned to Trinidad Patrick sold his bicycle to make up his passage money and travelled third-class on a cargo boat. He landed green and wobbly after the overnight crossing, a gaudily-coloured necktie looking oddly out of place against his sick face. He clutched a suitcase with all his clothes, and a kitbag with the tools of his trade.

Johnny installed him in a small back room next to the bathroom, and gave him a canvas cot to sleep on. He then detailed Patrick's duties and status with the household.

Patrick was to assist generally, not only in the workshop but with household chores. He would have to run errands for Mary. He would be given three meals a day. He was not to eat with the family; Mary was to put his food on the table and call him, and he was to eat alone. He was to use the passageway at the side of the house, and never enter or leave the house through the front door except by permission. He was to have nothing to do with any of Johnny's daughters. In the workshop, he was to do anything Johnny asked without grumbling. Around lunch time he was to come to the house and collect Johnny's lunch, and about four o'clock in the afternoon, return with the empty food-carriers and go back to work until five. And anything else that Johnny or Mary should think of at any time. He would earn five dollars a week.

Patrick listened to all this with a distracted air, and agreed to the conditions of employment. He was willing to please everybody, and he wasn't afraid of work.

But no matter how hard he tried, he was always receiving rebuffs. Every morning before he went to the workshop Mary sent him to the market to buy beef (from a special butcher who had performed all the religious rites before slaughtering the animal) and she was never satisfied with what he brought back. She accused him of robbing her.

In the workshop, Johnny made him work hard, doing all the intricate jobs for which his own hands were not steady enough. This encouraged Patrick to hide his abilities and show a false ignorance for the jobs he could have done in a few minutes.

By and by Patrick fell into a pattern of existence. The first week, he broke away a little of the rotting wood between a crack in the wall, and was able to peep into the bathroom when the girls were taking a bath. Rena caught him at it one evening and she went up against the wooden partition so she couldn't miss and she spat right in the crack, in Patrick's eye. Later the crack was sealed with a piece of newspaper—a deliberately flimsy job, so that if Patrick punched the paper it would be easily observed. But he was no fool; he sought out another less obvious spy hole in the rotting wood, and for the duration of his stay in Johnny's house he was able to watch the girls.

Patrick spent most of his leisure sitting on the canvas cot and cutting out pictures of girls in bathing suits and other scanty costumes from magazines; when the bikini came into vogue Patrick was a happy man. He used to do that during the week, and over the weekend paste them on the walls. As time went by you couldn't see the walls for pictures. He used to stick them on the ceiling too, so that he could see them when he was in bed. He had a torchlight and when he lay down with the electric light out in the night, he used to flash the torch like a projecting beam around the room from picture to picture until he fell asleep.

Mary waged a wordless war against what she called "this nudeness." She never told Patrick anything; he would come in from work to find the pictures torn from the walls. But he had infinite patience and an inexhaustible supply of magazines, and in a short time scantily-clad limbs would be decorating the room again. Mary had to give up after a few weeks, though if she was ever sweeping the room she kept her eyes fixed firmly on the broom handle or the floor, and she never allowed any of her daughters to enter the room under any pretext.

The workshop was situated in a busy part of the city. It was a small place, not more than eighteen feet by eighteen, but a great deal of work went on there. There was a cinema and a rumshop, and the way Johnny's shop was, it looked as if it was just wedged in between those two buildings out of a mad caprice; indeed, one of the cinema walls did for the northern side of the shop, and the cinema manager used to look into the shop every now and then to see if Johnny was disfiguring his part. The front of the shop was closed by one of those folding steel doors; Johnny always locked it himself until he could trust Patrick. There was a glass show-case, in which he displayed miscellaneous jewellery and wristwatches. Then a counter on which he accepted repair work and transacted business. Under the counter there were countless empty rum bottles. One of the distilling firms gave a full bottle for ten empty ones, and when Patrick came to work for him Johnny began to cash in all the empties that he had. On the eleventh day Patrick would gather the ten bottles in the handbag and Johnny would give him twelve cents for the bus fare to go to and from the firm's works for the exchange. In his eagerness to please Patrick did this job as quickly as he could—it was only afterwards he realised that he should have taken an extra hour, just in case he wanted time of his own on one of these journeys. As it was, Johnny noted how long he took the first time and made it clear that he expected Patrick back at the same time on further trips.

Behind the counter was a table stool on which Johnny sat before a small table covered with tiny spin-wheels and springs and other parts from the guts of a wristwatch. The sides of the table were scarred—over and over again in some places—where Johnny left his cigarettes to burn away into ash. He felt that ashtrays disciplined his smoking and deprived his pleasure, and he kept none in the shop, though Mary insisted on keeping them at home "for visitors." Johnny would light a cigarette and then become so engrossed in his work that when he would put out his hand for it he only rubbed the ashes. He would take instant alarm, jumping off the stool and slapping his clothes all over crying: "I just had a cigarette here, which part it gone to?" And he would look to see if his clothes were smoking. The fear of fire always haunted him.

Or else, he lit the cigarette and held it between his lips, so that it burned away until the ash bent and finally fell on his hand. Completely absorbed in say, examining a defective watch, he would spring to life with an oath, as the burning cigarette reached his lips, spitting out the butt and looking around for the responsible agency.

Although Johnny had a reputation as one of the heaviest smokers in Trinidad, it was rare that he inhaled the nicotine; it seemed that all he really wanted was the companionship of the smoke rising from his lips, and it is doubtful whether he was aware even of that.

The shop was in a poor and slummy area, patronised by people who were often ill-mannered and rough. Groups of idlers loitered the pavement. When Johnny first opened the shop he was scared of the neighbourhood, and with good reason, for there were fights and arguments in front of the shop nearly every day, and drunks often came hurtling out of the rum shop next door.

Then one day Fingers Charles came into the shop. He leaned his big, bad self over the counter and told Johnny that he could see that none of "the boys" played the fool around the shop. Johnny knew that Fingers was leader of one of the biggest gangs in the district. A tacit agreement was reached. Fingers collected a dollar from Johnny every Friday, and peace was preserved. Fingers kept his side of the bargain well, and Johnny was never disturbed. Fingers sometimes brought along a stolen watch or necklace, and placed them silently on the counter. Johnny paid for them without fuss, dismounting the articles and using the parts for repairs.

Even when Patrick came to work for him, Johnny still found it difficult to deliver a job on time. There was always something more to be done, or he hadn't got the spare part, or it was a bigger job than he thought.

"Come back tomorrow evening five o'clock," he would tell the customer, "and I finish it sure."

"Yesterday you tell me come today," the customer would grumble, "today you tell me come tomorrow."

When Patrick became an accustomed sight in the shop Johnny started firing him every two or three months. "I tired of seeing your damn face around—you fired, go away."

This usually happened after a bout of steady drinking, and Patrick came to expect it. He went home and loafed around for a week. Then on the Monday morning Johnny would tell him to turn out to work.

17

Patrick got disgusted. The next time Johnny fired him, he went out and got another job with a well-known firm of jewellers in Frederick Street.

Johnny called Patrick into the house that Sunday morning. Johnny was sitting at the desk where he dealt with all his correspondence and read the Sunday newspapers.

Patrick stood near the desk in a defiant attitude, ready to defend his independence.

"So you have a new work now? How you getting on?" Johnny played with the letters on his desk, speaking in a tolerant voice, as if he really wasn't interested.

"I'm making plenty more money than when I used to work for you," Patrick muttered.

"You lie!" Johnny cried, "I know them jewellers good, they don't pay the staff much at all." Then he asked: "So you don't want to work with me again?"

"Yes, I want to work with you," Patrick said, "but all the time you only firing me for nothing at all, and you treating me like a messenger boy. You must realise I getting big. You must realise I have ideas."

Johnny nodded, more to himself than to Patrick. He picked up a letter and appeared to be reading it.

"So when you coming back to work for me?" he asked, pretending to be busy with the papers on his desk, as if he were only wasting time with the interview.

"Well, in the first place is nearly a year I working for you now and is still five dollars a week. Things hard now, cost of living gone up. I want more money."

Johnny grunted. "How much you was getting at this other place?" He spoke as if Patrick had already given up the job.

"Twelve dollars a week."

"I know you lying," Johnny said. "I give you ten."

"I getting twelve."

"I bet I put you out of the house! Then you have to pay big rent to live somewhere else."

"All right, I take ten."

Johnny instantly changed the subject. "The last time I was drunk and you bring me home, I had twenty dollars in my pocket. When I wake up in the morning I only find ten. You know anything about it?"

"No, I don't know anything about it."

"I know you lying," Johnny said.

Patrick smiled as he turned and walked away. Johnny knew he would have to treat Patrick with some respect in the future.

When Patrick came back to work for Johnny, he began to take in private jobs of which he told Johnny nothing, and he made a little extra money on the side. For even with the rise he found it hard to meet expenses—he was making friends, he had to spend money. Before he left British Guiana his mother had told him that he should send some money for her every week. But Patrick never intended doing that, and from the first he wrote her a long letter saying how things were expensive in Trinidad, and that his salary was too small, he could hardly manage. Thinking her son was having a rough time, whenever she could she sent him a postal order for a few dollars, which Patrick instantly spent on buying gaudily-coloured neckties.

Patrick had an easy way with private customers. He knew the district was poor and he charged them as little as he could: also because he was afraid that they might tell Johnny about his private deals. Sometimes a girl or woman came with a broken necklace and he did the job for nothing. But in the night, he called at their houses to pay a friendly visit, and he got a big thrill out of it, especially if it was a married woman.

Patrick liked his drink, but he couldn't take it. Two small shots would have him gay and merry. He didn't mind—it cost less that way. When he was drunk, he used to quote history. It had been his favourite subject at school, and he had memorised pages and pages about the Battle of Waterloo, and how it was during the French Revolution. None of this he remembered in the normal course of his life, but once he had taken a few drinks, there was no holding him back, he would quote long passages, fluent and loud-mouthed, the spittle flying from his mouth as his tongue loosened.

Patrick liked cricket. He joined a club and managed to get some practice if he got off early from work. He was not a good player, but he talked a lot about the game. He wore his cricket apparel well and with an air of pride, strolling on to the pitch with an easy air to be bowled for duck.

Any matches he played in had to be on a Sunday, as it was his only day off. Even so Mary was apt to call upon him to do something on that day, but Patrick refused unless he felt like doing it.

On Sunday evenings, he dressed himself in a double-breasted suit and put on one of those flashy neckties and went for a stroll around the Queen's Park Savannah, looking at all the girls that passed by.

Chapter Two

Johnny's youngest daughter, Jennifer, was prettier than her sister Rena. She was just seventeen, with a shapely body and large, luminous eyes and the curve of her father's upper lip. Jennifer used to sleep with Rena in the big bedroom next to her parents' room.

Rena was self-willed and stubborn, accustomed to having her own way. But Jennifer was Mary's pet, and Mary was determined that Jennifer should marry a rich man with a profession.

Every morning, even before Johnny saw the paper, Mary put on her glasses and sat in the rocking chair in the drawing-room for a few minutes, eagerly scanning the columns of the Trinidad Guardian to see which son of whom had returned qualified from England or the United States. Mary preferred doctors, but these were hard days, and she wouldn't mind letting Jennifer go to a lawyer or a barrister. She frowned on qualified engineers; she imagined them in dirty greasy clothes, oiling engines.

Every now and again as her eye caught a headline: Student Returns to Practice Profession, she took steps to arrange for the man to visit the house, speaking to friends who knew the person. And if it happened that a party or a dance was being held at which it was likely he would be, Jennifer was bedizened and painted with lipstick and rouge and sent out to try and make a catch.

But Jennifer had her own ideas about marriage. "These are modern times," she told herself, not quite knowing what she meant, "and if Ma thinks she's going to arrange a marriage for me she's mistaken."

Days were, to Jennifer, long stretches of time when she daydreamed about boys and dances and parties.

She used to help Mary in the kitchen and clean out the house. When she finished her chores she sat near a window facing the street, a True Story magazine in her hand, watching people go by.

That was most of Jennifer's world until Johnny decided that the girl was only wasting time, and should learn to do something.

Mary reluctantly agreed, and sent her daughter to take commercial lessons at a private school in Tragerite Road.

The world opened up a little for Jennifer, but she walked in the street with blind eyes, conscious of her beauty and her poise. She never saw the morning rich with sunlight, blown by sweet wind from the hills, and though she had to pass through a park on her way to school, she never had eyes for the poui trees when they were in blossom.

A young man saw Jennifer in the park one day and fell in love with her. Jennifer treated him calmly, she was never flustered or bright-eyed or singing and dancing, her face still registered blank. The man made dates with her: he used to meet her in the evenings when she was going to a private library to borrow novels. She tried to discourage the man, telling him that if her father or mother got to find out she would be thrashed. But he met her secretly.

One evening in a cinema, they were sitting in the back seats. All he did was hold her hands: Jennifer had the look of someone to be worshipped, and he was afraid to even caress her. She was bored. She whispered to him, "I don't know what pleasure there is in feeling a woman's breast, I don't get any. Here, touch me and see," and she thrust out her breast at him. His lips trembled and his hand shook. He caressed her and nothing happened; she didn't sigh or nestle closer to him.

"You see," she whispered, "and kissing too."

When he was seeing her home in the back streets a relative of the family met them and told Mary later.

Jennifer never went for commercial lessons again, and she only left the house if she was chaperoned by Rena or Mary herself. She sulked about the house, but she didn't dare rebel, because Mary threatened to tell Johnny everything.

For a few days the man passed near the house, and she saw him when she was sitting near the window.

Mary now realised that Jennifer was reaching a stage where she would be out of hand like Rena, so she doubled her efforts to find a suitable husband. Day in, day out she scanned the columns. Then at last one morning she saw a prize of a student returning to practice law. He was from a good Indian family, he was wealthy. But she mustn't rush him, she knew that from experience. Give him time to settle down a little. The trouble was, most of these young Trinidadians who went abroad returned with English or American wives, perhaps. . . She read the news item slowly. No, he wasn't married.

Mary made it her business to see that Jennifer learned to cook properly. "No man won't want you if you can't cook," she told her daughter in the kitchen, "see how I kneading the flour, watch how I making the curry."

A sort of dinner party was arranged, and Jennifer wore a low-cut dress which showed the dawn of her breasts, and she borrowed a jewel brooch from Rena.

When Mr Ranjit came Jennifer took one look and turned her head away. He might have money and a profession, but he wasn't the sort of man she dreamed about in the night.

Mary gave her a meaningful glance and left them alone in the drawing room.

"I say, awful hot weather we're having, isn't it?" Ranjit, schooled for five years in the usual opening sentences about the weather English people use when they get together, had forgotten that Trinidadians don't really give a blast if it's hot or cool. He sat and crossed his legs, pulling up his trousers from the knees to preserve the seams. He spoke with a pseudo-Oxford accent.

Jennifer typed him at once in her mind, as she had typed all others. The way they all spoke was ridiculous. It might have sounded all right in England; here in the house it always sounded pretentious, as if they were no longer Trinidadians but tourists paying the island a visit.

She decided to give him the usual treatment. "I ain't notice dat it making hot," she said in a flat voice, "must be how you just come back."

"Yes, that must be it," he agreed uneasily. He gazed around the room. He knew the object of the meeting was for him to decide whether this girl would make him a good wife: he had already been to several parties in different parts of the island. "Tell me something about yourself," he said.

"Me? I ain't have nothing interesting at all to talk about, man. I don't do nothing, I does only stay home and clean the house and cook. But how 'bout you? Tell me something 'bout England."

She wished she could put her fingers to her ears so she couldn't hear. They all said the same things, how London and New York were so vastly different from Port of Spain that she wouldn't understand. It always made her feel small, stifled, cheated. If it was that Americans or Englishmen came to Trinidad to look for wives, she would be the first to get away from the small island. She would go with any sort of man, just to live in New York or London, and see snow and travel in underground trains.

Ranjit observed a lost look in her eyes and stopped talking. He went across the room, to the radiogram in the corner, and he stood there looking at the record albums. Before he left Trinidad Ranjit didn't know anything about music. He still didn't know anything, but while he was in London he saw that people went to concerts and art exhibitions and the theatre as a matter of course. It was the done thing, and he did it too. It made him feel—as it probably made the others feel—cultured, refined. The music and the paintings didn't make any impression on his mind, but all the same he used to go now and then. It was good to be able to say, "I went to the theatre last night," or "have you seen that exhibition by contemporary artists?"

The record albums were mostly of Indian songs and dances, but there was a record of a piece by Sibelius which Johnny had brought home one day when he was drunk. It had never been played.

Ranjit held this record in his hand and turned to Jennifer. "Do you mind if I play?" he asked. He had already switched on the set.

"You best hads be careful wid dem records," Jennifer was still in a bad mood, "all them records belong to Pa. But anyway he not here now."

"Do you like Sibelius?" he asked, hesitating.

"Who name so?" Jennifer frowned. "I does only like to listen to jive, man, and we ain't have no jive records."

"Oh well, this will only bore you." He switched off the set and sat down on the sofa, next to her.

At that moment Mary peeped through the door and thought everything was going all right.

Jennifer's beauty impressed Ranjit, despite her attitude. He thought he would make another effort. He began to talk about a film he had seen recently, dropping the false accent from his voice. Jennifer listened with glazed eyes, her mind ruminating in London and New York.

When they went into the dining room her attitude became friendly because Mary was there. The table was neatly arranged,

24

and the Indian dishes Mary had made Jennifer prepare smelled good.

"Is Jennifer who cook the dinner, you know," Mary said, fussing around Ranjit, "she is a good cook. She is a good, obedient girl—the best daughter I have."

All might have gone well, Mary was already picturing the wedding and hoping her daughter would bear many sons.

But Johnny came in then.

That morning Mary had begged him: "We having guest this evening, try and don't get drunk, try and don't let your family down in front of a stranger."

If Mary hadn't said anything, there was a fair enough chance that Johnny might have turned up sober from work. But just because she spoke to him he got drunk.

Johnny staggered into the drawing room, stumbling against a chair. "Jesus Christ," he said. If there had been another entrance to the bedroom, he might have taken it. As it was he had to pass through the dining room to get to his own room.

In a desperate attempt to save the situation Mary rose from the table and held on to him tightly when he appeared.

But Johnny shook her off roughly. He went to the box he kept behind the refrigerator and searched for rum.

Ranjit maintained an uneasy silence. Jennifer was indifferent from the experience.

Finding the box empty Johnny straightened up and looked around, swaying from side to side, as if he enjoyed the swaying. Then he saw Ranjit for the first time. His eyes opened wide in amazement, he put his hands on the back of a chair for support and leaning forward, he asked slowly: "Who the *hell* is that in my house? Who is you, boy? What you doing here?"

"Allow me to introduce myself—" Ranjit began, smiling feebly.

"Allow you to introduce yourself!" Johnny repeated. "I don't know you at all. Who is your father? You better get out of my house, man."

"Why you don't behave your drunken self!" Mary screamed, tugging at his arm. "Come come, go and sleep and you will feel better."

But Johnny pushed her off again. He glanced at the table.

"But you-all haven't offered the guest a drink! You does drink boy?"

Ranjit had already risen from his chair in readiness to leave.

"Mr. Ranjit doesn't drink strong," Jennifer said quietly.

Johnny sneered broadly, then began talking to himself.

"Always inviting people in the house! Always spending up money we can't afford! Is which part you hide the rum, eh?"

He leaned heavily on Mary, and she seized the opportunity and pulled him towards the bedroom door.

"I think I had better leave," Ranjit said to Jennifer.

"Good-night," she said, and went on with her dinner.

Rena woke to find sunlight on her face—rich, brilliant sunlight that promised another sweltering day of heat. She stirred for a few seconds, squinted her eyes and frowned at the glare. She had been to a dutch party in Cascade the night before, and didn't get home until two o'clock.

She turned and tried to go back to sleep though she knew it was no use, the light had wakened her fully, it must be after nine. But every morning when she awoke she tried to go back to sleep. Sometimes she got under the sheet, drawing it over her head and shutting out everything. But she couldn't stay crouched like that for long, though it was a pleasant feeling while it lasted, as if nothing could happen to you.

Rena was slim. She had small feet, a narrow waist, attractive breasts, and she always looked as if she liked excitement. Her brown eyes sparkled alike at gossip and the prospect of a dance. Her lips curved sensuously like her father's, and she had long wavy hair which fell behind her neck.

She was like a kitten in the morning, writhing and twisting the sleep out of her body. She lay diagonally across the double bed. Rena used to always imagine that someone was looking at her, and she fixed herself accordingly. In the bath, she rubbed the soap on to her body with graceful movements: before the mirror she sort of tossed her head back while brushing her hair: whenever she awoke she stretched luxuriously and smiled for the unseen spectator, as if she had been sleeping with a lover.

She adopted a posture for thinking now, crossing her hands behind her head and staring up at the whitewashed ceiling through the mosquito net. She was wondering whether she should get married to the man from British Guiana who came to the house to see Johnny. This fellow used to carry on long conversations with her father about the jewellery business, and Johnny was impressed. "I want you to marry this man," he told

Rena, "you like him?"

Rena didn't give a definite reply. For all his faults, Johnny didn't want to force a marriage on his daughter. But he said, "You better make up your mind quick."

But Rena was in no hurry to get married. She was having a good time, what was the rush? And besides, it was good to know that a man wanted to marry you, and you have the power to say "yes" or "no". She knew she could get around Johnny if she had to: he would make a big scene and shout and curse, but in the end he would carry on as if nothing had happened. In any case, from the very beginning she had set herself up as a girl with her own way, stubborn and self-willed. Rena wasn't really like that, but the attitude served a purpose: her parents left her alone.

She was going to a dance in St James tonight with this fellow for the first time. She hoped he could dance well. She would wear her blue organdie dress, and put a white gardenia in her hair.

Chapter Three

In a hilly town called San Fernando forty miles south of Port of Spain, Rufus got up one morning shortly after war broke out and asked his brother Foster what he was going to do. Roused from sleep to answer the gigantic problem: What To Do, Foster blinked and looked at his brother foolishly.

Rufus had deliberately shaken awake, hoping to get a sensible reply instead of one of the usual evasive statements Foster seemed always to be making to any query during the day.

Rufus had tried to understand Foster and given it up. Though they were brothers, they had entirely different lines of reasoning. When they were children Foster asked Rufus one day:

"How do you do what?"

"What do you mean?" Rufus asked.

"Well, that fellow who was just here asked you 'How do you do.' That sentence was not complete?"

"Who say it not complete?"

"Well it look so to me."

"It mean, 'How are you,' if you are well. You too stupid. You stand up there like you dumb when the man ask you, not saying a word."

"I don't know what to say."

"People ask you that already, and you answer all right. What happen just now?"

"Nothing. Rufus?"

"What?"

"Nothing. I mean, you mustn't think I'm shy. I just don't know what to say, sometimes. And it struck me as being foolish to ask a person 'How do you do.' That's why I hesitated. I have plenty to say, but I can't always be like you, though I try."

Rufus never forgot that conversation, and as they grew up he realised with alarm that Foster was still hesitant with words, as if he were puzzling over great problems in his mind at the simplest question. Foster was pretending an awkwardness and embarrassment which Rufus knew were false.

Reproaching him once after they had been introduced to a girl,

28

Rufus didn't know what to say when Foster told him, "I wanted to say I wasn't pleased to meet her, I wanted to say, 'you look stupid, although you are attractive. I don't think I could get any pleasure in your company, though I'd like to have you.' I was debating in my mind whether I should, that's why I was slow to respond."

Foster's youth was very miserable.

"I asked what are you going to do," Rufus repeated, shaking Foster again.

"I don't know," Foster said.

"They want recruits for the forces. A lot of the boys have already joined up. It's a chance to get out of this hole, to go abroad. They're taking recruits for the RAF, and you could go to England."

"War is a hell of a thing," Foster said.

"Come again," Rufus sneered. "You're corny."

"Yes," Foster agreed, "but I mean—look, how about you? Are you signing up?"

"I have a better idea."

Foster didn't want to know the idea. He said, "Well, don't worry about me. I appreciate your big-brotherly attitude, but I'll be all right."

"I don't really give a damn about you," Rufus said. "But I'll be going to live in Port of Spain. I hear that the Americans are paying loads of money at Chaguaramus. I'm going to try and get a job."

Rufus was working in the oil fields in Point-a-Pierre. Foster didn't have a job at present, he was staying with his brother in a small room.

"Are you urging me to join up to ease up your conscience?"

"No. To ease yours. You haven't had a steady job for more than two years now. And you could show your loyalty to the King at the same time."

"Balls."

"Well anyway you've got to do something—you can't go on living like that, you know, wandering around from here to there, as if you can't make up your mind about anything. The army or the navy will take care of you. You won't have to bother about meals, or a place to sleep, or what to do. They'll do it for you."

"There's a lot in what you say."

"And don't give me any of those smart-aleck replies, either.

Anyway, why the hell should I worry about what you do? It's none of my business."

"You always wanted to go away, why don't you join the RAF?"

"I could take care of myself. When I am already I will go. I'm going to America when I get the chance later on."

Rufus went to live in Woodbrook, one of the districts in Port of Spain, and he worked with the Americans. And Foster wandered into a local branch of the Royal Navy, wondering all the time why he was doing it, but saying at the same time, To hell with it, I've got to do something.

Rufus had a cheap room and he tried to save his money. He lived as miserly as he could. He bought biscuits and bread and tinned meat and kept them in a drawer in his room to eat when he was hungry.

Foster came to see him when he was on leave.

One evening Rufus told Foster: "I'm going to get married."

Foster said: "You making joke man!"

"No, serious. She's on the way."

"Just like that? Out of the blue?"

"How do you mean out of the blue?"

"Well you never told me about this girl before."

"So what? I met her at a dance in St James one night, about three months ago."

"And you getting married so quick?"

"Man I tell you she on the way! You don't understand?"

"But where you going to live and all that?"

"She trying to get the old man to give us a room in the house. I am going round there tonight, why don't you come with me? I've told them about you.

"This getting married—is that what you want to do?"

"Jesus, I keep telling you the girl is going to have a baby."

"No, I mean you've made up your mind? It's just that—well, I was only thinking about what I would have done, if it was me."

"What would you have done?"

"I don't know."

"One day you will find yourself in a 'mooch' and I wonder what will happen to you."

"Oh, I'll find a way out, don't worry. I know you think I'm slow, but it's just that I can't seem to get things worked out properly in my own mind, that's all."

The night before he got married, Rufus invited all his male

friends to a party. He wanted to drink with each and every one as a bachelor for the last time.

He had many friends, so he was very drunk.

He woke with a splitting headache on his wedding day. Holding his head and moaning softly, he went into the bathroom and spent fifteen minutes under the cold shower.

He didn't feel much better. He got dressed and went to a chemist friend in St James.

"Look man, I feel like hell and I'm getting married today," he said. "Fix up something for me—anything, just so I could get through the day."

Mary begged Johnny, as guests began to arrive, to behave himself and not to disgrace the whole family. But already Johnny was high. He was dressed as if he were the bridegroom, in a double-breasted vicuna suit, and he wore a heavy gold chain in his fob pocket.

Johnny had reconciled himself to the marriage, knowing there was nothing he could do. He was philosophical about it. As far was he was concerned, the wedding reception was a chance to drink like hell, and watch the silly guests talking and giggling.

He had allowed Patrick the freedom of the house for the occasion, and Patrick was there, mixing familiarly with the crowd, keeping an eye on a tight dress or a pretty face. He had a few drinks with Foster, and in a short while he was prattling historical data, about Henry the Eighth. Poor Patrick passed out shortly after and Foster had to take him to his room behind the kitchen, where he fell on the canvas cot and went to sleep in all his pretty clothes.

Rufus couldn't touch a drink, he was feeling that sick. Nor anything to eat. His stomach muscles contracted at the thought of food. He moved about the guests in a daze, receiving congratulations and shaking hands.

When he told Johnny how he was feeling, Johnny said: "Never mind, I will drink with the guests and them for you." And strengthened with this excuse Johnny ignored the eye of Mary and kept the rum flowing.

Rena sat on a high chair, so that everyone could see her. Now and then Rufus came near and she asked him how he was feeling. He rubbed his forehead woefully.

"Well, don't touch a drop of rum," she said, "not even with

Foster. He seems well charged up."

"He can hold his own," Rufus replied, glancing at Foster who was in a group around the table with the drinks.

It was a sober time for Rufus in a gay crowd.

"Ah," Foster said, getting a moment with him alone, "I bet you never thought you would be unable to take a drink on your wedding day. Take a little shot, it will put you right."

But Rufus shook his head then grimaced as if the shaking hurt.

Foster bent forward a little, "Jennifer isn't such a bad-looking girl. I wouldn't mind. . ."

"Careful what you say," Rufus digged him in the ribs, "the room's full of people. You had better go easy on the bottle."

"Oh I'm all right. How does it feel to be a married man?"

"Like hell."

"Already? But tonight you'll be in Bombshell Bay on your honeymoon—'honeymoon' is an exciting word, isn't it?"

"Boy, I'm feeling hellish. I haven't recovered from last night yet."

Foster looked sympathetic. "Well, conserve your strength for tonight. Look—"

"What?"

"I was just wondering if there are many people in the world who do it for the first time on their honeymoon."

"Sometimes I wonder if you are ever serious."

"But I am, truly. Only, I don't want to be serious now. Forget it. How long are you going to be away?"

"Only a week."

"Well, that's a long time. You know the one about seven days—I hate smutty jokes, especially when they're corny."

"I think you're drinking too much. I wish you wouldn't talk in this damn manner. After all it's my wedding day."

Rufus was obviously annoyed, and Foster was instantly repentant. "Sorry, boy. By the way, I shan't be seeing you for some time. We're going to dry-dock in Barbados for two or three months."

"Righto. I'll see you later before I leave."

Foster went across to Rena and kissed her lightly on the cheek. "How is the happy, blushing bride?"

Rena laughed gaily. "You seem in good spirits. I never saw you so talkative. What does it, the rum?"

"It helps." Foster blew cigarette smoke over her head. "Your father can certainly imbibe," he observed.

"He drinks too much."

Rufus brought her a small glass of wine. She hesitated. "I've had three already, darling. Do you think?"

"Oh, it's all right. Won't harm you," Rufus said.

Foster went away and filled a glass and quickly returned. "I'll drink with you," he said, "here's to—here's to—"

He had been doing all right, he thought suddenly. He had been doing all right, and now all of a sudden he didn't know what to say. He looked at Rufus and licked his lips. They probably think I'm drunk, he thought, and maybe that's a way out, but I'll be damned if I'll take it.

"—a happy partnership," he waved his glass at the couple.

"Thank you." Rena sipped the wine delicately. She didn't give any sign that she had observed Foster's hesitation. "Oh, I almost forgot to thank you for the lovely music box you gave us. Where did you get it? I've never seen one like it before."

"Picked it up from a Panamanian ship a couple of weeks ago," Foster replied.

"You should have seen what Aunt Matilda gave us!" She drew near to Rufus and whispered something in his ear. He winked at Foster.

Rena laughed and said, "When are you going to follow Rufus?"

"He's not the marrying type," Rufus answered for him.

"Let him answer for himself."

"I'm not the marrying type," Foster said, and grinned. Perhaps Rufus thought he wouldn't have been able to answer that one.

"You and Jennifer would make a good match. But Ma wants her to marry someone with a profession."

"That counts me out."

"You must come and see us whenever you're on leave. We're going to live here. Pa's giving us half the drawing room and the first bedroom."

"It would have been nicer to get your own place," Foster ventured.

"You know what the housing situation is like," Rufus said. "It isn't for want of trying. I could get a place down Diego Martin, but Rena doesn't want to leave Port of Spain."

"Boy Foster," she said, "your brother wants me to go and live in the bush. All my friends living in Port of Spain, I don't believe I could live anywhere else."

Diego Martin is a town a few miles from Port of Spain, but to Rena anywhere outside the city in the island was bush and uncivilisation. She spoke as if she expected Foster to agree with her, and once again the feeling of hesitation came over him. He didn't quite know how to go on. It didn't matter a damn to him where they lived. People always wanted you to agree with them, to share in their problems and show an interest.

He was beginning to feel depressed, and he went off to get drunk.

When he returned from the honeymoon Rufus made a wall of celotex and he put it up in the drawing room, separating his part of the house from Johnny's. They had received many wedding gifts—most of them useless except at parties or special occasions. Rena put them on display on a sideboard and Rufus looked at them in the evening and wondered why people didn't give useful gifts that you could use every day, instead of elaborate carving knives and big fruit bowls.

Rufus had to be very careful with Johnny, his moods were so unpredictable. One moment Johnny would say how it was a good thing that Rena was married, that Rufus was a hard-working man, and the next he would be abusing Rufus, why the hell didn't Rufus get his own place to live, instead of living like a parasite in Johnny's house.

One Sunday morning Johnny wanted to use the lavatory, but Rufus was there. Johnny kicked up hell. He had laid down a rule that around half-past nine in the morning, no one should use the lavatory, because that was usually when he got his motion. The others had adjusted themselves accordingly. All of them were up before nine, anyway. But on Sundays everyone lingered in bed, and then if it was after nine o'clock they would peep into Johnny's room to see if he was still asleep, and take turns watching while the others went.

Rufus didn't know anything about this, and Johnny was enraged when he found the lavatory occupied.

"Is my fault, Pa," Rena said, "I did forget to tell Rufus."

"This family too big for one lavatory now," Johnny stormed, "you better get one for your own self, Rufus."

But in a way, Johnny was glad there was another man in the

house. If there was any little quarrel, he went to Rufus for understanding. "They say I drinking too much," he said, "boy, come and fire one with the old man."

Rufus was unwillingly drawn into all the family's business, with reservations.

One night Mary's sister was visiting with her, when her husband stood up on the pavement outside the house and cursed Johnny, saying that he was carrying on with his wife, that was why she was always coming to see her sister.

He tried to get into the house, but Johnny locked the door.

"Look at trouble here tonight," Johnny said, "this man really looking for trouble, yes."

For a long time Lala stood there cursing and shouting and threatening to cut off Johnny's head. Then because no one responded—Johnny had turned off all the lights to try and make him believe they were going to sleep—he pushed open the gate near the pavement and came into the front yard. He took up Mary's flower pots which adorned the steps and threw them against the house.

Rufus's room was at the side of the front door. He listened to the commotion.

"Why don't you do something?" Rena whispered to him.

"What the hell you expect me to do?" he said irritably.

"Well go and tell Pa to open the door," Rena suggested, "otherwise that man won't go 'way. Go tell Pa to open the door and let him come inside."

"Why don't you leave them alone, it's not our worry."

"Man, Lala won't go away at all. He will stay there whole night. We won't be able to sleep."

Rufus got out of bed and went to Johnny.

"You better open the door," he said, "and settle this thing quietly with Lala."

There was a mahogany stick which Johnny took to work with him standing in the corner. Johnny looked at it.

"No no," Rufus said, "you will only cause trouble. Leave the stick alone. Call Lala inside and you-all talk and try to settle things."

With his son-in-law to back him up if there was any trouble, Johnny flung the door open and Lala staggered in drunkenly.

"I go kill you here tonight!" he screamed. "You have my wife here, eh? Every day she making excuse and saying she coming to see her sister."

In the back room, Mary and her sister held on to one another. "You better go and let Lala see you," she said, "he might go away quietly. Go and tell him to behave himself."

When Lala saw his wife his rage doubled. He advanced with two weights in his hands which he had snatched up from his own jeweller's shop.

Realising the danger Rufus sprang between them and held Lala's hands. Meantime Johnny had grabbed the mahogany stick and he now belaboured Lala with blows, swinging the stick furiously.

"Oh God oh!" Lala screamed, "look Johnny and his son-in-law killing me here tonight!"

Rufus was extremely upset by the incident, but he couldn't stop Johnny and hold Lala at the same time.

Johnny pushed Lala towards the door and as Rufus let loose shoved him with the stick down the steps and bolted the door.

The incident seemed to have given Lala more strength than frighten him.

"Oh God!" he shouted in the street in front of the house. "Johnny and his son-in-law break my foot! Oh God! Look at advantage! Johnny have my wife lock up in his house! That nasty coolie son of a bitch!"

A small crowd of idlers gathered, and they egged Lala on.

Inside the house Johnny told Rufus: "You better go to the police station and report this man. Say that he creating a disturbance, and let them send a policeman to take him away. You better pass by the side, through the back, so he won't see you."

Rufus was very tired, and he knew that if nothing was done Lala was the sort of man to stay out there until morning.

Wearily he got dressed and left by the back door, passing through the narrow passage at the side of the house. Lala was threatening his life too and he wasn't in the mood to encounter him.

About an hour after he made the report at the police station, a policeman came and took Lala away.

After another hour of wrangling and argument, Johnny began to feel sorry for what he had done. Lala was a relative of the family and it was a disgrace for him to be locked up in the police station.

By this time Rufus had turned in and was trying to go to sleep. Johnny woke him up.

"Get dress boy, and let we go and see if we can't get him out, he must be learn his lesson by now."

Rufus swore under his breath as he got up for the second time.

When they got to the police station Johnny explained to the sergeant in charge how it was just a family quarrel, and that he was sure Lala had learned his lesson.

"Don't lock him up any more, just let him promise to go home quiet and sleep," Johnny said.

Lala was released and he went home, but Rufus didn't hear the last of the night's activities for a long time. Lala's sons and daughters refused to speak to him for months. They were all under the impression that he had deliberately held down their father while Johnny beat him with the walking stick.

Rufus had to get up early every morning to catch the truck at Green Corner which took him to the American base. He had sandwiches for lunch, then ate a big meal in the evening when he came home.

Rena got up much later and had her breakfast alone. Then she cleaned up the apartment and either idled about or dressed and went shopping in Frederick Street. In the evening she cooked and waited for Rufus. Cooking was a problem, for she had to wait until Mary did hers before she could use the kitchen.

For a few months the newness of married life kept Rena quiet. But as her belly became big with child she wanted to attend every party or dance held in Port of Spain.

"Soon I can't go any place, I will get so big," she told Rufus.

He was usually tired out in the evenings, and found it hard to control his temper if he came in and found her all dressed up for a dance he didn't know anything about.

One night she promised they'd return early, but when they got there she forgot all about it. Rufus tapped her shoulder about eleven o'clock.

"We'd better be going now—I have to get up early to go to work."

She protested it was much too early, the dance had just begun.

Rufus lost his temper. "Well, stay as long as you like, but I'm going. You can come home with one of your relatives."

One night Foster dropped in to see them, and after dinner Rufus suggested going to play ping-pong at a club.

"You going to play ping-pong nearly every night now," Rena said.

"I got to have some recreation," Rufus pointed out.

When they got outside Rufus turned to Foster.

"I don't think I'm going to the club. Have you got anything to do?"

"Nothing in particular."

"Well, find something to do. I'm going out."

"Where?"

"To see somebody."

"A woman?"

"Well, yes. A girl working down at the base."

"You will get in trouble."

"To hell with you."

Rena had the child—a boy—in a clinic. For a few weeks she and Rufus seemed to get close together again. Then Rufus began to go out alone in the nights. Rena instructed Jennifer in the ways of babies, and left the child with her while she went out on her own. She had many friends, and there was always something to do.

A casual relationship now existed between Rufus and herself. If he came home and she wasn't there, he just went ahead and prepared something to eat. If she was there, the moment he entered she thrust the wailing baby into his arms and said, "I had the baby to mind whole day, is your turn now." And she dressed and went out.

Of the rest of them living in the house, Jennifer was the only one aware of the breach.

As for Johnny, when the child was born he was delighted. True, it was not his own son, but it was a boy anyway, and he was in the family. He used to sneak into the room when no one was about and play with the child, and bring sweets for it. Johnny thought: If this was my child I could tell him about the big invention when he grow up.

Tim learned to say "Grandpa" before he could say "Daddy" or "Mummy."

The old ambition to go abroad smoked again in Rufus when he got a rise in salary. He kept quiet about it and saved the money.

One day he told Rena he was going to the States to study dentistry.

"All of a sudden so you deciding to go away?" she asked.

"Oh, I always wanted to go."

She pointed out numerous obstacles which Rufus waved aside.

"What about your son?"

"When I settled in America I could send for you and Tim."

"You have enough money to go America?"

"I am saving as much as I could. I think I'll make it."

Rena considered the idea. That her husband was going away to study dentistry would enhance her social status. And she was a little tired of married life, anyway.

When Johnny heard about it he said, "This man will go away and leave you, he won't come back." But another time he would say: "What the hell I care? Is none of my business what you all do, I don't give a damn."

A few weeks later Rufus told Rena, "I haven't got enough money."

"Well, I can't help you. Only if I pawn my jewelries. And if Pa hear he will get vex."

All the same she did it, but even then Rufus was short.

"Once you told me your father has some money keeping for you," Rufus said, "you can't get it from him?"

By this time he had repeated his intention of going abroad so often that it was all they talked about.

When she was a little younger, Rena used to attend not only social functions but club meetings and group gatherings. She only went because she was flattered by the attention the young men paid her. Once a club was going to San Fernando to debate on the topic: Is Britain a Fallen or a Falling Nation, and Rena went with them. Half-way to San Fernando the bus skidded round a curve and turned turtle. Rena suffered a deep gash in her head and had to stay in hospital for two weeks. Johnny sued the bus company and got two hundred dollars. He told Rena: "That is your money, and I will keep it for you."

It was this money that Rufus was urging Rena to try and get.

At first Johnny refused, warning Rena that she should try and stop Rufus from going away.

"Everything decide already. It too late now to turn back," she told her father. "Is my money, Pa, why you don't want to give me?"

"Well all right then. But don't say I didn't warn you."

But as the time drew nearer Rena was a little frightened. She wasn't quite sure it was the right thing to let Rufus go. He had to reassure her time and again.

"You will send for me and Tim? You sure?"

And Rufus, visions of freedom floating in his mind, answered: "Sure, sure, as soon as I get settled."

"You better get a job quick in America so you could send some money for me regular."

"Yes, yes, of course."

"And don't forget Tim. He growing up, he will need a lot of clothes."

A week before his departure the office staff where he worked arranged to throw a farewell party for him.

When Rena heard she went to the wardrobe to pick a dress, her eyes bright with excitement. She had never been to the American base, it was a prohibited area.

There would be American officers at the party, it was sure to be a lavish affair.

She hummed as she got dressed. When Rufus came back from the bathroom he said: "What are you getting dressed for?"

"Why, I'm going with you!"

"Oh, I really forgot to tell you, it's a stag party. Only men."

Rena almost ripped the stocking she was putting on. "Well it's a big shame. Your own wife and I can't go with you—" she started to cry.

"But it's a stag party. You know what a stag party is?"

She sniffed and glared at him. Then she said, "I might as well go to the pictures, seeing that I nearly dressed. Jennifer could keep Tim until I return."

A sudden suspicion came to her mind and she looked at Rufus closely.

"You sure is a stag party? You not lying to me?"

Rufus laughed uneasily. "Why should I lie to you? The boys in the office are meeting to have a few drinks with me, that's all."

It was no stag party. Rufus took the girl with whom he was going around. He had a wonderful time, the staff presented him with a Parker 51 pen. When the party broke up about midnight a few of them got together to carry on. They went to one house where there was a pickup, and they danced and drank until four o'clock in the morning.

"You're a lying bitch," Rena was sitting up waiting for him

when he got home. "It was no stag party. You went with that girl from the office. Don't worry with how I find out! I know you've been going out with her all the time, making excuses and saying you going to play ping-pong by the club with Foster."

Rufus got into bed silently. Only six days to go, he thought, and all this would belong to the past.

She kept on at him, and he said, "You'll wake Tim, talking loud like that."

"I don't care! Why you didn't spend the night with her, instead of coming back here?"

"I don't like to quarrel in bed," he said. "It reminds me about when I was a little boy. My father and mother used to quarrel in bed. All day it would be all right, but when they got in bed, like it was a signal not to sleep but quarrel. I don't even like to talk in bed. They used to do that too. Talk about what they had done for the day, and what they were going to do tomorrow, and about guests we were going to have for the weekend. I don't like to talk in bed. I want to sleep. I'm tired."

But Rena was inflamed by his attitude. "Just because you going away and leaving your wife and son," she sobbed, "is no reason for you to shame the whole family."

A small party was held the night before his departure. Rena invited as many friends as possible so that they could spread the news that her husband was going away to America to study dentistry.

"How long are you going to be away?" Foster asked Rufus.

"About five years. Maybe more."

"The war might be over by then."

"Yes. What are you going to do then?"

"I don't know. I haven't the faintest notion. Rufus, I wish I were like you. To marry and settle down, to go to America. I don't mean the courage to do those things—I have the courage all right. I mean the belief."

"The belief?"

"Yes. How did you know your marriage would work out? Don't you have a little fear about leaving everything you have, everyone you know, and going to a strange country?"

"My marriage didn't work out, I believe you know. But one learns from experience, I guess."

"Corny?"

"So what? It's true, anyway."

"What about Rena and Tim?"

"What else can I do? I'll try to send for them later. You talked about belief just now. Of course I believed in my marriage, and I tried to make it work. Things didn't seem to come out as I had expected, that's all. Maybe this separation will bring us nearer to each other, if you see what I mean. And as for being afraid of leaving Trinidad, why should I be? You ask some damn funny questions, boy. Were you afraid when you joined the Navy?"

"I just sort of drifted into it. I didn't think about it."

"Good. You continue to do things that way. You like to think too blasted much, sitting on your tail all day and puzzling about why this and why that. What about a job after the war? Haven't you thought about that?"

"I am saying 'why fret about tomorrow'; et cetera, and you are going to say I am evading the question. You know, Rufus, if you were a different person you could help me out of a lot of difficulty."

"How do you mean?"

"Well, there are some things in life which baffle me. One of them is marriage. If you knew you were going to America, why did you get married at all?"

"Oh Christ, there you go again. I told you Rena was on the way. The situation forced my hand. But that isn't enough for you, is it? You want something abstract, you want to know how my mind has been functioning all the time, you want to know the motive, and what actuated me. You have got to get it into your head that people do things for certain reasons. Life is full of beaten paths, and if you take one of those you're pretty safe. You don't want to go bothering yourself too much."

"Well what's the use of experience if someone can't put it to some use?"

"Get married yourself and you'll find out all about it. Push your own hand in the fire."

"Ah, we shouldn't be talking like this tonight, anyhow. Let's fire one—oh, wait a minute, there's Jennifer. I must have a word with the girl. She's looking hearts tonight."

Rufus frowned as Foster walked off.

"Hello Jennifer," Foster sat on the sofa as she swept her dress out of the way. "I was just telling Rufus that you're looking hearts tonight. Dream. Song."

"I haven't seen you for a long time," she said, smiling. She liked Foster, in a careful way. She wasn't sure yet what sort of a person he was. Mary had warned her not to be interested in him, that there was no future for her with a man like Foster. She was ignoring Mary now on the strength that she and Foster were related by her sister's marriage.

"I've been deep-sea fishing," Foster said.

"You look good in ordinary clothes. I don't like to see you in your uniform."

"But you like to see Americans and Englishmen in theirs. Why is that? What's wrong with my uniform? Is it because I am a Trinidadian?"

"No, I just mean you, I didn't think about all that."

Jennifer's tone was apologetic as Foster had spoken with a sudden vehemence.

He realised he'd been a fool. The girl had just made an innocent observation and he had pounced at her. Still, he couldn't help being on guard against the stupid attitude of some people. It was all right for a foreigner to be in uniform, but some people thought there was something ludicrous about a Trinidadian wearing a sailor suit. They didn't seem to have any pride that their own kind was helping to win the war.

"We're not supposed to take off our uniforms on leave," he said, smiling to cover up the blunder, "but I felt like taking a chance, as it is Rufus's last night in Trinidad. Can I get you anything? What about some wine?"

"A little please."

Foster pushed through the crowd of people. He hardly knew any of them. He had met some at the wedding, and they had drunk together, but that was all. He saw Patrick and called out: "How is the history?" But Patrick was taking things easy, there were a lot of girls present and he didn't want to pass out quickly like he had at the wedding. He was hoping that later on they could roll up the carpet and dance, if Johnny got drunk enough not to care.

Foster met Johnny at the table hovering like a guardian angel over four bottles of rum.

When he saw Foster he said: "But we haven't had a drink together for the night, man! Call your brother and let we fire one together."

Foster signalled to Rufus and he came over, and Johnny

poured drinks.

"You know," he said, addressing Foster but looking at Rufus, "I have a feeling your brother not going to come back to Trinidad. You don't think so?" And he looked Foster in the eye as he handed him the drink.

"Where else could he return to?" Foster laughed, determined not to be drawn into giving opinion. "Unless he sends for Rena and the child and they live in America."

"Ah!" Johnny swallowed his drink quickly to get on with the conversation, as if Foster had struck the heart of the matter. "And who going to keep them while he in America? Who going to buy clothes and food for the boy? Who going to mind the two of them while he looking for job over there, and studying at the same time?"

Foster had an irritating feeling that he was supposed to answer these questions. Why did people put their problems to you as if they expected you to solve them? What the hell could he say to Johnny?

"Rena could get a job," he suggested tentatively.

"None of my daughters ever work before," Johnny said proudly.

"Well, it's time. They'll get a lot of experience," Foster found himself saying.

"Young men too worthless these days," Johnny grumbled irrelevantly, "they married and leave their wife and go away, they don't realise their responsibilities."

Rufus laughed uncomfortably and glanced around to see if anyone had heard. He cleared his throat and said, "Cheers," raising his glass.

"I agree with you," Foster said, filling the glasses again and enjoying Rufus's uneasiness, "they should stay at home with their wives. I don't know why this man going to America at all!"

"I am going to study dentistry," Rufus said loudly. "I'll send for my wife and child as soon as I get settled." And he glared at Foster.

"Excuse me—I have to take Jennifer some wine." Foster winked at Rufus and walked away.

A little later Rufus dragged Foster away from Jennifer into a corner and said in a low voice, "You're a helluva man, man. You had a man in an embarrassing position. I don't like your sense of humour at all."

"Oh, never mind. Nothing serious happened, and it's too late now to hold you back."

"That's what you think. Rena told me Johnny was considering letting me have a cheque for a hundred dollars as a sort of gift. He was to give it to me tonight, if at all. But the party is almost ended and I haven't seen him make a move. On top of that, you had to go and talk to him."

"He must have changed his mind."

"You cause the whole damn thing, man! Trying to be clever! You helped him to decide not to give me. It's your fault if I don't get it."

"Look boy, I'm really sorry, I didn't mean any harm, you know that. You should have told me as soon as I came. Is it too late to do something? What about if I go and old-talk him, and fire a few? You think I could soften him up?"

"Boy, things desperate. I am willing to try anything at all, I could really use that hundred dollars. But be careful how you talk to him, don't let the others hear you."

Foster found Johnny in the usual place. Johnny never sat at these house parties. He always stood near the drinks. Now and then he would venture a walk around the room, talking to no one, but smiling to himself as if he alone knew what life was all about and everyone else was a fool.

"I have a watch that needs repairing," Foster faltered for an opening.

"Come and fire one," Johnny ignored the remark. "I know is rum you come for, you don't have to make excuse."

Foster drank with him. "This is a nice party," he said, trying again.

"These young men can't drink," Johnny grumbled, "they only come here because the rum free, and they could get something to eat for nothing."

It was as if they were both talking to themselves. Foster wondered what he could say to connect up with Johnny. He decided to take the plunge.

"This boy Rufus, I don't know why he didn't save up enough money before he decide to go away. But you know how it is with we Indian people—we always have to help out one another. As for me, I had about eighty dollars in the bank, and I had to take it out to give him. He say 'lend', but when you think I will ever get that money back?"

Johnny seemed to be listening for the first time. "Well, he is your own brother. You shouldn't be looking for that again."

Foster laughed and tilted the bottle: the rum gurgled. "How about you, eh? He stick you for anything? You must be give him two—three hundred dollars!"

Johnny looked up startled. He looked at Foster suspiciously, but Foster was pouring drinks. He put his hand in his pocket, and seemed to consider for a moment.

"If you really want to know," he spoke in a whisper, leaning near to Foster, "I have a cheque here now. But I wondering if I should give the scamp?"

"That is up to you," Foster said casually.

"Everybody does say that I mingy with my money," Johnny muttered.

"Well, why you don't show them?" Foster drove in desperately. "You could make a big presentation, with a big farewell speech, after all, he married to your daughter."

Johnny looked suspiciously again at Foster, but Foster had turned his back and was walking away.

Rufus was sitting with Rena.

"You manage to old-talk Pa?" she asked Foster as he came up.

Foster glanced over his shoulder to see what Johnny was doing before answering. Johnny still had his hand in his pocket, a look of indecision on his face.

"I'm not so sure. Look. Rufus, you and Rena must hand round drinks to everybody, and say you want to make a farewell speech—"

"I hate that sort of thing," Rufus groaned.

"Well, it's up to you now. He's got that cheque in his pocket, and if he's going to give you it will be now. But he can't make up his mind. You must lay the land for Johnny to make a big presentation. Say how you have been proud to have a man like Johnny for a father-in-law, and how you have been happy living here in his house, and how if it wasn't for him you would have been in plenty trouble. You don't want me to tell you what to say? Make it good, lay it on thick."

"Go and try to bring me a big drink," Rufus said. "A tall one. Don't let Johnny see you if you can help. Then I'll see if I could do it."

Foster got the drink and Rufus took it in one gulp. Rena was

46

already distributing wine to the ladies. A sort of restless quiet came over the crowd as Rufus stood up to address them.

"Relatives and friends—" he began nervously.

"Hear hear hear!" Foster couldn't contain himself as he thought how funny the situation was. He bit his lip to prevent himself from laughing out loud. Everyone in the room made a little laugh, as if he had said something funny, but Johnny shouted: "Behave yourself and let the boy talk!"

Thus encouraged Rufus got through a sort of rambling farewell speech in which he praised Johnny effusively. He kept his eyes averted from Foster, who had his face buried in his hands.

But Foster was listening, and as the clapping died down he rose solemnly. "Perhaps the father of the house would like to say a few words in reply," he suggested, and sat down, bending his head.

For a moment Johnny appeared confused, but he had been drinking all the evening and couldn't resist the opportunity to address the cheering guests.

And in the course of his thick-voiced tirade on the ways of youth today, his hand unconsciously came out of his pocket, and the envelope with the cheque was in his hand. He looked at it foolishly for a second.

"Nevertheless," he changed direction, "we are family, and must help out one another. Nobody could say that Johnny didn't help to send his son-in-law to America to study. I have a small cheque here. . ."

Long after the guests departed Rufus and Foster sat around the table with Johnny mopping up the remains of rum. Then Foster passed out completely. Rufus put him to sleep on the sofa.

"I think he has to report back to his ship by six o'clock in the morning," he told Johnny, "and it's almost three now."

"To hell with that, man. All you young people can't take your liquor. Let we finish up this bottle here."

"No more for me," Rufus said firmly. "I'm going to sleep. I have to get up early to finish packing."

He left Johnny muttering to himself, his hands stretched out full length on the table.

Rufus was dead tired as he got into bed. He didn't have the energy to put on his pyjamas, he got under the sheet in his drawers, and sighed loudly as his body sank into the soft mattress.

"You did say you was coming to bed early." Rena turned over and whispered, her eyes bright with anticipation. She had had an hour's sleep which had taken the edge off her tiredness.

"I know. But I just couldn't get away from Johnny and Foster. Lord, your father could drink!"

He raised himself on an elbow limply and looked at her. Her eyes were bright in the dark, like a cat's. He wondered if he could control his tired body. He had a feeling of to hell with it, he wanted to sleep and wake refreshed. But he knew he couldn't do that. Not tonight. She began fondling his body, sliding her hands along the hairs on his chest.

And with everything piling up in his mind, the oh-Christ thought of everything that had happened to him, he knew he had to do it with her for the last time. His muscles stiffened and quivered as she threw her legs over him.

Almost savagely he cast the sheet aside and stood on his knees and elbows over her.

When Foster got up two hours later with a splitting head he heard the bed creaking through the celotex wall and he hesitated to say good-bye. He shrugged and lit a cigarette and ran his fingers through his hair.

Then he opened the front door quietly and slipped out. The early morning wind felt cold on his face.

He didn't see Rufus again for five years.

Chapter Four

Foster wished he had joined the RAF instead of the local branch of the Royal Navy. He was a little tired of it all—the lazy months of inaction just cruising around the Caribbean, the strict discipline, and the attitude of the foreigners. He had mixed with all the islanders in the Caribbean, with the US servicemen and with the English, with homosexuals and prostitutes. It struck him that the Americans and English never thought of themselves as foreigners, it was as if they expected the local people to conform with their ideas and not the other way round. In the first place they didn't know anything about the West Indies. They came expecting savages and dusky girls in grass skirts. One enthusiastic Englishman wrote an article for a London magazine about how they were staying in a base in the bush where snakes crawled around and lepers walked freely—and the natives sang calypsoes and drank rum all day long. Other chaps came ashore covered in mosquito nets and with their feet encased in long rubber leggings, expecting swamp and jungle.

Once a Canadian officer saw Foster using a drinking glass and the man got on like a primitive savage. "What!" he roared, "you natives don't know how to use a drinking glass—take it back to the galley at once!"

The situation was so ridiculous that Foster could only laugh foolishly: he was detained ashore for fourteen days at the Army barracks in St James for insubordination.

There were a lot of other incidents like this, but Foster put it down to ignorance rather than anything else. As a matter of fact, he used to get along fine with them after they had been in the island for a few months.

In the conglomeration of personnel which made up the force, there never existed a feeling of unity or oneness among the islanders that they were helping to win the war. The Trinidadian was better than the Grenadian, but the Jamaican was better than the Trinidadian, and as for the British Guianese, they came from the continent of South America they weren't "small island" like the other West Indians. They were in a class by themselves.

Foster still sought his common ground, looking for a level where man could meet a man on equal terms. But he was miserable most of the time. He had had no word from Rufus, and since his brother's departure he never bothered to go around by Johnny's house.

The future was hazy. Days made months and months years, and he wasn't nearer to anything in his mind. Just stick around, something will happen, he told himself. He sprawled on the deck on warm nights with a million stars over his head, and he saw the world, spinning off there in space, and he wondered what he was going to do when the war was over. He had a few distant relatives here and there—two cousins in San Fernando, another in San Juan. He hadn't seen any of them for a long time. If the worse came to the worse, he could live for a couple of months with each of them until he decided what to do.

He had made no real friends except Andrews, an artist. The English sailors were astounded that Andrews, a Trinidadian, could paint.

"My dear fellow," Foster said to one in an argument one day, "what do you think we are, savages? Don't you know we think—" But he never bothered to finish. Let them think what the hell they wanted to think, to hell with them. He wasn't going to educate a pack of ignorant Englishmen who believed cannibals lurked in the hills. "Yes, we have lions," he told another viciously some other time, "and tigers too. You'd better keep near to Port of Spain."

But whenever he talked like that he repented, and afterwards apologised. Only, it didn't seem fair that West Indians had to know all about England in the schools, and on the other hand Englishmen didn't know anything about the West Indies.

He read a lot, but spasmodically: all the books in the world used to pile up in his mind, and he knew a futility and a fear at not being able to read them all.

And in those days in the service his mornings began to be fearful. The moment he awoke his mind began a restless pacing, what were people doing and why, was it a sunny morning, and a host of other unrelated thoughts. He transferred from ship to ship until he met Andrews on an MTB. They were the only natives, the rest of the crew were English. He stayed there for the remaining six months of the war.

One day while he was ashore drinking with Andrews he asked

him what plans he had for afterwards.

"I think I'd like to teach," Andrews said. "Not in one school—a sort of roving art teacher, going all over the island. I always had a fancy for teaching, I suppose because I was never well taught myself!"

"We could use some good teachers," Foster said, sipping beer. "I think you could make a good job of it."

"How about you?"

"It's funny, about me," Foster gave a little laugh and twirled his glass, looking at the beer. "I can't seem to make up my mind about anything."

"I don't know why you treat everything so seriously," Andrews said. "You have to think out each little detail, each why and wherefore."

"It isn't that really," Foster said earnestly, "and you know it. Why, I could be as practical as any man, I could make up my mind quickly if I have to. And I could have a good time, same as you or anybody else. Remember last month in Barbados?"

"Boy, that was time! Four of us on one bed! But in the end you had to go asking Dorothy why she prostituted her body, and spoil it all."

"Well, I wanted to find out, that's all."

"And you were morbid in the morning. I tried to get you out of bed, but you said for Christ sake to leave you alone—and we had to report back aboard at seven o'clock, too."

"But we had a good time at Bathsheba, though. We drank four bottles of rum, and we made love in the water."

"And you remember the night we barged into a dance, and made the orchestra accompany us while we sang 'Night and Day'?"

"We must have been drunk as hell." Foster poured another beer, and smiled wearily.

"So we start off as we have done many a time to discuss one thing, and ramble off into pleasant irrelevancies. But one thing. When it's over, we must still get together now and then to exchange ideas. Andrews, do you think I'm an escapist? That I run away by pretending I'm puzzled?"

"I won't say that. But you do waste a lot of time making yourself accept accepted things. To make a point, this is beer we're drinking in glasses. That's OK by me, I don't give a second's thought to it. But you, you're different. I can see you pouring beer and watching it fall in the glass and foaming, and your eyes tell me that you can discuss at length the subject of beer and glasses. And not only that. You'd want to ask questions, funny questions that people don't ask at all. Like, Why are we drinking beer in glasses? Now I know you don't mean that we might as well drink from the bottle, or any other container for that matter. What you mean by Christ, is What are we doing here. What you mean is something fundamental and deep, that has nothing to do with beer and glasses. It would please you if in answer to your question I say, 'Bread and butter, fire and water', or make some other utterly remote reply. Your face would beam, you would say Wonderful! Giant! But I am telling you, to hell with all that balls. I am drinking beer and having a good time, and that's all there is to it."

Foster threw back his head and laughed loudly. "Wonderful! Giant! Andrews, you are my friend for life. And you must be thirsty after that. Let me get more—er, bread."

Foster went to the bar.

They were in a servicemen's canteen on the waterfront. The room was crowded with uniforms and thick with smoke, but they had managed to drag a small table into a corner.

"My friend," Foster said, returning with six chilled bottles, "you do not know how happy I am. Tonight we celebrate to an everlasting friendship. We accept, and are accepted. Wait a minute—didn't someone say that before?"

"Pour the blasted beer man."

"Don't be so primitive, boy, what will all these foreigners think?"

He sat down. Andrews offered him a cigarette.

"I find," Foster spoke as if he were joining up to a matter already discussed, "that I often think or say things which are original only to myself. When I discover that someone else has already been that way—and broadcast his findings, to boot—it is most frustrating. Has that ever happened to you?"

"Yes. Just last month I was trying out a new idea on a landscape, and I was all excited until I found out it wasn't new at all. I expect that happens to many people."

"Well then," Foster said, leaning across the table, "supposing I wanted to write a book telling about some of these thoughts I have, do you mean to say I'll have to check every blasted book that has already been written to make sure I don't repeat someone's ideas?"

"Not only that. Think of the thousands like you who may be contemplating writing. First dog in is the winner. Have you started?"

"Who said I was writing a book? I'm merely discussing the idea with you. But to get back, you can go to hell if you expect me to believe that writers do that."

"Of course not. Writing is different from thinking. I don't know what we're talking about anyway. We seem to be mixed up."

"Well, who cares? Let's talk all the same."

But they fell into an embarrassed silence. They knew they were getting tight.

Foster said: "Do you think I am under the influence?"

Andrews looked puzzled, and Foster laughed. "I've done with that balls we were talking."

Andrews said, "I wasn't quite sure what you meant. One can't be too careful with you. No, I think you're just 'sweet'."

"And you?"

"In like vein."

"Then let's do something. Come play some ping-pong."

"Too much fellars around the table man."

"Well, the piano then."

"OK. But first I want to do something."

"Me too."

They returned and went to the piano, which was on a platform in one corner of the canteen. The piano was dilapidated and had seen its days, but when struck the keys emitted sounds. It had been donated by a wealthy local English woman who wanted to clear her drawing room for a radiogram to decorate her room. The canteen manager was thankful for the gift until he found out he had to get it tuned every month.

An English soldier had just swung off the stool in disgust. Foster said to him, "It's no damned good, but I'm accustomed to it." He sat down and struck a few chords. Andrews leaned against the piano.

"I bet you haven't enough guts to play some de Bussy here and now."

"What're you betting?"

"A beer."

"Go bring it."

But when Andrews came back Foster was tinkling away a hot

calypso tune with a crowd around him.

"Do you know that one about rum and coca-cola mate?" a sailor asked him.

Foster nodded and swung into the calypso. He was not a good player, but in the atmosphere it didn't matter. Everyone sang and hummed, and bottles of beer appeared as if by magic on the piano, brought by convivial spirits.

Then after the calypsoes he struck a chord and played 'Drink to Me Only with Thine Eyes'. That one brought all the English servicemen around the piano. They sang slowly and thickly, waving their glasses of beer. When he got up there was so much protest that he sat down again and played 'Annie Laurie.' Then he saw someone he knew could play and called him.

"Take over for the boys—you'll get loads of free beer," he whispered. He slid off the stool with his hands still busy and the fellow took the keys off his fingers and went on playing.

Foster and Andrews were deliberating whether they should go to look for whores in George Street when the fight broke out.

As usual, no one knew how it had started, but all of a sudden men were scrambling around and swinging fists and chairs. There were no Colonials involved, the fight was between English sailors from two ships.

But Foster grabbed Andrews' arm and shouted, "It's our men, boy! There's Smitty and the bo'sun!"

"Let's clear out, it's not our fight," Andrews began, but Foster had already swung into action, jabbing with his elbows and fists until he was in the centre of the fight. Andrews started after him.

The West Indians in the canteen saw Foster and Andrews in the melee and downed glasses to join the fray.

Foster saw them from the corner of his eye and shouted: "Keep out!" But if they heard they paid no attention. They thought it was the old problem once again, and several of them waded into the battle.

It lasted for fifteen minutes before sufficient military policemen arrived to restore order. Bottles and chairs had come into play, but except for a few gashes and bruises no one was seriously hurt.

"You know," Andrews said as they walked along the waterfront with the rest of the MTB crew, "you got me into that fight almost against my will. Before I knew what was happening I was there. And you are one hell of a man, last week when I tried to get you into that fight by Green Corner you refused."

"That was a black and white fight—I don't waste my energy fighting for stupid causes, I told you that before. This black and white business is a lot of wind. If a white man doesn't want to accept me as a human being, I pity his ignorance and reach, that's all. It doesn't get me angry or make me see red. In any case a man must be colour blind to call me black—as we are to call pink white."

"All right, all right. But just because you refuse to admit it doesn't mean that a colour bar doesn't exist."

"So what? Look old man, I am tired. Let's don't talk any more tonight. We're sailing at four o'clock in the morning, and it's after one now."

The war was over. One morning Foster was sitting on the deck in a pair of shorts, his chest bare, leaning over the gunwale and watching the water in the sea.

"What are you doing?" Andrews had been ashore to get his demobilisation papers fixed up.

"Taking a tan," Foster replied without looking up.

"Ha, ha, ha. If you used to make jokes for a living you would surely starve."

"Are you fixed up now?"

"Yes. I can see you drifting around Port of Spain catching your royal. You'd better get into something quickly—any sort of job."

"I hear we're getting some money."

"Boy, maybe two or three hundred dollars. Where are you going to live?"

Foster looked up for the first time. "No idea. I have some things in a room in Woodbrook where I used to stay with my brother. I may be there for a while if the room's vacant."

"Why don't you come and stay with me in Tacarigua until you get fixed?"

"Thanks. But I'd rather be on my own for a while. Look, things aren't as bad with me as I make you seem to think. I have relatives here and there, I'll get by."

The morning he was demobilised Foster walked out of the naval base in Port of Spain with a duffle bag on his shoulder and three hundred dollars in his pocket. Other ratings were laughing and singing about that they called freedom, saying they'd never join up again, not even if Germany invaded Trinidad. Some who had volunteered to stay on as long as possible were jeered at—"we love this place oh lord." They had nothing to complain of really, but it was the "tough" thing to pretend that life had been hell in the navy, and take every opportunity to decry the service. Indeed, some young men had never enjoyed themselves as much as when they joined up, but they were afraid to say so. Nothing complimentary was ever said about the force, it was grumble and complain all through the war, and no one was brave enough to say anything else. So they joked and laughed a little uncertainly, not sure what civilian life would be like, but whatever it was, they were sure it would be better than rotting in the navy.

With six others Foster went into a Chinese restaurant and they ate a huge meal while getting drunk. Then someone suggested they should go to a film.

When Foster got into the cinema and sat down nausea overcame him. He went into the lavatory and was sick for five minutes. He staggered outside and went up Park Street. His legs were wobbly. He was very drunk.

Patrick was going home from work and saw him leaning against a wall.

"Boy Foster, what happen man?"

Foster said something.

"Boy, you drunk as hell. You better wait here let me get a soda water from the parlour."

Patrick ran into a cafe and came back with a bottle of soda water. He dashed the effervescing water on Foster's face and forced some down his throat.

"You better come with me boy, you look as if you ready to fall down."

He put an arm around Foster's shoulder and led him to a nearby taxi-stand. He sat in the back of the car with Foster sprawled all over him.

Patrick stopped the car a little way from Johnny's house, and he led Foster by the side entrance to his room. No one had seen him enter, he was glad for that, because he hadn't formulated a good excuse.

He threw Foster on the canvas cot and took off his shoes.

Patrick remembered the time of the party when he was drunk and Foster had taken care of him.

Some hours later Foster opened his eyes. He watched the long-legged girl on the wall putting on her nylons. He turned his head and there was another girl. This one was naked, but she had coyly clasped her hands and placed them together between her legs. He shook his head, and it was as if he had shaken a tambourine, a jangling started in his head.

He moaned and rolled over. He almost fell off the narrow cot. He got his knees braced against the wall and he fell asleep again.

Chapter Five

For a few weeks Foster floundered hopelessly around the city, out of tune with the population and the things they did, unable to fit in with people he had known before joining the navy. He was sorely tempted to look up Andrews, but he put the idea aside: he would see him only after he was working in some job, so Andrews wouldn't say clever things. He spent some of his demobilisation money on clothing. The rest he banked—for a sunny day, he thought with a smile.

He spent some time in San Fernando with one of his cousins. But he got fed up with free meals and lodging and circular conversations. One day he met a man much older than himself, and in the casual exchange of conversation he felt there was some intelligence there. The man invited Foster home. He was a prominent man in the town, well-off and in good social standing. But when they were having drinks the man stood up near to Foster. Foster finished his drink and went away. As soon as a homosexual discovers that you are a free thinker he believes you are easy prey. Foster knew he should feel pity for the man, but he only felt revulsion.

He left San Fernando and went to San Juan to stay with another cousin, Regald. It was much better here. Regald was happily married to Muriel. They had two girls and two boys. They hadn't intended to have so many, but these things happen.

Regald was a middle-aged man, but somehow time seemed to pass him by. He had a boyish face and he thought young. He worked steadily at his job, conscious of his responsibilities. He was never morbid or terribly angry. And though he never probed too deeply into anything, he was intelligent and witty and honest with the knowledge he had, backing out of an argument if he knew he couldn't hold his own.

Regald had married, settled down, and his wife had borne four children. He was contented in a way. He knew there were perhaps better things in the world than what he possessed: he had the capacity to gain those things if he wanted. There were sometimes minutes of regret and wistfulness, but Regald had learned to accept life.

Foster liked and admired Regald. He had been to see them now and then, and at those times he had mentioned in a joking manner (though he was in earnest) the likelihood of his putting up with them for a while when the war was over.

And Regald had told him anytime, so his appearance wasn't altogether a surprise.

Foster did odd chores about the house. He weeded the kitchen garden. He took the children to school in the morning, and went for them in the afternoon if he was free. He kept them if Regald and Muriel wanted to go out.

In this happy, domestic setting Foster patterned in his imagination his own life: do the same thing, get married, have children, to hell with the spinning world. The children scrambled on to his bed in the mornings and broke his reverie: they screamed out that he was a fool, that all he had to do was find a nice girl and such contentment could be his.

"When are you going to look for a job?" Muriel asked one day. "You only idling your time away writing. Regald could get you a job in the office where he works. Tomorrow, if you like."

One morning Foster was surprised to get a letter from Andrews. He had got the address through someone who worked with Regald.

"Come and spend Sunday with me," Andrews wrote, "you must be morbid and frustrated and melancholy for rich companionship."

That Sunday Foster went. It was only seven miles from San Juan to Tacarigua, and the bus took him there in a few minutes.

He saw Andrews sitting in an easy chair on the verandah. He had on a white merino and a pair of khaki trousers held up with a necktie. He was reading a book.

Foster walked up quietly and said: "Is this where Mr Andrews lives?"

"You thought I didn't see you coming," Andrews said calmly, still looking at the book, "but I saw you all the time." Then he closed the book and jumped up with a grin.

"Well, you old dog, how are you?"

Andrews asked that deliberately because Foster had told him how he found the query difficult to answer when he was a boy. But Foster only replied, "Not bad, boy. Catching my royal."

"I can see that. But come inside and meet my mother and

sister."

When the formalities were over they went back to the verandah and Foster took off his shoes and sat on the floor. "What have you got in the line of entertainment? Gin? Rum? Whisky?"

"Gin and coconut water. It will come out in a minute."

"Ah, you're a good host. I should have taken you up on that invitation to spend some time in Tacarigua."

"If you're serious you're welcome, you know. We have a spare room."

"Thanks. But I think I've loafed around enough. I must get a job." It was what he had been telling himself all the time: the words came from his mouth almost unconsciously.

"What about the Resettlement Office?"

"I haven't made an honest effort anywhere."

"Look Foster, if I give you a letter of introduction to a man I know in Port of Spain, will you go to see him?"

"What sort of job?"

"Probably clerical. I know you'll be bored to death, but you have to do something, man, you can't go around like this all the time."

"You know I won't stay there long."

"That doesn't matter. You ought to be doing something."

"All right. I'll go tomorrow." And then, as if a thought had just struck him, he said, "Have I been sounding as if I'm not grateful for what you're doing, as if I don't care?"

"I don't think so."

"It suddenly struck me that people may think I'm ungrateful by my attitude."

"Well, this isn't costing me anything. Don't say you'll go tomorrow and then forget all about it."

"No, good talk. How about you? Are you working?"

Andrews poured gin and coconut water. "Doing what I want to do—teach children art. It's a great job. I love teaching."

"It's a funny thing. I wanted to see you so we could have a long talk, and now I don't feel like talking at all. Oh well. Have you been painting?"

"Yes. Want to see?"

"You know I am not interested in painting."

They sat in silence, drinking gin and smoking. The house was near to the mainroad; from where they sat they could see traffic plying the road.

After four gins Foster began to feel better. "I've been staying with my cousin in San Juan," he said. "He lives a happy life. Wife, children, piece of land to garden, steady job. Maybe I should follow suit, eh? Maybe I should become domesticated."

"What's the hurry? Look at me. I know many girls I'd like to marry, but imagine being tied to one woman for all the days of your life. Imagine going out to parties and seeing dozens of girls you'd like to—"

"You're talking too loudly."

"Anyway, marriage is a resigned state of life. I'm not ready for it yet."

"I bet you get married before me, though."

Foster got up suddenly. "Let's do something. You told me Tacarigua was beautiful. Show me the landscape."

"Oh hell, I'll have to get dressed."

"Put on a shirt."

Andrews rose from the easy chair with a sigh. "There's a savannah across the road, near the railway line. It's nice out there. We could sit under a tree."

He went inside and returned in a minute, pushing a shirt down his trousers. "What about the gin?"

"How do you mean what about the gin? We'll take it with us." Foster put the bottle in his back pocket and slipped two glasses in his side ones. "Get a bottle and put the coconut water in."

They crossed the road and went over a wire fencing. The savannah was green and lush, with a few grazing cattle. There was a muddy pond with water lilies.

Foster flung himself under a cannonball tree and rolled to a stop against the trunk.

" 'Youth is not a time of life'," Andrews observed, smiling and dropping down himself.

"Ah," Foster said, "we should be grateful for the chance to breathe and watch the sky. Think of all the people who work in dark dusty rooms where a ray of the sun never shines."

They lay on the grass, pressing their bodies into the earth. They had propped the bottle and glasses against the trunk of the tree.

"I want to tell you something," Foster murmured, "but it's difficult. You'll just have to listen. Give me a cigarette."

Andrews peeled the cellophane wrapping off a pack of Anchor

Specials and tapped the bottom of the pack to loosen the cigarettes. With minimum effort he stretched his hand to Foster. They lit up and blew smoke which danced crazily in the breeze and vanished. Foster looked up and saw the glare of the sun spread in a circle in the sky, and there was a blue whiteness in that circle, but outside of it the colour mellowed and softened into pure blue, and clouds came over the Northern Range and rushed towards the sun like it was a vacuum.

"Oh kiss me the universal kiss," Foster murmured, "and there's an end to the world's wrangle."

"Quote?" Andrews asked.

"I hope not. I just thought of it."

"I like it." He repeated the words to himself. "Yes, I really like it."

Foster wondered if he told Andrews about what he was thinking, if he would understand, because he didn't himself. He felt the earth with his hands and it was cool, despite the sun.

"What I wanted to talk about doesn't seem important now," he said. "It was, a few minutes ago, and it is, at the time when I think of it. But I'm not in that frame of mind again."

But Foster knew he would tell Andrews. Not passionately, as he would like it, but as if he didn't care, as if he were only talking to pass the time away. The immensity of it, by God. He trembled a little, and then he said, as indifferently as he could, "Have you ever been afraid, Andrews? I mean really? A kind of feeling inside you, linked up with life itself."

"You mean like if you lose faith with yourself?" Andrews didn't speak as if he were particularly interested, and Foster was glad, it would be easier to tell him.

"That's near, you're on the right track, but I don't think it's that at all. Oh hell, forget it."

"You mean remember it. That's what people mean when they say forget it that way."

"Well, I don't know if I can impress you. It's difficult to explain. It's a fear of—well, life. Everything in life. Wars. Music. Death. The Wind. Does that make sense?"

"In a way."

Foster hesitated a little, then went on, "Just sort of follow me, see, don't give with clever interruptions. Just keep track of what I say. I mean, waking in the morning and just lying there thinking about life, about work, about the millions of people who will meet millions of people and the things they'd say. About the world, spinning in space. And how life is so damned funny. Wars and governments and art and a piece of chalk—look, all this sounds screwy, but you follow me?"

Foster chewed the soft, undeveloped white bottom of a blade of grass and waited to hear the tone of Andrews' voice. "Sure go on."

"Well, I mean all those things. They sort of make you think that it's all a hell of a joke, and you want to laugh and then suddenly you're frightened not at any one thing but at everything. You remember what you've learned of history, thousands of years of Man's existence. Do you know how many people live without awareness of Time? Without thinking, 'nineteen fifty-two?' Why the hell should I be bothered?"

He was speaking too intensely. He tried to forget everything and watched a butterfly trying to right itself in a gust of wind. If he were Andrews, he knew what he would say—"Why are you telling me all this Foster? For God's sake, why? On a brilliant day like this, with clouds moving in the sky and a clean wind blowing and your heart pumping blood into your veins?"

Andrews said, "I would like to recommend a snowball. Look, over yonder near the edge of the savannah sits a vendor drowsing in the heat—"

But Foster had said too much to stop now. "I have a fear sometimes. I don't know why. I can't pin it down and say it is this or that. The way lips move, the creak of an ageing limb, the mind filled with the pictures of fields of rotting bodies lost in war, and sunsets and flowers. You follow?"

"I'm trying hard," Andrews said, "what about a drink?"

"A lot of things, like different beliefs. You for one say that the mind is the root."

"And what do you say?"

"Me? Why, to hell with all of it; I don't say anything at all. It's got so a man can't live wondering which is the most nutritious food to eat, the right way to talk, the proper clothes to wear, even what he should think about."

"Well," Andrews said, "you must live outside of all that, like I do."

"But I'm afraid. There's a sameness about life which gets you—"

"Ah, we stray like yonder cattle, hither and thither."

"This sameness you discover when you're outside. A pattern which is followed, and you can't do anything about it. It's like trying to escape from yourself. You live, and the pattern exists with you, the shadow thrown before you when you walk, your bed companion in the night."

"My bed companion is usually an ordinary woman, shapely, preferably with a skin soft to the touch."

"Ah, my friend, you joke when I seek hope and consolation. But I'll tell you, all the same. Because if there is a change, it always looks predestined, as if it were there all the time waiting. If I move my hand at this moment from here to there, I will feel as if I had to do it. And if I oppose this desire, afterwards it will seem that I was predestined not to move it in the very first place and there was really no concrete opposition. And if I say again, that in fact I could have moved my hand in opposition to a desire not to, it would be the same thing the other way round."

"Philosophy in a nutshell," Andrews murmured in spite of himself, "metaphysical obscurity made clear. Let me see," he sat up and pressed a dry twig between his fingers and it popped loudly. He broke it again. "You're covering a pretty wide field, and jumping from point to point without any explanation."

"That's the way it has to be. If I tell you I'm afraid of Life, do you expect me to explain that? It's everything and nothing. It's sun shining and man eating, wind blowing, the sound of gurgling water. It's an ant and a giant, and a telephone conversation and the cow that jumped over the moon. It's poetry and music and the smell of dirty drains and the flight of birds over the sea."

"And all these things, when you think of them, make you afraid?"

"All these things, and all manner of things, action and inaction, animation and inanimation, the spin of the world on its axis, a woman's underwear, saxophones and gramophones, and how some words sound like macabre slip gristle crispy."

"And this fear, what is it like?"

"It's like a sickness. Say it's more hopelessness than fear if you like. And I keep telling myself that actually there's nothing to be afraid of. But I can't help. Especially on mornings. My mind broadens immediately I awaken. I rise with the world and I begin to think about what men are doing, how they will be going to work, and what they would say and do during the day; the old office chair, the worn pencils, invoices, and receipts. If you could freeze the moment with the toothbrush and see hundreds killed in everlasting war, babies born, the million acts occurring at the precise moment as you squeeze the toothpaste onto the brush. You think of eras gone and eras to come and someone calls out to you to hurry up or breakfast will be cold, and the sun shines outside and birds sing, and a car horn blows shrilly in the road and you exist."

The wind moved a cloud, the sun was brighter, the cattle in the savannah moved restlessly from grass to grass, the panorama from under the cannonball tree was filled with things the eye could linger upon—scattered trees, a cane field blurred by distance, houses, movement created by the wind.

Foster lay there tightly on the grass, aware of a burning shame, glad that Andrews was silent, but wondering what he would say when he did speak, knowing that whatever his friend said he would categorise under a mental heading: The Things People Say, and knowing it would be unimportant, because one is only concerned with the immediate needs of life: If I want to wake refreshed tomorrow, I must sleep well tonight. If I want fresh bread for breakfast, I must get up early and go to the bakery. I must hurry up and get that job done, I must go to see Doris tonight, and I mustn't forget the football match next week. A man could live in a little world, concerned with a few things, and he would be well satisfied, there wouldn't be great blanks of time when he wouldn't have nothing to think about, or ever reach a stage where he has to tell himself, Where do I go from here? A man could say, What the hell have I got to do with London and New York and Paris, or the war in Korea or the fact that Mrs Bellflent had a baby last week? And the fact of the matter is, that he doesn't even go so far as to ask himself those questions, his little world is self-contained, and he takes part in the routine activity of his life, and one day he dies.

Andrews laughed suddenly, kicking up his feet in the air. "Well, when it come to talking real bull, boy, you is hearts. You take the cake, as they say. Look, what about this snowball? Let we go over by the cart and buy some."

Foster shook his head and stretched. "No."

"Well, done this kind of talk?"

"Why is it that sometimes we speak properly, and then lapse into broken English?"

"Because we feel more at home with it, I expect."

"I think it's because we're too lazy. That's one of the reasons. The way you spoke just now, you insinuated that we should dismiss the topic of conversation. Whenever we're talking and we find ourselves losing ground, we fall back on broken English."

"Wat happen for dat?"

"Well, nothing. Don't get aggressive. That's another trait we have. Hiding our ignorance behind 'to hell wid you' and 'wat I have to do wid dat.' "

Andrews went on deliberately. "You going for this snowball, yes or no?"

"All right, all right."

Foster hung his head as they dragged their feet across the grass. He thought with a sickening feeling that he had spoilt the morning for both of them; they would have to fall back heavily on the gin.

Andrews made a joke. He said, "I will ask my sister to burn a candle for you when she goes to church."

And Foster, realising they had got no place at all, thought: Maybe she should set the world on fire.

One morning when he was going to work Foster met Rena in Woodford Square. He was glad to see her; it was more than three years since Rufus had been away, and he had had no news about him for a long time.

"You don't come by us again at all," Rena said, then asked him a series of questions.

He led her to a vacant bench under a weeping willow tree and they sat down.

"Have you heard anything from Rufus lately?" he asked.

"Your brother is a nasty man. He stop sending me money regularly. I got a letter last week. He say he studying hard, but I feel he running around with women over there. You know America is a fast country."

Foster smiled. "Isn't he coming back for a holiday?"

"He didn't say anything about that. He always ask for you, but I tell him that since he went away you never come home by us. What you doing now? Where you working?"

"I have a small job at Jennings."

"And where you living? By your cousin in San Juan?"

"Yes."

"Why you don't come and live by us? Is a long time now since I move out of the room we used to stay in. And it empty, Ma ask me to try and get somebody good to take it."

It sounded like a good idea to Foster. He didn't like travelling the six miles to work everyday, though he didn't have to pay any rent to Regald.

"How much for the room?"

"Twelve dollars. But as is you, Ma might make it ten."

"Look, I'll let you know tomorrow."

"You could ring me up," Rena said. "I working now, you know. Since your brother don't send enough money I have to work. I have a job at Emils, the jewellers. Ring 32454 any time, and ask for me."

"All right, I'll ring you tomorrow. How is Tim?"

"He growing big. I have to start sending him to school just now."

Foster moved from San Juan and went to live in Johnny's house. It was a week before he encountered Johnny, though he heard him often enough.

"Aye, you scamp," Johnny greeted him, "I hear you come here to live. What about your worthless brother, he ain't coming back?"

Foster thought: How can I reply to that question, fool? But aloud he laughed.

"Come and fire a drink with me," Johnny invited.

Foster used the drawing room, but only at nights, when the others were asleep. He bought a selection of records and kept them on the table near the radiogram, and in the night he played it softly. He loved listening to music.

"I don't know why this stupid man Foster don't buy some good jive records," Jennifer grumbled when she was cleaning out the house, "he only have some stupid classical records here." She used to hear the music softly in the night when she couldn't sleep.

Foster noticed that Rena was out most evenings until late, leaving Tim with Jennifer.

Johnny liked the little boy, though he tried to hide his feelings. When Johnny came home Tim would shout: "Granpa, you old drunkard!" and run to hide. And Johnny would chase him and beat him on the bottom with his open palm. But he petted him if no one was around.

Foster kept out of the way of the family as much as he could. He avoided having anything to say to Jennifer, for fear of complications if he became involved with the girl.

One evening he met Andrews and they had dinner in a Chinese restaurant. After some drinks Foster asked: "Want to listen to some music?"

"I don't mind," Andrews replied.

"Well we'll go in late. That man Johnny is hell, I don't like to play the radiogram until they're all asleep."

They went in about half-past eleven.

"Quietness we must have," Foster whispered, tip-toeing across the carpet, "if we make noise and wake Johnny there's no telling what will happen. If you have to talk, whisper."

"I see you have a collection of popular classics," Andrews spoke low, as he looked through the record albums.

"What's wrong with popular classics?" Foster hissed.

"Nothing. Only I thought you'd have had heavier music."

"I see you've fallen prey to the idea that because a piece of music is well-loved by the millions, it becomes popular and trite, and isn't worth listening to."

"Not that exactly—"

"Oh yes, it's that exactly." Foster held a Swan Lake movement in his hand and stood over the radiogram. "It seems that because a piece of music is melodious and easy to understand, it becomes classified as a popular classic, not to be bothered with by intelligent people who want something more complicated to chew on. I say that is balls. To hell with the critics; if I like a certain piece I like it, I'm not going to be swayed by any sophisticated opinion. I hate to hear people say: 'Oh, the Dance of the Hours, yes, but I prefer to listen to Beethoven.' All this time, they don't understand Beethoven a damn, but just because it is said that the music they love is popular, they forsake it and try to fathom something out of their depth. Not me, old man. I play what I like."

He put on the records and sat down on the carpet. "Better to sit here," he whispered, "you could stretch out if you like."

While the music was playing he went on, "Mark you, I have nothing against difficult music, after all, the enjoyment is in putting effort towards an interpretation. But I think a lot of them get away with murder. Perhaps I can better illustrate with painting. With this mania for what is called modern art, some fellows paint rot which is acclaimed masterpieces. Their work is hung upside down and applauded. Also, take verse. I heard about two Australians who got hold of a dictionary and strung a lot of words together. They were put in the field of modern contemporaries—surrealistic verse. It seems as if all you have to do is write or paint something which no one can understand, and you become one of the moderns."

"But I think you have a wrong conception," Andrews said. "The movement is towards something different, something not yet entirely in our grasp. And that is why you get so much faked work, because we are biting off more than we can chew. But that does not seem to me to be important, so long as we advance towards more understanding eventually. This period of charlatans and fakes may well be worth tolerating if we emerge to a deeper understanding of art."

"I agree with you." Foster lay back on the carpet with his hands clasped behind his head. "And I see a big point, but it isn't quite settled in my mind. I wish it were—it's worth talking about, I feel. But maybe another time, when I've thought it over."

"Who the hell is that making all that noise when a man trying to get some sleep?" Johnny shouted.

Foster snatched the arm off the record and Johnny's voice echoed in the sudden silence.

They lay quietly after that, smoking.

Foster went out with Andrews when he was leaving. It was a cool night, brilliant with stars. They walked up Park Street, then down Frederick Street.

"How is the job?" Andrews asked.

Foster whistled a bar of 'You may Not be an Angel.'

Andrews laughed. "Are you doing any writing?"

"Trying my hand at verse."

"Charlatan?"

"Go take a running jump," Foster said.

Andrews laughed again. "I forgot to tell you, I'm showing some of my work at an exhibition at the Victoria Institute next month. You must come along one evening."

"I've told you before I'm not interested in painting. I don't know anything about it."

"All the better. I'll get an honest opinion from you."

"Well, I don't know. I won't promise."

Chapter Six

There is a beautiful place in Trinidad called Caura Valley, and there's a village there named Veronica, and it is surrounded by green hills, and small streams sparkle in the valley.

It stayed beautiful a long time, because only poor peasants lived there, and because it was difficult to get to, the road zig-zagged crazily around the hills, with no sort of protection against hairpin curves and sudden precipices. In the season of pouis, the valley was yellow or mauve from head to toe, except where flaming red immortelle blossoms rose high for sunlight. The people there lived simply and worked hard, tilling the land and rearing a few odd head of livestock.

Father Hope lived in that valley for sixteen years, and he was just another ragged boy helping his father in the fields, except that he was more silent than most. When he got to that age, his parents sent him to a college in Port of Spain. Hope had seen his parents sweat and strain to save money for his education, and in turn he sweated and strained, and he won a scholarship, and he went away to study for a priesthood.

Hope stayed away a long time, but he never forgot Veronica. He wrote his father often, though it was a hardship for the old man to get letters to and from the village, the nearest post office was seven miles away. It was not easy for Hope to explain in his letters the things he wanted to find out. It was about the land itself, if the shape of the valley had changed, if the orange trees still blossomed in profusion of sweet smell, and whether the sunlight was still falling on the waters of the streams. But the old man for all his years couldn't understand: when he did write, in a slow laborious hand, it was to tell his son about a birth or a death in the village, and to ask him when he was coming back.

Two years went by, and Hope got no letters, and he didn't need anyone to tell him that his parents had died. To Hope, living in one of the great continents of the world, it was hard to imagine the funeral and the burial of his kin in a small island thousands of miles away.

Five more years went by, and no one knew what had happened

to Hope, or if he had been ordained a priest or anything. But one day he came back to the island quietly, and he went to the village of his birth. Hope climbed a little hill he remembered in his youth, and he sat down under a mango tree and he looked at Veronica. Nothing had changed. Old people had died, but there were births. Trees had dried and rotted, but new ones sprang from the earth.

It was here, on this little hill, that he would build his church. There were rocks on the hill—all he needed was cement to weld them together.

Oh yes, there were rocks, the villagers agreed, but cement cost money, where would the get the money?

I have money, Hope told them, and he bought the cement. The villagers built the church, and Hope took off his jacket and helped them.

Six months after his return Hope stood on the little hill one Sunday morning and pulled the rope which rang the bell summoning the people to church. The bellnotes echoed in the valley: they struck a hill opposite and came back, as if someone else in another church was ringing a bell there.

Hope preached to the small congregation and they went back to the land with high hearts.

He was satisfied. A man couldn't save the world but perhaps he could save a few souls. Fifty or sixty villagers were enough. By and by he would know them well—their individual sadness, their excitement, their happiness—and he would be able to do more good.

Seasons came and went, and Father Hope was a loved man in the valley. And no one thought it strange that a man had come to the valley, built a church, and resided with them as their intermediary with God. Because the way it was, any man could have done the same thing, if he had the money to buy the cement. But it is questionable whether he would have gained the love of the people as Father Hope did.

Father Hope never left Veronica to go and preach elsewhere. He had come back to the valley to be alone. And he remained alone, out of touch with the world or even the local happenings in the island.

Andrews, visiting the small school in Veronica, met Father Hope and they became good friends.

"No matter how you try to drill it into them," Andrews told

Father Hope, "these children still say 'dis' and 'dat.' "

Father Hope smiled. "I know. It's because from the very beginning they were never taught properly. Remember our own education?"

Andrews chuckled. "Yes. When I used to go to school, the teachers themselves never spoke proper English."

"And here in this very valley, pupils graduated into teachers."

"Do you know Father, I don't like to talk about it. We Trinidadians already have a reputation for being great talkers, even among ourselves. But our education system is rotten. They don't seem to realise or care that it isn't enough for a child to know that two and two makes four. The children leave school entirely unprepared for life, believing that the facts and figures they were forced to memorise will see them through. There is no play for imagination, no real exercise for the mind." Andrews waved his hand helplessly and went on, "I can see nothing but a general upheaval, a complete uprooting of old systems of teaching. Teachers in this island don't realise their responsibility. They don't think, These are the future citizens of Trinidad and I will see they get a better education than I did. To them it's a bread-and-butter job, nothing else. They see no nobility in their profession, and that's funny, because I can think of no other profession in which the fruit of labour is so rewarding."

"On the other hand," Father Hope said, "think of the meagre pay they get, it acts as no incentive. Those with a little sense leave the schools as soon as they could get a better paying job."

"Ah, it's a frustrating business."

"All over this island, little knots of intelligent men get together and talk as we are talking now, deploring the systems and methods of education, labour, politics, social service. Then they finish their cigarettes and go off to a film or a football match. There is a lot of fury and indignation on the surface, but no one does anything. It's a pity about Trinidad. She builds on a rotten foundation, introducing new ideas to fool herself and the world that she is progressing. Every man can vote now, but what is the good when there are men who don't know what the privilege is, who don't even know the meaning of the word 'vote'? But there, let us finish our lemonade, but remember what we have spoken about."

Andrews was so impressed with Father Hope that he asked Foster to go along with him one Sunday afternoon for what he

72

called "an old talk."

Foster demurred. "I don't want to have anything to do with priests," he said.

"Oh, he isn't like that at all," Andrews said, "he's travelled a lot, and he's very intelligent. Besides, it would be nice to spend the afternoon in the village."

So Foster went with him and met Father Hope. "Andrews told me about you," Father Hope said, shaking his hand warmly.

"What did he say? That I was a lost soul groping in the dark?"

"No. But are you?"

"Who isn't?" Foster countered.

"A lot of people," Father Hope looked at him keenly.

"But let us go and sit under a tree in the yard; we'll have grapefruit juice later. I know it's a poor substitute, but you won't mind."

"I like grapefruit juice."

They sat comfortably on the grass, and Foster said, "Tell us about the big countries of the world that you have visited."

"He is being cynical, Father," Andrews said. "He envies those big countries, and the people who live in them."

Father Hope looked at Foster questioningly, but Foster kept silent. It seemed as good a start as any for a conversation.

"I used to be that way too," Father Hope said. "I used to feel as if this island was too small, that my mind reached the sea as soon as it began to expand."

"Why did you come back to this island, and lock your self away in Veronica?" Foster asked. "I would have thought that someone of your capabilities would be crushed by the smallness of the place."

"People are the same all over the world," Father Hope said. "It does not matter where you are, you encounter sadness, happiness, love, hate. An island is a world, and everywhere that people live, they create their own worlds."

"But sometimes that world is small," Foster said. "Sometimes you feel as if you are at the top of it, and you want more. Your mind is cramped, your vision limited."

"What you want is variety," Father Hope said. "But you could stay in one place and have that. Think of all the things you could occupy your mind with. You might feel that I am bored living in this small village. But I despair of ever being able to cope with half the problems I am daily confronted with. My son, when you grow older you will realise that Man's span is so short that his activities are limited, you will look back and realise how very little you know about anything. You will say, 'I thought I was at the top of my world, but I am only now beginning to learn how to live.'

"Why should you feel that people in a big country are better off than you? The bigger the country, the bigger its problems. The more the people, the more the sin and corruption—"

"The more the happiness too," Foster broke in.

"Yes, but not *more* happiness to each individual. And if the one strives side by side with the other, where is the improvement?"

"But aren't we trying to outbalance sin?" Foster said. "People in progressive countries get food, work, a place to sleep. They get more of a chance to be happy."

"But what happens in a welfare state? You give a man food and shelter, and he becomes too lazy to work. You offer him amenities, and he makes no effort to attain them himself. Anything 'good' in the world may appear new to us, sinners that we all are. But is there anything new about evil? It keeps abreast of the times, that is all.

"And yet our concepts change. At one time it was a 'good' thing to offer your seat to a woman in a crowded bus. Now, you think you are a fool if you do it."

Andrews spoke for the first time. "I see I must act as mediator. You all are straying from the subject."

"Father Hope sounds cynical to me," Foster said, "if sin is always there, why does he devote his life to fighting a useless battle against it?"

"Because we must always fight," Father Hope said, "it is easier to sin, than to do good. One has to help the weak to be strong, the fool to be wise."

Andrews, seeing that they would ramble and get off course, thought he might as well clear up one or two points in his own mind, so he asked: "Father, you seem to have answers to all the questions. How is it that you always maintain such equanimity, such objectiveness?"

"I have my beliefs, and my faith. I have religion."

Foster said: "But religion does not teach happiness, it teaches one to tolerate unhappiness. The life of Christ seems to have been a struggle against the evils of the world, with promise of

74

happiness in the hereafter. And even this land of milk and honey sounds fantastic to me: I cannot conceive of a world where man lives in a state of perpetual bliss and joy, it is incompatible with his very nature. It is easier to believe in Hell: a man can imagine himself in a world of continuous suffering and misery."

"Well," Father Hope smiled, "even if Heaven falls short of your expectations, surely it is a better place than Hell?"

"What I would like," Andrews broke in again, "is some philosophy, religious or otherwise, which I could apply to everyday life."

"Whatever philosophy you have," Father Hope said, "it changes with time. As you grow older, your views are different, your eye sees events through experience. You are young men, and I would not preach God to you, because I know how hard it is for you to believe and have faith now. I cannot hasten the process of experience, you will have to make your own decisions, follow your own paths to the end. And that is a bitter irony, for with all my warning you will seek the experience yourself. If children used to heed us, they could start off so much nearer the goal, but tell them fire burns and what do they do but thrust their own hands in to find out for themselves.

"Yet I will tell you this. Learn tolerance, and learn humility. Youth is impatient and arrogant, eager and enthusiastic to get ahead, unmindful of trampling others on the way up. Learn tolerance because you will find that we aren't all alike, that we have different creeds and beliefs, and each believes his is the truth and the best. Such people are around you every day. They will laugh at your beliefs, and try to convert you to theirs. Learn humility, so that if you find that they are right and you are wrong, it will not be such a blow to your own pride and confidence to reject your own ideas and start again."

The two young men were silent, then Foster asked: "What made you turn to religion, Father?"

"What else is there?" Father Hope said. "But of course you will not appreciate that now. When I was a young man, I went through the same stages as you are going through now, I too knew the pulse, the heartbeat, the song, the kiss. I was in and out of love many times: I found faith difficult: I immersed myself in all the metaphysical theories I could find, I pursued my ideals down every possible avenue. When I went abroad, I tried out all my own ideas of life, and found they weren't satisfactory. A man can get so far under his own steam, and then he reaches a wall, and realises his own limitations."

"So you took to religion as a way out," Foster mused.

"I took religion as the *only* way out," Father Hope said. "But I did more than that. I didn't accept all the dogmas and tenets that have been accepted. In a way, I am an outlaw. I try to remodel religion so that it could help people like you and me. That is why you must not be surprised at some of the arguments that I put forth.

"You see how honest I am being with you. It is usually held that a man of God is a tower of strength and faith who helps you out of your problems, and points out the right direction when you are lost. That I do, but in my own way, with the help of God. I have a faith and belief which is my defence against the world. I wish you could have that too, but I think it is wrong to force you to my way of thinking. You must come to an understanding with your own soul."

"Ah," Foster said, "I am sorry you said all that, because I have always dreamed of religion as being flawless, the one perfect thing I could fall back on if and when I am ready for it. Now I fear that if I reach that wall of which you spoke, I will remember your words and hesitate."

"It is my honesty which has created your doubt, and I thought it would increase your belief. But I didn't argue with you about your conception of heaven and hell, and I won't argue with you now. I have told you so much because of your intelligence, and, I am sure, your ability to sift the chaff from the grain. If even religion proves imperfect, you will find it is the least imperfect of all beliefs in the world, and the only one from which you could get any lasting consolation.

"But there. I am sure that Andrews didn't bring you here to listen to me talk all the time! It is a nice afternoon, let us take a walk. Have you ever been to Veronica before?"

"No," Foster said.

"You see," Father Hope said, "you want to go to another country, but you don't know this small island yet."

But he added, smiling, "I was only fooling."

"What a lot of things we have talked about," Andrews grumbled, kicking at a stone, "one never seems in line with what one started out with in such discussions."

And Foster gave him a knowing look.

Chapter Seven

Foster was about to give up his job at Jennings—he was rather surprised that a drab job filing letters and invoices kept him so long—when a girl came to work in the office.

Foster saw a lot of Marleen, besides working with her in the office. She was a light-hearted girl, full of humour, taking life as it came. He found much solace in her company, and for a while he forgot himself as he marvelled at her willy-nilly attitude.

He became so engrossed that when Marleen told him there was a vacant room in the house where she lived with her mother, Foster moved over.

Rena said: "You think I didn't hear about that brown-skin girl you going around with. Everybody know, everybody see you all holding hands in the streets. And now you going there to live."

Foster didn't reply. He took away everything but his records, which he left on the radiogram in the drawing room.

Living in the same house with Marleen wasn't as pleasant as he had anticipated. Her mother had a daughter fixation and she watched them carefully. She made Foster pay for the privilege. She borrowed money from him and didn't pay back, as if she had forgotten all about it. Many times she didn't bother to prepare any food, although he was with them in the capacity of a paying guest. If he left any money on the dressing table in his room, it mysteriously disappeared.

There was a dog, and it slept in Foster's room.

All these things he tolerated because he was attracted to the girl. Sometimes her mother had to go out, to visit friends or shop. Early in the morning, before the others awoke, she went to the market. Marleen slept in the same bed: when her mother went she used to slip into Foster's room for a few minutes.

Foster had a narrow single bed, but he used to move up against the wall and Marleen would lay down with him.

But nothing ever happened, they were afraid her mother would come back suddenly. She had a soft step and a way of moving about the house like a phantom.

One evening after work he took Marleen to the botanical

gardens. A shower of rain had dampened the ground, a valiant evening sun was trying to dry it.

"What about if I have a baby?" she whispered as he loomed over her.

When they were leaving he saw his shirt was muddy at the elbows. He rolled up his sleeves.

Next morning he changed his shirt. When he came in from work the shirt was missing. He had rolled it into a bundle and tossed it in the corner, to take to the laundry later. Marleen's mother was out.

"Did you take my shirt?" he asked Marleen.

She burst into tears.

"Ma took it," she sobbed, leaning on his chest. "She said she knew we had been to the gardens."

"But why did she take my shirt?"

"She said she was going to keep it as evidence."

"She's a fool," he said. And then he softened, "Hush, don't cry. Everything will be all right."

"You don't know," Marleen sobbed, "all night she kept me awake, holding me and shaking me and asking if you had anything to do with me. She said, 'You understand what I mean?' And I said, 'Yes.' She said, 'You sure, because I could tell you out plain. What I want to know is if—' "

"Never mind darling," Foster broke in, holding her tightly and patting her shoulder like she was a child. "What's that you're holding behind your back? Here, let me see."

But Marleen pulled away from him and sort of put her whole body in front to defend her hands. Foster forced her hands forward and tore at her clinched fists. It was a bottle of iodine.

"I hope you haven't done anything silly," he said quietly.

"I—I don't know what to do. I'm going to poison myself!" And she tugged away and ran into the bathroom, slamming the door and bolting it.

"Jesus Christ," Foster muttered.

He pounded on the door. "Don't be a fool," he shouted, "come out of there at once."

She kept silent.

Foster swallowed saliva but his throat still felt dry. "Darling," he said softly, "it isn't as bad as all that. Please I love you. Your mother will be coming back at any moment. Please open the door darling."

"What's the use of us going on?" she sobbed. "I may as well kill myself."

"A lot of people think like that," he said, trying to keep calm but anxiously looking about to see if he could get into the bathroom by any other means but the door.

He began to climb the door to get in from the top. And he talked to her, softly saying silly things, as much to keep himself going as to hold her attention.

"Why, I myself once thought of committing suicide. I looked down into the sea from the deck of a ship, and it looked so easy to jump over the side—" He stopped, realising with a start that he had intended to make up a little story, and in fact he had been speaking the truth. It was funny how, if you wanted to commit suicide, your arguments were infallible, but you could always find reasons for other people to live. Marleen was just being dramatic, of course, but you never could tell. Once there was a girl in San Fernando who said she would jump in the sea if he didn't go out with her. She didn't jump in the sea, because he got to her just in time when she was on the jetty. But he always had a feeling afterwards that she would not have jumped anyway. He had had to argue with that girl, as he was arguing with Marleen now, and even as he drew himself over the top of the door he had time to think: This is the second time this thing has happened to me.

But he panicked for a moment as he saw Marleen huddled up in the corner of the bathroom. The bottle was on the ground. It was empty.

As he stood there it was as if the last month in this house had never been: he looked at Marleen as if he were seeing her for the first time, and a feeling of dispassionateness ran over him for a minute.

"Did you drink it?" he asked wearily.

She nodded, her body shaking with movement.

He looked in the wash basin and saw a streak of iodine. "You're lying," he said, but there was no relief in his voice. He felt disappointed, he had primed his body and his mind for a calamity, and now it was only a farce.

"You're lying," he said again, making a fresh start, as if he had just come in, "you poured it down the drain."

Marleen began to sob. It was as if each individual movement she made had to be by her whole body, like she'd lost control and her brain was making crazy signals to her nerves.

"Why did you lie?" he asked, and the question comforted him: there was something to be learnt, after all.

"I wanted to see how much you cared," she sobbed, and the words jerked out, like a car making a bad start and bucking.

"Christ," he said, "you really had me scared that time."

"You don't care what happens to me."

"Of course I do."

"Oh, men are all the same." Her voice was quite resigned now. "I used to know someone before I met you, and I thought he loved me too. He worked in the same office with me at the American base in Chaguaramus."

"And what happened?"

"Oh, he was just like you, he resembled you a lot. That's why I liked you in the first place. You remind me of him."

"And what happened?" he asked again.

"He went away to the States to study."

"Ah," Foster said, "you are talking about Rufus."

"How did you know?" Her eyes opened wide in wonder.

"Oh no," Foster said, "oh no."

Andrews brought one foot up on the bench in Woodford Square, wrapping his hands around the knee.

"So what happened about the shirt eventually?"

"Well, she made a hell of a scene. She threatened to shoot me. Yesterday she came into the office and sat down behind me with her hand in her purse, waiting for Marleen. I was frightened like hell, in case she had a gun in her purse. You know how it is with people, they're apt to do crazy things at times."

Andrews laughed.

"This is a serious thing boy, no joke."

Andrews laughed louder.

"You could laugh skiff-skiff if you like, but if you were in my place a monkey would have smoked your pipe."

"Did she really have a gun?"

"How the hell do I know? I couldn't call her bluff. Anyway she tossed the shirt at me right there in the office without saying a word. Marleen herself was so frightened she kept her head down to the typewriter all the time. Oh, the things that happen to me."

"Ah, you laugh about my experiences, but look at you."

"That's no comparison at all."

"So now, what are you going to do?"

"Well, I think I'll take a job on a ship. I wanted to tell you about it. You know, one of the ships we used during the war is still here. She was being repaired, and now that she's fixed they want a crew—preferably ex-servicemen—to take her to England."

"How melodramatic it sounds. You get in trouble with this girl, then you go to sea and desert her—"

"Oh, shut up."

"Well, that is the way it is, whether you like it or not."

"Listen, why don't you come with me?"

Andrews changed feet on the bench. "It's different with me. You've just been drifting around and all you have to do is pack a suitcase and go abroad. I have become involved in a lot of things—teaching, painting, meeting the important people in the island."

Foster snorted.

"Well, it's true anyway. Do you know that I have been asked by prominent citizens if I'd like to be put up for nomination in the next elections?"

"No kidding?"

"Look, are we just exchanging words?"

"I'm sorry. But I never thought you were getting around so much. What are you going to do?"

"I'm seriously thinking about it."

One evening some time later they met in a rumshop in Charlotte Street to talk some more about it. Andrews had made up his mind. He said, "Imagine yourself in my place. You've been nominated for election to the Legislative Council, among other reasons, because you've always been talking about bettering conditions in the island. Now what?"

"Make sure of your votes," Foster said.

"But how?"

"Listen boy, I don't know anything about politics. You have to do as the others do. Tour your district, make speeches. Let the people see the man they're going to vote for. In any case, it should be a pushover. Promise them a few things. Better water supply. Electric lights. Better wages—you know the line to hand them."

"I am not going to make any promise I won't be able to keep," Andrews said.

And Foster thought to himself about the greatness of the thing they were talking about, how to make people happy. He thought how people talked great things in funny places, like rumshops. And he saw the smallness of Trinidad, and the people moving about on the shape of the island, from Port of Spain to Toco, down to Mayaro and Icacos, the two bottom points. The island was so small, he could step from it to the continent of South America.

"One thing," he said, "you'll have to be practical. Tell me, what is your manifesto like? What party are you affiliated to? The Caribbean Socialists? The Political Progress Party, the Labour Party, the Butler Party? Do you claim to be working for a strong and prosperous Trinidad? Will you do all you can to strengthen the national economy, and what will be your manner of approach? Do you think it practical to have fiscal autonomy for the West Indies on a regional basis? Will you advocate no personal victimisation? What are your views on: a, Public Health; b, Housing and Slum Clearance; c, Social Security; d, Education; e—"

Andrews had been listening wide-eyed as Foster spoke, but now he interrupted.

"You bitch. You've been reading some book or pamphlet. You don't know yourself what the hell all that means—"

"e, Federation; f, Labour and Unemployment—"

Foster had been leaning forward and jabbing Andrews with a grave air, and now he rocked back in his chair and laughed.

"I wish you could be serious for once," Andrews said, shaking his glass to make the ice melt quicker in the rum punch he was drinking.

"I'm sorry." Foster sat up. "Maybe I reflect this attitude because I'm going away soon. But let's think about the election. You'll have to pass money."

"That's out."

"Don't be silly. Money talks loudest in Trinidad. Pass a couple of dollars around—"

"I tell you that's out. I mean it."

"All the others will be doing it."

"I'm surprised at you offering that as justification."

"My point is this. I sincerely believe you'd be able to do a great

82

deal of good if you get on the council. And if some people will vote for you if you pay them, then pay them, if that's the only way. The thing is to get there where you'll be able to do something."

"You mean I'll be able to make amends if I get there? To hell with it. I am thinking about what I'll feel about myself."

"Suppose it makes a difference between getting in and staying out?"

"I'm not buying votes."

"There'll be plenty for sale. You understand that I am only persisting on this point because of the people's mentality? It isn't that I agree with the principle myself. It is like leading a blind man in the right path. Money is the light."

"Ah, you have a very poor opinion of Trinidadians. Your cynicism will get you into trouble one day."

"I have it," Foster went on, ignoring the remark, "hand them a new line. Say that others have promised them so much, but you are promising nothing. Say: 'I am not going to tell you that I will do this and do that. But with all the sincerity and honesty possible, I will try to better our lot in this island.' How does that sound?"

"A new angle might certainly help."

"Of course! All you have to do is stress your newness to it all, make them feel that you're as much a stranger to politics as they are, and that you're going in there as one of them might go, indecisive, uncertain of anything, only spurred by a sincere desire to do good. They'll put themselves in your place, they'll feel you are the genuine thing at least."

"It sounds all right, but I can imagine some fellows in the crowd saying: 'What happen to he at all? He stupid in life? You don't see he is a young man who ain't know what he talking about? Why he don't go back where he come from and leave the people politics alone?'"

"Aha, and who's being cynical now?" Foster moved suddenly for the pack of cigarettes on the table. The movement was rather a gesture, as if he were stretching out his hand about to say more and only pick up the cigarettes on the way. Andrews raised his eyebrows in anticipation, but Foster only gave a forced laugh.

"I don't think I'm of much help to you, old man," he said. "But I certainly wish you luck. It'll be hard going, but I have a feeling you'll succeed."

There was so much on his mind, and he didn't want to bother Andrews. After all, he had his worries too.

When he got home that evening Muriel said: "A girl was here to see you."

"Oh," he said listlessly.

"We know about her. Rena came the other day and she said how you used to live with this girl. Is true?"

"Yes."

"You must think of other people sometimes. You don't think we feel shame when you do a thing like that?"

Faced with simple human emotion, what could he say? What does an intelligent and wise man say, when he comes up against something like this? Does he laugh lightly and brush it aside? Does he make an esoteric remark, absolving himself from any responsibility, or generalise and say that it doesn't really matter about one or two people being unhappy in the world? Try, by all means, to maintain equilibrium, and if possible, get out of it with grace. But what did it boil down to?

"I think you put that girl in trouble, Foster," Muriel went on. "She look distress. Suppose she make a child for you when you go away? We don't even know the girl family or anything."

"Did she say that?" he asked, because he had to say something.

"Well she didn't say so, but it could be nothing else, I know that look. You have a few days still, you better do something."

"Do something?"

"What happen, you lose your tongue? You know well what I mean. Don't beat around the bush, man."

He hesitated for a moment then he said, "Yes, I know. But I can't do that, Muriel. I know I seem to have very few principles, but there are one or two things I hold firm to. And right now I can't afford to let them go, Muriel. If she's having a child let her have it."

"You must be crazy. Think of the humiliation, the shame, the worry and responsibility you'll put on this girl. She won't be able to bear it."

"You mean a life isn't worth all that bother," he said slowly, "yet we ourselves live through worse hardships clinging desperately to life. Ever heard of a man called Bernard Shaw?"

"No. But I don't see—"

"He is one of the men in the world who speaks and people listen. He said that children take up too much of our time, that they are a nuisance and a hindrance to our progress. I don't believe that, Muriel. I think he was talking balls. If we let children alone they'd grow up as stupid as we and there won't be any progress—"

"Ah, I don't know what you talking about, you trying to avoid the issue. I am not like you, Foster, I can only see the trouble all this will cause. Who going to support the child? Who going to buy food and clothes and medicine, and see about all the expense? The trouble with people like you is you live in the world, and you have your own ideas, and you think you could do as you like. Too besides, what about the girl? Suppose she don't want the baby? Suppose she want to throw it away?"

"As I see it," Foster said, "there isn't very much I can do. I'll be going away in a few days. I have about two hundred dollars in the bank. I'll leave it with you, and you could give it to her."

"You adopting the manner of the rich, you trying to pay yourself out of this."

"No, no," Foster said quickly, "it isn't that at all. But out of all the wrong things, I consider it the least wrong. Put it that way if you like."

"Well, is your life, boy. You was always a funny person, I can't understand you. But I don't want to be mixed up in this business. You better talk to Regald when he come home from work, and hear what he say."

Over a flask of Vat 19 later that night, Regald agreed to take the money.

"Though I think you should see Marleen and give her yourself," he said.

"I don't think there's any point in seeing her," Foster said. "Nothing may come of all this, you know. I feel her mother won't let her have a baby. And I'm not sure how Marleen feels herself."

"It will be a bastard child," Regald said.

"Well, I'm not disclaiming it. I think a child shouldn't be called a bastard unless the father disclaims it."

Regald smiled and poured a drink with elaborate care. "What you think doesn't change the laws of society."

"I talk too much, don't I? I suppose it's because I was so silent as a boy."

But he was thinking about Rufus, who had said, "One day you

will find yourself in a 'mooch' and I wonder what will happen to you."

"Oh, I'll find a way out, don't worry. I know you think I'm slow, but it's just that I can't seem to get things worked out properly in my own mind, that's all."

But had he found a way out? Why was he really taking this opportunity to go to England? I am running away, he thought, but it isn't only from this.

Andrews saw him off the morning he was sailing.

"You must keep in touch," Andrews said. "And I hope you've practised some calypsoes. The English think all we can do is sing calypsoes and play cricket."

"I'll write you."

"Tell me if you prefer seeing a symphony orchestra in action than listening to the music on records. And I hope you've checked up on your West Indian geography and history. They don't know anything about us. They believe all West Indians come from Jamaica."

Foster nodded to all this. The night before he and Regald had drunk two bottles of rum. The sun made his head ache. They were standing near to the entrance of the wharf.

Andrews went on, "If I were you I'd lose my passport after I landed. I heard that a West Indian went on the continent and none of the countries there would recognise his passport. They wanted to know who was Governor—. Said they'd never heard of him. Better get one from Britain, signed by Bevin."

"This here passport," Foster patted his pocket, "is good enough for me. It says I'm a citizen of the United Kingdom and Colonies. If they don't know the Governor I'll tell them about him."

They stood silent for a minute. Then Andrews said, "Father Hope wishes you bon voyage."

"Tell him I'm sorry I didn't get a chance to see him before I left."

"He said he had a lot of faith in you."

"I wish I had some in myself."

"Oh, you'll get by."

"By the time I come back you'll be a big politician, with a car and plenty money!"

"But think of you in London, all the white meat you'll be eating!"

"Ah what's the difference between a white woman and a black one, when it comes to that?"

"These are famous last words."

They laughed and shook hands.

"Keep the home fires burning," Foster said, and he turned and walked away.

Andrews stood for a minute watching him, then he flicked a cigarette end away and went back to his life.

Three hours later, when the vessel had cleared the Dragon's Mouth, Foster stood on the deck and watched the island. The hills rose green and irregular. The sky was blue with fleecy clouds.

He thought it was very beautiful.

PART TWO

Chapter Eight

The first night he was in America Rufus forgot where he was and went out in an open-necked shirt and white flannels, and he had to run all the way to a cafe, and when he burst inside shivering everyone looked at him as if he were a madman, going around in summer clothing in the winter. He used to laugh afterwards, because he had landed in two pairs of socks, two underpants, pyjama pants, two pairs of trousers, two undershirts, a shirt, sweater and a jacket.

He had been so anxious to get away from Trinidad that he hadn't let the time of year deter him, and it was like stepping out of a hot bath into a refrigerator.

He managed a reservation on a Pullman going into the Midwest, and waited at the Philadelphia Railway for his train. It was a nightmarish experience. Cold biting winds followed screaming trains. Thousands of civilians and servicemen commotioned on the platforms and stairways, and loudspeakers blasted arrivals and departures. Rufus hugged himself to keep warm, kidding himself that all this was exciting and important.

For twenty-one and a half hours he journeyed through a landscape of snow-capped houses, factories and industrial centres. Thousands of vehicles were snowbound on the roads. Rufus got into conversation with a passenger who said it was the worse winter for many years. After a few winters in America, Rufus got to know that every year they said the same thing, and if he met any West Indians who had newly arrived and they complained about the cold, he used to say, "Ah, this is nothing. You should have been here last year."

He was staying in a small town, according to the Americans, but to him it was a big city, with brick-paved streets, giant buildings, never-ending streams of traffic, and factories all around. Rufus had never seen traffic lights and once when the traffic stopped, as it seemed, for him to cross, he was amazed.

Other little experiences like this he kept to himself, or shared only with West Indians as new as himself at the school. He couldn't get used to the food at first; he ate hot dogs and hamburgers, which he knew, but he was afraid that if he ordered a T-bone steak he'd get a glorified bone in the shape of a T.

He bought his books and sharpened his pencils, and he felt like a boy going to school for the first time, but his resolution was firm.

He took a part-time job in a restaurant as a busboy, clearing the used plates and dishes from the tables.

One night he wrote his first letter back home:

Dearest Rena, I hope you and the baby are keeping well. I miss you both terribly. After a thirteen-day crossing I arrived here in this strange but nice country. You would be glad to hear that I was not seasick at any time, but the trip was not without incident.

We had a fire aboard. The cargo consisted of wools and hides, and fire broke out in the hold. We stopped twice, once for one and a half hours and another time for half an hour. It was quite an experience for me, but I was in no way panicky. The crew fought the fire gallantly, and they poured thousands of gallons of water into the hold.

Then there was terrible weather for two days, and a thick fog set in. It was difficult for the ship to steer a true course. At meal times the dishes on the table rattled and fell on the floor, and some passengers were unseated when the ship rolled.

Those two days I spent in my cabin going out only for meals. I had quite a time moving around with my suitcases. The straps on the black one broke and I couldn't get it closed again, so I had to tie it with a piece of rope.

It was annoying at the Customs the way they made me take things out of my bags and then I had to put them in again and shut them all by myself. You remember that it took both Patrick and myself to shut them, the way they bulged with things.

I have started school and am working part-time at a downtown restaurant—a swanky place, good food. In the evening an orchestra entertains the customers. It is quite a bustling business for me but I am gradually getting used to the routine.

Most of the hot pepper sauce landed intact, but the bottle of mango pickle broke and made a mess with two of my shirts.

I did not need the two limes and the orange you packed as I was not seasick at any time. In any case they had oranges galore aboard.

I am anxious to hear from you and looking forward eagerly to your letter. Give my regards to all the boys. I hope that my brother Foster comes around now and then to see you and the family. He is such a funny fellow, God knows how he will end up. If you see my cousin Regald tell him I will write later.

Write soon, love to baby and your dear self.

P.S. The winter is terrible—cold, cold, cold. I bought a heavy topcoat, scarf, gloves and earmuffs, so I am well set now. Will tell you more about it in my next letter.

Rufus put a ten-dollar bill with the letter, but when he was licking the flap of the envelope he changed his mind and took it out.

On the whole Rufus got along well with the Americans.

He found he didn't have to take on an accent: he was a foreigner and they expected him to speak differently and have customs and a culture of his own. With the women, these differences were fascinating and even enchanting, and Rufus played his foreignism for what it was worth.

But he was shocked at the ignorance of a lot of Americans who knew absolutely nothing of geography. Many times he was asked if he ever saw ice before coming to America, and if there were electric lights and cars in his country. Like Foster in the navy, Rufus was infuriated at times and alternated between truth and fantasy according to the person he was speaking to.

Thousands of American servicemen were flocking to schools for free education under the GI Bill of Rights, and in Rufus's class there were sixty-eight of them and the instructor was never able to cope.

Somehow or other Rufus got through his first examination, and felt justified in widening the fields of his recreation. He used to go to the Friday night dances at the YWCA, but now he began to do the taverns with the boys. Beer was the cheapest drink, though it was tame after all the rum he used to drink.

There was the 'Green Frog' and 'The Old Mill,' and near to closing time they got around the piano and sang at the top of their voices 'Down by the Old Mill Stream' and 'Paper Moon.'

Rufus and another Trinidadian called Malcolm became very friendly: they were the only two in the crowd who could empty a glass of beer at one go.

After a late snack at the White Pig or the Steeplejack Burgehouse (he got into a habit of making a special mental note of these names) they would go back drunk to the "Y".

Malcolm always seemed to suffer worse with hangovers. Many nights Rufus had to go and extricate his head from the waste paper basket. Malcolm used to put the basket at the side of his bed so if he felt sick during the night he wouldn't have to get up, and sometimes he fell asleep with his head in the basket.

One night after hard work at the restaurant Rufus was on his way home when a man approached him and asked: "Could you tell me the nearest place a man can get a drink around here? I'm a stranger."

Pleased that he had a knowledge of the vicinity to help, Rufus said, "Just around the corner. I'm passing that way, I'll show you."

On the way the man said he could tell Rufus was a foreigner, and asked him how he liked the country.

When they got to the Grid Iron Rufus pointed the way down the stairs, anxious to get home quickly as he was very tired.

"Have a drink with me," the stranger said.

"I really shouldn't, you know," Rufus said. "I'm a student and only drink on a weekend."

"Ah, come on and have one with me," the man insisted.

So to humour him Rufus went inside, thinking: It isn't going to cost me anything.

The orchestra was playing Symphony and the place was packed. Couples were dancing in a haze of smoke.

The stranger picked out a table in a corner and ordered a couple of beers. In the garish light now, Rufus could see that the man was slightly drunk.

He paid the waitress and pushed the change along the table-top and left it near to Rufus's elbow.

Rufus sipped his beer slowly, sizing up the situation, not quite sure what the position was. The man said very little.

The waitress came and the man ordered another round of beer quickly to get rid of her. He smiled broadly, and again pushed the change near to Rufus when she brought it.

"Don't you want this money," he said, "I could give you a lot more."

Rufus knew then that the man was being blunt because he thought he was a stupid foreigner, it wasn't a straight-forward invitation, it was just that he thought he was ignorant and uncultured.

"I could use some money," Rufus said, "things aren't very good with me these days. How much money have you got?"

The man took out his wallet and bent it and flicked the notes.

All the time Rufus was wondering how he would get out of it, though he was feeling reckless and wanted to find out as much as he could about this specimen.

"Have another drink," the man encouraged.

"I'll have a double scotch and soda," Rufus said.

The man was delighted. He placed the order and drew up his chair.

Rufus thought about all the rum he used to drink with Johnny and Foster, and he laughed aloud. The man laughed too, as if there was a joke.

"Another double scotch and soda," Rufus said. By now he wasn't even polite: he almost demanded the drinks.

After this had gone on for some minutes and the man had paid for six whiskeys and soda, Rufus took the money from the table and put it in his pocket.

"Order another whiskey and soda for me," he whispered. "Excuse me a minute, I won't be long."

He slipped out a back entrance and when he got home he took off his clothes and stood before the mirror examining his body.

Then he burst out laughing. "It's a damned good thing I left when I did," he told his reflection, "how much whiskeys and sodas I would have lasted, I wonder?"

The next day he got a letter from Rena asking him for a divorce.

LONDON

Dear Dog,

Here I am, little man in big country, and though I hadn't intended writing many letters, I have a feeling I will.

It was good to be at sea again, but it was a wonder our matchbox stayed afloat, as we had foul weather most of the time. An English officer aboard proved intelligent and we had long talks about the West Indies. He gave me a few letters of introduction to people in London; I haven't used any yet.

Well, I do not exempt myself from that feeling of strangeness and wonder which possesses anyone in a strange country for the first time, though I am rather suspicious of these early emotions. It is April now and supposed to be spring, but snow fell last night. It's real cold, I can't yet get over the fact that I breathe out vapour, when I walk in the streets I am constantly breathing out through my mouth, and I know this may sound ridiculous, but I think about St George and the Dragon, I guess because the dragon used to breath out fire and smoke.

I am sitting before a gas fire writing this. I am full of first impressions, but I am wary of telling you these, as I feel they will change and I don't want to give you any wrong ideas—nor have any myself.

Funds are running low: I hear tell the State supports you here until you get something to do—remember Father Hope on the Welfare State? I must begin hunting a job next month; the weather is too depressive now and I don't go out much.

There are many West Indians staying in this hostel, and inter-island feelings and differences are minimised, as would be expected: we are all birds of a feather, fighting against the injustices of the Mother Country. Some complain bitterly about the colour bar, they say it's hard for a coloured man to get a decent job. A lot of them are on the dole—getting assistance from the government.

Already I am getting tired of their grumbling, though. They would like to take me in hand and say do this and don't do that, go here but don't go there. But I won't have any of it.

I am getting lost like hell every time I go out. You're walking up a street and suddenly they change the name and you're in another street. So far I've had to ask the way back to the place where I stay more often than not, but I suppose I'll be able to get around after a while.

Every where I go people are drinking tea, and if you ask for a drink of water they look at you as if you're mad. Cocoa is a more nutritious drink, and makes you warmer—why isn't it used instead of tea? It is easier to make, too. What with all this tea drinking, and the amount of ale that is consumed, it is no wonder that every time you swing a corner you see a convenience. Must be something to do with the temperature too, 'cause I've been using them like hell since I came.

Well, I suppose the natives of this country have their peculiarities, same as we have ours.

I haven't been to any places of interest: as I said, I'm laying low until the weather changes. But I've used the underground trains a lot, and it's a wonderful transport system. You've only seconds to get on and off, and in a couple of minutes you get from one place to another. All the passengers are supposed to read newspapers: even in the rush hours when they are packed like sardines they manage to get an inch or two of newsprint before their eyes. You get the impression their minds would instantly go blank if the newspapers were taken away. I bought one evening paper and I am keeping it in my pocket, so I won't have to buy one every time I travel by tube.

And now perk up, you hot-blooded dog, 'cause I'm going to tell you about the women. So far I've seen more middle-aged and old than young ones. Must be a result of the war. It struck me as peculiar; many times I've boarded a bus and seen only old women on it.

But have no fear, lad, there are lots of luscious beauties to choose from. Wonder of wonders: pretty young girls going about with black Africans! These fellows grow their hair long, and comb it high so it sticks out in the air.

If you expect a tirade on the colour problem to follow, I am sorry to disappoint you. Apart from my lack of interest I don't know anything about it. I know you will deplore my attitude, but I have far greater problems to occupy myself with than to pause and consider the colour of my skin. Maybe one day I shall come up against it myself (should I consider myself lucky so far?) but all I hope for is to exist with grace.

But it is so cold now that the girls are all wrapped up in great coats, and you can't see a blessed thing but their faces and an inch or two of calf. I hear that in the summer it is different—you see quite a lot of them.

There is much food in London, but I am starving for a well-cooked meal. Everything here is boiled or roasted. There is not a drop of seasoning in the food, it is insipid. I tried to explain the use of salt and garlic to my landlady one morning. She listened politely, but all the same shoved the joint of beef into the oven just as it came from the butcher's. I have a gas-ring in my room and I am allowed to cook if I like; sooner or later I'll have to. You would have thought reading about the magnificent feasts that used to be held in the days of yore, that they would know how to prepare food, but if meat was cooked as it is today, give me a humble West Indian stew or curry any day. Even the oriental restaurants fail to give me any real satisfaction, catering as they are for the local palate.

Other West Indians tell me that they are accustomed to the fare, and that I would be too, after some time. I daresay they are right; one could become accustomed to anything with time, eh?

One evening I was lost on my way home and I passed near to the Royal Albert Hall. I noticed that a symphony concert was on that night—your friend Tchaikovsky was billed, so I attended. I found watching the orchestra distracting. I was part of an audience watching and listening to a performance, I wasn't myself. What matters if A moves a bow more gracefully than B? Surely it is the sound which results that is the thing? And I thought that maybe one might be unjustly prejudiced in thinking that one likes to listen to one artist in favour of another, when in fact one prefers to see the one in action to another.

That answers one of the questions you asked me, doesn't it? It may be different with you, but as far as I am concerned listening is the thing. You may say that reproduction by radio or record robs the music; bosh, if you have a good set you're well off. Indeed, you could reduce the volume and mellow the tone to suit your taste, whereas in the hall you have to take what the orchestra dishes out. So give me a good radio and a personal atmosphere any day.

Well, that's all the news. They allowed me to land with two hundred cigarettes (I got away with four). But they're almost finished, and they cost over here. So what I want you to do one of these good days is to stow away a hundred or so Anchor Specials in some newspapers, wrapping them up tightly. The boys tell me they get cigarettes regularly that way from home.

Also, rum costs. The angle with this is to put a couple of prunes in a bottle then fill it with the good grape and label it "preserved fruit."

I shan't be expecting these things, you must pleasantly surprise me one day.

I know you must be busy with the elections, but if you have any time to spare I wonder if you'd look up Marleen for me, and do anything you could to help? My cousin has some money I left behind and it may come in useful.

Have you told Father Hope about Marleen, and has he passed verdict on me?

Dear Glass Bottle Electric Machine,

I can tell from the trend of your letter that you are catching your royal in the Mother Country although you have hardly wiped your feet on the mat, hence I hasten to your rescue with much blah.

While your bones rattle and you clutch clothing about you, flowers are blooming and the sun is a constant in this fair isle. (How is that for a beginning, but I must stop now).

A week has gone by since I began to write this letter. During that week I won the elections by a narrow margin (you will say I write 'narrow margin' to make it sound more interesting, but it's true, I barely got in).

I never worked so hard in all my life nor been more objective (a double meaning here) than I have been these past weeks. I have seen enough conniving, scheming and dirty work to last me a lifetime, and I feel a different man. You used to say that this is a small island but enough corruption and graft goes on to fill a continent. Already I have been threatened that if I don't play ball things will go bad with me.

The dirty struggle is over, and I am glad my hands are clean: I can think of few who could say the same thing. Do you know, I almost gave it up in disgust at one stage when hooligans went around threatening people if they didn't vote for X.

I don't think I have many friends around me. They look on me as an intruder and a complete stranger. Which is true in a way, because I don't know any of them personally. They're trying to cow me into submission and put me in my place right from the beginning. They aren't even going about it tactfully, or feeling me out to see which way I lean. At least I know how I stand! But I wonder if I deserve this victory, with my poor knowledge of politics and administration.

However, that is only one side of the matter: of course I feel proud and triumphant, and I am hopeful that I will meet some honesty and sincerity as I get into stride.

It sounds as if I alone am going to run the affairs of the island, doesn't it? And that hitherto there has only been chaos and confusion! But I only speak to you this way 'cause I think you'll understand how I feel.

I spent last Sunday with Father Hope and we had a long talk about everything in general. He has been of great moral

98

assistance to me, and but for his hope and encouragement I might well have chucked in the sponge and called it a day. He says you must write to him, and I think you should: he is a wise man and a rare one, it beats me why he stays locked away in Veronica when he could be doing so much good outside. He won't leave the place, acts like an old hermit in that respect. But his name is spreading afield. Do you know there are well-to-do socialites who've been going to the valley to see him, seeking solace and guidance. He says you must write to him, and I think you should: he may be able to shed some light on your problems—*quien sabe?* (I hope that's right and rightly used).

I saw Rena a few days ago and she said you were one hell of a man going off like that without telling anyone goodbye. She asked me if I knew your address and I said no, but that you had promised to write me and as soon as you did I'd let her know. Shall I give her your address? I see no harm in it, but your relationship with people here is so complicated that I hesitate to say anything concerning you.

I haven't had a chance to see Marleen yet. I don't know what you expect me to do, I don't know the girl at all and she mightn't like the idea of a stranger prying into her affairs, especially at this time. However, I shall make an effort to get in touch with her soon. All well and good for you to sit on your tail in London and say befriend her.

I saw Regald—he voted for me! I passed on the tips about the cigarettes and rum, and he promised to do something.

That's all the news. I hope you get what you're after—whatever it is. Keep in touch . . .

Chapter Nine

In her letter to Rufus, Rena said that she was young and in the prime of her life, and couldn't spend the best years waiting. There was a successful lawyer from British Guiana who loved her and wanted to marry her.

Although in the beginning Rufus had wanted to get away, the idea of divorce had never entered his head, and now that the prospect was before him he hesitated in a sort of bewilderment, as if he had never thought the rift would widen that far.

He was well in stride at this stage, settled in the routine of things and making good progress at school, sure of something to return to in Trinidad. The separation had made him realise that after all he did love Rena, and the idea that she might want to leave him was so remote that he never thought of it.

"Your letter was not only a big shock to me," he wrote, "but it hurt to the core. What is this sudden business all about. Is it a matter of love at first sight. Do you know what you are doing? Are you really serious? You must indeed be terribly in love with this man to hurt me in this way.

"I am asking you to think this thing out clearly. Do you think he was serious when he told you to get a divorce, and he would marry you. I guess I have the right to ask you how long this thing has been going on. I know you love a gay time, but I did not think you would be going out with anyone while I was away.

"Anyway whether it is because I am selfish or jealous I do not know, but I surely cannot say yes to the divorce. You would probably say at some later date, 'I was only trying him out to see what he would say.'

"You say that he can really make you happy. I suppose your life with me was nothing short of misery and unhappiness. But what can I say, you know my financial position, it is true I could not give you all you wanted, and probably deserved—but I think that it is the reason why I am here, thousands of miles away, to try and better my position for the ultimate good of the three of us.

"Have you thought about the baby, or did you write that letter in haste? I am not condemning you, I guess I am to blame to a great extent. Maybe I am asking too much of you, to wait for me. Think this thing out clearly, and if you want me to come back, I will just pack my bags, give up my quest for bettering myself, and catch the next boat home.

"That might sound like a lot of big talk to you. But it can be done. All I have to do is quit school now, or wait for the end of the term which is two weeks away, and then work full-time in a factory, and in three or four weeks I could earn enough for a passage home.

"You have it all. You make the decision. The next move is yours."

It wasn't a satisfactory letter, but Christ, what was a man supposed to say when his wife asked for a divorce. He made the offer to return home wholeheartedly, because he knew Rena wouldn't accept it.

And he was filled with that feeling of importance and bigness that overcomes one at a time of grave decision, making one willing to forget one's own wishes in a grand gesture of self-sacrifice. There was something about self-sacrifice: if you made a show of it, people didn't like it. And if you were quiet about it, they said it was false modesty. So he wasn't sure what sort of attitude to adopt about the matter. But during the weeks he waited for a letter from Rena, it was a pleasant sort of anxiety, he saw himself packing his bags, telling his teacher at school: "I am sorry, but I have to return home at once, my affairs are in chaos," and seeing the looks of concern on the faces of the friends he had made, and hearing them say: "Hard luck, boy, I hope you'll be able to come back quickly." For trouble segregates you from the herd, you become a special individual: "You see that chap over there, he looks just an ordinary sort of guy, but he's got a world of worry on his head." And people who never knew you existed want to know what you are thinking of now, and if there isn't anything they could do to help. (They know there is anything, but they ask all the same).

And in his mind he made the trip back to Trinidad, and Rena and Tim were there on the quayside to meet him, and he held her in his arms and said, "Darling, what is all this nonsense?" And she said, "Oh darling, you shouldn't have come, I must have been crazy to tell you I wanted a divorce. Everything is all right. You must go back and finish your studies. You must."

"You fool," she wrote, "you are still a little boy and scared of what people will say if you agree to a divorce. There would be a lot of talk at first, but it will soon die out, and people will forget." She made no comment on his offer to return to Trinidad.

Knowing Rena as he did, Rufus was sure she would take advantage of the fact that she was virtually free to do as she pleased. By asking for a divorce she had cleared her conscience. The marriage was now a farce, though a legal matter in the law books.

Rufus thought seriously about what he should do. Getting a divorce was exceedingly difficult in Trinidad—bigamy, insanity or adultery were the only grounds. A man would have to have a fabricated, pre-arranged affair and a witness to state under oath to the court that he actually saw the act of misconduct.

To hell with all of it, thought Rufus, let her do whatever she likes. But in the months to follow he regretted that he hadn't allowed her to go ahead—that BG lawyer would have found a way out without much trouble.

He never bothered to write Rena again. And she kept silent, and the matter rested like that.

In the restaurant where he worked, it was good business for the proprietor to have attractive waitresses. He had them. One evening during a lull a blonde named Florence asked Rufus: "What do you do after work?"

"I have lessons to do. But on Fridays I am free and usually go out with the boys for a drink."

Florence looked disappointed. "I didn't know you drink," she said, "you look so quiet and reserved."

It was a cue, but Rufus didn't take it until two nights later.

"What are you doing tonight after work?" he asked Florence.

"I'm tired. I'm going straight home, wash a couple pairs of nylon and straight to bed."

"Maybe we could go some place for a drink?"

"Well, you could take me home. I have a little whiskey left there. But you must promise to behave, because the landlady is a bitch, she doesn't like me to have men in the apartment."

"I'll be good," Rufus lied.

"Then it's a date. Meet me outside the Greyhound bus terminal after work."

When they were walking slowly down the avenue she said, "You are walking on the wrong side of the road."

"Let's cross over then," he said.

"No. I mean you should be walking on the other side of me, don't you know that?"

"I didn't think it mattered," he said. But he went on the other side.

Walking home with Florence, he lost all sense of direction. He was used to a set pattern of roads, and after some turnings he didn't know where he was.

"Are you living far?" he asked.

She seemed to understand by that that he was tired, and she hailed a taxi without saying anything to him, and they got in and she gave the driver her address.

Florence was staying in a large boarding house. They went along a corridor and she stopped at number 77 and opened the door quietly.

"Don't make any noise," she told Rufus, motioning him in with her head.

Rufus looked around at the expensive furniture and said, "This flat must have cost you a tidy bit."

"Oh, it will do for now." Florence went into the kitchen and opened the refrigerator and took out a half-filled bottle of whiskey.

She poured two drinks and said, "Take your coat off."

Rufus unbuttoned his jacket slowly.

"Hurry up," she said impatiently, "you have to leave early."

"What's all the rush?" Rufus asked, gulping down the drink.

"Take it easy with the whiskey, though, don't think you are going to finish the bottle for me."

They sat down on a sofa and Florence looked at him silently for a minute. Suddenly she started to prattle Spanish at Rufus, the whole expression of her face changing as she changed languages, so that she looked a different person altogether.

Rufus was a little startled with this development.

"I don't understand Spanish," he said.

"Stop kidding me, say something," Florence said.

"But I tell you, I don't speak Spanish. I'm Indian, not a Spaniard."

America came back slowly into Florence's face.

"Well, I certainly deceived myself. I could have sworn you were a Puerto Rican."

"Do you like Puerto Ricans?"

"I was married to one once," Florence said. "He looked a lot like you. Or rather, you look a lot like him."

Rufus helped himself to another drink.

"Is that why you spoke to me that first time?"

Florence nodded.

"Well, to tell you the truth," Rufus lied, "I do have some Spanish blood in me. Other people have made the same mistake."

"On which side?"

"What? Oh, my mother."

Rufus moved up nearer on the sofa and put his arms around her. She leaned her head back and he kissed her slowly and long.

"You are a fast worker," she said the first thing that came to her mind. "But if you have any ideas you'd better forget them. It is late. You had better be going. I want to go to bed."

"I'm tired too," Rufus said, moving his hands hither and thither, "where's the bed?"

Florence sat up and ran her fingers through her hair. "Listen," she said. "I am so tired I could die. Why don't you be a gentleman and just go. If you do, I promise I'll see you again."

"I don't feel very gentlemanly tonight. Why don't you have another drink?"

"If you don't go, I won't ever see you or speak to you again."

"Have another drink?"

"Please go."

"No."

"I am going to bed," she said. "I don't know what you are going to do."

She went to the bedroom.

Rufus had another whiskey and sat thinking about how he was in America, and in a room alone with an America girl. The thought was like a luxury, so that when Florence called out: "Aren't you coming?" he went on thinking for a minute or so before he got up and went into the bedroom.

Some hours later there was a soft tapping on the glass pane of the living room window. Rufus pretended not to hear. But the noise persisted and he asked Florence: "Do you hear that noise?"

"Quiet, you fool. Don't say anything, and he would go away."

But Rufus sat up and said, "I'd better see who it is."

Florence held on to him excitedly. "Don't be a damn fool," she hissed. "It is Chester, your boss and mine. We would both be fired if he knows that you are here. What the hell does he mean by coming here at this hour of the morning, does he think I am running a brothel."

Rufus relaxed on the bed, feeling more comfortable and safe because Chester was out there in the cold.

After a few minutes the tapping stopped. They waited a little while then Florence said: "You'd better go now."

It took him more than a hour to get back to the "Y", because he didn't know where he was and he didn't have a dime in his pockets.

And Florence kept her word. She never went out with him again.

LONDON

It is six months since I last wrote you, but I am making no apology. Instead, I will tell you frankly that from now on when I do write it won't be so much to give you news as to be an outlet for my thoughts. Nevertheless I do hope that things are going all right with you, though thousands of miles away as I am and enmeshed in the struggle to find myself, I say that only as a saving grace.

Once or twice I have seen some Trinidad newspapers, and read about your "lone stand" against this and that proposal, or your agitation for steps to be taken in such and such direction.

I find it difficult to write with any relish of what has happened these past months. I find myself drinking cups of tea and I say: What the hell is so funny about that? And I have adopted all the little things which struck me as peculiar at first. It is quite obvious that I will soon be as those other West Indians before me, who move about London's streets with the confidence and casualness of an ordinary citizen.

I will tell you, that important as we Trinidadians think we are (in the sense that we are human beings too) there are people in this country who have never heard of our existence, nor know in what hemisphere the West Indies lay. One evening I went to a club and they asked me to tell them about the West Indies. I said all right, you ask me questions and I'll try to answer.

Do the people live in houses?

Do they wear clothes?

Are there lions and tigers in the jungles?

What language do they speak?

Have you ever eaten human flesh?

Over here you don't say you come from Trinidad, because no one knows where or what Trinidad is. You have to say the West Indies, and then they take it that you are from Jamaica.

We have a task to build up a national feeling, living as we are in scattered islands with our petty differences. Hitherto I have always been a little proud that in Trinidad we never felt very strongly about belonging to the island. (Or so it appeared to me.) Mixing with so many other nationalities, we have a sort of carefree political philosophy: this is a place to eat and sleep and work and get some fun out of life, and that's all. We never sort of visualised Trinidad as part of the world, a place to build history, a young country which could reap the benefit of the bitter experiences of older countries.

But sometimes a man feels as if he hasn't got a country, and it's a lonely feeling, as if you don't really belong nowhere. I used to think that this had merit, that we'd be able to fit in anywhere, with anybody, that we wouldn't have prejudices or narrow feelings of loyalty to contract our minds. I used to think we belonged to the world, that a Trinidadian could go to Alaska and fit in, or eat with chopsticks in Hong Kong, and he wouldn't be disturbed by the thought that he belonged somewhere else. I used to think of this philosophy as being the broadest, the most universal, that if it ever came to making a decision on an issue involving humanity itself, we'd have an advantage with this disadvantage, as it were, that we'd be able to see the way clearer, unbounded by any ties to a country or even a race or a creed.

But when you leave the country of your birth, it isn't like that at all. Other people belong. They are not human beings, they are Englishmen and Frenchmen and Americans, and you've got to have something to fall back on too, you can't just go up and say, "Hello fellow being, I'm new here, and I'm looking for a job." Or you can't go to the United Nations and say, "Look, I don't belong to any country, I have no ties of any sort to any particular nation. Maybe I could help you sort out some of your problems."

And so I don't know that there's any pride in a being a Trinidadian, or even a West Indian. I feel that if I had come to this country and said I was from Gagazendoom, it wouldn't have made any difference.

Other people belong, and they haven't time with you, they have their own pots on the fire. "West Indies, eh? Oh yes,

Jamaica, where the rum comes from. Well so long, drop in for a cup of tea some time."

So I feel now, that all those idealistic arguments we used to have at home don't mean a thing. You can't belong to the world, because the world won't have you. The world is made up of different nations, and you've got to belong to one of them, and to hell with the others.

Was a time when I used to be a little amused at the Englishman's thraldom to tradition, his love of ancient pomp and ceremony with all the colour and pageantry of a bygone era. But I don't know, boy. It is theirs, it belongs to them, and they'd fight and lose their lives for it.

The very aspect of London is ancient. It has been standing for hundreds of years and it will continue to stand. The cold, grey weather-beaten buildings, the ancient monuments. The uncomfortable, ludicrous uniforms some wear, the rites that will not change with time, the jealous way they preserve old papers and "guard" the towers. It is all well and good to stand on the outskirts and guffaw, but they like these things, and to hell with you, this is their country and if they choose to dress in a ludicrous costume and march in the streets, then that is their own blasted business, haul your tail if you don't like it.

We have nothing, and we thought having nothing could be an asset in a world where those who have don't seem to get any place.

A man will tell you, "Oh, you should be happy in your ignorance, living in a green tropical island without care, you don't know how well off you are." But the dog only tells you that because he has tasted of the fruit himself. What man in a state of ignorance calls ignorance bliss? What foolish man says " 'tis folly to be wise"?

We used to think we could put open minds to the world's problems, not mindful of anything in particular ourselves. But watch that ochro tree in your own back garden, and see how it is thriving. That post under your house which is rottening, you'd better take it away and put in a new one.

All that talk of universal understanding is only good when you have a bottle of Vat 19 near you, and you are old-talking with the boys.

Which reminds me of something else. One night in a pub in Chelsea I was having a discussion with two English writers. We were in good form and took the discussion and some bottles of beer to a flat to continue when the pub closed.

You know how one thing leads to another. We were talking at random about music and painting, when Paul—the more talkative of the two—smiled at me and said: "How naive can you be?"

And that set me off, because I've had some thoughts on naivete, and it strikes me that unless you can affect a sophisticated attitude, especially with regard to art, whatever you say is received with a condescending smile.

These fools feel they know the answer to everything, because they are full of knowledge. The pure mind, uncluttered with false ideas and theories (if you could find such a one these days) is called naive. Such a mind giving expression is laughed at and debunked. You mustn't look at a picture and say: "Oh what a beautiful painting." You must frown as you look at it, and bite your lip and rub your chin, and mutter, "Too much light . . . rather Marxist, don't you think?"

But they don't know one damn thing about what they are talking about, because some artists get their pictures hung upside down and they are praised just the same. A famous artist goes into the gallery and says: "I want that picture of mine hung from one corner, so that it looks lop-sided—that is the way it is meant to be seen." "Oh certainly, Mr—, ha-ha, of course, there, let me see . . . hmm, yes, I see what you mean, yes, the angle does make a difference, doesn't it?"

My friend, become famous, and you can talk bull and the people will listen avidly.

Don't be innocent, don't be simple. Don't say: Be kind to dumb animals—that is too naive. Tie the same thought up with big words—or richer yet, say: Deep purple hoipolloy ladeda, and if they are brave enough to ask you what you mean, look at them as if they're naive and say, Oh, that means be kind to dumb animals.

It is a crime to be simple, to be astonished, to be sentimental. See how people disguise their natural feelings, as if they were ashamed to be moved or touched by anything, quickly brushing away a tear, as if they have succumbed to a weakness by crying. See them in the cinema, surreptitiously wiping an eye and glancing around uneasily to see if anyone has noticed.

In such a world, in such a time I find myself. The wind is ruthless, the sun bitter, the sky weeps rain. Don't dare to be sentimental. If you like Tchaikovsky's music, you don't know what good music is. But listen to some of the stuff that Bach wrote, or play keen to any music which is not popular, and the critics will say you are a man of discernment.

The fundamental things of life aren't fundamental anymore. They wouldn't dare to ask you how you figger that out, because they believe artists are special people, that they must have privileges. An artist could wear a trousers with a tear in the bottom, and nobody will say anything. He could f____ your wife, and it would be all right. He could sit on his tail all day scratching while you are sweating in the sun, and it would be all right, he's waiting for inspiration. But you expect something from him, so one day he opens a dictionary at random and strings some words together and he calls it "Aspen Tree" or "One Pound of Beef, Please." And when you're finished toiling you go to the bookshop and you buy a book for ten shillings, and you go home and read "One Pound of Beef, Please," and you wish you could write like that fellar.

Because you've been taught from ever since that people who write and paint and compose music are little gods above you, that they live on a higher plane of life.

But that is bull, because I who write can't do your job in the sun, and you are as much an artist in your own right, doing a job to the best of your ability. I don't know anything about higher planes of life, but I suppose that if I ask you what is the secret of life, you may grin and look at me and say: Hard work, a wife, a home. And that is what you think, and what you think you believe, so for you the problem of life is solved.

But I playing hide and seek with words don't know, and I feel I will never know. All my life, while I wrestle with problems in my mind and debate the whys and wherefores, you will be going to your job and getting contentment out of your existence.

And I whom you think of as a little god will be still catching my royal, wondering why a man does as he does, or meditating on the shape of a rose. And that is a naive exposition. And it is the truth . . .

When Andrews finally got around to looking up Marleen, he found that she had left home, and her mother didn't know or care where she was.

After some inquiry he found her living in a room in St James, one of the districts of the city.

Marleen was still working. She wore a tight corset to hide her pregnancy. Foster's desertion, and the attitude of her own mother and friends had strengthened her into a resolve to stand on her own feet and face the world. She avoided people she knew, keeping to herself as much as possible.

She opened the door to Andrew's knock and stood there, her whole body a gesture of defiance and defence. She didn't know if the world was against her, but she was against the world.

"I don't think you know me," he began uneasily, "but may I come in? I'd like to speak to you."

She closed the door and motioned him to a chair. She sat down too, waiting for him to speak.

"I don't see any point in beating about the bush," Andrews spoke rapidly. "I'm Foster's friend. I know all about you and him. He asked me to help you if I could. Is there anything I could do?"

"I've seen your picture in the papers," she said, as if she hadn't heard him. "You're a councillor."

"Yes. I knew Foster well. He isn't really a bad sort of guy, just muddled up in his own mind, that's all. Are you living here now?"

"My mother threw me out."

"Is—is there anything I could do? I mean to help you."

"What could you do?" Marleen asked bitterly.

"I don't know really. I just want to help if I could. He left some money for you with his cousin. If you need anything—"

"I'm working."

"You're a brave girl. I mean that. But you just can't lock yourself away from everything, especially at a time like this."

"What do you want me to do, wear a placard in Frederick Street?"

She was making it difficult for him.

"Are you—that is, are you going to have the baby?"

"Yes."

"Is it—look, you mustn't mind my asking these questions, it's only because I want to help, you understand? I mean, is it because you don't know anyone who would—well, you know."

"Ah, Foster put you up to this, didn't he? He doesn't want me to have his child."

"No no, he never told me anything." Andrews knew he was

110

making a mess of everything, floundering around, not sure what was the right thing to say.

"I'm going to have the baby," Marleen said. "I don't care what happens."

"I could get the money for you from Foster's cousin," Andrews said.

"Why are you so concerned in something that's none of your business?"

"That's a pertinent question. I don't really know, honestly. You're quite right when you say it's none of my business. But Foster is my friend."

"There isn't anything you could do," Marleen said. "You nor anybody else. But thank you all the same."

Andrews got up. "At least let me give you the money he left."

"I don't want it. Good-bye."

Andrews went to the door, not clear in his mind what he should do, his feet moving automatically.

But when he opened it and turned to say good-bye, he saw Marleen sitting with her head on her knees, sobbing noiselessly.

He shut the door quickly and came towards her.

"Is anything the matter?" he asked foolishly.

"I don't know what to do, oh God," she sobbed.

"Haven't you got any friends?" he asked, wondering why he didn't think of that before.

"Yes, but they can't do anything."

"Look, I have to go now. But will you let me come to see you again? I'll come tomorrow evening if I may."

Marleen nodded.

"And don't worry about anything. I'll help you."

He went away, thinking to Foster thousands of miles away: You see what the hell you've put me into, you son of a bitch.

Four weeks later he wrote a letter to Foster:

. . . While you walk about the streets of that great city and seek balm for your frustrations, I have the business of life to attend to. I have been trying to hear your plaintive cries above the sun's brilliance and the roar of the foam-crested waves, and it seems as if you're in a different world, I can't tune to your wavelength.

And I am wondering why I should make the effort, if the thoughts you have have no bearing on the immediate problems of existence in this colony. It appears to me, as if the things we

111

discuss, the ideas we have, are a sort of part-time occupation or recreation, set apart from the business of living. You think philosophy, but even while you think you're on the way to the office to make entries in a ledger, or in the cinema watching a film, or you're with a woman. And day after day the routine goes on and on, and how does philosophy apply? Where room for "common ground" between the figures of a ledger sheet?

It is truly amazing how very little a man can concern himself with and get by, or get to the top of his little sphere and reign there serenely. Life doesn't make many demands, it is we who have balls-ed up the works and we blame everything and everyone but ourselves.

I imagine that sooner or later you will come to terms with your problems, at least reach a stage where you will realise the futility of abstraction in a material world and the importance of being accepted and accepting.

There is something wrong in our method of trying to shear argument and discussion of abstruse reasoning and getting a simple result to apply to life. Philosophy cannot be applied to life as it is: it may be applicable to life as it should be, or as we would like it to be.

But why should I wrangle with you? I have my hands filled with the ordinary business of living; and that is complicated enough.

You have hauled your tail off "to see the world" and left Marleen with child, depending on your good friend Andrews to see that all goes well with her. You are one son of a bitch, you know. Do you think you could just push your head in the clouds (and murky clouds at that, God knows) and leave your relationships and responsibilities to take care of themselves?

Do you think, when Marleen's mother threw her tail out when she discovered she was having a child, that Marleen could have said, Art is long, life is fleeting?

And you think was easy for me to explain to my mother and sister, that I want them to take she in because I promise you to· take care of she? You think while my mother was 'busing me for interfering in peoples business, that I had time to think of the universal kiss? You think, when my mother say: "I don't want to have anything to do with this business," that I could have said, "Adopt a philosophical attitude to the problem, mother?"

Well old man, if you think so, you damned wrong. And many

a night I have sat up and tried to reason this thing out. Is it because of friendship? Is it because of sentiment, or is it because I am a "good" person?

I went to Father Hope, and I said, "Father, do you think that Foster should have done this to me?"

And he said, "Foster didn't do it, you did it yourself."

I saw what he was getting at, but I wanted to make sure. So I asked, "How do you mean?"

He said, "Well, you didn't have to take the girl's worries onto your own shoulders. You had a choice."

"But the alternative never occurred to me. As I saw it, there was only one thing to be done."

Father Hope said, "Well, that's the kind of man you are."

"You mean I'm a sucker? That anyone could pour out their troubles and I'd push my hand in my pocket?"

"It's nothing to be ashamed of, my son. I would have done the same thing. Only, I wouldn't have had any doubts, as you have.

"You see Andrews," he went on, "the trouble with you and Foster is that you have nothing to believe in. Life can't be like that, because sometimes you're going to come up against things where you can't reason yourself out, and you're going to panic, and whimper, because for all your intelligence you can't see a solution. If a tree could have given you the courage and strength you need then, or fire, or woman, or anything at all, I would feel you're justified in worshipping that thing, and you haven't any need of God. I am not trying to convert you, don't look so humbled and ashamed. I believe that you have sense, and one day you'll see things in their true perspective.

"In the meantime, you are playing safe by befriending this girl. You aren't doing it out of genuine concern, you're doing it because you're not sure you won't be committing a sin if you leave her in the lurch.

"Foster now. He's stronger—or weaker, depending on how you look at it. He's flung everything aside in his search for truth. Foster isn't sure himself; perhaps he will have a lot to be repentant for.

"You know, what Foster is hoping for is something big and dramatic in his life, which will test his capabilities to the limit and force the truth on him, as it were. But it doesn't have to happen like that at all. Perhaps one day, walking in a field, the truth will dawn on him, just like that. It will creep up without a sign or a blare, one day when he hasn't got anything particular on his mind, when he least expects it.

"It's hard for a man like Foster. He's like Saul—he wants a vision in the sky. Saul was a lucky man, God gave him one. I hope Foster is lucky too."

Well, a man can't surround himself with wise words only and hope for the best.

But Father Hope did more than just counsel. He offered to take Marleen in. I had wanted to suggest that, and I was greatly relieved when he made the suggestion himself.

Marleen is a wonderful girl. She has shown great spirit and strong will all this time.

She didn't want to leave Port of Spain for Veronica, but I persuaded her, and in the end she agreed.

So now you have it all. Any time now she's going to bear your child. I don't know what that means to you. In your letters you don't ever mention anything about what I tell you—you only burden me with your own thoughts and problems. You are acting as if your life in Trinidad never was; at least as if you don't want to have anything to do with it.

Like Father Hope, I too wish that you'd get a vision. We need men like you here, but you just can't ride roughshod over other people or behave as if they don't exist . . .

Chapter Ten

Rufus was doing all right. He had taken a full-time job as a stock-keeper, and now went to night school, where progress continued.

Then the Immigration Authorities wrote to him, saying that he must cease working or be subject to deportation from the United States.

He talked over the matter with the school's Student Adviser, and accepted an offer to live at a wealthy home—free meals, lodging and laundry with five dollars pocket money weekly—in exchange for waiting at the table, washing dishes, cleaning the house on Saturdays, and doing odd chores.

Rufus was doing too well at school to baulk at any sort of proposition, and he fell to with a will. The American family were kind to him. But all his spare time and holidays had to be occupied painting and sawing logs or washing the walls and ceilings.

Then another problem confronted him. His permit to stay in the country was due to expire in five months. The only way to get an extension was to carry on with his studies, and for that he needed money.

And to get money, he had to chuck up everything and spend all his time working. He began lecturing at clubs, fabricating when his knowledge of West Indian affairs was exhausted: no one knew the difference. He cleared dishes in restaurants for meals.

The kindly American family offered to take him back, but Rufus knew that wouldn't be a way out of his difficulty.

One summer day he met Sylvia at a friend's home, and he went out often with her in the weeks that followed. He never told Sylvia he was married. And when he did want to tell her, he found he couldn't because he was afraid she'd leave him. In his mind everything was a great jumble which he refused to recognise, having eyes only for what was to him a real love. When he remembered Trinidad, it seemed so far away as to be harmless. He exonerated himself from his marriage to Rena, bossing conventional law and order in his mind, creating new standards for all those people who were in like situations.

He wrote Rena a letter:

It is over a year now since last I heard from you, and I feel like a stranger towards you. I do not know exactly what has been in your mind, or what you have been doing.

But I want you to know that it is entirely over as far as you and I are concerned.

I have been living the life of a bachelor for a long time now, and want you to know that you can do as you please, not that I think you have been doing differently.

But I want to make it clear that you are free of the responsibility of being my wife. You know that our marriage exists now only on paper, and is a legal obstacle. As soon as it is possible we shall be divorced, as you requested long ago, and I was fool enough to deny you.

I wish you the best of luck.

Thus Rufus, like Rena, cleared his conscience with a few words on a piece of paper.

If he had been in Trinidad, he would have gone to the office of the *Trinidad Guardian* and said he wanted to put in a classified advertisement. And the next day, under the heading of "Personal Notices," his conscience would have been cleared with these famous words, which appear every so often in that newspaper:

The public is hereby notified that I am no longer responsible for my wife—, and that I do not hold myself responsible for any debt or debts contracted by her.

Potent words like these would appear in tiny print on the back page, next to advertisements for rooms and buildings for sale and "Livestock—General."

Sylvia worked second shift at a factory and Rufus used to meet her after work, and they would walk around, dropping in at cafes for coffee and pie. She drank very little, she would toy with a glass of wine all evening just to keep Rufus company.

One weekend some friends went out of town and left the keys of their house with Rufus. When he met Sylvia after work, he took her there, saying they would dance to music on the radio.

But what they did was to sit on the divan and make a lot of love.

"Would you like a drink?" he asked her.

"Not particularly. Where would you get one at this time of night, anyway?"

Rufus went into the kitchen and took a bottle of wine from the refrigerator. He had a quick one by himself, then filled two glasses.

"You have a lot of nerve helping yourself to the people's drink like that," she said when he returned.

"They're good friends of mine—they won't mind," he said.

He had bought the wine himself, earlier in the day.

Sylvia held the glass of wine so long in her hands that Rufus said, "Go on, finish that and have another."

"Listen," Sylvia said, putting down the glass and looking him straight in the eye, "you don't have to try to get me tight with wine to get what you want. I love you body and soul, you know it would make me sick to drink too much."

It was about a month later when Sylvia told Rufus that she hadn't seen her time and knew she was pregnant.

"Let's get married, darling," she said.

LONDON

In a world fishing for peace, how can any individual find peace? Each day there are reports of war, murder, unrest. Each day, if you read the newspapers, you could find enough occupation for your mind, enough hopelessness to swamp the puny efforts you make towards happiness.

There is not one day in the world's existence when man is completely at peace with his brother. What a great thing it would be, if all the nations said they would observe just one day of complete friendliness throughout the world, if only to honour those who died for the false dream of a better world. If for that one day warring nations downed arms, statesmen rested their wrangling, murderers held their weapons, and you said to your neighbour, "This one day let there be peace between us."

I would fight and give my small life willingly for that one day. I won't even ask that there be a great peace, or that my country wins, or that there won't be another war. All I would ask is just one day when the sun shines and the wind blows and a man could feel that today there's real peace, today there's no fear.

But they won't do it even for God, much less themselves.

You could feel a tensity and a crazy anxiety for movement in the people, as if they felt that to stop and take stock would be to court disaster. One day of any day, if you stand still in Oxford Street or lean against a wall in Piccadilly Circus, you would see the English people rushing about madly. You would say to yourself: This is a great country and a great people, but if they are like this, what hope for us? You would see them, full of no purpose, sure of no destination, streaming in the streets of London, going to the theatre, to the cinema, going to the security of jobs. But always they are going.

I have myself been conscious of a feeling of fear and insecurity while I have not been working at a regular job. Apart from the influence of a steady income, there is the thought that millions of people are working, and there is safety in numbers. Everyone else is unconcerned with the spin of the world. They are somewhere out there, filing papers, writing stories for tomorrow's news, taking notes in shorthand, typing letters. They are selling behind counters, making clothes, cleaning the public conveniences, sweeping the streets, weighing the weekend joint.

And they are all looking at the clock anxiously, longing for elevenses, when they will smoke a cigarette and drink a cup of tea.

That is the pattern to follow for security. And indeed, there is a comfort to be in an office with your fellow workers, a sort of "here we all are" feeling, and "nothing can happen to me here. If something happens, it will happen to everybody."

I had been hoping to find something in this country, mature and great as it is. Instead, each day the newspapers tell you what your horoscope says, and if it will be a good day for romance or business, and if the weather will be fine. Do you wear size eight shoes? Then you are a man of strong character. Do you cut your hair long or short? Then you will be happy in love. Do you eat macaroni? Do you sleep under the blankets? Is your nose flat? Then you are a sharp businessman. Then you will be unhappy in love. Then you will go on a long voyage soon.

Ah, they have it all cut and dried for you. Now you don't even know what food to eat or what clothes to wear, or whether an innocent, unconscious gesture of the hand or a slight tilt of the head will type you as a man who has a strong personality, but is weak willed with women.

118

If you read the type of newspapers which enjoy the larger circulations in this country, you will weep. You will stand aghast at the muck and tripe which millions look forward to eagerly. It will surprise you to know how many, particularly young girls, base the day's activities on what the stars foretell, going out of their way to do as Taurus or Pisces command.

Apart from that, valuable space is covered with pictures and stories about animals. If an animal in the zoo is pregnant, that is big news. Progress is anxiously followed, each day there is a sort of news bulletin about how Bruno the bear is getting on. Meantime the kind-hearted people swamp the zoo with gifts for the animal, until the caretaker has to turn away boxes of presents.

On the great day Press photographers go and take pictures of Bruno playing with cubs, and the pictures are published extensively for all the people to see and acclaim this addition to the zoo, and they breathe a great sigh of relief that all has gone well.

I would tell you, there were times when I was hungered and I saw my landlady go out and buy rabbit for her cat (she doesn't like fish, the little dear, isn't that strange?) and meat for the dog. And for all the fuss and attention paid to them, one could find time to wish one were a dog instead of a suffering human being.

But as if that were not enough, rich people stretch their hands from the grave, bequeathing thousands of pounds for Flossie to live in comfort and luxury.

My God, how ridiculous could people be?

As for fashions, there is something new or old every day. If Paris wears no panties, then London follows suit as a matter of course. A man designs some ludicrous costume, and instantly it is on the Woman's Page: What YOU will be wearing in the autumn. A famous designer says skirts must be shorter and the slaves pick up their hems obediently. The Queen wears a new hat, and next day the shop windows are full of them, and women fall over each other to get one.

Each day there are new recipes and new ideas about how to cook the "humble" herring or what to do with leftovers, but I am yet to eat an English meal which is tasty.

Wear this, don't wear that. Eat this, don't eat that. Make love this way, not that way. What kind of toilet paper do you use? And this is a mentality which is supposed to be better than mine, for I am only a poor coloured colonial from a backward island far across the world, come to learn about life in the great city of London, where the cream of the white people live.

"Do you think Marleen is happy in Veronica?" Andrews asked Father Hope while he was sketching him sitting under a mango tree and looking up at the hills. He still found time to draw and paint, though it was only for recreation now.

"It is difficult to say. She is reconciled, at least. And now that everything is over, she is peaceful."

"You are very kind to her."

"I try to be kind to everybody. That way, you get on well, they like you, they would do things for you. At first Marleen was shy, a little afraid, not her real self. It was as if she had given up and others had to live for her. I don't think she was ever her real self before this misfortune happened to her."

"The baby looks like Foster."

"Of every new-born babe it is said that it resembles the parents. How can you tell? She looks just like a little monkey to me."

"Well, she looks like Foster, anyway. Especially the eyes. You only saw Foster once."

Father Hope got up and came near to look at the sketch. Andrews made a few finishing strokes then said casually, "I had a chance to make some quick, easy money yesterday."

Father Hope waited.

"All I have to do is back a proposition that's going to come up at a meeting next week."

"I'm glad you're not going to do it," Father Hope said.

"Don't credit me too much," Andrews said. "It's a big temptation. Actually I've thought about it a lot. Just by saying 'aye' instead of 'nay' I could make a thousand dollars, and no one would know the difference."

"No one but you."

"True. It makes me think how badly off we are, if the leaders in the island can be like that. At first you are full of ideals, and pledge yourself to do all you can for the upliftment of the people. You are keen and enthusiastic, wanting to contribute all you've got. Then you get an insight into what has been going on all the time, and you feel helpless, because there's nothing solid to work on. Before anything can be done we will have to purge the administration. I'm a bit tired of it all."

"You've just started. You have a long way to go yet. If the set-up is as bad as you say—and I don't doubt it is—it should incite you to try and bring about a change for the better."

"I know." Andrews looked around at the day, how it was in Veronica, with the hills covered in sunlight and the valley a dark green in the shade.

"I'm going to talk to Marleen," he said. "It's a nice morning to go for a walk. I'll encourage her."

"I'll be down at the school if you want to see me before you leave," Father Hope said. "I promised to do the Bible lessons today."

Andrews went into the house. Marleen had re-arranged Father Hope's few possessions about the house so it wouldn't look so bare, and she kept the rooms clean and filled with flowers.

She was sweeping when he came in and said, without preliminary greeting, "Would you like to go for a walk."

She put down the broom eagerly. "I saw you outside with Father Hope," she said. "I wondered if you were going to come in."

"You don't think I'd come all this way and not say hello to you?"

"Well, you're an important man, you know. You have a lot of things to attend to, you're always very busy."

He laughed. "You sound like Foster."

She looked at him. "Some weeks ago if you had said that I might not have liked it. But it didn't bother me just now."

"I'm glad. How is the baby?"

"She's sleeping. She had a bad cold, but it's better now. Don't go and wake her."

"Would you like to go for a walk?" he asked again.

"Where shall we go? In the village?"

"The day's too nice for that. Let's go up the hill."

"Wait until I put on my shoes." She was always barefooted in the house.

"I heard from Foster the other day," he called out when she was in the bedroom.

"Oh? How is he?"

"Still trying to find out what makes the world go round."

"That's good." She came out with a new skirt, smoothing down the front with her hands. "Shall we go?"

They took the trail behind the church and climbed slowly, Andrews in the lead. Now and then he waited at the side, getting a bird's-eye view of Marleen as she climbed the steep trail. She walked with her hands on her knees, as if that helped.

"Have you ever been this way before?" he asked.

"I've rambled about a bit, but I've never come so far. Do you know where you're going?"

"No. And I don't care. Let's just walk. Tell me when you're tired, then we'll stop wherever we are."

She tired about a half mile on, and they found a shady spot with a view for miles around the valley. Behind them a stream tumbled over smooth rocks into a small pool, and colourful butterflies flitted about in the cool shade.

They sat for a while in a pleasant silence, she with her legs drawn under her and resting on one hand so that that shoulder hunched, he supine.

"Are you happy with Father Hope?"

"Yes."

"No regrets?"

"None so far."

"Don't you miss your mother and your friends? Don't you miss Port of Spain?"

"I suppose I do, sometimes."

"Would you like to stay here? Always?"

"I can't do that! I've been a burden to Father Hope all this time, he'll be glad to get rid of me."

"You know that isn't true. He thinks you are a wonderful girl, and you could stay as long as you like."

"I mustn't take advantage of his kindness. Or yours."

"But what will you do if you leave Veronica?"

"Oh, I'll find something to do. I could go back to my old job, if they'd have me. I could get a room to live in some place."

"Father Hope told me you are always working, and that you've been of great assistance to him one way or another. Why don't you stay?"

Marleen didn't answer, and he went on, "At least for the time being."

"I still can't get over your interest," she said. "The way you've taken care of everything for me, and made it easy. Why have you done all this? Is it because of Foster?"

It was a question he had been asking himself for some time

now, and he wasn't sure of the answer. In the beginning his friendship with Foster had motivated him—that and a desire to do the right thing by a person who was in trouble. Having done far more than was expected of him, he should have left Marleen a long time ago to take care of her own affairs. Instead he had been coming to see her at every opportunity on the pretext that he wanted to see Father Hope. What further concern was it of his?

"It's partly because of Foster," he said slowly, "but I guess it's because of me, too."

"How do you mean?" she asked, though she suspected what he meant, and her heart quickened at the suspicion.

"How else can I tell you?" he blurted out uncomfortably, "I'm—well, that is, I'm fond of you, Marleen." His voice steadied when he got that bit over with. "In spite of everything—or rather, because of everything. I never thought it would turn out this way."

He put his hand under her chin and turned her face to look into her eyes.

"This is very real to me," he said, struggling to keep control of his voice. "I want you to know that. I'm not just saying it because we're alone here." He dropped his head as he went on. "But I don't know how it is with you. I don't know how you feel about Foster—I feel rather ashamed of his not being here right now—or if there's anyone else in your life."

He heard her voice over his head as he looked down at the grass.

"Foster doesn't mean anything to me." Her voice was soft and low. "There's nobody else in my life."

"I'm not very good at this sort of thing," he said. "I've known a lot of girls but it's never been like this. Those times I knew what to say and do. With you I can hardly bear to talk."

"Don't say things you'll regret later on," she said. "You're in a different world to me. You have a career and social position to think about. You're endangering your standing as a councillor by keeping my company—"

"That has nothing to do with it."

"Let me finish. I've given myself for far less than all you've done for me, and if you want me, I'll be happy to give myself to you. You don't have to fool yourself or fool me about anything. You don't want to say things that will cause hurt and sorrow

123

afterwards."

"It isn't like that at all," he said. "I love you."

"Oh, I want to believe you." She was crying, silently, he wouldn't have known if he hadn't looked at her and seen the tears in her eyes. "How can I believe you in the face of everything that has happened to me?"

"All that has happened makes no difference—"

"I've just borne another man's child."

"If all this hadn't happened, I might never have known you. I don't regret anything."

"It is only pity you feel."

"I've felt pity before. It wasn't like this."

"What do you want?" she cried. "Why don't you just take me without speaking words we may both live to regret, why are you saying things you can't mean?"

"Perhaps it is that you don't care for me. I've sort of taken that for granted foolishly."

"Care for you! Oh, the nights I've never slept, thinking of you, knowing that if it hadn't been for you I would have been lost and helpless. But I couldn't imagine you caring for me this way. I am so utterly unworthy of you."

"Marleen, darling, will you—will you marry me?"

Chapter Eleven

"How can I marry you?" Rufus asked helplessly. "I have no money, and they won't allow me to work in this country."

"But I am working," Sylvia said, "and we would have enough to get by on until you get permission to work. And if we're married they're bound to let you work."

Rufus stretched the argument over as many days as he could, stalling for time to think, refusing Sylvia's suggestion that she be the breadwinner, all the time remembering how one day some years ago a minister in Trinidad had pronounced him and Rena man and wife, and it was too late now to tell Sylvia anything.

"What are we going to do then? I am beginning to feel sick at work and some of the girls there are asking all sorts of embarrassing questions."

"You will have to lose it," he said, drinking beer in a cafe, and after he said it he thought: Why didn't I tell her so all the time?

"I'll stand by you all the way," he offered as remission.

Sylvia showed her remission by refusing to see him for two weeks, during which time Rufus paced floors and smoked hundreds of cigarettes. Then the phone rang one night.

"I'll go through with it," she said, "but only for your sake. You must stay by me all the time."

They tried several doctors. Rufus used to sit in the waiting rooms, biting his nails when he was out of cigarettes, while Sylvia went inside to see the doctor. She didn't have to tell him the result, he could tell by the look on her face.

Then one morning she went in and he waited as usual. He was quite used to it now, sitting there turning the pages of a magazine while behind the closed door Sylvia was telling the doctor she didn't want the baby.

This time when she opened the door and looked at him he saw hope in her eyes, and he could hardly wait for them to be outside before asking her.

"If you testify that your earnings are very frugal, and if the doctor finds I am not physically well enough, he would do it for a special fee."

"How much?"

"Seventy-five dollars."

"I haven't got it."

"I've been saving money for the past two years. I never thought it would be for this. It isn't enough, but I'll borrow the rest."

"No. I'll get the difference somehow."

After the doctor attended to Sylvia they had to wait for about three weeks before anything could happen. She took a week off from work and moved into an hotel. But nothing happened, and she went back to work, because at this stage she had ceased to care very much about anything.

She had to go back to the doctor before anything happened. Then one Saturday night they were in a tavern, and the jukebox was blaring, and Rufus was drinking beers. Sylvia wanted to be excused, and when she came back from the Ladies her face was pale.

"Hurry up and let's get out of here," she said, biting her lip.

"What's wrong?" Rufus asked.

"Let's get out of here," she said again.

He finished his drink and took her arm.

As soon as they got outside she gasped, "It has started."

"Where shall we go?" Rufus asked. He was glad he wasn't cold sober. Sylvia had been lingering over her glass of wine as usual and he had mixed it with his beer. The effect had dulled his senses. He was ready to do anything she suggested. Just tell him.

"Oh anywhere. Let's go to an hotel. We can't just stand here like this. Are you scared?"

"I don't know," he said truthfully, "I don't know how I feel."

"I'll just die if you leave me now. I feel terrible."

Rufus stopped a taxi and they got in. "Which hotel?" the driver asked when Rufus told him to drive to one.

Sylvia called out the name of the nearest one and sank back on the seat.

It was only a short drive, but Rufus thought it would never end. Sylvia was moaning and sinking her nails into his arm. There was nothing he could do; he kept rubbing her forehead. His head was clearer now, and with soberness came fear. He wanted a smoke badly, but Sylvia's head was resting on his arm. Her eyes were shut and her face looked like it didn't have any blood.

When they got to the hotel he told the driver to wait. Sylvia leaned heavily on him as they got out.

She dropped into a chair in the lobby as Rufus went to the desk.

There were no rooms available until one thirty. Rufus looked at his watch. It was almost midnight.

"Would you like to reserve a room that will be empty then?" the attendant asked.

"Just a minute." Rufus went across to Sylvia to see what she thought. Before he could open his mouth she muttered, her hands clasped to her face, "Take me to the hospital. I feel as if I'm dying."

A wave of fear swept away the last effects of the beer and his body felt like ice. "My wife is ill," Rufus said to the wide-eyed attendant. "I'll have to take her to the hospital right away."

He was relieved that the attendant didn't say a word. He went and got the taxi driver to help him carry Sylvia to the car.

"The hospital, quickly," Rufus told the driver.

"Which one?" the driver asked blankly.

"What? Oh, the nearest one, the nearest."

Sylvia lay back in the car and groaned with pain. Rufus supported her head and held her hands. His throat felt dry and he ran his tongue over his lips, but there wasn't any sensation. It didn't look like Sylvia would survive the journey to the hospital: he tried to imagine it was like when they were going to the hotel, but this time she was gasping and fighting for breath, and her eyes were rolling wildly.

He didn't know they were at the hospital until the driver opened the door, and there was a nurse with him. They put Sylvia on a stretcher and took her inside.

Rufus's face was bathed in sweat as he waited while the nurse attended to Sylvia behind a screen.

The nurse came out and asked: "Where's the taxi? Is it still there?"

"I guess it must still be outside," Rufus said. "I haven't paid the driver yet."

The nurse told Rufus to take her to the car.

She opened the door and went in.

"Haven't you got a light in this car?" she asked the driver irritably.

The driver took a torchlight from the glove compartment and handed it to her silently.

Whenever and wherever he thought about it, there was a brilliant beginning, and if he were a composer he could have set it down to music. But every sally ended in frustration, because he knew the flash would die (as many flashes did) and that there would be other times, other places. And on each recurrence he remembered and smiled in a resigned way. As if he had all the time in the world, he locked each leaping phrase away, telling himself, "All right, stay there and mellow until I am ready." But he knew they would be forgotten by then (Will I ever be readier than now?) so he never really bothered.

Living eagerly was what he did, thinking that when the time came he would have lived so vividly that every experience would be a source to draw upon. He had formulated a theory at last. It was this: Too many people forget the actuality of life, the exact moments of existence. Each action is mechanical, habit charting a beaten, circular course, criss-crossing over the beaten, circular courses of every man. The done things are done again and again, the ground of the world is covered with the footprints of people who will walk and walk on the same spot, footprint on footprint: it is hard to say "This one is mine and that yours."

Action is mechanical, a man is not aware that he is walking, or talking, or breathing. A man does not close his eyes and shut out the world and say, "What a wonderful thing sight is." Life is taken for granted, no man goes to sleep dreading that he will not wake on the morrow.

To escape from this, dream dreams, write books, compose music, paint pictures, is not the way out. There is something false and hollow about each creation of the artist, something lifeless and useless, inapplicable to the common-place, everyday actions, kissing or walking down the street on your way to the cinema, or to play a game of billiards with the boys. In the actuality of life, an invention like a vehicle to transport one's self from place to place is of use: a painting of the sunset, a brilliant sonnet is useless. If it came to a matter of choosing between the works of T S Eliot and Graham Greene, and No. 88 or No. 2 bus, how many would walk? If all the art galleries in London were shut for a year, and if no books were published and no music played, how many people going about their businesses would notice the difference? But if one electric train goes out of action for fifteen minutes on the lines, chaos and confusion is instant.

Life as it intrinsically is cannot be depicted. The artist steps over life to get at the person: the person is willing to listen, but wait a minute, he has to retire for a moment, or he has to put through an urgent telephone call, or he will come to the exhibition, certainly, but not tomorrow—he has an appointment with the dentist, a tooth has been aching and torturing him, and he must pull it out. Any attempt to present life as it is either recounts events which have already happened, or speculates on what is to come. The present, in truth, is a farce. It does not exist, the tense could be done away with altogether.

The one thing to be done then was to try and live in a state of acute consciousness of being. Not to let life sweep like a wind pass you and go on to the twenty-first century, but to have your mental faculties fully awake in constant appreciation. Let all concentration be on life, it being the only tangible reality. Be forever conscious of living. The world spins, and somewhere on that globe you are, a microscopic dot in a land mass, with the oceans of the world flowing about you, existing because you exist, existing as long as you exist.

Thus, each morning was a fresh if monotonous venture. Looking at faces in a crowd. Or drinking deeply the twenty-odd seconds of emptiness the lift took to carry underground passengers to the surface. There was something here, he could feel it. What goes on in the minds of those travellers who are suddenly herded together, standing in an embarrassed lot, eyes clashing and glancing quickly away?

He was working now, through necessity as much as fear, and it did not matter how the mornings began, going out in the world always took care of them. Going out to catch the bus, and meeting people with purposes, business to attend to, friends to visit. He was always grateful for that, for talking and reading newspapers and going places. Hating the pattern, he himself was a mark, though he liked to console himself that he was a little different from the rest. (Does everyone think that?) It gave him the confidence that existed for everyone: he used to stop thinking, "I am going forward in the day," and think: "*We* are going forward in the day." And almost with relief he sat or stood hanging with the rest of the world in the bus, feeling habit and daily activity coming over him like a shot of rum coursing through his body, drugging his senses, dulling perception, making him think of the office and the others, whether he'd be late, joining the hour with the last bit of work done yesterday: I must finish checking those vouchers.

"This will never do," he told himself time and again, and hurried off to write down a few thoughts. "I shall call my work 'Ha-ha,' " he said, "or 'Skiff-skiff' or 'Hello How Are You This Morning,' " and he would sprawl over the typewriter with all his life pressing down on him, wondering which of the brilliant beginnings to use. Oh, he had the shape of the whole thing in his mind, there was no doubt about that. It would be a slow, painstaking effort, hesitation and memory, each sentence capable of standing on its own feet away from the others. The greatest compliment would be to hear someone say, "Ah, that's *life* for you."

He used to find time to think about those parts of the pavements which have never felt the pressure of a foot. When he walked on them, he looked for these places. Up near the base of the wall, where dust and dirt and moss gathered, where people never walked. He used to walk there deliberately, his trousers wiping the dirty walls, ankles knocking each other as he trod virgin ground. Just for the hell of it.

That September was one of many months, but the leaves, turning yellow and brown and golden on the trees and falling to be wind-driven on the pavements and swirled in the air, helped to urge him towards. Waiting for something to happen, you never really know what it is, or what it will be. But one day birds in a tree chirp lustily and there you have it. Or a ray of forgotten sunshine falls across the desk in the office where you work.

Many days he saw them burning the brown leaves in the park. Raking them together in heaps and setting them on fire, and the smoke straight as a rod. The old man leaned against the rake and smoked a cigarette and watched the leaves burning.

When the leaves began to fall there was no stopping them. One day he saw a tree leafy and in the evening the branches were naked. The wind twisted and spun and lashed out at him; it waited around corners and outside doors. When it was behind him he didn't have to walk, and in front it braked him with a gusty force, so he had to lean and step off again.

For some nights, pacing the streets, he found it bracing and invigorating, for though it was powerful it was not yet very cold, and when it swept him it left him feeling clean. He walked in it, groping for an intangibility to lead him out of the drear dampness he was in. He was indescribably lonely. You could meet a man on the street, and you would glance at him as you pass by, and you couldn't know what he was thinking. You couldn't know anything about anybody in the restless sea of movement, movement, hesitation for tea, washed into Piccadilly Circus, (short time or long time, mister?) floating up the Strand, watching show windows: the long queues of strained faces waiting to go into the theatre, because a good play was on, the critics had said it was good, everyone was talking about it, so I must go too.

One night it was foggy and he went on Waterloo Bridge and he spat in the Thames, and he watched the buildings and the lights. A man came up and rested his elbows on the parapet and watched too, and said it was a picture; he was a painter from Holland, and he was going to Ireland the next day; he had been to the West Indies; would you like to go to my flat to see some of my pictures, it isn't far off.

He was watching a barge part water as it made headway. Darkness was quick in those days: by four o'clock in the afternoon, a quiet dark would fall and lights go on in the mist and the fog. It seemed there was never daylight, you got up in the morning and it was like night was still there, and you went out looking for the sun. If it ever came it was a sick, yellow orange at which you could stare unblinking, and you went through the day in a grey fog, as if you didn't exist entirely, as if it were a sort of half-life, a dream.

And then snow fell. He went out in it, turning up the collar of his coat. He went in the park and he scraped snow off the ground and heaped it up. While he was doing it he thought it was a hell of a thing for him to be doing, but he went on all the same. There were a few children doing the same thing and hurling snowballs, and they must have thought him funny, a grown man scraping snow into little heaps, because the way he was doing it was kind of thoughtful, not as if he was enjoying himself.

One day he went to Kew Gardens to see amber and gold on the trees. It was beautiful. He soaked in it (I mustn't forget to live life) but he didn't make any effort to impose the picture on his mind, because he wanted that if he thought of it in the future, he would only remember hazily that it was beautiful, and not be able to recall any detail about a leaf or the shape of a branch. Sometimes when things happen to you that's the way you like it to be, because sometimes when you think back about a thing too much or try to remember everything, you lose everything, and it might as well have not happened.

Julia came into all this like a breath of fresh air. He met her one night at a dance in Chelsea. He was just passing by, and he went in.

Julia didn't love him at first, he had to wait a long time for that. But he waited, finding in her company the solace he couldn't find in himself.

He loved her very much, he loved her desperately because it seemed to him then that there was little else in the world, and he wanted to make a big thing of it. He went through all the stages of love. And all the time he told her, "Let us live. Let us be aware of each other, the things we do and the things we say."

She was London to him; he forgot everything gladly in her company.

And then about two weeks after they spent a night together she met him one morning, and in a roundabout way, she told him she hadn't seen her time, and she was worried.

He was surprised at his calmness when he heard, it was almost as if she had said: It's a fine day.

But he got to thinking about it later on, though still he was not alarmed, almost as if it were something which had happened to other people, so you could feel the comfort of knowing it hadn't happened to you. He remembered Marleen in Trinidad, and he thought how everything seemed to happen twice with him. But drugged with Julia, he couldn't clear his mind to look at the situation as a problem.

Late that evening he was seeing her home, walking slowly, holding hands.

She told him it had happened before that she hadn't seen her time, but on those occasions there hadn't been anything to worry about, it was different now, wasn't it, and she asked him to tell her that nothing happened that night they spent together.

He thought it was a funny question, he thought she ought to know same as him, and he said: "How can I honestly tell you nothing happened?"

And she said straight away that if it was a baby she wasn't going to have it, that she didn't have the courage to go through with it.

He was silent at that; he watched a tree new in leaf and he thought how wonderful it was to be able to make up your mind just like that, without pondering and sleeplessness. But he was wide open to the poignant emotions of love, he felt hurt that she hadn't asked: What shall we do, she just said she wasn't going to have it, as if he didn't have anything to do with it.

But he gave a little laugh and he said: "You'd better wait until you know for sure, all this may be unnecessary worry after all."

All the time she was talking as if he were completely out of the picture, and he kept on feeling hurt, because he loved her and he wanted to be part of it.

Love for Julia was like an escape from the baffling problems which confronted him every day, and he loved her wholeheartedly, flowing every thought in her direction, refusing to think of anything else. But always he had the hollow feeling that perhaps she didn't love him.

He used to ask her, and she said: "I don't know."

And now this thing was happening. The time with Marleen, it hadn't been this way at all. He had never felt a love for her as he did for Julia. Julia had come into his life at a time when he was lonely and miserable. He was happy with her, as happy as he ever hoped to be.

No matter under what circumstances, if there was love first there should be the miracle of it to think about, then afterwards the dread. But not just the dread, and the fear; that could well mean there wasn't any love. And it would be talked about with hands holding, and in-between kisses and words of love, not just thrown at you like that, as if it were a broken arm or a cold or something.

But he never wanted to think she didn't love him, so he pushed all those feelings aside, and he tried to get inside her, to sort of let her know that she didn't have to be that way, that come hell or high water he was going to stand by her.

One day she told him she had been getting up nights, worrying.

She said: "I'm going to drink a bottle of gin."

When he asked her who told her that helps, she waved her hand in the air and said: "Oh, everybody knows."

He said: "If you feel like that you'd better do it yourself."

But Julia wanted him to be with her. She said they'd get some sandwiches and the bottle of gin, and spend an evening out in the country, and she added as a joke that if she got drunk he could take her home.

He said he wasn't going to have any part of it, but all the time he knew he would, only, there was just this one idea of seeking safety, never any talk of waiting to see if it would be all right next month.

The idea of marrying never seemed to occur to her. He wanted to marry her—she knew that. But they never talked about it as a solution. In his heart he was glad—he didn't want that if he ever married it would be because he had to. Yet he knew that he loved her enough to do it if she wanted. But she had it down pat what she was going to do, and once he tried to show her how he felt and she said: "Don't be ridiculous."

They went one evening into a wood, and sat under a tree. They ate the sandwiches and then had a big shot of the gin. She began to joke about the whole affair, and time and again she asked him if he thought she was going to have a baby, and he said no, he didn't think so.

They made a lot of love, and they came near to doing it again, and undoing everything.

But she told him no, please.

After three shots of gin she began to cry. Not because of anything, it was just that she was that way when she drank.

It made him sad to see her cry, he had to kiss her and tell her that he loved her, and after a few minutes she dried her tears and kissed him back.

After they had been about an hour she told him she loved him.

It was the first time she'd ever said that, and he wanted to believe her more than anything else in the world.

"Do you think it's possible to love two people at the same time?" she went on. He knew then that it wasn't only him. It was bitter to bear, after he had one-tracked his life for her.

He wouldn't look at her after that, he kept looking at her lips and her hair when she raised her head, but he wouldn't look her in the eye at all.

She began to cry again and tell him that she loved him, and he made her say that she loved him alone, and no one else.

But after a few kisses she said she was drunk, and didn't know what she was saying.

When they were ready to leave the wood it came back what they had come for, and she said it would be a hell of a thing if nothing happened after all this, and she said it was a crazy idea, wasn't it.

Coming back to London in the bus, she slept all the way on his arm, and he watched how peaceful she was, and got to thinking back about the things she'd said, about loving him and being drunk, and loving two people at the same time.

The next day he phoned her. He thought of something light-hearted to say while he was waiting, and when she answered he said: "Hello darling, anything to report on the efficacy of gin?"

She said: "No darling, isn't it a shame, after all that. I feel awful, I just had a bath, but my head hurts."

He said: "Darling, you're not worried still?"

She said: "No darling."

"You remember everything you told me yesterday?"

"What?"

"I mean about you and me," he said, feeling uneasy.

"Yes darling."

"And you take good care of yourself," he said. "Rest a lot today."

She gave a little laugh. "Yes darling. Good-bye."

"If you have made up your mind," Father Hope said, "there isn't very much I can do about it."

"You could let me know what you think," Andrews said.

He had driven into Veronica that morning to show Father Hope the new Vauxhall Eight he had bought. It wasn't the car they were talking about. It was Andrews' decision to marry Marleen.

Father Hope sighed. "What makes you think I have the power to see into the future?"

"We love each other, Father. There is no reason why we should not marry."

"How much do you really know about Marleen, Andrews?"

"All that I need to know. She's told me about herself. I know about Foster, and his brother Rufus. I know she hasn't been what you call a good girl. I've considered everything and I still want to marry her."

"Do you think Foster would like that?"

"He has nothing to do with it. He has forgotten all about Marleen. It's more than a year since he's been away. There wasn't very much for either of them to remember, anyway."

"Except that Marleen has borne Foster's child."

"She is quite dispassionate about it. The child will live with us."

"Does he know about this?"

"Who, Foster? Why, it hasn't even occurred to me that I should write and tell him."

"Perhaps you should."

"If Foster is your only objection, I don't see there's anything to worry about."

"What about your career? Such a marriage won't do you any good. It might be a handicap more than anything else. You're a public figure, you know."

"What am I supposed to do? Forget my personal happiness and dedicate myself to local politics?"

"It might be rewarding to more people in the long run."

"I won't do it. I'm not that sort of man, Father. Maybe I've given you the wrong impression. I have my ideals and my ambitions, but I'm very human too. I want the simple pleasures of life as much as the next man. I want a wife and a home and children, and a piece of land to raise corn. Why should I sacrifice all that for a worthless cause? Do you think Trinidadians care very much whether the island progresses or continues to rot? Do you think I care?"

"Yes. You care. And that's the difference. When someone like you comes along, it's a great pity to see you go the way of all the others. This island needs men like you to pull it out of the stagnation it's been in all these years. It needs selfless, honest men."

"I don't see what this has to do with my marrying Marleen, anyway."

"You'll forgive me if I speak bluntly. Marleen is a common girl. By that I mean that she's not of your class, Andrews. You come from a good family which has its roots deep in the island. If you marry at all, the people expect it to be a social event for a man of your standing."

"My private life has nothing to do with the people. You seem to forget that this is Trinidad. The ethical view doesn't come into it at all, they don't really care if I marry a George Street whore."

"That has always been our failing. Whenever a question involving the finer principles of life is involved, we say, 'Oh, this is Trinidad, corruption and dishonesty goes on left and right,' and we justify our own selfish motives. We never try to make a better island, because the conditions offer excuses for all our failings. We blame everything on some sort of mythical evil existing all around, we wave our hands helplessly in the air and say, 'What else could you expect in this place?' "

"Substitute 'real' for 'mythical' and I agree with you. But I still don't see that it concerns Marleen and I."

"Maybe it doesn't concern her. But you're different. I wouldn't like you to do anything with the attitude that it doesn't matter because this is Trinidad. We have too much of that attitude already. That's the very thing you're fighting against."

"All right. I made a mistake, I shouldn't have said that."

"Don't blame yourself too much. It comes to our lips as a ready excuse for anything."

"But I'm not asking Marleen to marry me for any other reason than that I love her, and she loves me. Isn't love enough, Father?"

"I can't answer that. Love isn't always getting the thing we want. Sometimes it takes everything we've got and we get nothing in return. But I won't keep you here arguing. You want to show her your new car."

He took Marleen for a drive into Port of Spain.

"Any place in particular you'd like to go, darling?" he asked.

"Let's go up on Chancellor Hill," she said. "There's a lovely view from there."

"I know. I had to go up there to pass my driving test, I hope I can do it again."

The road was a narrow, winding one. Andrews drove slowly, not yet sure of the feel of the car. He parked at the top, on a cleared spot off the road. They got out and sat on the grass. Port of Spain was spread out under them, and the sea was like gold in the path of the setting sun on the horizon.

Marleen was so quiet that Andrews looked at her. Her eyes were moist. Instantly he put his arms around her and held her close.

"What is it darling?" he whispered. "Why are you crying?"

"I was in the next room," she said, wiping her eyes and trying to smile a little. "I couldn't help hearing what you and Father Hope were talking about."

"That's nothing to cry over. You don't have to mind what he said, darling."

"But you told me he was a wise man. You've always said how Father Hope was the most intelligent man you ever met, and how you always go to him for advice when you're in trouble. And you can't deny that all he said was true."

"Nothing he said or says can ever make a difference with us, Marleen."

"Ah, you are on the other side of the wall, you can't know how I felt when I heard him say I was a common girl. It's so true. You've had to come down to get to know me. Father Hope thinks you are a great man. It's funny, but I never thought I'd ever to get to know a great man. And least of all that he'd be a Trinidadian. I've learnt a lot since I have been in Veronica—isn't that strange? I leave the city and go to a small village in the country, and I learn more in a few months there than I ever learnt in my lifetime in the city. It's not so much the place as the people you meet, isn't it? I think I know what he meant when he said that you're great."

"I wish you'd stop speaking like that, Marleen. I'm just an ordinary person like you, and I want to marry you because I love you and I'd be happy trying to make you happy."

"But there's so much more to it than that, and you know it. You're being deliberately blind. You think I'm the most wonderful girl in the world, but I'm not. Even your parents have spoken against me. We would be defying everything to get married."

"Look, Marleen." Andrews's voice was serious, and he looked straight at her when he spoke. "We don't have to make this thing complicated. Just because I'm a councillor doesn't mean that I'm great, God knows, it could mean the very opposite in Trinidad."

"Remember what Father Hope said."

"Stop referring to him as if he is a god or something. What I've said is true, anyway, though it mayn't be loyal. But darling, can't you see that being with you means everything to me? What does it matter who I am or what I am if we love each other? Isn't love enough?"

"You asked Father Hope that same question. Now you're asking me."

"Yes. I'm not marrying Father Hope."

138

"Oh, you know how happy I would be to be your wife, and how proud. This love we have for each other, will it always last? Will it be strong enough to keep us together always?"

"Always and always. Don't say no, Marleen. It would break my heart."

"When I'm with you I feel sure it is the right thing to do."

"You'll always be with me, dearest. Say you will, Marleen. You'll make me happier than I've ever been."

"Sweet darling, you are so sure everything will be all right."

"Say yes, Marleen."

"Oh, yes, yes," she cried, falling back on the grass, "I love you too much to let you go. Today, tomorrow, whenever you like."

They stayed a long time on the hill, and when the sun sank and darkness fell they were still there, locked in each other's arms.

The new car shone in the darkness.

Chapter Twelve

Two weeks later Sylvia was back at work, and she and Rufus
were talking about what had happened as people do after their
experiences, examining themselves to find out why it was that
it didn't matter as much as it did at the time, a little amazed
that the passage of a few weeks could so take care of everything,
fooling themselves that if it ever happened again, they'd know
what to do, they'd be calm and collected, because after a while
they'd forget it had ever happened, as how now it was a thing
of the past.

Instead of drifting them apart, the incident drew them even
closer together. Passion hadn't gone its natural course and died,
it had been aborted, and there was more to come, there was
plenty love remaining. Now it was deeper, smoother, like after
a happy honeymoon.

When Rufus suggested living together, Sylvia raised no
objection, and they took a room in a flat. She went out to work,
and he stayed at home and kept house.

It only needed a week of this arrangement for Rufus to become
restless. Preying on his mind was the fact that he only had three
more months legal stay in the country. There was no way of
getting the time extended: when the three months were up, what
the hell was he going to do? Like his marriage to Rena, he had
kept this news from Sylvia.

He made up his mind to take a job until the time was up. He
went to work in a big factory that manufactured parts for cars.
Though he had no definite plan, he knew that whatever he
decided he would need money. He worked like a slave, putting
in overtime, and in a month's time he had saved quite a bit.

It was then that an idea came to him. He would go on
working—night and day if necessary—and save up enough
money to return to Trinidad. There he would try to get a quick
divorce from Rena (or give her one—anything at all, as long as
it was quick and didn't take much time) and return to America
and marry Sylvia, and continue his studies when things were
settled. When he thought of this plan it seemed the most

140

workable of any he could imagine.

But a change came over Sylvia as the weeks went by. She was silent and moody, bursting into tears at the slightest incident. "What's the matter, honey?" he asked her one evening. "Is something bothering you?"

"It's all right for you—I'm the one the neighbours talk about," she said, as if she had been waiting all this time for a signal from him to speak. "You're a stranger to this country. But I'm an American. They keep asking me where I met you, and when we were married. Last Saturday the landlady took the rent from me, and when she was making out the receipt I gave her my name instead of yours. I had to cover up with a lie. Oh, I'm tired of lies and deceit. You don't really love me, you don't care what they say about me. The milkman smirks at me, the grocer serves me with a leer in his eyes. Even my best friends at work know I'm lying to them. You expect me to be happy living like this? Do you think we can go on fooling people all the time? Why can't we get married, darling, why, why? We have enough money now to marry and live like decent people."

"We'll get married, honey," he said. "Only we've got to wait a little."

"Why have we got to wait? Why can't we get married now? At first you said we didn't have enough money. What is the excuse now?"

He didn't know what to tell her. The more she talked, the more he remembered his marriage in Trinidad, and more imminent, that in a couple of months' time he would have to leave the country. He would have to do it before the Immigration Authorities came knocking at the door.

Trying to sleep at night, with Sylvia tossing beside him, he reviewed his years in America, seeing the complications of his life like a net which he clawed in vain. And yet in spite of the circumstances he was in, there was a sort of not unpleasant feeling, encouraged by his belief that all his experiences had had to be, there was nothing he could have done. If he had the choice at the moment of thinking of being happily settled in Trinidad with Rena and his son, or lying in bed with Sylvia in a rented room in America, he knew which he'd choose. Tangled in the net, he was crazily tempted to ensnare himself still further. How much worse off would he be if he got married? The idea of this was so impractical that it intrigued him. Apart from the fact that he loved Sylvia and would willingly marry her if he could, the thought of involving himself more hopelessly into an already complex state of affairs attracted him like a magnet. With clear and lucid reasoning he saw what a fool he would be if he got married to Sylvia now.

Sometimes, in those nights he couldn't sleep for Sylvia's stifled sobbing in the sheets, Trinidad seemed so far away he felt as if he were a completely different person, a stranger to the man who had left the island years ago. The separation was not only time and distance. It was in everything but memory, and what was memory but reflection on a past which could never be recaptured? Rena must be living her own life. For all he knew, she must be living with the lawyer from British Guiana; perhaps they had begotten children of their own. Everything must have changed for her too.

One night, wearied out with such thoughts and unable to bear the unhappy state Sylvia was in, he woke her.

"We'll get married," he said. "Tomorrow, if you like."

A Justice of the Peace did it, out in the country. He had never seen Sylvia happier, her joy filled out some of the hollowness in his own heart.

Why didn't I do this all the time? he wondered, as he had wondered when he kept putting off telling her they couldn't have the baby.

And a few weeks later, "Why did I marry her? Why couldn't it wait until I went to Trinidad and came back?"

For there was no more compromise or putting off: he had to leave the country shortly or be thrown out. If events had happened in a way to employ only his own resources, he might have carried on living side by side with deceit. One day it would have become unbearable, but by that time he would have worked out a solution. But it wasn't only himself, one day there'd be a knock on the door, and they'd give him a day or two to clear out of America. A man or men he didn't know would do that, people out of the conspiracy of his life, unconcerned with what happened to him. That was what everything had come to, in the end. After all he'd been through. And he knew that if they threw him out of America, it would be hell to get back in again.

As the deadline drew nearer, he felt as if everything had been useless and in vain. He had lived lies so long that he didn't even know how to tell Sylvia. They had been together so long without her knowing anything and no big catastrophe had happened, that he was led to believe she need never know the whole truth.

Nevertheless, she had to be told that he had to leave the country.

It was not until some time after that he realised the dimensions of the matter. Accepting it had been easy, so that when the realisation came it came like a new problem, as if he were facing it for the first time. Though, not really. It was like keeping your shadow behind you, but one day the sun threw it out in front of you and it went and flattened itself against a wall so that as you walked forward it too seemed to stride like a live thing and the two of you collided.

But always, as they discussed the problem, it seemed to him that the heart of the matter was not the important thing, that what was important was the background of the days they lived, the places where they walked, the way she looked. Thus, at a crucial moment when he should have been sharply tuned to the deliberation of a solution, he was aware only of the wind that blew (if the wind was blowing) or the way the day looked. It was as if the unreality was the reality; background was foreground; when she spoke, asking him what they were going to do, her voice was a sound heard in the distance, like how they do it on the radio or a film when a person is hearing something in a dream.

And as in a dream he would come back (but hiding the dreaminess, for to appear distracted might hurt Julia) and he would nod slowly, so that if distraction did show on his face it would appear instead to be absorption with the problem.

Yet it was no lack of concern, and for all the twilight of his reception he heard every word; they came back long after she had spoken, it was as if he trailed behind. And if she were that kind of person, he could have answered today's questions yesterday, and show her he was ready for tomorrow's answers.

But because Julia was not that kind of person he had always to be on the ball, to offer quick reply (it was not as difficult as it used to be) and at times even to take the matter in hand himself and hold the reins of the conversation.

All this, in a time of summer and sunlight, when they should have been revelling in a happiness he had planned all winter.

The day he went to see the doctor, he sat in the office cracking his knuckles abstractedly, and he put the problem to the doctor, who said it was indeed a problem. The doctor observed the while a completely impersonal interest, as if he were a friend who could offer nothing but sympathy (but that wholeheartedly) though he knew what it was all about, what was required of him. "I have heard this story many times before," his eyes said, "but he listened to the numerous reasons why he should commit himself, folding his hands across his stomach in a gesture of eternal patience.

And all the time they both knew an agreement would be reached; he hated the doctor for making him carry on the preamble, losing more dignity and respect with each word. Though, too, dignity and respect were distant things, but not so far that he couldn't feel a pang every now and then.

Before the matter reached this stage he had sat with Julia one evening on a culvert in a lonely lane, and their backs rested against a strong wire netting, and it was a balmy evening, with a touch of early summer, and he said, "Let's not do this thing, let's go away or anything, but not that."

But she cried and said how it was impossible, and it was funny, but the more she said that, the more possible it became to him that they could go away or do something (when he thought "something" he unconsciously waved his hand in a gesture suggesting "anything"), perhaps stay and face the issue, holding on tightly to love, because people always said how love could make you do anything, and that was how he felt.

It would have made all the difference in the world if she had said, "Yes, yes, let us go away, as long as you are with me, that's all that matters." Then afterwards, through a process of warm mutuality, they could have both decided on doing it, and it would have been all right. But she never said anything like that, from the very beginning her mind was one-tracked.

There was the sound of children playing outside; the doctor said, "Those are my children, you want me to risk that?"

He pleaded with the doctor (he will agree eventually, why does he make me go on and on?) until he said he would examine Julia. He said if he did that and found she was pregnant, he wasn't going to do anything about it.

He took Julia to see the doctor. He sat outside, and his flesh crawled when he thought how the doctor must be touching her.

The doctor said yes.

Julia cried in the street as they were coming away, and he had to hold her close.

Another day they went to see another doctor, to make sure, because there was always the last hope that the diagnosis was wrong, don't worry darling.

The doctor made sure.

And now there was nothing and everything to do.

He went back to the first doctor, and he said, "You've got to help me out."

But all the fine things in the world were crumbling, and he wished his attitude could be like Julia's, for she was hell-bent on it, and he was still vaguely hoping, fooling himself like a man who was inevitably committing a crime but kept doping himself with hope of a last-minute reprieve.

"Doc," he said, starting all over again. "By God, I know how you feel, I know the big risk you will be taking. But you've got to help me out. I haven't much money, but whatever you say, doc."

He kept saying "doc," because it sounded intimate and friendly. There was a bottom, and he and the doctor had reached it. By casting aside all reservations and personal characteristics and whining like a whipped dog, and the doctor by preaching the ethics of his profession which he knew all the time he would forgo. And his hatred of the doctor doubled, because there shouldn't have been any need for that—he could have been businesslike and agreed to do it, and leave the nakedness for when they were separated one from the other, each in his own temple. That would have left him a little dignity and manhood, to keep the chin up halfway.

But his head was bowed to the pavement when he left, it was as if he had come away from an evil conspiracy, and he turned up the collar of his coat, and pushed his hands in the pockets against the comfort of his legs, feeling the muscles work his feet forward.

Julia was relieved, the way out was arrowed, all they had to do was walk along it. And now for her most of the terror and anxiety and uncertainty abated, now that it wasn't going to happen she acted as if it were going to happen. She felt a glow of security, like how sometimes a person in bed pulls the sheets up and feels everything's all right, nothing could happen. She imagined all she'd ever heard or read happening to her, living

145

in a world of expectation. She became wistful at the thought of losing the child, and used to stand naked before the mirror and look at her body, moving her hands tenderly over her belly, pressing it a little to see if she could feel anything.

He as in a mist walked beside her in those days, knowing only love for Julia, doing what she wanted. Julia was tender and loving, needing tenderness and love herself. They crept through the streets of London on silent feet, holding hands, whispering in cafes over cups of tea, united in their dread and in their love.

The day she came from the doctor he was waiting outside, hunched in a chair.

Two weeks went by, and nothing happened, except that fear, worry and anxiety increased. Summer came cruelly to London, the days were long and sunny, the sky blue and clouds fleecy. They spent the evenings together, sitting on park benches, or on the grass, or on stools in cafes.

He went back again to the doctor.

Doc, he said, nothing's happened.

Bring her back, the doctor said.

Julia went.

And then one day about a week after, she came to see him and said, It happened yesterday.

Yesterday, he echoed, and you come today to tell me?

I couldn't find you yesterday, Julia said. Does it matter?

No, he said slowly, of course not.

PORT OF SPAIN

Almost six months since I heard from you, what's the matter? Have you found the secret of life in London and don't want to share it with your friends? Mayhap you've found some rich dowager, and you're taking things easy, preparing a great philosophical work to spring on the world.

On the other hand I don't think you have any good reason for not writing, it's just sheer laziness. I had thought we'd keep up a regular correspondence, sharing experiences. There are so many things you could tell me of which you know I'd be interested. In particular, I was wanting to ask you if you would look into the problem of West Indian emigration to England. I wanted some first-hand information on this, you could have gone around and seen some people, and got their views. We hear so many stories down here . . .

146

Well, anyway I hope things are all right with you, and you're not scattering little Fosters all over London.

Over here things are moving slowly as usual. Federation, the big move to put us on the map, is treated with suspicion and mistrust: each island is waiting to see what the other does, and no one does anything. It is difficult to have any idea of what is happening in the other islands. You know how we have our differences. There is no news about what is going on at "headquarters" in London.

Do you know how this matter appears to me? West Indians clamour for self-government. They're not so sure what it is; they know it's a step in the right direction. So what does Britain do? She proposes federation as a compromise. And instantly there is confusion, what shall we do, what is federation, what is this all about, what have we put ourselves into? They don't know their backside from their elbow, each island waits, afraid to say yes or no, watching to see what the others will do. The small islands watch Trinidad, Trinidad watches Jamaica, Jamaica plays ball with the Colonial Office. That proposal will keep them quiet for a while, Britain rightly thinks, now let them argue about it among themselves.

Oh, we have a long way to go. The idea of federation is nothing new, but who has done anything about it in the past? Meanwhile our own administration is corrupted and dishonest, each individual selfishly seeking his own ends. I get sick when I think of it. We can't even manage our own internal affairs properly, there is constant bickering and accusation. Hard as I am trying, I can't seem to get a clear picture in my mind of what it is we're after. As far as I can make out, it is only necessary for me to learn a few parliamentary phrases with which to clothe anything I have to say. "Is the Hon. member aware . . . alleged that various projects have been deferred . . . needs of the taxpayers . . . unanimously accepted an interim report of a committee appointed to inquire into the possibilities of developing . . . "

I went into this business with my eyes wide open, and I have faith in Trinidad, and in the destiny of the West Indies. But I'm not keeping my head in the clouds while my feet wallow in mud. When I look on the scene I lose hope. While others talk about "our progress" and "our ultimate goal," I am going to fight hard for an investigation into the local administration, for what we need first of all is a purge. There is no honour here, no ideal, no great sincerity or desire to make conditions any better. As Father Hope told me, the conditions that exist offer excuse for all our failings, so why should we bother to make things better?

Are you interested in all this? Well, to more personal talk. I've got me a little Vauxhall, which I haven't finished paying for yet. When Father Hope saw it he said he hoped I wasn't taking advantage of my position to do any shady business! But I got it honestly, by sweating off my brow, believe it or not. I am breaking her in slowly, so far I've only done sixty on the Churchill-Roosevelt Highway; I nearly ran off the road one night, near Claxton Bay, when I was coming back from a meeting down south.

Marleen and I were married some time ago. Don't think I am mentioning this *en passant*, only, it seemed the best thing to talk about it just as it came along. This may be a surprise for you—if you can be surprised by anything. I know you never cared for her that way. So you see, it happened to me earlier than I expected. I remember how we used to talk about settling down, and you wagered I'd do it before you. Well, you've won! I never thought it would be like this—on the other hand, I never thought about it at all, it just happened. I love Marleen, and she loves me, and we got married, and that's all there is to it. Don't expect any long dissertation on the subject. I bought a lovely house in St Joseph, near the river, where we are living.

Father Hope was against the marriage, but when he saw I was determined he gave us his blessing. I haven't seen him for some time, but Marleen wants us to go this Sunday, and now that I have a car it isn't much of a bother getting there, though the last time I almost ran over a precipice, you know how narrow and dangerous it is once you get off the main road, with hairpin curves and deep drops on either side.

I saw Rena once or twice in Port of Spain, but she acted as if she didn't know me. I don't know why, I never did her anything!

That is all the news in a nutshell. Of course, we have the baby with us. She is a sweet little girl, and growing up very quickly. We had quite a time when it came to giving her a name. While Marleen and I were talking about it, Father Hope reminded us that you should have a say in the matter too! Marleen had about six names from which to choose, I had three, and Father Hope had one or two ideas of his own. So we wrote all the names on pieces of paper and put them in a hat, and Marleen drew one out. It was Julia. I hope you like it. It seemed rather a capricious way to decide on a name, but I remembered how you used to say that names weren't very important, and as you weren't here it seemed the fairest way.

Have you made any plans for the future? What are you going to do? Stay in England? Are you writing a lot? Have you sold anything? What about taking time off from chasing blondes and dropping a line?

Chapter Thirteen

If time hadn't been running short for Rufus, he might well have gone on and on living in America with Sylvia, without telling her anything. But what might be collided with the hard, solid fact that he had to go back to Trinidad.

He put off telling Sylvia as long as he could. Each evening he formed the opening phrase in his mind, and he spoke it out to himself. Until one evening, when he wasn't even aware, the words came out.

"I really think I have to go back to Trinidad," he said, and he was ruminating out loud. "I must get this immigration business straightened out. They tell me that I cannot have my status in the country changed from student to resident unless I leave and re-enter under a 'resident status' visa." He sighed. "That could only be issued by the American Consul in Trinidad."

Sylvia was knitting. She was contentedly settled in the domestic routine of married life now. Rufus was hers, by the laws of the land. Nothing could take him away from her. To his surprise, she took the news rationally. She was upset by the idea of his leaving, but when he showed her there was nothing else to do, she accepted his plan.

As he set about the business of departure, he also prepared a reasonable refusal to give her if she suggested going with him. Each day he expected her to ask, until he could stand it no longer, so that he had to tell her, "I'm sorry you can't come along," to bring the subject up.

"That's all right," Sylvia said. "You won't be gone long, will you darling?"

"Oh no. Only a couple of months."

He had two more weeks. He concluded all his arrangements, and packed a suitcase.

"Surely you'll need more clothes than that," Sylvia said.

"I don't intend staying in Trinidad one hour longer than I have to," he said. He had almost added "when I get my divorce." He bit his lip at the thought.

"I'll miss you a lot, darling."

"I'll miss you too. It won't be long. When I come back we'll really settle down and make a go of life together."

"You must come back before our child is born," Sylvia said anxiously. She was beginning to show a little fear now; Rufus thought that if she made any trouble, he would just have to go, there wasn't any turning back at this point.

"I'll come back quickly, darling," he said. "I'll begin working on things as soon as I get there, and I'll write you very often to let you know how I am getting on."

"Where will you stay? In Port of Spain?"

"No. I'll put up at my cousin in Petite Bourg—that's just a little way from the city. I'll send you the address as soon as I get there."

"They'll be surprised that you're married to an American girl. Do you think they'd like the idea?"

He thought: All this is conversation, to fill in the gaps of time before I leave.

"Sure they'll like the idea."

"One day we'll go to Trinidad together. I've always wanted to see a tropical island. How do you feel, going back?"

"Not any way particular. It might have been different if I were going back to stay, or for a long time. But darling, my only reason for going is to get proper papers so that I could live in America. I don't imagine that would take more than a few weeks."

"Don't spend your time looking up all your old girl friends."

When Sylvia said that, for the first time in years Rufus thought about Marleen.

"Did you get that?"

"Yes, sure. I haven't anybody to look up."

He knew he would return, come what may. Of that he was certain. Nothing could keep him from Sylvia and America. Here was a country he had grown to love, and here was Sylvia waiting for him to return—Sylvia, and the child she was bearing.

So that when he left America, he wasn't looking forward to Trinidad at all. All his thoughts were on the great continent behind him, not the small Caribbean island he was heading for. On the friends he'd made in America, the people he'd met and liked, not the inhabitants of the island where he was born.

It was as if the ship were travelling backwards all the way to Trinidad, the way he kept his mind on America and the life he was leaving behind.

151

If only there were some creed to hold on to, some culture, some doctrine that offered hope, something worth dying for. Supposing he jerked a man out of his equanimity, stopped him on his way to work one morning and said, "Excuse me sir, do you know anything worth dying for?" what would the man say? Or selected one in the thousands racing for the tube station and asked: "Excuse me, but why are you living?" what would that man answer, if he stopped at all to answer? A bit naive, he smiled to himself, but a question to limit. Where are the people going, when they circle and jostle each other along the pavements, when they circle and turn left and turn right in Piccadilly Circus, when they hop on No. 2 and No. 46? Why must they always be moving, going some place, all these people, all these buses and cars and taxis, jamming the streets, while even under their very feet trains shoot into the darkness in endless movement to and fro?

You son of a bitch, he answered himself viciously, they have purpose, they have aim. They are going to their jobs, or going home, or seeking to entertain themselves for the evening. To hell with you, if you haven't got anything better to do than to stand up there and wonder where they're going, and why. They know, they are satisfied, they have little destinations in their minds, little goals and ambitions. That girl in the high-heeled shoes, swinging a handbag, she wants to be an efficient stenographer. Her time—her days and her nights—is filled with hope of reaching her goal. She goes for commercial lessons in the evening. She has an old typewriter and she practises at home; she gets her sister to read out passages from a newspaper and she learns shorthand. Sometimes she goes to a dance or the pictures with her boyfriend.

That man over there with the flabby face under a bowler hat, and a briefcase under his arm, he is a business executive. He has an office "in the city," he goes to work every day, he spends his time thinking how to make money. In the evening he goes home to his family, and they look at television in the drawing-room.

That fellow in the dirty mackintosh, rolling a cigarette, he is a porter. He lugs things around, all day. In the evening he goes for a "mild and bitter" in the pub, and he plays a game of darts.

What the hell are you worrying about, what concerns is it of yours?

152

In and out of the frenzied bustling of London, threads of West Indian lives ran. Sometimes he lost track of them, they were swallowed up and disappeared behind a million white faces. There were those who worked at anything they could get, the railways, factories; living in cheap dirty rooms, meeting the boys now and then for a game of rummy or poker. Out of the frying pan into the fire. No sense of gain or loss, no backward glance. No hope of making progress in the old "Brit'n," but it was better than living on the "rock." Here and there they slouched about the streets, men without future or hope or destiny, lost in London, fooling themselves into a way of life because there were so many people and they seemed to be doing the same thing; picking up a prostitute and half a pound of salted codfish on the way home; begging the landlord to wait another week for the rent because things were "reel bad."

"Boy, I was walking down the road yesterday with a sharp woman, and a white man was passing in a car and he look out and say 'You black bastard.' Just like that, old man, I don't even know the man or anything at all, he just look at me and say, 'You black bastard.' "

"Boy, you lucky to have a place to live in, I seeing hell to get a place, them landlords and landladies only saying they don't want black people. This is a hell of a country, boy."

"Boy, I can't get a work no way, they not taking the boys."

"Man, you lucky that nothing like this ever happen to you. But you know in this country they don't care what you is, as long as you not white, you black. Boy, I is a Indian, and the people does call me a black man."

"If you want to write a book, boy, come and see me, I will give you my experience in this country as a black man."

If it wasn't one thing, it was another.

He still saw a lot of Julia, but things were different now, though he tried not to show her how he felt. One day they were walking on Hampstead Heath, and she said, "Darling, I don't know what's come over you, you're so moody and depressed these days."

"It will pass."

"But really, I've never seen you like this before. We've been together so long, and done so many things, and yet we don't know much about each other. Let's sit and talk."

"It's too cold to sit."

"Just for a little while. Here, under that tree."

When they were seated she said, "You never told me why you came to England in the first place."

He relaxed on the grass. "I just wanted to see the place and the people. I thought perhaps I'd find a different way of life, something to offer hope for the future."

"Have you found it?"

"No. Only the same safety in numbers."

"What do you mean?"

"Being one among millions who don't know why they live."

"I don't think I understand."

"It doesn't matter. Let's go, I'm cold."

"No, wait. Tell me more. What did you do in Jamaica?"

"Trinidad, darling, Trinidad. Nothing much. I had a job, I went to work, I slept, I ate, I lived."

"You sound so hopeless. Hasn't coming to England made any difference, then? Here in London, in the centre of the world, where we have nearly everything we want, books, music, art."

"I'm after a way of living that has a purpose. I've tried to figure out what all these millions of people in London are after, and I can't. Everything looks aimless to me, a general movement to nowhere."

"Perhaps the fault lies in you. Perhaps it is you who have no aim in life. Everyone seems contented. I've never heard anyone speak like this before."

"You are right. I want so desperately to be happy—I suppose everyone wants that, too. When I fell in love with you, I thought for a while that we'd be happy. But we can't marry because your skin is white and mine is black. Don't think I am bitter about that. It's so stupid that I despair. I wish with all my heart that there was some other reason. Much as I try to ignore this question of colour, it forces itself upon me. It's no use, Julia. It won't ever work out. In a way I am glad I found out."

"I'll go away with you. We'll go to Trinidad and live."

"No. No one person could fill the hollow that's in my heart. It's the world we live in that bothers me. The wars that go on, the cheating and the killing and all the evil that exists. We were born in this, Julia, and sometimes I wonder if we stand a chance."

"Of course we do! But darling why do you take so much to account? Why can't you be like other people?"

154

"I've tried to follow little trails here and there, but it's useless. We are old from the time we are born; twenty centuries of man's existence press down on us, we stagger along with all that has ever happened and been recorded since time began. If a man puts forward some brilliant idea for a better world, people say: "Oh, let it take its course, for great changes have always evolved slowly over a period of years.' Even if they see the benefit of the idea for all mankind, that won't shake them into action. Like how they've been trying to change the calendar, and can't agree about it. Do you know why? No one thinks of the world. I am an Englishman. I am an American. I am a white man. I am a black man. No one thinks: 'I am a human being, and you are another.'"

"I've never heard you talk like this before. You make me frightened. I feel as if I don't know you at all, I feel as if one day you'll just fade out of my life and I'll never see you again. I love you, I won't allow you to clutter up your mind with all this foolish philanthropy, if that's the right word. Leave that for philosophers and statesmen. You can't do anything about the state of the world, even if you don't like it."

"You talk about my being hopeless, but what's more hopeless than what you've just said? It's defeat from the beginning. You talk about the state of the world as if it belonged to somebody else, and we're just renting a room."

"I find that just living my own life is enough trouble as it is."

"Ah, how many millions must have said the same thing, and lived their miserable little lives to the end, and left the world as they found it. Placing values on the week's rent, a day by the sea, the latest song hit, the Saturday night date. But let's not talk any more. Let's go. Doesn't the sun ever shine in this country?"

Julia got up slowly and he took up his mackintosh.

"Are you taking me to the pictures tonight?" she asked him.

"If you like. I'll meet you at the tube station at seven."

She put her hand on his arm. "Don't be unhappy."

"I'm not, you know. It's just that things are out of place in my mind. One day the pieces of scattered thought will mesh, and I'll be able to build a lasting sense of values."

But being with Julia now was not as important as it used to be.

One day about six months after this conversation with Julia he wrote Andrews a long letter, and ended ". . . so don't be surprised if one day you see me walking down Frederick Street. Maybe I shall come back for only a short time, maybe I'll be just as restless there as here. One thing I do know. If I come back to Trinidad, it will either be to stay for the rest of my life or to leave and never return. I'm not sure when I'll come—I have to get some money first. I'll write and tell you how things shape up."

Even after he'd written that letter to Andrews he wasn't decided firmly about returning to Trinidad, but he worked a night-shift in a factory and saved the money. He hardly saw Julia now, except she phoned and asked him to come around to her place.

"You don't care for me any more," she said. "I see less and less of you now."

"Why do you go on pretending?" he asked her, "you know it's all over between us. I'm going back to Trinidad soon."

"But why are you going back? I thought you were going to live in England."

He didn't bother to answer that.

The night before he sailed he phoned her to get together for a good-bye drink, but she wasn't at home. He walked the streets of London alone, for the last time.

PART THREE

Chapter Fourteen

Sometimes if Johnny became too engrossed in his work, he jerked his head up as a tired man fighting off sleep, and his hands would shake and scatter the tiny parts of the mechanism he was working on, and he would have to ask Patrick to help him find them. Johnny would start out of this engrossment because the thought used to prick him like a pin: Why the hell am I working so hard? And he would put down his instruments and take a quick swig from the bottle under the counter, bending down so no one would see him.

"Take over this job, boy," he told Patrick.

"But I am working on something urgent," Patrick would protest. "I fixing the chain for the woman who coming this afternoon."

"Well, when you finish then."

"I have a lot of other work to do, how much things you expect me to do at one time?"

"Find time, boy, find time. Take it home with you this evening."

Johnny had grown a little fatter around the waist, and a double chin rounded out his face. These were local signs of prosperity and didn't bother him. Business was neither up nor down, and the daily routine was undisturbed by the passage of time.

Also, he had made no progress on the Great Invention. This point worried Johnny, and he was wont to brood over it at work, he used to drop things and watch Gravity pull them to the ground: Patrick was quite convinced he was going mad, and once asked him, "What you doing that for?"

"Gravity, boy, gravity."

"Sure, everybody know that, if you drop something it must fall down."

"What pulling it to the ground?"

"Gravity, you know that."

"Suppose you could get Gravity to pull sideways, eh! Suppose you could harness that force, and make it do things."

Johnny was sure Patrick didn't have enough sense to understand about a big thing like Gravity, so he wasn't afraid to talk about it with him. As the years went by, the image of his invention in action had become clearer, though he was as far as he would ever be from making it work. The more he thought about it, the more he saw what a simple idea it was, and he racked his brains to create some machine that would do the job. Scores of sketches and secret drawings had been destroyed one day in a drunken rage; he tried afterwards to join the pieces together, but it was useless. Often he determined to forget all about it, but he could find nothing else to occupy his mind, and he would begin all over again, only to rip up the plans at some stage when frustration got the better of him.

There was only one distraction from this—the little boy Tim. Johnny was fond of him. Tim used to hide by the front door waiting for Johnny in the evening, and scream, "Grandpa, you drunk again!"

"Aaye, you little scamp, come here!" But Tim used to tease him and hide, though if Johnny caught him he gave him a few sound slaps on the bottom, telling him he should have more respect for his elders.

While the others bolted their doors and kept out of Johnny's way, Tim would walk around with him as he staggered from place to place, laughing as Johnny stumbled and fell, tugging at his trousers, singing, "Drunken old man, drunken old man," until Johnny gave him a clout behind the head and sent him crying to Rena.

With no one to talk to, Johnny sometimes sat down in the drawing room and put Tim on his knee.

"Where your father, boy?"

"Don't know."

"How you don't know?"

"My daddy in America."

"Ah, so you know! Your father is a worthless man, boy. He gone away and left you and your mother. I did tell your mother that would happen, but she won't listen to me. Now look at you. Nobody to look after you."

"You is a drunken old man."

"What? I bet I give you some good blows here tonight, eh! Where your mother, she gone out?"

"Ma inside. If you hit me I will tell Ma."

"Go on, tell! You don't get enough licks, that's what wrong with you."

Tim had a pacifying effect on Johnny even in his wildest moods which the others in the house were quick to observe. If Johnny was making trouble, they opened the door and sent Tim outside, and as soon as Johnny saw the boy he usually quietened down.

One morning Johnny announced that he was coming home early to take Tim for a walk in the gardens. Mary was so shocked she was speechless; Rena thought her father was making a joke because it wasn't often that she took him out herself. But in the evening Johnny came, sober to the point of sadness, and he took the boy and they went for a tram ride around the savannah. This was so out of character for Johnny that they now treated him as if he was out of his head.

"Grandpa take me for a tram ride!" Tim shouted for days afterwards.

No one knew about Johnny's longing for a son. He used to look at Tim and think: If I had a son like you, things would have been different. But it is only girls that Mary give me. And in his heart he loved the little boy dearly, with all the love he had stored up in vain for a son of his own.

Outside of Tim, there was nothing in the house to interest Johnny. He was quite indifferent to the affairs of the family. Rena never told him directly when she decided to ask Rufus for a divorce. It was through Mary that he heard the story. Rena told Mary, then Mary, afraid to bear the responsibility by herself told Johnny. Not that she expected him to do anything, but it was just like him to say that they were hiding things from him. It was difficult to tell Johnny anything at all, because as soon as she began he would say, "Look, don't bother my brains with foolishness, I don't want to hear anything, you-all is a set of stupid people, always getting in trouble and then coming to me for help."

"But if I don't tell you, and you hear it from somebody else, you will come back and say I should have told you."

"Ah, you think I foolish. You think I haven't eyes to see. I know you want to tell me about your daughter."

"Is your daughter too."

"You think I don't know she going around with this fellar from BG? All-you won't listen to me from the beginning. I did say how she should have married that man, but she went and married

160

Rufus."

"She say she want to divorce Rufus and married this man."

"What the hell you telling me that for? What you expect me to do?"

"Well is a bad thing to have divorce in the family. I don't know what to tell she. I say, 'Girl, you better hear what your father have to say about this.' "

"So what the hell you expect Johnny to say, eh? I don't care nothing. Let she do whatever she want to do."

"She say since Rufus went away he ain't send any money for she."

"Look, you still going on with this story? Why you don't leave me in peace, woman?"

"Well, don't say I didn't tell you about it. You know you, how you does be sometimes, getting on like a madman and saying things happening that you don't know anything about."

The day when India got her independence, all the Indians in Trinidad celebrated, and Johnny made it a day to remember. He put up the Indian flag over the door of the shop, and he gave Patrick the day off. A little later he himself closed the shop and went into the rumshop where he met dozens of other celebrants. Nothing could be more to his liking: after a bottle or two, he invited about a dozen Indian strangers to come to his house. Mary was startled when they all walked into her drawing room singing "Jana-Gana-Mana" in Hindi at the top of their voices: "I bow to thee mother richly-watered, richly-fruited, Cool with the winds of the south, Dark with the crops of the harvest . . ." However, she herself was caught up in the gaiety and excitement which was prevailing, and for once she allowed Johnny to do as he liked without a quarrel. "Aaye, we must all go back to India now," Johnny said, waving his glass at his sudden friends, "now we have independence."

It was a long time after that Johnny remembered his words, and many things happened. Among them was the appointment of an Indian Commissioner to the West Indies. When this happened, men who had forgotten their nationality in the cosmopolitan population became aware of themselves as Indian. A flame of nostalgia began to spread. Men who had forgotten who they were dusted their memories and began to talk about going back home.

The original Indians had come to the island as indentured

labourers, and free passage back to India had been promised to them and their children. Those who were still alive were old and feeble; those who had died had made sure their children knew of this. But it was such a long time ago, no one really remembered until just like that, it seemed, everyone was talking about it, and the local newspapers carried stories about the Indians in the community.

Suddenly it seemed to Johnny that what he wanted to do was to go to India. True, he was not entitled to the free passage, but he could easily fix that, the government would have a hard job saying who was and who wasn't entitled after all this time. The idea took root in Johnny's mind and grew. No love of country or tie to custom and tradition nurtured it. It was just that life was becoming monotonous in Trinidad, and if he could wangle a passage to India for nothing, he saw no reason why he shouldn't go. Besides, by showing an interest in the matter he attached importance to himself in the eyes of the others.

Now his drunken talk took up the theme in the house, going something like this: "All of you better start packing your things and making plans, because we going back to India, where we come from."

Mary: "What stupidness come in your head now? You well settle here in the shop, and everything going all right. We not making a lot of money, but still, we not starving. You minding those old people who making trouble saying they want to go back. What you go do in India? You better keep yourself quiet."

Rena (in an aside to Mary): "You better get that foolish idea out of Pa head. You know he mad enough to do something stupid like that. But I for one not going any place. It's you I studying, Ma, you and Jennifer. What Pa want to go back India for? You better get that foolish idea out of his head."

Jennifer (thinking): Up to now none of them don't know Pa, is just an idea to frighten them, he only saying that for so, he ain't really serious.

But if Johnny wasn't serious, other Indians in the island were. Groups met and discussed the situation. Johnny became affiliated with a Back to India Society, and started to attend meetings twice a week. This really frightened Mary, it was the first time Johnny had ever sobered up enough to do such a thing. Relatives advised Mary to leave him alone. "Give him enough rope and he go hang heself," they told her. They all felt that he would get over this crazy idea, and perhaps if their attitude was different, Johnny might have forgotten the whole thing. But the more silent contempt they displayed, the more determined he became.

Knowing too that he was not legally entitled to the free trip, Johnny got on as if he were the first Indian who ever set foot in Trinidad, making the loudest noise and demanding his rights with the zeal of a fanatic, so that in time it became confused in people's minds whether he was, after all, a relative of one of the original indentured labourers. Johnny's past was a mystery to most, anyway, and even Mary began to have doubts as he carried on with unflagging energy. Until it reached a stage where Johnny, with no talent for leadership, found himself at the front of discussions when the society met, though the most he did was to keep repeating, "We must stand up for we rights. The government bound to send we back."

When Johnny joined a band of Indians marching in the city with 'Back to India' placards, a relative rushed into the house and told Mary. "Look Johnny walking about in the streets with a placard, like a common man. Your husband must be gone out of his senses."

But worse was to come. Johnny didn't know what the final outcome would be, but while it lasted he intended to take part in everything. Representations had been made to the government, but no decision seemed forthcoming. Now they got a politician in Port of Spain to cable Pandit Nehru explaining the position. Back came a reply to the effect that India was just getting on her feet and things would be very difficult for them, why didn't they stay and help to build up the West Indies?

But nothing could quench the fire now. Men were dreaming about dying on the banks of the Ganges.

In these days Johnny was excited and full of talk, and he told Mary, "You know what we going to do now? Everybody going to threaten to commit suicide. So you better watch out. If the government don't send we back, all of we going to kill weself."

Johnny offered this information like a martyr, sticking out his chest. In fact, this latest move had him apprehensive. When it was decided he acclaimed it along with the others at the meeting. An old diehard Indian next to him had nudged him and said, "Is a good idea, we old and we ain't have long to live again, anyway." And Johnny had thought, H'm, I not so old as all that. This talk of mass suicide scared him, though he kept up the show that he intended to be among the first to leave the island.

"You hear what I telling you?" he told Mary, enjoying the fear and concern he was causing, "if things don't go right you will lose your husband. I going to commit suicide."

What with repeating this threat time and again, Johnny began to have a genuine fear that if it really came to a matter of taking his own life, he might have no choice after his zealous behaviour. He now missed a meeting or two on the pretext that he wasn't feeling very well, and locked himself up in his room to think out the situation with a bottle of rum.

"Well, anyway," he told himself as he fell back to the old pattern of drunkenness, "I better have a good time while I could. Everybody would give me hell if I back out now. I wonder how all of we would commit suicide? I suppose we would go and jump in the sea, or something."

But there was no doubt that some of the Indians in the island were set on returning to India, and people knew that the government would have to do something about it when mass suicide was threatened.

Chapter Fifteen

One morning in San Juan Muriel was washing dirty clothes in the kitchen sink. These days the rain fell heavy and unexpected, and as the sun was shining she wanted to get it finished as soon as she could, so they could dry by evening if the rain held. She was rinsing them under the tap when she heard a knock on the front door.

Wiping her hands in an apron around her waist, she went to the door and saw Rufus.

For a minute she couldn't believe her eyes, she just stood there, looking, and Rufus pushed open the door and came in and put down his suitcase, grinning.

"Rufus!" Muriel exclaimed at last. "What it this, boy? What you doing here? Well I never! Wait a minute, boy, until I catch myself."

She sat down and Rufus stood smiling, not saying a word. Then she jumped up and gave him a big hug. "I couldn't believe it was you, boy. What are you doing here? How long you come back to Trinidad?"

"I just came," Rufus said. "This morning."

"This morning!" Muriel repeated. "But you didn't write or anything. You have me confuse, man. What happen? You taking a holiday or what?"

"Well yes, it is a holiday, in a way. Just for a little while."

"But why you didn't tell me you was coming? You have me so excited I could hardly talk. But look at you, how big you get! You mean to say that you just land from the ship, and you come straight here? Regald will be shock to see you. You hungry?"

"Well, I could eat something," he replied to the last question, ignoring the rest.

"It have some fry bake and saltfish leave over from breakfast. We will kill a chicken this evening. But boy, up to now I can't believe is you."

She went to the cupboard in the kitchen, glad for something to do to cover up her fluster at sight of Rufus, whom she hadn't seen for five years.

Rufus lit a cigarette and sprawled in an armchair with a sigh. But he didn't relax completely: his mind was still awhirl as it had been leaving America, and he intended to keep it that way in Trinidad, because he wasn't going to stay long. If it was all right with Regald and Muriel, he could stay here and stretch the little money he had. He gave himself two months to get things straightened out with Rena, and he allowed another month for any unseen complication. Three months. He had to have everything settled by then, or else he would have to get a job. He would have to see Rena. Soon. When the ship docked in Port of Spain he had a wild desire to rush off and find her the moment he landed, to tell her he was here and she must see about the divorce right away. He should have written to her to say he was coming, then she would have gone ahead with all the little details and saved precious time. I was too impetuous, he thought.

"Did you go home before you came here?" Muriel asked from the kitchen. And he felt ashamed that he was so taken up in his own affairs, even before he had time to get the feel of his legs after the long trip. He got up with a sense of guilt and stood near the door of the kitchen.

"No, I came straight to San Juan."

"Then you haven't seen Rena or Tim! But why you do that, boy?"

He flushed unconsciously. There would be a lot of awkward questions like that to answer. Even if he wanted to forget the whole thing for a while, they wouldn't let him, they'd be asking questions all the time.

"I suppose you know how it is with Rena and me," he said.

"Well, we hear that things weren't going too good. Rena came to see us a few times. She said that everything was over between you. But she didn't give any details, and we didn't think it was anything too serious. So you mean to say you didn't write her at all? She don't know that you over here?"

"No."

"Well I don't know what to say. I really can't understand you. I thought Foster was bad, but you beat him. The way you two young men live is a puzzle to me."

Ah, Foster! What had happened to Foster? For the first time in years Rufus really thought about him. Now and then, his face had cropped up on the screen of his mind—like the faces of all those he had left in Trinidad—but he had been far too occupied to bother. He remembered him now, indecisive, wondering what road to take, hesitant to say yes and no, finding reasons for this and reasons for that, groping like a blind man.

"Where is Foster?" he asked. "Where is he working?"

"Ah, you playing as if you don't know Foster in England."

"Oh yes," he stammered a little, feeling again the sense of guilt, that he didn't know about Foster when he should. This thing would keep on happening, they'd take it that he knew certain things and wouldn't bother to mention them, or they'd throw a question at him which he couldn't answer.

"I knew he was in England," he lied, "but we haven't been writing each other. How long has he been away, I can't remember?"

"Is about five years since you went America, and is about three years he in England now. How you can't remember? It was a little while after the war. But you mean to tell me, he didn't write you or anything? You-all never wonder about each other, or want to know what happening?"

"I suppose I am to blame for that—I never wrote to him. But don't you hear from him? Don't you know how he's getting on? What's he doing over there, anyway?"

"Oh, he's just like you—he don't write us at all. Is only now and then that Regald get a little news from some friend that he write to—some councillor in Port of Spain. And what news? Just the usual thing, he getting on all right. We don't get no details at all. To tell you the truth, we forget all about you and Foster. Regald say you-all are big men, and that you went away to make a future. And now, suddenly, you come back, and start asking a lot of questions I can't answer. For all we know Foster must be dead in England."

"Regald could have got his address from this friend."

"I suppose so. But why we should bother, when Foster don't write us? And it was the same thing with you, we could have got your address from Rena, but you never write us neither."

But he wasn't going to allow any sentiment to hinder him. If Foster was in England, he couldn't see him, that was all. Foster didn't have anything to do with why he was in Trinidad, anyway. All this talk about why you didn't write, what about Foster, and the slight reproach in Muriel's tone—all that could go to hell. His best plan lay in action. To see Rena as soon as possible, and return to Sylvia. No idling around and wasting time. There weren't any old friends he wanted to look up, or any place he wanted to visit. He hoped that Regald and Muriel wouldn't ask too many questions when they learnt he had come back for a divorce. He would have to prepare for a lot of tiring talk, why he wanted a divorce, what about Tim, what about the future, the disgrace of the whole affair, and all that sort of thing. He felt like shuddering.

Already Muriel was saying, "So what about Tim, you don't want to see your son? He growing big, boy, and he resemble you a lot."

"I'll see him in time," Rufus said. "But tell me about Rena. When last did you see her?"

"Come and sit down and eat," Muriel said, laying the table. She was much better at doing things than talking. "I hope you still like saltfish and bake."

While he was eating the guilty feeling returned: he hadn't even asked Muriel how she was, and if Regald and the children were in good health. The ordinary, natural questions one would expect. He wanted to minimise all that, if it were possible to spend one night in Trinidad and fix things and return, he would do it. But he had to go slow. For the first time he relaxed properly. He finished eating and lit a cigarette.

"I haven't even asked about the children," he said, "are they all right? Going to school now, I expect." There was no interest in his voice.

"Oh yes. You should see them now, getting into mischief all the time. Once Rena brought Tim and he spent a few days with them. But it's a long time since I saw her." She got up and went to the cupboard. "I must offer you some rum! When last you had a good drink?"

"A long time. Rum is very expensive over there. I drank beer most of the time."

"Plenty snow over there, eh? One thing I want to do before I die is to see snow, and walk in it, and pick it up and crush it in my hand. You do all that, I suppose?"

"Oh yes." He had a drink, and he wanted to tell her what he thought would interest her about his stay abroad. He was relieved when she brought up the matter of Rena herself instead.

"What happen between you and Rena? Is serious?"

"It's serious all right. As a matter of fact, I might as well tell you that I've come back to see about a divorce."

168

"What! Boy, I didn't know it was so bad. You can't patch things up, for the sake of Tim?"

"I know how you feel, Muriel, but you've got to get this straight. There isn't a chance. I want that divorce as badly as she wants it herself. And there's no sense in talking about it. I've made up my mind and I know what's best."

Muriel knew that Rufus didn't like her asking so many questions, but it was all she could do. She felt it was her duty, in a way. It didn't matter about Rufus being irritated, or thinking she was stupid and didn't understand. She understood all right, but it wasn't the sort of thing to accept without protest.

"What about Tim?" she asked firmly.

"You must try to understand. There's no future here for me in Trinidad. I'm going to return to America as soon as it's over."

"I not even going to try to understand," Muriel said. "But I'm not going to worry you about it. You and your brother are two people that live your own life, and is as if is a kind of life apart from the one I know. You-all do things, and don't look back. As if you-all belong to another world. Well, as Regald say, is your own life, and you have to live it your own way. You think it going to be easy to get a divorce?"

"I hope so. I'll do anything."

"What about Rena? She don't even know you in Trinidad?"

"I was thinking maybe you could ask her to come here," Rufus said on a brainwave.

"What for?"

"So she and I could have a talk. That is, if you don't mind."

"Why I should mind? But why you want her to come here, why you don't go home and see her?"

"I'd rather meet her outside. If I go there you know what it will be like. I'll have to answer so many questions from Mary and Johnny, and you know what he is like."

"Like how I asking you so many questions, eh?" Muriel was persistent.

"Yes," he said, a little shortly.

"And you don't expect people to ask questions? You want to do as you like and nobody must ask you anything?"

Rufus bowed his head wearily, propping his chin with his hands.

"All right, all right," Muriel said. "You want me to tell her that you here, and you want to see her. Suppose she don't want to come?"

"She'll come all right."

"When you want her to come?"

"Tonight, if it's all right with you."

"But man, you just land in the place! Regald hasn't seen you for so many years, he will want to have a few drinks and talk! And besides that suppose Rena has to go someway else? Why you don't wait a few days until you get settled down before seeing about all that?" She knew she would irritate him again, but she couldn't help, she was tackling the situation in her own way.

"I haven't got much time, Muriel. I don't want to stay away from Sylvia very long." It came out before he knew what he was saying, and Muriel snatched it up.

"Who is Sylvia?"

"A girl I know over there."

"You just come to Trinidad to divorce Rena and go back to this Sylvia?"

"It amounts to that."

"A white girl? A American?"

"Oh Muriel, I wish you wouldn't keep on at me like this. When Regald comes home I'll have to go over everything again. Wait until he comes, and then we'll all have a long talk."

"All right. You must be tired after that long journey. The sea was rough?"

He ignored that. He said: "How are you going to see Rena?"

"I could phone her at work. They have a telephone by the post office."

"Will you phone now?"

"If you like. But I have to change this frock." She left him and went into the bedroom.

But while Muriel went inside he thought, Why can't I ring her myself? And he called out, "Never mind. Give me the number and I'll do it."

"I don't know the number. I was going to look it up in the directory."

Rufus rose and went to the door. "Where is the post office?"

"You mean to say you forgot that already? Is just up the road. Go to the main road and turn left."

When he left Muriel returned to her washing, making up her

170

mind not to ask Rufus one single question again.

The sun struck him sharply, but he hardly felt it. It was easy to forget what he was here for, to lounge around from place to place, have a drink here and another there, lay on a sunny beach and forget everything. Trinidad was the place for that. Why should he put off seeing Rena? There wasn't anything else he had to do. He wasn't tired, he didn't want to rest for a few days.

As he walked on the main road he thought about Foster. Perhaps later on he would get in touch with this friend that Foster wrote to, and get his address and drop him a line.

When you haven't seen a person for years you could speculate according to what you know of the person, and the place he's in. Trouble was, he didn't know Foster very well. Foster's puzzlement with life baffled him.

He went into the phone booth in the post office and he found the number of the firm where Muriel had said Rena was working. He lit a cigarette while the connection was being made, and he spoke to Sylvia in his mind: 'You see darling, I'm not wasting one minute. It's just two hours or so since I landed, and I'm going ahead with what I have to do.' Unconsciously he was keeping up the lie to Sylvia, referring to the divorce as 'what I have to do.'

And there in the phone booth in San Juan in Trinidad, thousands of miles away from Sylvia, he felt cold along his spine as he thought about how he was married to two women. He felt cramped in the booth, he couldn't breathe.

"Hello?"

He kept quiet, the 'hello' echoing in him, trying to remember how her voice sounded in the past, suddenly afraid.

"Hello?"

"Hello. Is that you Rena?" There wasn't a damned thing to be frightened of, he was behaving like a fool.

"Yes. Who is it, please?"

"Don't you recognise the voice?" he knew he was stalling, and he didn't like it.

"No-o. Who is it, please?"

She was talking in a special way over the telephone—he should have expected that from her. Trying to speak in a cultured sort of voice which was unnatural.

"It's Rufus," he said, almost savagely.

"What did you say?"

"It's me, Rufus." He couldn't bear the unnatural tone of her voice. He wanted to shock her out of it.

"Who? Rufus? Is that what you say?" Her voice was returning to normalcy, and he smiled.

"Yeah," he said, trying hard not to be impatient; after all, it was a long time. "Listen, I came back this morning."

"You come back this morning?"

"Yes. I want to see you, Rena."

"Want to see me?"

"Yes. I wish you wouldn't repeat what I say like that." He bit his lip and softened his voice. "Look, I know this must be a shock to you, but you'll get over it. I am here, in San Juan. I'm staying with Muriel for the time being. Can you come this evening?"

"I—oh, it's really you?"

"Yeah," he said, deliberately putting on an American accent, "it's me all right."

"But—why didn't you tell me you were coming? Why you didn't come home? It sound too good to be true."

"What do you mean?" he asked sharply.

"I mean—oh darling, it's so wonderful to have you back! I'll come right away. I'll get the rest of the day off—"

"Hold on, hold on," he said. "Those are strange sentiments, coming from you."

"But I wrote you. Didn't you get my letters?"

"No. Look, we can't talk now, over the phone. But you know what I've come for?"

"Oh darling, we haven't seen each other for a long time, and your first words are unkind."

He hadn't expected this. It sounded like a trap. "I haven't changed my mind about anything," he said. "By that I mean I've come back for a divorce. Get that straight."

"We can't talk now. This phone is right in the boss' office and he's coming back in a few minutes."

"Can you come this evening, then?"

"Don't you want me to come now?"

"No." That was too quick for him. He was puzzled by her attitude. "Come this evening, after work."

"I won't be able to do any more work today," Rena said, and her voice was soft and warm.

Rufus felt furious. "I don't know what's the matter with you," he said roughly, "or what you're trying to do. But I've come back

172

to fix things between us once and for all. I'm going to give you a divorce, whether you like it or not."

"I'll come this evening, then," she said, as if she hadn't heard him, "and we'll talk then. Are you all right?" her voice was anxious now. "Are you all right, darling?"

"Of course I'm all right," he snapped. "What do you think? I'll see you this evening." He slammed the phone down and came out of the booth quickly.

He was sweating. He lit another cigarette and inhaled deeply. Rena was going to make trouble, he felt it. Her 'oh darling, it's so wonderful to have you back' still rang in his ears; he shook his head vigorously. It had never occurred to him that she might have changed her mind about the divorce. He imagined her coming to San Juan in the evening, a sad, lost look on her face, probably holding Tim by the hand, and she would say, 'that's your daddy, son,' and she would look at him and say something like 'you're all we have in the world.'

He wasn't going to have any of it, by God. He was going to push that divorce down her throat and clear out of Trinidad and go back to Sylvia, and he was going to do it quickly. He wasn't going to wait around for things to happen, he was going to make them happen.

When he got back Muriel had unpacked his suitcase and made the bed in the spare room.

"I think I'll rest a little, after all," he said.

What if Rena said she didn't want a divorce again, that it was all a mistake? What if she refused to cooperate? Instead of indifference or even fear, she had expressed a strange delight at his return, and her voice had been full of hope—hope for what? What did it mean? I should take a few days off, he thought, and take it easy for a while. It wouldn't make all that difference. He hadn't yet got over the feel of the ship's rolling and already he had contacted her. What are you moaning about? he thought angrily, isn't this how you wanted it?

He closed his eyes, lest Muriel felt tempted to talk to him. He wanted time to think, alone.

But Muriel only watched him for a moment and shrugged her shoulders and went into the kitchen.

Chapter Sixteen

The day Foster landed back in Trinidad, the sun was brilliant in the sky, and he went ashore with a high head, buoyed with the false confidence each new day presents, as if what had happened didn't matter, the 'now' of the day offering fresh fields, tomorrow too distant to be bothered about. Of this he was aware, of the falseness of each new resolution, but he was prepared to accept it as a way of life; and he took his time walking into the city. This is my country, he was thinking, and I've come back, and it's good to feel the sun in my face. But he would have felt a lot better if he knew for sure why he'd come back. It isn't as if I've been all over the world and decided to return to live here, he thought. I shall see how things go for a while, and if I don't like it I could always leave. Like a man bored with the routine of his life, getting up each morning and going to work, chaining himself with the thought, Oh, I could always leave this job and get another. And all his life this thought comforts him—he stays because he could leave.

What do others do when they think like that? he wondered. Perhaps life in the long run is only a reconciliation to circumstances, made bearable by the thought that a freedom exists at hand always available.

Now, he thought, everyone will ask: 'But why did you come back to Trinidad?' And he would have to find a reason that they could accept. It would sound ridiculous to say, 'I was just exercising my freedom, I felt like coming back, so I did.' He said those words aloud, to hear how they would sound, and a man passing by heard and turned his head and looked at him curiously.

However—, he thought, and took a taxi to San Juan. Going to San Juan, to Regald and Muriel, was the first thing that occurred to him, and he felt ashamed that he had never written them, and they were his first thought of comfort. On a sudden impulse he stopped the taxi and went into a store. He bought some toys for the children, and a dress for Muriel. He tore up the bills and when he was in the taxi again he unwrapped the parcels and he opened his suitcase and stuffed the things at the bottom. It was unlikely that they would ask where he had bought the toys, and if Muriel asked about the dress he would say he bought it in a shop in Bond Street in London.

In due course he would get in touch with Andrews. They would talk about this and that, and he would ask Andrews to get him a job. That would take care of the weeks and months ahead until—what?

Never mind, he told himself, settling back with relief, it looks very easy, and it will do for the time being.

When he got to the house he felt as though he'd just been away for a holiday. That was what it amounted to, he would have to guard against the tendency to believe that things and people had changed, it was best to act casual, as if he were just paying an ordinary visit, and not to expect too warm or surprised a welcome.

But when Rufus opened the door for him he was really astounded: they stood looking at one another for a minute, both of them stifling the surprise they felt, each wanting the other to be the one to exclaim, 'What! You here?' And so each said nothing, and Foster came inside and Rufus closed the door, and Foster calmed himself and asked, "Where's Muriel?"

"I thought you were in England!" Rufus conceded.

"I didn't know you were in Trinidad," Foster said.

And then they shook hands self-consciously.

"It's good to see you," Rufus said, clapping Foster on the back, "but you don't look so well. Are you ill or something?"

"I'm all right. Must be the long sea voyage and the beastly food aboard. It was a French ship. What are you doing here?"

"A sort of holiday," Rufus said.

We aren't acting naturally, Foster thought. After all these years we should be falling over each other and asking scores of questions. But I haven't seen him for such a long time, it's like meeting a stranger.

He voiced this thought, and Rufus said, "I feel like that, too. Maybe we'll thaw out after a few minutes. It's the suddenness, I imagine. I never dreamed I'd see you. I heard you were in England."

"Funny," Foster went on, "I forgot all about you when you went away to America, I thought perhaps I'd never see you again. I never wondered what it would be like if we ever got together, but certainly just standing here and talking like this would never have occurred to me."

"Ah, you haven't changed at all," Rufus said. "You're still the same Foster I left behind."

"Do you really think so?" Foster smiled. "But where's Muriel?"

"She's gone to town to do some shopping. She said she'll be back by two or three, but you know what that means, she probably won't get here until four o'clock."

"Are you staying here, then?" Foster asked, seeing that Rufus had on a pair of shorts and a sports shirt, and was barefoot.

"Yes. Look boy, we have a lot to talk about. I'll go and get a bottle of Vat 19. Regald had an end here, but I polished it off on my own."

Rufus put on a pair of soft shoes and went out for the rum. Foster sat down and lit a cigarette. The way he felt, he wasn't going to be surprised by anything. It wasn't very difficult to imagine that the past five years hadn't been. The relationship between Rufus and himself had been at best a strained one which the years had only accentuated. Foster liked Rufus—he had always liked him, but they had never seemed to get on well together. He went back a few minutes, to his arrival, how strange it was meeting Rufus, and not knowing what to say, standing there and looking at his brother. 'We must get on better than this,' he told himself, 'I must make an effort.'

Rufus returned and they made rum punches and sat at the dining table.

"Have you finished your studies, then?" Foster asked, instead of saying what he thought: What are you doing here in San Juan? "Are you a doctor now, or something?"

"Boy, I've got a long way to go yet." Rufus lit a cigarette and pushed the pack to Foster. "The things that happened to me in America! It would take days to tell you."

"Go on, I have time," Foster said.

Rufus was glad he had someone to talk to; he had a feeling that Foster might be able to help him, though he wasn't sure how. "Too much to tell," he said. "You'll hear about my experiences later. But right now I am in big trouble. I suppose you know the position between Rena and myself?"

Foster shook his head. "Don't take anything for granted. Remember I've been away too."

176

"Well anyway it's all finished. Couple years ago she wrote me asking me for a divorce. Naturally I was shocked—"

"Naturally."

"Ah, still the old Foster, as I said. Never mind. I refused—foolishly, as later events proved. Well we stopped writing each other, and I gave her up completely, living as if I had never been married to her. My permit to stay in the United States was up, and I had to return. I was glad—I wanted to settle this business with Rena. But for some stupid reason she seems to have changed her mind. The girl is a fool. It has me worried." He wanted to tell Foster about Sylvia, but he hesitated. No one in Trinidad knew he was married to Sylvia. "There's a girl in America I want to marry," he added.

"And you can't unless Rena gives you a divorce," Foster said, "Is that it?"

Rufus nodded and rattled the ice in his glass.

"Well, keep pegging away at Rena. She isn't quite a fool, she ought to see there's no hope of getting you back. Does she know about this other girl?"

"Oh yes. I didn't see any reason to hide it from her. The whole trouble is, this fellow from BG has left her flat, so she wants to hold on to what she's got. Or to what she thinks she's got."

"You've got a problem there," Foster said, "but a man of your talent could get out of it."

Rufus gave a forced laugh. "You're all right, you have nothing to worry about. Your attitude has always been to take things easy and drift through life. It's just an irresponsible game, and you go through it like you're in a dream all the time. Say, why did you go to England, anyway?"

"As you say, I take things easy. Have I got to have a reason?"

"I just wondered, not that I'm particularly interested."

"I went," Foster said, "because I wanted to have a look around. I had a look around, and I've come back. Satisfied?"

"There you are. Just as I said. You mean to say that up to now you haven't decided what you want to do? You intend to go on like this for the rest of your life? Look at me. I have ambition. I went away to study for a profession—I know what I want out of life. What did you do while you were in England?"

Foster smiled. What reply would please Rufus? "I started to write a book," he said.

"Is that all? You didn't have to go away to do that."

"I know. But let's don't argue about me, boy. The way we're talking, one wouldn't think we hadn't seen each other for five years. Let's get tight, these rum punches are good. How did you make out for drinks in the US?"

"Rum is expensive as hell."

They talked about the things they could remember. Rufus said, "Boy, you want to come with me to America when I'm going back. That's a country for you, I don't know why you chose to go to England. Come with me and get a good job over there. Bags of women in the States, boy."

"Bags of women in London, too. Funny thing about London. Over-populated. Can't find yourself. Met a damned nice girl. Which reminds me. Big joke for you. Remember that girl you used to go with before you went away?"

"What girl?"

"The one who used to work down at the base with you. Marleen."

"Oh, yes! I haven't given her a thought! I wonder how she is? I must look her up."

"Well, the big joke is that I used to live at her place. I didn't know she used to be your girl, and she didn't know I was your brother. Can you imagine that, in a small place like Port of Spain?"

"So what happened?"

"What happened?" Foster repeated. "A hell of a thing happened, boy. She had a child for me."

"No!"

"Yes. We're getting drunk—at least I am."

"Never mind that. What happened?"

"Well, I went away, and I asked Andrews to look after her."

"That's the councillor who's your friend?"

"Yes. A fine fellow, Andrews. You must meet him sometime."

"What happened?"

"You sound like a repeater asking what happened like that. Don't, it unnerves me, it makes me wish that things happened when they didn't. Andrews married Marleen."

"Ah well. Why didn't you marry her yourself?"

"I didn't love her. Did you?"

"No, not that way."

"Anyway, she's happy now."

"I must see her sometime."

"Don't go bursting up anything for Andrews."

"Look who's talking! You were the last one with her."

"Well it's all past and forgotten as far as I'm concerned."

"What about your child?"

"Oh, I must tell you this, too. The girl I used to know in London was called Julia. And what do you think Marleen and Andrews called the child?"

"Not Julia?"

"Yes."

"Let's both visit them suddenly, and watch Marleen's face."

"How heartless you are. Can't you leave well enough alone? You've got your own affairs to attend to. Marleen isn't the sort of girl who would allow either of us to break up her happiness with Andrews."

"That's what you think. I bet if I see her once—"

"You'd better keep away and don't cause any trouble." Foster pressed the palm of his hand against his forehead and drew it slowly across. "Christ, what a conversation, on my first day."

But Rufus, though he didn't mean any of what he was saying, kept on at him. "The way you talk, it's as if you're still soft on Marleen. Oh, I know you all right. Still waters. You can't fool me. What business is it of yours if I do go to see her, anyway?"

Foster suspected that Rufus was only feeling him out; he was sure his brother had no intention of going to look for Marleen. He changed the subject abruptly, asking Rufus about Regald and Muriel.

Muriel returned from her shopping and exhibited the same surprise at seeing Foster, but he put off talking much until the evening.

"You have to stay in the spare room with Rufus," she said, "it ain't have no more room. One of you will have to sleep on the floor."

She went about her household duties, but every now and then she couldn't resist calling out, "I can't get over this. The two of you here at one time."

Rufus dressed and went into Port of Spain later. Muriel asked him to stay because she was having curried chicken for dinner, but he said he had to see Rena.

Foster got through the evening quieter than he expected, and turned in early, saying he was very tired.

He was almost asleep on the floor when he thought, To hell

with Rufus, he can sleep here tonight, and I'll have the bed.

He slept soundly.

It wasn't until he was washing his face the next morning that he realised that Rufus hadn't come in for the night.

"Many nights he don't come home," Muriel said when he asked her about it.

Andrews picked Foster up in Frederick Street two days later, after Foster had phoned him to say he was back.

"Of course, I'm surprised and all that," Andrews said as they drove off, "but one gets used to the idea of meeting people unexpectedly, and besides, I knew you'd turn up one day. Where shall we go?"

"You should know the better places by now."

"Well, I haven't got much time. There's a lounge in George Street that's nice, despite the environment. But it's too early for it to be opened. Let's go for a drive around the savannah, by the gardens."

When they got there Andrews parked the car and they went inside and found a shady spot under a bay tree.

"Cigarette?" Andrews offered.

"Thanks."

"When did you get back?"

"Last week Friday."

"Good trip?"

"Not bad."

"What are your plans now?"

"I haven't any. Can you get me a job?"

"That shouldn't be difficult." Andrews looked at Foster. He still had that same restless look, and humour in the eyes, though it wasn't so easy to tell now.

People go away, Foster was thinking, and they come back, and they talk. But nothing is the same.

"I could get you a job in a library—I think so, anyway. But don't walk out suddenly one day and say you're fed up."

"No, I won't do that. At least, it won't happen suddenly, I'll think about it a long time first."

It would take some time for Andrews and I to get attuned to each other, he thought.

"How are things with you?" he asked.

"Could be worse. Have you seen the news about some people wanting to go back to India?"

"Yes. I was talking about it with Regald. What's it all about?"

"Oh, the old Indians have this crazy idea about that they want to go back to India after all these years. I've been trying to discourage the move through one or two influential people, but the matter is quite out of hand now. Of course, they have the right, but I don't think it's a wise thing. How do you feel about it, by the way, you being an Indian yourself?"

Foster shrugged. "Don't ask me, you know I'm an individualist. I don't know anything about India. I've never thought of myself as belonging to any particular race of people. I'm a Trinidadian, whatever that means."

"It'll mean something one day," Andrews said.

Foster smiled. "You still have hope for us."

"And why not? If we could only get rid of those selfish, dishonest leaders whose only thought is of wealth and local fame. If we could have a purge, and throw out the fools and the grafters, and get men whose minds are not set on personal gain. And if we could get rid of this stupid, apathetic feeling which prevails in the whole island. Well, anyway, let's don't talk about that. But these Indians have toiled away their lives here, and now they want to leave."

"Well, why not? What has Trinidad got to offer them, but more toiling and no fruit?"

"Oh, this is their country, and they should help to build it, and suffer with it, and go through all the struggles that we have to undergo before we find a place on the map."

"That lounge in George Street must be open by now. Are we going to spend the whole morning talking, or are you taking me for a drink?"

"Of course."

But while they were drinking in the lounge they lost the amiableness they had recovered, and Foster wondered if Andrews thought there might still be something between Marleen and himself.

"How's Marleen?" he asked.

"Oh, she's fine." Was there a slight change in Andrews' voice?

"Listen," Foster said, putting down his glass, "what I have to say isn't going to be roundabout. You appear to have something on your mind, and I hope it isn't that you think some bond still exists between Marleen and me, and that my coming back to Trinidad will cause trouble. I could take anything but that."

"Of course not. What a one-track mind you have." But Andrews searched himself and couldn't deny that he was jealous of the happiness Marleen had given him.

"Well, just remember that. Did you know that Rufus is here too?"

"Why, no. I didn't think he would ever come back."

"His affairs are in a mess. He's back to get a divorce, if he could. Look at your face! I don't think you need lose any sleep about him and Marleen, either. In fact, set yourself at ease for goodness sake and stop worrying. When are you inviting me home?"

"Any time at all. Tonight, if you like."

"What about Sunday? I could spend the whole day then."

"That's a good idea. Come in the morning, and after lunch we could go to Veronica and see Father Hope."

"Ah yes, Father Hope. I want to see a lot of him, his theories interest me."

"That's settled then. I have to go off to a meeting now."

"Will you come to San Juan and pick me up?"

"You're still a lazy dog. You could take a bus or a taxi."

"Why should I, when you have a car?" Foster added, smiling, "If it won't put you out."

"I always sleep late on Sundays. But I'll come." He wanted to assure Foster that it wasn't because of Marleen he was so cool in his welcome, that he knew everything would be all right. Foster and Rufus were both in Trinidad, so what? It wouldn't interfere with their lives. After a week or so Foster would fall into a pattern with his job at the library. As for Rufus, he had his own affairs to attend to—in fact, he had never met Rufus, and wouldn't recognise him if he saw him. He wasn't giving Marleen any credit; he was ashamed that this fear for their happiness should upset him, as if he expected Marleen to run off with one of the brothers as soon as she knew they were in Trinidad. What sort of love was that? What had happened to his confidence and trust?

When he left Foster he was angry with himself for being such a fool, but he was very much in love with Marleen and it was a struggle to compose himself.

Chapter Seventeen

Johnny knew that Rufus was in Trinidad, but he acted as if he didn't know anything, amused to see how the others tried to keep the news from him at first, as if they thought he would go into the kitchen and take up the cutlass and go after Rufus. What the hell did he care if Rufus had come back? So he allowed the others to believe he knew nothing; yet, by his very blatant indifference, led them to think that after all he must know something. What gave them the idea that he would attack Rufus he didn't know, but it was quite obvious that they expected him to do something drastic. That was the whole trouble, they were always ready to think the worse of him, to feel that if he was upset he was likely to behave like a madman. But Johnny himself had fostered this impression, because he found that they left him alone in peace.

But the price for peace was loneliness, he was cut off from the rest of the family. It was a loneliness Johnny never showed. He hid it under a bluster of threats and drunkenness. No one had ever thought of asking Johnny, "Are you lonely?" If they had, Johnny might have confessed that he was indeed lonely, unloved by his family, treated with respect only because they feared him.

Sometimes Jennifer wanted to ask him. Sometimes she wanted to go to her father and comfort him and tell him that she knew how it was, that she knew he wasn't really a bad man, that he was only putting up a front. She was the only one who had any affection for him, and it was secret because Johnny was never approachable enough for her to risk speaking to him.

Johnny, on his part, was aware that his younger daughter was different from the rest, but instead of letting it give him some solace he pushed the thought roughly aside. "I don't need any damn love," he told himself, "I don't want anything from anybody."

He ignored Jennifer more than the rest, because she knew what sort of man he was. However, without openly showing his hand, he granted little favours to her through Mary. "I think is time that girl had a new dress," he would say, giving Mary the money to buy it. Or, "Why the hell this girl stick in the house all the time? You don't let she go nowhere? You must let she go out sometime—this house does have too much women in it when I come home."

Whenever Mary relayed these concessions, however, she always did as if she were responsible, and Johnny had nothing to do with it. She would say, "Girl, I think you need a new dress. I have a few dollars here, go and buy one." Or, "You don't want to go to the dance with Rena tonight? Is all right, your father too strict, but I will send you."

Jennifer never revealed that she knew Mary was only a go-between for her father and herself. She felt sorry for her mother, and affection was such a scarce thing in the house that she couldn't rob Mary of any pleasure.

When she wanted to resume commercial lessons, she told Mary, knowing fully well that her father would be the one to do the deciding. Mary came back and said, "I think about the matter carefully, I had a lot of trouble with your father, but I think I will send you."

Afterwards, when she wanted to go out to work, it wasn't so easy. Johnny didn't like the idea of her working, and at first he refused. Jennifer stayed in her room for two days, then Mary came and said, "I manage to persuade your father."

By the time Rufus returned to Trinidad she was working a year in the Public Library.

Jennifer went out sometimes with Rena to a dance or a party, but she never met anyone who interested her, and for the most part she kept to herself, spending her spare time reading books from the library.

She was quite grown-up now, and more beautiful than her sister. Mary was still anxious to have her marry a man with a profession, but Jennifer didn't like any that she invited to the house. If Mary was persistent she made sure that Johnny knew how she felt, and once Johnny found out that a man was visiting the house in whom his daughter wasn't the least interested, that was the end of that.

Now that Johnny had taken up this idea of returning to India, Jennifer wasn't quite sure if it would fizzle out. It was the first time he had shown such determination, and though her intuition told her he would give it up, this time he was carrying it a bit too far, and she was afraid. There was romance in the thought of going to India, but it was a big step, and she wasn't sure that she wanted to go. She had noticed Johnny's concern at the threat of mass suicide, and she knew in her heart that if it came to that in the end, her father had enough pride to go through with it after his big show of patriotism. Now, more than at any other time, Johnny needed a friend, and he didn't have any. She felt it was time to do away with pretension and get together with her father before he did anything foolish.

One lunch hour she had a quick snack at a cafe in Green Corner and she went to Johnny's shop. It was no use waiting for him to come home in the evening, when he would be drunk and difficult.

Johnny had just sent Patrick out with ten empty bottles to collect a full one, and he was busily engaged in putting together a small wristwatch.

"Pa, I want to talk to you," Jennifer said straight away.

"Just a minute." Johnny went on with what he was doing, his head bent to the desk. The words and the voice hadn't penetrated, he thought it was a customer.

Jennifer watched her father. She hadn't seen him like this before, at work and sober. There were a few gray strands of hair in Johnny's head that she hadn't noticed before. He looked like a different man, he might have been any man working away at his occupation.

Johnny finished and looked up. The eye-glass fell from his face like a monocle and rolled on the ground.

"What the hell you doing here, girl? What happen? Somebody dead?"

"Look Pa, I want to have a talk with you," Jennifer said. She came behind the counter and stood near to him.

The next thought to occur to Johnny was that she was in some sort of trouble, and he washed his hands of it right away.

"Don't come to me for any help," he said. "You working now, you have money of your own. If you in any trouble I can't help you at all."

"I'm not in any trouble," Jennifer said.

"Well, what happen then? Something wrong? Something happen at home?"

"No, everything is all right. I just want to talk to you."

"Well, this sound suspicious. What you want to talk about?"

Jennifer realised that Johnny would never give way, he would go on blustering and threatening, hiding himself from her. Already they had wasted so much of their lives that way.

"It's about this India business, Pa."

"Well, you know about it. Is suicide for everybody if the government don't send we back."

He was still keeping the show up, and he would go on like that, she knew, because it was too late to turn back.

It was awkward talking to her father like this. She tried to frame proper sentences in her mind, but nothing seemed applicable to the occasion; all the things she wanted to say piled up in confusion in her mind.

"Pa, I understand about everything. You don't have to try to fool me like the others. I just want you to know that."

"Fool you? I don't fool nobody."

And because what she had planned to say wouldn't come out of her mouth, she cried, "Stop it, do you hear? Stop getting on like an old fool and be reasonable."

Johnny looked at Jennifer, too astonished to speak. He was still sitting and her had to look up at her. Jennifer drew away a little for fear he might strike her.

For a minute Johnny was silent. And then his shoulders sagged like a beaten man, and he opened the palms of his hands and held them up as if there was a message there.

"Ah, I see you not a little girl again. You grow big now, big enough to treat your father with disrespect, like your sister."

It was pitiful to hear him talk like that, with all the life gone from his voice.

"I didn't come here to quarrel," Jennifer said. She knew he would listen if she spoke calmly and womanly, but her voice was full of emotion. "I want to talk to you about this wild idea you have. Are you going through with it?" She felt sorry she had come and broken his guard, he looked so hopeless and lost now that he couldn't bluster his way out. And perhaps he was ashamed that it was his own daughter who had done it; he might have recovered from a stranger, but it was so different with Jennifer.

Yet Johnny gathered himself for a last effort. He said angrily, "Why you don't go back before you lose your job and stop this foolishness."

But Jennifer knew she was winning. She put her hand on his shoulder and said, "Don't you think it's time that we had a talk about everything? You think I wouldn't understand, Pa, but I will. You've got to get it in your head that I'm grown up."

"I don't want to talk about anything."

"You do. I won't laugh at what you have to say. I want to help you if I could, Pa."

"What could you do? You can't do anything."

Patrick returned with the bottle wrapped in newspaper, and he put it under the counter without a word. He went and sat on his stool, casting sidelong glances at Jennifer, admiring her figure and wondering what she was doing in the shop.

Jennifer looked at the time. "Promise me we'll talk this evening," she said. "I have to go now, or I'll be late. But promise you won't drink and come home drunk."

"All right, all right." He wanted to get rid of her quickly. But before Jennifer could leave the shop he got up and rushed after her. "No, not this evening. We must talk now. Now or never."

"But I have to go back to work," she said.

"To hell with the work. Girl, you won't get Johnny in this mood again. I will tell Patrick to look after the shop, and we will go somewhere and talk. I don't care where, in the park up the road if you like. Wait while I put on my jacket."

He rejoined Jennifer and they went up the street together. Patrick was eyeing the bottle under the counter, gauging his chances of drawing the cork and having a drink and re-topping with water so Johnny wouldn't know.

It was a strange feeling Johnny had, walking up the street with his daughter holding on to his arm, and several times before they got to the park his spirit failed him and he wanted to turn back. But Jennifer as if she sensed what was in his mind squeezed his arm and led him on.

Johnny sat down on the first available bench and said, "I change my mind. I don't want to talk. Come go back."

Jennifer sat close to him. "How like a child you are, Pa. I wish you would stop all this pretending between us. You know," she went on, changing the subject and giving him a chance to talk, "I feel sure that the government will agree to send the Indians back home."

"You think so? But is a long time now and they ain't do nothing."

"Well, don't worry. They will agree in the end. So don't let this suicide business prey on your mind."

"Is not that so much I worried about." He had to do as if he were talking to himself for the words to come out. "Is everything. Things didn't turn out like how I plan. What you think about going back to India?"

"I don't know, Pa. You talk as if I belong there, but I don't know anything about the country, except what I read and hear about."

"Is a good country, girl. I should have stayed there. You will like it, you will get on better over there. In this place you is nobody. All sorts of people living here, so that you don't know what you belong to."

"I don't think I want to leave Trinidad, Pa. I born and grow up here and is home to me. Even if what you say is true, I would still like to remain."

"Well, I won't force you. I would like you to come with me, but I won't force you." He hesitated then said, "Is funny how we sit down here talking, you and me, for the first time."

Jennifer put her face against his arm. "It's not funny. It's the most natural thing, we should have done it long ago. Have you been very lonely, Pa?"

"Who me? Lonely? Why—yes. Nobody to talk to. Everybody saying that Johnny is a drunken old fool."

"You won't be lonely any more, Pa. You have me now."

"Yes." It was the first time in his life that he had thought about his loneliness, no one to talk to, no one with whom to share his dreams and his fears. The flood of emotion inside him was choking. He wanted to tell his daughter everything, but his throat was tight and he kept swallowing all the time.

"Pa, you have enough money to go to India?"

He nodded.

"What about your business? What about the shop?"

"Well, I was thinking about that," he said slowly, wondering if he should tell her. "You know," he sat up straight now, "I have a scheme about the shop. I think I going to burn it down."

"Burn it down!" Jennifer repeated. "But why Pa?"

"Well, I pay big insurance on it, and is time I collect something back. Burn it down, the whole damn shop, and collect the insurance before I go away."

"But that is a crime! You'll get in trouble with the police if they find out!"

"How they will find out? Nobody know about it. I could start the fire in the night. I making a little contraption now, that I could leave in the shop one evening. Then in the night it will catch the place on fire and burn down everything."

"But Pa you know how those buildings jammed up together, you might destroy the whole block."

"Ah, somebody sure to see the fire and call the fire brigade. They will put it out before it spread."

"That is a big risk to take. Don't do it, Pa. Why you don't sell the shop to somebody? Lala would buy it from you."

"Lala is a crook, he won't give me enough money."

"You can't be sure the fire won't spread," Jennifer said, frightened by the idea.

"I make up my mind about this," Johnny said. "Not even you could make me change it. I tell you round there always full of people in the night, somebody sure to call the fire brigade."

She knew that nothing she said could stop him if he had decided to burn down the shop. There was no point in arguing about it now, perhaps later on she would try to dissuade him. Right now it was important that her father know she was his friend, that he had someone he could talk to when he wanted, that he didn't have to drown his loneliness in drink.

"Forget about that for the time being, Pa," she said. "I want you to promise me you won't drink so much, you don't know how worried Ma does be about you."

"Ah, a little drink now and then don't do any harm."

"But you take too much. Nearly every evening you come home drunk. You must try to drink less, for my sake."

"You only trying to wheedle me now because I feeling soft."

"No. You mustn't think that. I don't want anything but your own happiness and welfare. We've wasted so much time already, hiding our true selves from one another. All these years I've wanted to talk to you, and perhaps you needed someone, too. We can't go on living like strangers, Pa. I tell you what. You take me to the pictures this evening."

"What!" This struck Johnny as being so funny that he couldn't help laughing out loud.

"It's no joke. You'll take me and Ma. We are going to be dressed and waiting, so don't disappoint us."

"Girl, your mother will think I going mad when you tell she that I taking you-all to the pictures."

"Don't let that disturb you. Don't you think it will be fun for a change? From now on, I am going to see that you have a lot of things to do, so that you won't feel lonely and go drinking yourself to death. Tomorrow evening you will take Ma round by Lala—"

"That man is a crook. I don't go around there at all."

"He is not a crook. It's time you took Ma out visiting her friends. Besides, Lala always has a bottle of whiskey at home for his friends."

"Ah, he so tight, you think he will offer me a drink?"

"On Sunday we'll all go to Maracas Bay and spend the day by the sea."

"You notice I not saying 'yes' to any of these things."

"But I trusting you to make an effort, Pa. Think of all the things we could do together, all you wanted to do but didn't because you felt we were all against you. You're getting old, Pa, let's try to get a little fun out of life."

"Well, I don't know. We will see. You make everything sound good, but I don't know how it will work out."

"I'll go back to work now," she said. "I hope they won't quarrel because I'm late."

"If they tell you anything, just say you is Johnny's daughter and send them to me."

Jennifer smiled happily. "I think this is the happiest day I've ever known," she said. "Look, I'll walk across the savannah—it will be quicker. Now you go back to the shop and do your work."

She kissed Johnny on his cheek. She was almost as tall as he was and only tilted her head to do it.

Johnny stood in the park and watched her going, confused feelings in his heart. His hand softly rubbed the spot where his daughter's lips had brushed. A tramcar came clanging up from Park Street. The sky was blue and the grass on the lawn was green. A few birds darted in the air.

Johnny felt like a new man.

When Jennifer got back to the library she was called into the office. She prepared an excuse for being late as she went in, but she was so happy she didn't care if she was fired.

"We've got a new man with us," her boss said. "He's starting tomorrow, and I'd like you to help him for a while until he gets used to things."

She turned sideways and saw Foster standing there, a faint smile of surprise on his face.

Chapter Eighteen

Rufus used to go to Johnny's house to see Rena late in the night. She was occupying the front room and it was possible to get in without anyone else in the house knowing. These meetings were far from romantic and they usually spent the time in long arguments, with Rufus making little headway towards a divorce. When the man from BG left Rena she had found an American accountant, but he was working in Venezuela, and it wasn't often she could take a plane and fly over there for the week-end. All this she told Rufus freely, but it didn't help matters. She sometimes said all right, then the night after said no. Rufus was in a quandary. "What do you think the bitch did?" he told Foster, "she said it would cost money for a divorce. She said she had been to see a lawyer, and he wanted fifty dollars. So I gave it to her like a sucker. When I asked her last night how things were going, she said she had taken the fifty dollars and gone to Venezuela to spend the week-end with this American."

"There seems to be a pleasant understanding between you two," Foster observed. "You mean she didn't make any excuse, she just told you point-blank she'd taken your money and gone to Venezuela?"

Rufus groaned. "Yes. She said she wanted to get something on me for a change. Boy, it's month now and I still can't see my way clearly."

"Well, she seems to have agreed about giving you a divorce, anyway. That's something, isn't it?"

"In a way. But it's like hell. She won't be definite."

"You don't want to rush things too much."

"That's what you think. I'm not like you, I have plans, boy. I'd like to get out of Trinidad tomorrow if I could."

"What about this lawyer, is he a good man?"

"Under the circumstances I couldn't have done better. He used to go around with Rena himself, so he has an interest."

Rufus went to see the lawyer himself. He had been leaving everything to Rena so far. They had a long talk together and the next day he took Rena with him and the three of them worked out a plan of action.

"As long as it's you who's doing everything, I don't mind," Rena said.

"Yes, yes," Rufus nodded.

"What about witnesses?" the lawyer asked. "You'll have to have two or more who actually see you in the act."

"I'll get my brother," Rufus said.

"No, that wouldn't do at all. The court might feel your brother is lying for you. Haven't you got any friends?"

"Patrick," Rena said, filing her nails, not looking up.

"Yes, but will he do it?" Rufus asked anxiously.

"You could pay him."

He could see the whole business was going to cost more than he had thought. He wondered if Foster had any money, and if he would lend it.

"How much do you want?" Foster asked when Rufus told him.

"About fifty dollars."

"When—or more interesting—how will I get it back?"

"Boy you see how desperate the situation is, and you know my position. You have a job in the library. I know that I myself should have got a job, but I need all my time to see about this thing. I can only promise you that one day you'll get it back, but how and exactly when I can't say."

"Why don't you ask Regald," Foster said, hedging.

"You know how much responsibilities he has with Muriel and the children."

But even before Rufus spoke Foster felt a burning shame for his hesitancy and was taking the money out of his suitcase.

"I shouldn't have asked you any questions," he said. "I should have given you the fifty dollars without a word when you came to me. I'm sorry."

"That's a hell of a thing to say," Rufus said, not understanding how Foster felt; but he pocketed the money, quite ordinarily.

"It doesn't matter. You've got the money, now hurry off and use it."

Rufus had a feeling that Foster was being superior, expressing amusement as he rushed around from place to place to fix his affairs. But every day the face of Sylvia was in front of him, and he didn't care what he did or what anyone thought as long as he could get the divorce matter settled and clear out of the island.

Patrick put on a show of reluctance until Rufus told him there was five dollars in the deal.

"You're my friend, I don't want your money," Patrick said.

Rufus helped him by pushing the bill into his pocket.

There was another witness, an old Indian woman who used to come and help around the house when Jennifer began to work—he gave Rena five dollars for her.

"Look, why don't we all meet here in your office and get everything clear so that there won't be any hitches," Rufus told the lawyer.

"No. Can't you see, the lot of you mustn't be seen together—especially here, in my office."

"Well, whatever you say, but for God's sake can't you hurry it up?"

"Everything is ready now. Tomorrow night you will do as I told you. The others know what they have to do."

Foster watched Rufus get dressed to go and commit adultery.

"This whole business is very interesting," he said. "Who knows, one day I may have to do the same thing myself. Do you know the woman you're going to er—sleep with?"

"No."

"Ah, most interesting, indeed. I must say."

"Haven't you got anything to do? No place to go?"

"Don't be like that. I seek knowledge. Now, what if this woman turns out to be an old, bent-up piece of wire?"

"It doesn't matter."

"But you have to be caught red-handed—there's a lovely French expression for it, I've forgotten at the moment. Do you mean to tell me you've actually got to fix up this unknown factor?"

"You seem to be in high glee at the prospect."

"Well, despite the seriousness of the matter I can't help but see the funny side. Like the time when you were going away and we were trying to make Johnny fork over that cheque for two hundred dollars."

"Come out to the rumshop with me and have a drink," Rufus said as he finished dressing. "I don't think I could go through with it if I'm sober."

"By all means."

Rufus bought a small bottle, selecting a cheap brand which was popular for quick effect.

"Ugh," Foster said, watching Rufus swallow the rum, "what does it taste like?"

"It's got a hell of a kick. I'll have another when I get into town, and by then I should be ready for anything."

"Foster saw his brother to the main road where he stopped a taxi going into Port of Spain.

"Well," Foster said solemnly, shaking his hand, "the best of luck."

Rufus tugged his hand away. "One thing I'll pray for always," he said, "is that if your day ever comes, I'll be there to watch you squirm and sweat like I'm doing now."

"But seriously," Foster said, laughing outright now and poking his head through the taxi window, "I wish you luck."

"You go to hell," Rufus said as the taxi drove off.

Foster thought to himself, walking back, It is really a grave matter, I hope my sense of humour doesn't fail me if my turn comes.

The rendezvous was an old, ramshackle house in St James, and when Rufus got there he saw with relief that Patrick and the Indian woman were standing on the other side of the road. He got out and paid the driver.

When he entered the house, Patrick and the woman followed him. He waited at the foot of the stairs for them; somewhere upstairs was the door he was supposed to enter.

"Look Patrick," he whispered, "you know exactly what to do?"

Patrick was shaking with fright. "No," he said loudly and then put his hand to his mouth as if amazed at his audacity. "I not sure what the lawyer say," he whispered.

"Listen." The rum was roaring in Rufus's head like a cataract, he suddenly remembered he was to have taken another bottle, and was glad that he hadn't. He had to keep his wits. Patrick was acting like a fool, as if he were the one who had to go upstairs. "Listen," he said again. "I am going upstairs. In a little while you and this woman have to come up, and open the door. You will see me and somebody else there. You understand?"

Rufus looked from one to the other. The Indian woman's face was impassive, as if he hadn't spoken.

"But how will we know when to come?" Patrick whispered. Now Rufus could hardly hear him.

"I will throw a shoe against the door," Rufus said, speaking slowly. "You will hear it, loud and distinct. I will throw it hard.

When you hear it, that is the time to come and open the door. You understand?"

"All right, all right," Patrick said. "But don't stop too long to throw it. I feeling funny in this house, like nobody here. The place dark, you sure the woman upstairs waiting for you?"

Rufus felt like knocking Patrick sideways. He left them and crept up the stairs. They didn't creak. He went to the door and he opened it. He felt quite calm, though his senses were getting dull with the rum.

He saw the woman sitting on the bed and he said, "My God," and sat down in an armchair.

"You is the mister?" the woman asked, getting up and coming close to Rufus. He got a whiff of sour staleness, as if she hadn't washed for weeks. She was middle-aged and flabby, and she had put on make-up in a hopeless attempt to appear attractive.

"Jesus Christ," Rufus said.

"My daughter was the one supposed to come," the woman said, "but she sick too bad, so I come instead. You bring the money?"

"The unknown factor," Rufus said, and he couldn't restrain a bitter smile as he remembered Foster.

"You bring the money?" the woman asked again.

"What money?"

"The lawyer say you will pay. He say you will pay five dollars."

"The dog," Rufus said. "I paid him already."

"No, he say you will pay," the woman insisted. "If you not pay, we do nothing."

"All right," he said wearily, giving her the money. "But look, you'd better go and take a wash. Go in the bathroom and clean yourself properly and come back."

The woman went into a side room, and Rufus got up and paced the floor, smoking. Could he go through with it? He conjured up the image of Sylvia in his mind, beseeching her to give him courage, thinking, I'm doing this for you, darling, because I want to come back to you more than anything else in the world. Suddenly he went to the door and opened it a little way.

"Patrick?" he hissed.

"Yes, yes, time to come?" Patrick began scrambling up the stairs.

"Go and buy a bottle of rum," Rufus told him, pushing a dollar into his hand, "go quickly and come back."

"But the lawyer didn't say anything about this," Patrick stood up in confusion.

"Go quickly, you fool. There must be a rumshop somewhere down the road."

Patrick came back out of breath. "I run all the way," he said. He tried to peep through the door but Rufus barred the opening and pushed him away.

"Good. Thanks. Now wait for the signal. You remember? I'll throw my shoe against the door. Then you and the Indian woman come up and open the door."

He could hardly wait to take a drink. He drew the cork out with his teeth and put the bottle to his mouth and emptied it. The woman had come back and was sitting on the bed, watching him.

"You ready now?" she asked.

He took off all his clothes, motioning her to do the same. He had to make things as simple as he could for Patrick.

"You want the light off?" the woman asked, putting her hand on the switch.

"No, leave it on."

He looked at her, and he thought, I've done a lot of things in my time, but this beats all. I must try to remember everything and see if I could find something to laugh at when it's all over.

The rum had him groggy and stupid, and he fought to fight the drowsiness that was threatening to overcome him.

It was only when he was on the bed for some minutes that he remembered Patrick and the Indian woman downstairs.

"Oh Christ," he cried, leaping up, "where's my shoes?"

He had left them near the chair, away from the bed. He got up quickly and took one up. He hurled it with all his strength against the door, and jumped back into the bed.

When the door opened Patrick pushed his head in first. He stood looking at them as if mesmerised until the Indian woman pushed him in so that she could see too. She looked over Patrick's shoulder and at once she cried out, "Oh Gawd!"

She hadn't been told what to expect, and her agitation was the only truth in the plan the lawyer had concocted.

Patrick was in the witness box, jittery and frightened, the palms of his hands wet with perspiration. Every now and then he wiped

them in the seat of his trousers. He hadn't bargained for all this.
"You say you know this man?"

He tried to imagine the films he had seen of court scenes,
where the stars giving evidence were calm and cool, even making
jokes with the lawyer.

He swallowed. "Yes sir, I know this man."

"You know him well, eh? He's a very good friend of yours?"

"Not so well, sir. A little bit." His eyes roved the court, but
he didn't see anything. Patrick had never been in court before,
not even to hear a case of rape or seduction. Only people in
trouble went to court. And what had he done? Nothing. Yet here
he was in the witness box, and the lawyer was asking him all
sorts of funny questions.

The case had been going on for some time—and going well,
Rufus thought, until Patrick began to give evidence. After all the
briefing, he was still fumbling to reply. Rufus was nervous, he
kept shaking his feet up and down like he was working a sewing
machine. Rena was sitting in front of him; he tried to read her
emotions by watching the movements of her head. The case was
revolving on Patrick's evidence now, and he was making a mess
of it.

Rufus glanced at the clock on the wall behind the judge's desk.
It was getting on to four o'clock, there was a slim chance that
the case might be carried over until the next morning.

"And what were you doing in the house yourself that night?"

"Who, me sir? Why, I was there, you know—"

Poor Patrick, Rufus thought. It hadn't been possible to put
him on guard against all the questions, he had had to rely on
Patrick using some of his own intelligence if he had any. Rufus
allowed his mind to wander from the case. In the beginning he
had hoped for so much, fancying that it would be just a few
weeks before he was on his way back to America, where Sylvia
was alone waiting for him. In about two months time she would
be having the baby. He felt a hatred for Rena, he pierced the
back of her head with his eyes. It was all her fault, he felt like
taking hold of her neck and shaking her.

He didn't hear when the judge said the case would have to
wait over until the next day, it was only when the clerk shouted
"Court rise!" for the judge to leave that he got to his feet with
a start.

The tension left him as he walked outside. For a minute the

glare of the sun dazzled his eyes, and he stood up near a wire fencing in St Vincent Street. It was a very hot afternoon; his collar and his armpits were wet.

In front of him Patrick was walking away dejectedly, his hands in his pockets, his head bent to the ground. It was as if Patrick was taking away his only hope, and Rufus hurried to catch up with him.

"Man, you made a good mess of everything," he said. "You didn't remember anything we told you."

"I finish with this business," Patrick said. "Is the first time I ever went to court. Boy, you does feel frighten in there, like you don't know what you doing."

"You'll feel better tomorrow," Rufus said, "we'll go over everything again. Take your time when you're answering. You haven't committed a crime, you don't have to be afraid."

"Yes, but suppose they find out that I lying."

"But you're not lying, don't you see? You just have to tell them what you saw with your own eyes."

"I don't remember what you and the lawyer say when I get in that box. Like if everything leave my head. You think I could have a drink before I talk tomorrow?"

"They'll smell it on your breath."

"I could talk good if I have one or two."

"No, that will cause trouble. Let's have one now, and we'll go over the whole case."

They went into a rumshop near Green Corner, and Rufus took his time and explained all the questions and answers he could think of in the simplest terms. After two drinks Patrick was replying swiftly to the questions Rufus shot at him, putting in a little historical data to show he was now at the peak of his intelligence.

"Now you're on the beam," Rufus told him. "But don't talk as if you've memorised all the answers. Take your time, speak slowly and plainly."

"You see how just two small drinks fix me up. Why I can't have a little in the morning before going to court?"

Rufus put his hands to his face impatiently. "Because, they will know you were drinking, and that would finish everything. Do you understand? Are you sure?"

But when Patrick got up the next morning the idea of facing the court again frightened him so much that he could hardly get dressed. Accomplishing this, he stood before the mirror studying his face. "I must have a drink," he told himself, and the urge became stronger as he realised it was too early for the rumshops to be opened. If he could slip into the house and get Johnny's box behind the refrigerator—Mary was in the kitchen, and Johnny was still in bed.

Afraid to take away the rum, he stood right there near the refrigerator and put the bottle to his head. He replaced the cork with difficulty, smarting from the straight drink. He hoped he hadn't taken too much, but he couldn't tell, four gulps might fill a glass.

"Tell the court exactly what you saw on the night in question."

"Well, I was there. I and another Indian woman. I know this fellow Rufus well, he married to Johnny daughter and he went away to the States, the exact date was February 16, 1944—"

"Yes, yes, but what happened on the night?"

"I remember that date well, I don't forget dates at all. Rufus was there and a woman was there. That was only afterwards that I find out after I went to buy the bottle of rum for him. I know Rufus well, the exact date he went away was February 16, 1944. I see everything that happen that night. My honour, what he say is true, I was in the house that night, I and another Indian woman—"

"The case was thrown out," Rufus told Foster afterwards, "the judge said the whole thing was a pack of lies."

"You should never have trusted Patrick," Foster said. "You know what sort of a fellow he is."

"I couldn't get anybody else. Boy, I'm worried. I haven't got any more money—I'll have to get a job to keep going. I must get a divorce, otherwise I can't go back to America. You see, I married that girl while I was over there." It had to come out at some time, and he was glad that it was Foster who heard it.

"But you said—"

"Forget what I said. I'm married to two women right now, so you see the position I'm in."

"You could go to jail for that, boy."

"Nobody knows. Rena knows about Sylvia, but not that I'm married to her. And Sylvia doesn't know anything about Rena. I came back to try and settle things with Rena and go back to Sylvia. You see how complicated the whole thing is."

He didn't only blame Rena, he felt that it was turning out this way because he was in Trinidad, a small island where everyone minded other people's business. He felt a dull hatred at having to remain in the colony; he had washed his hands of it long ago, and now he was back and stuck. He began to have misgivings about the whole venture, wishing he had never left Sylvia.

A month went by in which he wrote Sylvia every week, telling her that he was being delayed through no fault of his own, and that he was short of money. Sylvia sent him fifty American dollars and told him to hurry up, that she was going to have the baby soon.

And then his luck turned; Rena became pregnant after a weekend in Venezuela, and the divorce was only a matter of time. But precious time, because he wanted to return to Sylvia as quickly as he could. This time there would be no hitches— Rena was willing and ready.

Impatient to leave the island, Rufus arranged for the case to be heard in his absence and went off to see the American Consul to get his papers.

But events turned against him once more. They knew about his double marriage, and refused to validate his papers.

Meanwhile Sylvia was writing him urgent letters.

In the maelstrom of circumstances, Rufus could only see one thing clearly; he had to get back whatever the cost. He blinded himself to everything else deliberately.

"I'll go to Venezuela," he told Foster. "I'll go there and travel north. Somehow or other I'll make my way to Mexico, and I'll get across the border into the United States. Eagle Pass—that's what they call the point when you touch American soil. And that's my destination."

"You're really desperate to get back. Look at all the trouble you'll have to go through."

"What else is there for me to do?"

"They'll trace you down and throw you out of the country. I see a lot of news in the papers these days about how they are tightening up on restrictions and keeping a sharp lookout for illegal immigrants."

"That's a chance I'll have to take."

"Oh, what a penchant you have for getting into complications."

"Well, I've made up my mind. This is my future, as I see it: Get back to America and Sylvia. When I'm there we'll decide what's the best thing to be done."

"Why don't you send for Sylvia and live somewhere in the West Indies?"

"In these islands? There isn't anything here, boy. Nothing worth living for. You think I could settle down in one of these colonies after living in America for five years?"

"But what I don't see is the use of everything. All the time and energy you've spent going from place to place, wandering around without any money. You talk about me, but I don't see you getting on different. Where is all this leading to? What will eventually happen to you? You know, I think you must get some sort of unconscious pleasure in the way you live. However, I am not the one to advise you. Perhaps you see some reason for what you do, even if I don't."

Some force over which he had no control was driving him on, and there was no holding Rufus back. He packed his suitcase and he went to Venezuela, and three weeks later he was travelling north into Mexico. Some days he had a feeling of hopelessness, and a kind of fear as if he had been living uselessly, as if all the circumstances were piling up to form a barrier against which he didn't stand a chance. But he thought, Life is a different thing to different people, some go up, some go down, some go west, and some go east. And life for him now was with Sylvia. He had been through a lot, and whatever the future held he would go through with it together with Sylvia. There was to be no more looking back, no regrets. He would forsake Trinidad for the rest of his life, it wasn't a hard decision to make.

As for the future—Rufus faced north, across the thousands of miles of land which formed the continent of America.

Chapter Nineteen

When Andrews called for Foster on the Sunday morning he said that he had completely forgotten that he had promised to meet someone to whom he had been introduced at a party in Port of Spain.

"A chap by the name of Johnson, from England. Works for the police, I believe."

"Well, duty before pleasure, by all means," Foster declared. "Is he holidaying in our fair isle?"

"I think so. Say, why can't we all go to Veronica? I'm sure he'd like to meet Father Hope. Let's do that, we can pick him up on the way, he's staying at some friends in St Joseph."

Johnson was an affable middle-aged Englishman. Foster liked him at first sight. There was nothing about him to suggest he worked with the police. Foster imagined him in England, in a dirty mackintosh, with the collar turned up, wearing a bowler and smoking a pipe. The image wasn't one he drew from experience, but from the films he had seen of English detectives. Right now Johnson was dressed for the tropics in the prescribed manner—white shorts and a sports shirt open at the neck. He looked like a wealthy businessman taking a cruise in the West Indies.

It turned out that they had both travelled on the same boat from Liverpool.

"What brings you to this part of the world?" Foster asked him.

Johnson did in fact smoke a pipe and he took it out and filled it, declining Foster's offer of a cigarette.

"Holiday and business, you might say," he said. He got the pipe lighted and sat back comfortably.

Anyone else but Foster would have thought it strange that Andrews was showing Johnson around. Englishmen didn't come out to the tropics and make friends that easy with the natives, when they had their own kind and all the social amenities of the rich white in the island. Even though Andrews was a councillor and likely to be often meeting such people.

Johnson's easy manner made him say, "I bet you've worked

in the tropics before. Maybe in Africa."

"How did you guess?"

"Elementary—" he almost added "my dear Watson" but he went on, "—First, you have a tan which you couldn't possibly have acquired since your arrival. And second, I can tell you've mixed with colonials before by your easy manner."

"Foster once aspired to being a detective himself," Andrews turned his head a little to get in a word as he drove.

Johnson laughed and waved his pipe. "Clever deduction, unless Andrews told you."

"He didn't tell me anything. Are you looking for your man in Trinidad?"

"Oh dear me, no. There's an old, forgotten case on which I might get a lead, but chiefly I'm after pleasure and getting a look at the island."

"You chose a good man in Andrews," Foster said. "He loves this place, and he'll take a delight in showing you all the beauty spots, and our quaint customs."

"Foster is a cynic," Andrews said. "You don't have to listen to anything he says, because he doesn't really mean it."

They had to leave the car near the church and walk down to the village to look for Father Hope, who was visiting a sick man. He was delighted to see them, especially Foster, and said, "It won't be too much of a sin if we open a bottle of wine for the occasion. Take them to the house, Andrews, I will follow in a little while."

"Well," Andrews remarked when they got back, "fancy him suggesting a bottle of wine. He must think a lot of you, boy."

"I'm sure it isn't me," Foster said hurriedly, "it must be to welcome Johnson."

Johnson stood by a window admiring the view. "This is a beautiful spot," he observed.

Foster joined him. "Yes. Untouched by whatever we have of civilized amenities. No electricity, no transport, no contact with the outside world. Father Hope likes it that way, but Andrews feels that the area should be developed for the sake of progress."

"See the church over there?" Andrews pointed it out needlessly. "He built that himself. He and the peasants in this village. Rock by rock, with their own hands."

"Father Hope sounds like an interesting man. Are there many Catholics in the island?"

"Oh, he isn't a Catholic," Andrews explained. "Not in the true sense of the word, really. We call him 'Father' because everyone does. But he preaches his own ideas of religion."

"What do you mean?" Johnson frowned; he was a staunch Catholic himself.

"You tell him, Foster."

"Father Hope modifies religion," Foster said. "He doesn't accept all the Bible says. He believes in tolerance and humility, and fighting evil. But his methods are unorthodox. Perhaps he will tell you about it himself. He's a great talker. We all are, as a matter of fact."

When Father Hope came he opened a bottle of wine and he filled their glasses, pouring lemonade for himself.

"Do you think that is communion wine?" Foster whispered to Andrews at a moment when Father Hope's back was turned. Andrews dug him fiercely in the ribs.

"It is good to see you back," Father Hope told Foster. "Are you going to settle down and live here?"

"I don't know."

"Can't you help him to make up his mind, Andrews? We don't want to lose all our young citizens."

"Johnson here is interested in your teachings," Foster changed the subject.

Father Hope turned to Johnson. "Ah, yes. It is the first time that an Englishman has ever been here since I came. Do you like our country?"

The question sounded odd and unnatural to Foster, but Johnson said, "I haven't been here long enough to form an impression."

There was a strangeness in Johnson's face; Foster wondered why.

"I'm going to show Johnson around when I have the time," Andrews said. And added, "If he has the time, too. He's a detective, and he may have work to do while he's here."

"A detective?" Father Hope raised his eyebrows in a peculiar way. "All the way from England?"

Again it was an unnatural question coming from Father Hope. Foster felt he was deliberately putting Johnson off his ease.

"My occupation is only incidental to my being here," Johnson said, lighting his pipe. "Primarily I'm on a holiday."

The conversation turned to Father Hope's ideas of salvation, but Foster took little part in it. He couldn't help feeling that there was something between the Englishman and Father Hope. Was it disapproval on Johnson's part of disloyalty to Catholicism? It seemed a petty excuse, especially as he was appearing to agree with many points in Father Hope's brilliant reasoning. And what about Father Hope? Why was he acting strangely to Johnson?

Foster allowed himself to be tempted into the discussion and when they got up to leave it was after mid-day.

"You must come to Port of Spain and spend a day with me," Johnson invited.

"I've never known him to leave this valley before," Andrews said. "If he does for you I'll be jealous—I've been trying to get him to come out for years."

Father Hope coloured slightly and again Foster had the feeling that something was wrong; it was the first time he had ever seen disturbance on that face.

"Well, anyway, we shall meet again," Johnson said.

"You are always welcome. Get Andrews to bring you along." He turned to Foster. "And you, my son? You must spend a day with me, and tell me of your experiences in England. I too was there, you know. Perhaps we could exchange impressions."

Foster promised to come, and they left. On the way back Johnson asked Andrews, "How long have you known Father Hope?"

"Oh, a number of years."

"I was very impressed with him. Tell me, what sort of man is he? What do you know about him?"

Andrews kept his eye on the narrow road as he talked. "Well! It's funny you should ask that, because come to think of it, we don't know a great deal, do we Foster?"

"Well, you knew him first." Foster left it up to Andrews. He was looking at Johnson, who still seemed perturbed.

"Well, he was born here, if that's what you mean. In Veronica. He was a bright boy and he won a scholarship and went abroad for a long time. His parents died while he was away. He remembered Veronica and he came back to live—almost like a hermit, you might say, satisfied to spend his life in the valley. Something like that, anyway."

"All this is news to me," Foster said.

"You never asked," Andrews rejoined.

"He just returned and set up church in Veronica?" Johnson asked. "Wasn't he appointed by some local authority?"

"He's an individualist—you must have seen that for yourself. I don't think there are many people who even know of his existence."

"A man of his integrity and intelligence is wasted away in there," Johnson observed.

"I told him the same thing, but he wouldn't budge. He likes it there, doesn't ever come out. You don't know how funny it was when you asked him to spend a day in Port of Spain."

"I see." Johnson sat back and smoked his pipe, silent for the rest of the journey. He was having lunch with some friends, but he promised to meet them in town during the week for a drink, and he took Andrews's address and telephone number before they parted.

So preoccupied was Foster that he had forgotten completely that he was going to see Marleen for the first time since his return. But it didn't make any difference, she greeted him like an old friend with no trace of embarrassment. She had prepared a sumptuous West Indian lunch and they ate well.

Andrews lived in a small but roomy house. It was furnished simply, but with a graceful arrangement. Here and there he had stuck up some of his paintings on the walls.

"I don't have much time to do any work," he said, seeing Foster glance at the pictures.

After lunch Marleen brought Julia out for Foster to have a look. She was asleep. Foster held her tiny hand in his for a moment and his thoughts shot back to Julia in London. He didn't know what to say. It was an embarrassing minute for all of them until Marleen took her inside and went into the kitchen afterwards to wash the dishes.

Foster relaxed in one of the soft armchairs, a rum punch on a small table near to hand.

"You've done yourself well," he told Andrews.

"Oh, hard work, you know." Andrews laughed.

"I say, did you notice anything funny when Johnson met Father Hope?" Foster said up in the chair with an effort.

"No. Did you?"

"Maybe it was my imagination, but I'd swear there was something between them."

"Perhaps he was taken off guard to see an Englishman. I

didn't tell him I was bringing Johnson."

"Ah, that's nonsense, and you know it. It would take a lot to shake him out of his calm. Oh well, why worry?" Foster yawned and sank back into his soft chair. "How about a siesta?" he asked drowsily.

"Sure, stretch out on the sofa and sleep if you like."

Andrews stood for a moment watching Foster as he made himself comfortable. He was glad that the meeting between Foster and Marleen had gone so well. He was a fool to worry.

He started towards the bedroom and Foster called after him, "You lucky dog!"

Andrews smiled happily as he opened the door and went in.

Most evenings now Foster took her out, and he was surprised at the many things they had in common. It was a natural sort of companionship, they were free and easy with each other, and Jennifer was the sort of person who understood him and didn't ask too many questions. They went out as if it was meant to be, but Foster never made love to her, and she was content to share his thoughts and wait. Often he said how any day her parents would marry her off to some professional man, just to hear her laugh at the very idea, for he loved the freedom that she had made hers, and to hear her talk about it. He had never thought of Jennifer while he was away, nor ever dreamed that they would be together as they were now. Nothing was the same, did he expect that she would stand still in time? She had grown out of any bonds which held her, she was free, she could do what she liked.

"Will you be going back to India, then?" he asked her one day, for she had told him about Johnny's plans.

"I haven't made up my mind," she said. "Pa is a different man now, trying to make up for the years he lost. He wants me to go with him. Would it make any difference to you?"

"I'd like to go to India some time," he said, ignoring her question because he was afraid to answer it. "Not for any racial reason, but I'd like to see what it's like."

"There's a meeting tonight at the club about it," she said, "now that the government have decided to charter a ship. Afterwards there's dancing. Why don't you come?"

"Can I take you?"

"That's what I'm suggesting! Pick me up at eight o'clock."

That evening before leaving the shop Johnny put his contraption in a corner against the wooden wall and took a last look around. He had sent Patrick home early to have the place to himself. He was proud of his work and there wasn't any doubt in his mind that by midnight the shop would be on fire.

When he went to sleep that night he had a nightmare. He dreamt that the shop was on fire and he was in it, looking for something which he had forgotten to remove.

Johnny woke in a cold sweat and fumbled in the dark for cigarettes and matches on the table near the bed. He saw the time on the luminous dial of his watch. It was half-past eleven.

What was it that he had forgotten? The nightmare was so real that he sat up wide awake. The piercing wail of a siren made him jump with fear. That was the fire brigade, he knew. The shop was on fire. He had to get there, he had forgotten something. What was it?

He pulled on a pair of trousers and ran out of the house. There were other people running in the direction the fire brigade truck had taken and Johnny tried to keep up with them, his pyjama jacket billowing out behind him as he fumbled to keep his trousers from falling down.

There was a great crowd on the pavement opposite the shop when Johnny arrived gasping and sweating. The fire brigade was concentrating on the rumshop next door; there was no hope of saving the jewellery shop, which was a mass of mounting flame.

Jennifer and Foster pushed through the crowd to get to Johnny.

"Pa, I felt something was going to happen tonight, that is why we leave the dance so early."

She couldn't talk in front of the crowd.

"Look the mister there!" someone shouted and pointed to Johnny. "Is his shop that burning down!"

Foster held on to Johnny's arm and pulled him to the outskirts of the crowd.

Johnny was looking dazed and foolish, as if he didn't understand what was happening.

"What is it, Pa?" Jennifer asked.

"I forget something. I left something in the shop." Johnny's voice was dead and flat.

"No hope of saving anything now," Foster said. "What was

it?"

Johnny knew what he had forgotten. All the plans for the Great Invention. He had taken everything to the shop, every scrap of paper, and he had forgotten to take them away.

"Nothing. Nothing at all."

"It must be something to make you come running like that in your pyjama jacket," Jennifer said.

"No, is nothing, I tell you. I was sleeping, and I had a bad dream."

"Come and go back home, you can't do anything here. The fire brigade will put out the fire."

He allowed them to lead him away.

"I was going to take it with me to India," Johnny said, talking to himself. "I would of had a better chance there to make it work, I would of had more time. I was near to the end, too. Just a few more details and everything was finish. All this time I was working on it, and now it burn up in the fire."

"What's he talking about?" Foster asked in a whisper.

"What was it, Pa?"

"Nothing. It don't matter now. I spend all my life trying to make it work. I was really coming to the end. Just last week I work out a plan on a piece of paper, and I was going to take everything to India with me."

"Perhaps you'd better get him to bed," Foster murmured to Jennifer, "this must have upset him a great deal."

"I don't think I could sleep any more," Johnny said, overhearing him. "You-all don't realise what happen here tonight, you think I out of my head and talking foolishness. But if you only know!"

"Whatever it is Pa, you can't do anything about it now." Jennifer put her arms around his shoulders as they got to the house. "Go inside and try to get some sleep. Tomorrow we will see about it."

She handed Johnny over to Mary and came back to Foster who was waiting outside.

"I had a strange feeling something was going to happen," she said. "When he came home this evening I could tell."

"I should have listened to you when you kept asking me to take you home."

"Well, we wouldn't have been able to do anything, anyway."

"This must be a great shock to Johnny, losing all his goods."

"Oh, he knew about it."

"What do you mean?"

"Pa set fire to the shop himself to collect the insurance."

"What! You're fooling. How do you know?"

"He told me."

"He told you he was going to burn down the shop? Tonight?"

"He didn't tell me when."

"So you knew all the time! But—but you know it is a crime, Jennie. It's arson. The insurance people make full investigation before they pay out money like that. Suppose Johnny is caught?"

"Pa isn't a fool as most people think. He knew what he was doing. You won't tell anyone about this, will you?"

"Of course not. But he's taken a big risk, you know."

"I told him so and I tried to stop him, but he wouldn't listen. I wonder what it was he forgot to remove?"

In the bedroom Johnny was too grieved at the loss of his papers to heed Mary's noisy lamentation.

"What we will do now? The shop burn down! Everything gone! And you acting as if you in a daze, not saying anything!"

"Ah, the shop insure," he said at last to quieten her, "what you worried about? Leave me alone in peace. I have to think out some matters."

They came towards the city the night before the ship was due to sail, because they were afraid that it might go away and leave them behind. Old men and old women, some with their children sleepy-eyed and crying. With their bags and bundles of clothing, old ones with sticks to help them on the way, for some were near enough to walk. Others came by bus or train from the country districts of the island. And all of them had a light in their eyes, as if salvation had come at last. It was a moving sight, all these old Indians heading for the wharf in Port of Spain where the ship was tied up alongside. And yet no one was interested in watching them, no one in the island felt that this immigration was a big thing, that people were leaving the country in which they had worked their lives away, to go to distant India purely for sentimental reasons, to stand on the banks of the Ganges, to walk on holy land. No crowd gathered as when Johnny's shop was burning down.

In little groups of twos and threes they came out of the night, wanting to be there early, in case the ship sailed away and left them, though they well knew the date and time of sailing, but to them it was quite possible that such a thing could happen. Andrews heard about it and he took Foster along with him to the wharf.

"I want you to see this," he said, "the way these people are going away, as if it is for a short holiday to Tobago or Grenada." And in fact it didn't look like they knew the thousands of miles they would have to cross, or that they were going to a country which would be different from Trinidad. For they were dressed in their everyday clothes and their bundles contained very little—not that they had a lot to take away with them. And anyone seeing them would never have thought they were about to embark on a long voyage. They themselves seemed not to be quite aware of the undertaking. They were going to India as if they were going to spend a week or two at a relative or friend in another part of the island. Like how Christ had said take up thy bed and walk, and the cripple did that, so they were going away, without any fuss they had taken up their possessions and come to the city.

Andrews and Foster walked among them as they stood huddled against the sheds on the wharf.

"Where will they sleep for the night?" Foster asked his friend. "They can't stay out in the open like this until tomorrow."

"I'll see if I could get them to open one of the storage sheds," Andrews said, and he went off to the port authorities.

Foster looked about him, a strange emotion in his heart. He was one of them, and yet he couldn't feel the way they did, nor share in the kinship they knew. They were going back home. They had a home. It was far away, but they hadn't forgotten. When they had come to Trinidad they kept some of India hidden in their hearts. They had tried to live in Trinidad as they had lived in India, with their own customs and religion, shutting out the influences of the west. They had built their temples and taught their children the language of the motherland. They had something to return to, they had a country.

He had nothing. He had been brought up as a Trinidadian—a member of a cosmopolitan community who recognised no creed or race, a creature born of all the peoples in the world, in a small island that no one knew anything about. The world, in reality, consisted of the continents—the world was London, New York, Paris, and the big cities one read about every day in the newspapers. Who was interested in a few thousand people living on an island, when in one big city there were millions constantly moving to and fro, cheering the royal family, watching the bus fares rise, feeding the pigeons in Trafalgar Square? Of what material loss would it be to the world if the island suddenly sank under the sea? Who ever said that man cared what happened to his fellows? Indeed, who in Trinidad cared if these Indians wanted to go back home? As long as a man got his daily bread and a roof over his head, all was well with the world. He could belch after a hearty meal and pick his teeth and discuss the uncertainty of prevailing world conditions.

Andrews came back and got the shed opened and the immigrants went in to shelter. Some of the children were crying and some were asleep. One woman sat in a corner and took out her breast to feed her child. Old men made pillows of their bundles and tried to sleep.

"Look at this," Andrews cried irritably, "I don't know why they came here tonight. The ship isn't sailing until tomorrow morning."

"Oh, leave them alone," Foster said, "they're going back home, and that's all there is to it. To one of the oldest countries in the world, one with tradition and civilization. Anyway, I don't know why you're so interested."

"These people are Trinidadians."

"They're Indians, and they're going back to India."

"What would happen if everyone decided to go back? The negroes would return to Africa, the Chinese would go back to China, the Europeans to Europe—and who'd remain?"

"What about the Trinidadians you're always talking about? The true sons of the country?"

"It's up to us to produce such people. You think we haven't any, but I know a lot who are proud of belonging to these islands, and who would work to improve our lot. You wait until federation gets under way, and you'll see."

"Federation! Up to now the islands can't decide what to do—you told me so yourself. They don't know their backside from their elbow. British Guiana and British Honduras feel they belong to the continent of America and don't want to have any small-time dealings with the islands. Jamaica agrees because she's best off and will have the last say in any administration. The poorer islands have no alternative. And Trinidad sits back and waits to see what the others decide. Ah, with all the differences in these islands it will be one hell of a job to unify and have a common loyalty."

"Well, we're going to try, anyway. You can't expect us to progress in leaps and bounds."

"I don't know what we're arguing about anyway. It's a habit now, whenever we get together. I'm getting sleepy. You're not going to stay here all night, are you?"

"Don't back out of this. You know, old chap, you're always full of criticism, but this island is your home as well as mine."

"I know." Foster softened his voice. "I'd like to see it a better place, too. Don't think that I only talk and don't do anything. But I wish I could find myself first, boy. I wish things were as clear to me as they are to you."

"Why bother about obscure whys and wherefores? You could spend the rest of your life trying to reason out why the world is as it is, and be no nearer a conclusion at the end. I thought we were both agreed on that? Are you going on in this frustrated manner? You went away for two years. Are you nearer the truth now?"

"Ah, what sort of question is that? It wasn't a waste of time. However, you are quite right. If you've finished here let's go."

Andrews looked around at the Indians huddled on the ground. "I wonder what they're feeling now," he murmured, "I wonder if they have any doubts, if they would wish they had never left Trinidad. Tell me, boy, don't you feel any sort of alliance with these immigrants? Couldn't you go up to one of them and speak as one of their kind?"

"I see their position the same as I'd see it with any other nationality. They're human beings to me, not Indians or your Trinidadians. How now, you're a negro, why all this anxiety for their welfare?"

Andrews laughed. "I'm getting to be like you in that respect. I'm not as fervent as I used to be about my colour. But mark you, it's only because I know we are capable of great things. I still believe we are taken advantage of, and I'll fight against that until I die."

"I would have married a girl in England, but her parents didn't want a mixed marriage."

"You never told me about that."

"It isn't important."

"How did you feel when you found out?"

"To tell you the truth I wasn't prepared to let myself be upset by it. I think I was—tired, that's all."

"Let's go. Are you coming back in the morning to see the ship off?"

"What for?"

They went through the gate to the road where Andrews had his car parked.

When they got to San Juan and Foster was getting out, Andrews said, "I almost forgot to tell you that Father Hope wants to see you. He said this week."

"Didn't you tell him that I'm working?"

"He said you could come after work one evening."

"What does he want to see me for?"

"I don't know. Maybe he wants to give you his blessing."

"I'll go tomorrow evening. What are you doing, why don't you come, too?"

"I'm afraid I'll be busy. Come to think of it he sounded like he wanted to see you alone."

"Why the hell couldn't it wait until Sunday? I'll have to break a date with Jennie."

"Well, don't say I didn't give you the message. So long, we'll pick up later in the week. Come to the Red House on Friday if you have time and see how the councillors behave at a meeting."

In the morning the immigrants ate food they had with them and went on board the ship, due to sail within the hour.

Johnny came with Mary and Tim. Taking Tim away was Rena's idea, and as Johnny had no objections she got rid of the boy with less trouble than she had expected. He was quite excited by the adventure and kept Johnny busy answering questions. Mary was submissive and sad. She had been around to see all her friends, and told them, "I don't want to go to India, but if Johnny going, what I can do?"

Johnny was dressed in a smart suit and he was smoking a cigar. He and a few others like him represented the middle-class Indian who had prospered somewhat in the island. They knew what this business was all about, in contrast to the poor peasants who had spent the night on the wharf. Johnny had sent all his luggage ahead, he only had a briefcase with some necessary papers.

Jennifer was seeing them off.

"It not too late you know," Johnny said, "even now you could come if you like."

"I know Pa, but I'd rather stay in Trinidad."

"Look at all these people, I wonder if they know what they doing?" He glanced around as he made that remark, then turned to Jennifer again.

"I believe you making a fool about that boy Foster," he said. "He ain't ask you to marry him, he look like a fellar who can't make up his mind. You know what a worthless man his brother Rufus was. You see what happen to your other sister. You sure you will be all right?"

"Yes Pa. Don't worry about me, or Rena either. She is going to live in Venezuela next month."

"But what will happen to you alone in Trinidad, girl? You not afraid to live here by yourself?"

"Don't worry about me, Pa. I'll get along."

"Well, girl, I sorry that my family bursting up like this when we just start to get to know one another." He gave Tim a tap on the head to keep him quiet and went on, "But if you want to stay, Johnny won't stop you."

"Take good care of Ma and Tim. And write me as soon as you get there."

Johnny was only repeating what he had said in the past few days because he didn't know what else to talk about. It was awkward standing there telling his daughter goodbye. He knew he might never see her again. He wanted to tell her about the great sorrow he felt. And he wanted to give her some material token of his love, besides the house which he had left her. He was leaving the only person he loved behind him, and he racked his brain thinking of something he could give her.

"Listen girl," he said earnestly, holding his daughter's hand. "Is something I want to tell you. About Gravity."

"Gravity?"

"Yes. I work for years on it. That was the thing I had in the shop that get burn down in the fire. It was my invention, I had all the plans write down and I would of finish it in a short time. I have nothing more to give you but this idea. You have a piece of paper and pencil on you?"

"Yes Pa." Jennifer opened her handbag and searched.

"Good. Now write this down in case you forget it. You ready? Gravity is the force that pull everything down. Write fast, I don't want the ship to go away without me! If you throw something in the air, Gravity pull it down. You have all that? Now Gravity does only pull things down, but suppose a man could invent something so that Gravity pull things sideways? Suppose a man could harness that force and make it pull things like cars and trains? That would be a great invention. You have all that down?"

"Yes Pa."

"Well girl, that is the only secret I had in my life, and I give it to you. You can't tell, one day when you married you might think about it, and you and whoever your husband is might think is a good idea, and work on it. I know it could happen, because I was near to finding out the solution. I have no plans to give you, but you could think up how to start yourself."

"I know this means a great deal to you," Jennifer tried to say the right thing, "and I'm grateful that you've passed it on to me. Perhaps one day I'll find out how to make it work."

"Well, come on and go," Johnny said to Mary, "what you waiting for?"

Mary began to cry when Jennifer kissed her.

"Goodbye girl," Johnny said gruffly, looking over his daughter's head.

"Goodbye Pa." Jennifer threw herself into his arms.

"None of that stupidness," Johnny said, his own voice choking. "Come on, is time to go on board the ship."

And Johnny took Tim's hand and held him up the gangway, with Mary following.

Jennifer stayed until the ship sailed away, waving her handkerchief. She felt an immeasurable loneliness. She looked down at the piece of envelope on which she had written Johnny's last words and which she still clutched.

And then she began crying. She went out of the gate with the tears streaming down her face. She wished Foster had been with her, he was her only comfort now.

Chapter Twenty

Father Hope was sitting in his library reading when Foster walked in. Foster had told Jennifer that he would try to get back early. But it wasn't until late in the night that he left Veronica, and Jennifer was far from his thoughts then.

"Sit down," Father Hope said. "Smoke if you like. I'm glad you managed to come so quickly."

"I haven't got much time," Foster said, thinking of Jennifer waiting in town for him. "What is it you want to see me about?"

"How impatient you are, I am looking forward to a pleasant evening's conversation with you. We haven't had a good talk since you returned from England. How did you find it over there?"

Foster relaxed a little out of politeness and talked. An hour went by before he recalled that there should be something special he was wanted for.

"I'm sure you didn't want to see me just to hear what I've been doing in England," he said.

Father Hope got up and went to a drawer in his desk and came back with tobacco and a pipe.

"I don't smoke often," he said, ramming tobacco. "Thank you," as Foster offered him a light. He got the pipe going and walked over to the window.

"No, that wasn't what I wanted to talk about." He was looking over the valley as he talked. Night had fallen and the sky was brilliant with stars. Lights in the huts and small houses in the village glowed a dull yellow.

"Foster, how would you like to take over from me?"

There was a silence as Foster digested this. "How do you mean?" he asked at last.

"Take over. Live here, in this house. Preach in the church on Sundays. Offer consolation and words of encouragement when the people need advice."

Foster laughed a little and Father Hope turned from the window. "I really mean it," he said.

Foster looked at him dumbstruck for a minute. "Are you

leaving Veronica, then?"

"Yes, I'm going away. We'll come to that in time. But what do you think about the idea?"

"Think about it? Why, it—it's fantastic. Me here, in your place! That's impossible. I'm sure this is leading up to something else, you couldn't really mean that."

"Why not? Why is it impossible? Think for a moment. You are pursuing truth. You want a faith, a hope, a destination that will make your life worthwhile. Here in this valley you could live and learn and get to understand the things you believe in. I have lots of books, you'll never finish reading them."

"But me—of all people, why ask me?"

"I think you will be able to do it. For a while I had Andrews in mind. But no, he wouldn't do. Besides, he is well occupied. He isn't the sort of person who would be able to administer advice impartially. I could think of no one but you."

"Oh, the whole thing is fantastic." Foster got up and went to the window, and Father Hope moved away and sat down in the chair he had vacated. "Why, I haven't even figured out what I'm going to do. I don't know the answer to anything. You know me. I'm lost and puzzled and completely adrift. If you go to town and pick a man off the streets you'll get a more suitable person—at least someone who knows why he's alive and who would have reasons for the things he does. You might even say I have an inferiority complex with my chaotic thoughts, that I suffer from cynicism, that I find the world disordered only because I can't fit in. You can't really be serious about this."

"But I am."

"It isn't even as if I'm old—"

"Age has nothing to do with it. What does it matter how old you are, what your name is, what part of the world you come from?"

"But I'm not ready for this sort of life. I haven't even begun to live. You can't expect me to cast aside everything and spend my days here in Veronica. No, I'm not suited to this job."

"You say you're not ready. But will you ever be? No man formulates a theory of life to which he could adhere all the time. But in God you have a lasting belief. A remote Goodness, an almost forlorn hope that there's purpose behind it all."

"Ah, you offer God like a saving grace. There's nothing else to turn to for salvation. God has no rival, in the long run one turns to Him as the only light in a dark world, and I can't help telling you that I feel it's a bit unfair, because there are so many other things which offer some measure of comfort, but which could never attain the perfection which is God's and God's alone. And the fact is, we have a certain number of years to live, and it isn't as if he's giving you time to try other beliefs. Before you know it you're an old man ready for the grave, and you haven't come to terms with him not because you didn't believe but because there is so much confusion in the world it took you a long time to realise the truth."

"It didn't take you a long time, and you feel cheated because of that. It's like taking a shortcut and bypassing the pleasures of life. You think God is a time for old age, when you've given away your youth and the best years to worldly pursuits. Then when you have nothing more to offer but creaking joints and crinkled skin, and a mind tired with evanescent joys and fearful of the thought of death, you will seek to make your peace."

"Does God want all the people in the world to be priests then?"

"Ah Foster, you're so evasive. God doesn't want anything. It's you who's after a lasting belief. You say yourself that God is perfect. Why then waste time when the truth is before you? What I'm offering you here in Veronica is far from misery. You'll attain a spiritual peace—"

"I don't want to hear any more," Foster interrupted. "Why do you give me credit for being faithful and zealous when you know fully well that I'm quite the opposite? Supposing that I told you that I didn't believe in God, that I love the heartbeat, the pulse, the kiss, wine and the nearness of women? That I believe we were born to be happy and to make the most of these miserly years on earth?"

"Ah, but are you happy, that's the thing. Do you live without fear or thought of the morrow? Don't you ever pause and think, My God, what will happen to me when I die? Won't I ever kiss a woman again? Drink a glass of beer? Go to a cinema show?"

"Enough, enough," Foster cried. "In all this I still see the element of selfishness—God's and man's. Man serves God to save his own skin. After all, what is a life? Thousands die every day, cut off in a second from the solid realities they knew—chewing gum, a glass of water, the typewriter on the desk, the sound of another voice. Where do they go? What has happened to all the people in the world who have died? Who think of them, or wonder if they're quaffing milk and honey or shoving coal? There is nothing else to turn to—I have to console myself that when I die, if I've lived a good life I'll dwell in some celestial world where there's no evil or sin. Why do I have to believe that? Don't you see how God is forced upon man, making mock of all his efforts to attain happiness?"

"You are quite mixed up. We come back to the same point," Father Hope said patiently. "Why spend your life looking for an alternative when none exists? Why believe in man's power when man has failed, when you know that in the end there will be nothing else to turn to but the belief of which you were aware from the very beginning?"

"Well then, are we to assume a fatalistic approach to life, forsaking all for God?"

"Yes."

"I won't do it. The world isn't made that way—I'm not made that way. I question things, I want to know why, and when, and where. God will have to wait until I'm satisfied."

"We're going round in circles, you know."

"Well there you are."

"All these questions you ask, all the doubts you have—you'll have time and quiet to meditate on them here."

"Meditate! You think a young man like me could shut himself up in this valley and meditate?"

"Yes. I did it, and I'm not an old man, even now. I know you better than you know yourself, Foster."

"Ah, I don't know what we're talking about it for." Foster lowered his voice and calmed down. "One would think I had to do it, the way I've been carrying on. Still for a minute back there you almost had me considering the offer. Good work, Father."

"Apart from these vague misgivings, what other reasons have you for wanting to refuse?"

"Oh, I'm not going to give it any more thought."

"Tell me, just for the sake of argument."

"Well in the first place what qualifications have I got? Do you think I could just move in like that and take over the church in Veronica, and your duties?"

"Why not? My duties are self-imposed. No one sent me to Veronica. I just came and set up house, as it were."

"But you went away to study for the priesthood. You had certain qualities necessary for this sort of thing. Why do we go

220

on talking? The whole thing is impossible. I can't imagine myself in your place. Why, I have even begun to settle down somewhat. I've got a good job, and I may even get married soon."

"That's all right, you and your wife could live here. Listen Foster, you're writing a book—what better place for quiet than this valley? I myself have started a thesis on religion which I am sure will interest you. Perhaps you may even complete it for me."

"Ah, it's too much, this suggestion is beyond me, I can only marvel at your conceiving it."

Foster stopped walking up and down and turned to Father Hope. "But you haven't told me what has happened. Why are you going away?"

"I wish we had settled that other business before coming to this. But have it your own way, you can think about it and let me know later."

Father Hope's pipe had gone out and he took a light from Foster before going on.

"I committed a crime."

"You! What crime?"

"I killed a man."

"My God." Foster sank into a chair weakly.

"Oh, all this happened a long time ago." Now Father Hope was walking to and fro as Foster sat listening. "It was while I was abroad, before the war. I've paid in my soul for it, but the world wants more than that. An eye for an eye. That's the code of justice, and as far as the law is concerned I am a wanted murderer. Are you listening to me?"

"Yes. But your words aren't registering. Shock upon shock, this is. You don't happen to have any of that wine we had the other day remaining?"

Father Hope smiled and put down his pipe. He went out of the room and returned with a bottle of wine and a glass.

"You must learn to bear up without this dutch courage," he said. "But I daresay it will help you."

Foster poured a glass of wine and drank half of it gratefully. He lit a cigarette and felt better.

"It is ironic that Andrews was the one who brought Johnson here," Father Hope continued. "He came back to see me two days after. He said he wanted to make sure. It was rather a stroke of luck for him."

"But I don't understand. Why didn't he arrest you and take you away?"

"I gave him my word I wouldn't try to run away, and he gave me a week to get ready to leave."

Foster got up and now they were both walking around the room, Foster restless like a caged animal, Father Hope like he was following a funeral in slow, measured steps.

"We've got to do something about this. You don't have to keep your word. We could get you out of this jam, Andrews and I. You could go to another island. Oh, we'll think of something. Don't worry."

Father Hope stopped walking and looked at Foster and smiled. "But I gave my word," he said.

"That's nothing, forget it. By tomorrow Andrews and I will have you out of here, and somewhere where Johnson will never find you. We'll stall him, put him off the track completely. Don't worry—"

Foster was talking rapidly and he stopped suddenly and looked at Father Hope standing there serenely.

"You're going with Johnson," he said.

"Yes."

"But for heaven's sake, why? In the face of all that we've been talking, you turn around and tell me that once you killed a man, and now you're going to pay the penalty. What's one man's life to yours? You've more than paid the debt already. Look, all this happened years ago."

"Years and years ago," Father Hope mused. "Yes, I had almost forgotten about it. It was in London, you know, in the East End. A dark dismal night—you know what the weather can be like over there. He was attacking a woman, and I struck him down with a rusty piece of iron I found in the drain. The woman ran away. When I looked at him I knew he was dead. I panicked. I fled."

"What are you going to do, Father Hope?"

"All these years I've lived creating a philosophy which would stand me in good stead. See, I am not at all as agitated as you are. I accept my fate, because I have something to hold on to, a belief that I am close to God."

"But I can't accept this. It's ridiculous to think of a man like you, with your thoughts, being dragged off to face a murder charge."

"Why so! You walk in the streets and you see hundreds of people milling about, and you can't tell what is in their minds, you can't pick out one and say he's a murderer, or look at another and think he has just seduced an innocent girl and is on his way to the pictures. And why should it be different with me? Who am I, that I should escape justice when everyone else has to abide by the law?"

"No no, there are good men and bad men, and you have already suffered for what you did."

Father Hope sighed and sat down. "You must realise, Foster, that what will happen to me is unimportant. But I would like to think that there is someone else who would carry on where I leave off. In this room there is a great deal of my work. I have been writing for a long time. Some of what I have written you will agree with. The rest—well, I will have to sacrifice it to your own individual approach and thought. Andrews once told me about your universal kiss—how does it go? 'Oh kiss me the universal kiss, and there's and end to the world's wrangle.' I too passed through a phase when I felt it was my duty to save the world. I won't disillusion you with my own failures, you may well succeed where I have failed."

"All these things you keep repeating, Father, as if I am going to take your place. I tell you I am unworthy of any such trust as you would place in me. Perhaps we do think alike in some respects, but when you came here you had decided on a certain way of life. I still have to make my own decision, and when that will be I don't know. You have disciplined yourself and brought your emotions and feelings under control. Besides all that, you created a world in which you had found a way to the spiritual peace that all men seek, only to have it kicked from under your feet, and for what? Because some time in the past you killed a rogue by accident. People are killing one another every day and calling it war. Life is cheap. How can I reconcile these two things, your philosophy and the crime for which you may have to pay with your life?"

"Life, as you say, is cheap. You know that my spirit is free. It would not matter one jot if I were to die tomorrow. I believe that my soul will live on forever."

Foster went over to the window. Lights had gone out in the village and it was dark down there. A faint wind was moving the trees. The heat had gone from the land and it was cool when the wind blew through the window. More stars could be seen in the sky now.

"Does Andrews know all about this?" he asked, without turning his head.

"No. You will probably see him before I do."

"Do you want him to know everything?"

"But of course."

"I wonder how he'll take it," Foster said slowly.

"You'll explain everything to him. By the way, he was going to try and get electricity for Veronica. You'll find lamplight a strain on your eyes."

"You still talk as if I'm coming. You don't know what you're asking me to do."

"Take a couple of days to think it over, my son. But I hope you make the right decision."

"Think it over," Foster told Andrews, "as if I didn't know there and then that I wanted no part of it. Fancy, asking me of all people to take his place."

They were driving down the Churchill-Roosevelt Highway, and Andrews listened to Foster without interruption, which wasn't easy. He drove off the road and parked on a grassy spot. He lit a cigarette and passed the pack to Foster.

"What did you tell him?"

"I told him so. I didn't exactly say no—the idea was so preposterous it would have sounded grand to refuse outright. But he knows how I feel."

"I don't know how I look to you, but I feel numb and foolish by this news. What's to happen to Father Hope? There was always an air of mystery about him, come to think of it. Good God, who would have thought of it?"

"It seems so helpless that we can't do anything."

"I don't know." Andrews was thinking. "I must speak to Johnson. He isn't a bad sort, you know. I must find out what this is all about. After all, it was such a long time ago. There must be a way out. Listen, are you going to Veronica this evening?"

"No. I'm going out with Jennie. But I'd better go tomorrow and tell him that I made up my mind."

"Good. Tell you what. I can't go this evening either—I've got to attend a meeting. I'll try to see Johnson afterwards and have a word with him. Then tomorrow evening I'll pick you up after work and we'll go."

Jennifer waited for Foster in the drawing room. It was strange and lonely being in the big house Johnny had left for her. Rena was busy making plans to go to live in Venezuela, and Jennifer saw little of her. With Johnny away the house was dead, sometimes she was startled by the silence of the place. She had decided to sell the house as soon as she could, and live elsewhere. Whether Foster asked her to marry him or not.

"Jennie," Foster said as soon as he came, "laugh."

"Laugh?"

"Yes. Laugh. I want to hear the sound of your laughter. Let's go out and have a lavish dinner at a Chinese restaurant. And then we'll go dancing some place."

"What's the matter darling?" He looked so pale and worried. It was the first time she had called him 'darling' but he didn't seem to notice.

Foster sat down on Johnny's desk and swung his legs. "Oh nothing," he said wearily. "Jennie, you don't think the world's upside down, do you? And even if you do, you don't allow yourself to be bothered with it? I mean, there's war going on, and a lot of sin and unhappiness. Right here in Trinidad, all this business about progress for the people and better living conditions and the talk about federation, you aren't really interested, are you?"

"I don't always understand you," Jennifer said. "So unhappy and morose—is that word right? But I want to help you if I could. I know I'm not intelligent and bright and can't keep along with you, but I try. Even in speaking to you I talk carefully and take pains to use the right words. All I want out of life is to be happy. I love you, darling. I tell you that because I wasted a lot of years keeping silent with my father—he might have been a different man if I had told him I loved him. I don't feel any shame telling you, even if you don't want me."

"But I want you, Jennie, oh I want you very much." Foster took her in his arms and held her tight. "You don't know what it means to me that you care. Jennie, will you marry me?"

She could hear how his heart was beating loudly and for a minute she pressed against him. Then she loosened herself and said, "Something's happened. That's why you want to marry me."

"Oh, it isn't anything like what you're thinking," he said. But he thought, No, no it isn't, it's much more. This is what it had come to in the end—a decision to make, and he didn't know which way to turn. After all the thought and the reasoning, the long nights with the world spinning in his brain, he had to make a choice. Why was it so difficult? Why couldn't one say yes or no and have done with all the complexity? Why hesitate and ponder, why weigh each thought, why spend life going round and round in circles, never getting there, always thinking, wondering what was the right thing to do? To hell with Father Hope. It was all well and good to talk about the spirit, but one had a body of flesh and bone to contend with, too. And the world, spinning off there in space, the indifferent world, the millions of people utterly unconcerned. How many men were there like Father Hope?

"Marry me Jennie." There was anguish in his voice. "Marry me and we'll be happy. We'll be the happiest people in the world."

"Darling, is that what you really want?"

"Yes. I don't want anything else. Don't make me want anything else, Jennie. Make me want you and the happiness we could know together."

"All right. But if ever afterwards you change your mind, even when we're married, I—I'll let you go if you want. I know what I want to say, but I can't say it. You know how I mean?"

"Yes darling, I know. But I'll always stay with you." He kissed her and she clung to him.

After a while she asked, her words muffled against his chest, "But you look so worried. What's the matter?"

"It's nothing. A friend of mine is in trouble, and I only feel badly because I can't help him."

"Is it serious trouble?"

"Yes. I suppose you might say his world's fallen into little pieces at his feet. But let's not talk about trouble. Let's have a big celebration. Where would you like to go for dinner?"

"Anywhere, as long as it's with you."

The next afternoon Andrews phoned him to say that he would be delayed, as he would be meeting Johnson. "You catch a bus and go on," he told Foster, "and I'll come up later and meet you."

"What does Johnson say about it?"

"You'd be surprised. I hope I may have good news, but I'll let you know for sure when I come."

"What good news, boy?"

"I can't tell you yet, I have to talk again with Johnson. I'll come up as soon as I've seen him."

"Well, you can hear my good news, anyway. Jennie and I are going to be married."

"Really! Congratulations! You aren't rushing things, are you?"

"No. We just decided last night."

"Well, we'll talk when I see you."

After work Foster hurried to George Street to catch a bus. He wanted to get all doubt out of Father Hope as to what he intended to do.

Chapter Twenty-One

Foster was walking into Veronica from the main road as it was a pleasant afternoon and the sting was out of the sun. It was a winding, treacherous road through the hills, but now that he was walking it didn't appear as dangerous as when he was in a vehicle. There was an awesome beauty about the steep cliffs on either side, with the bush growing curiously from the angled faces, which he had never noticed before.

Breathing deeply with the uphill climb, he paused to rest on a low concrete culvert, wondering why it had been built because there were places all along the road as dangerous if not more so.

It was there Father Hope met him, each surprised to see the other. Father Hope answered the obvious question on Foster's lips.

"I'm stretching my legs a little," he said. "I've never been this far out the village yet. It is such a pleasant afternoon, I thought I would take a walk. Isn't it beautiful up here?"

Father Hope looked at the road winding down between the hills and small valleys to the main road in the distance.

"Andrews always complained about how dangerous this road is," he said. "And he also promised to try and get the government to erect walls along the sides. Always promising to do things, that boy."

"Well, you saved me walking to the house," Foster observed. "I didn't think I'd be so tired, else I'd have taken a taxi."

Father Hope sat on the culvert with him.

"Don't tell me what you've come for," he said, "not yet. Let's look at the land." His eyes swept the landscape. "When I was a little boy I used to work in the grapefruit fields with my father—down there," pointing. "And I told myself that wherever I wandered, I would return to live and die in Veronica. I love this place. There's nothing about the valley except a natural beauty, yet I'd rather stay here than live anywhere else in the world."

"You are a reconciled man—it doesn't matter where you are, your spirit is at ease. Father, I must tell you—"

"Oh, let it wait until we get back to the house. It is such a peaceful evening, and it looks as if we shall see the sun set from here."

A villager passed by with a basket laden with fruit and vegetables balanced on his head. He made a respectful sign with his hand to Father Hope.

"Ah, Rampaul. How is your child, is she better?"

"Yes Father. I pray for she."

"That is good. Now you must pray again, but this time with joy. Don't only pray when you are sad and full of trouble. You would not like your friend to visit you when he is in need, and keep away when his crops sell well in the market?"

"No Father."

"Well, God is like that too. Remember. Good-night, Rampaul."

"Yes, Father. Good-night Father."

The villager went on his way, and Father Hope said to Foster, "You see how easy it is. Simple minds, simple people who believe only in right and wrong, and do not allow the world and its ways to intrude on their lives, like you and me. You will like these people, Foster. You will be amazed that they are happy while you, equipped with so much that they haven't got, go on searching endlessly."

"Look Father, I've made up my mind—"

"We will talk about your decision later. I don't want to hear it now. Let us walk a little way."

Foster followed Father Hope resignedly, thinking, If he hopes to talk me into anything he's mistaken. I've made up my mind.

"Tell me Foster," Father Hope clasped his hands behind his back as they walked along, "if you were facing death, what would be your last words?"

"Why, I don't know. I've never thought about it. Wise ones, I hope. Words that will prove I haven't lived in vain. Words that might help the future. But death is more often sudden or brutal, while you're still with the taste of fresh bread you've just eaten, or struggling to save your life. A man doesn't have much time then."

Father Hope had a way of drawing him into conversation but it wasn't going to do any harm to talk.

"Too true. What an awful thing it must be to leave the world with a curse on your lips."

"Do you think the thousands who die every day are singing

'God Save the Queen' or 'The Cuban Love Song' when they fall shattered and bleeding?"

"Ah Foster, you must learn to clean your soul of bitterness and modify your views. You have a most peculiar way of stating yourself. I think I'll be selfish if I had the chance for a few words. I'll be busy making peace with God, not that I would be afraid to die. But I would like to be assured of a place in the hereafter."

"Come to think of it, I'd be terribly afraid to die when the moment comes."

"That's because you have so little faith. Oh there's nothing else, nothing else, my son. You say so yourself, in a roundabout way, and yet you want to go on wasting precious time. Will you not see you are deliberately blinding yourself? Do you expect faith to come surging up like a fountain on your death-bed?"

"I don't want to talk any more, Father. You said yourself it's a pleasant evening, and these are morbid thoughts. Look, the sun is sinking."

"So it is. Perhaps it was that that brought the thought of death to my head. That, or this cliff we are standing on. See how steeply it descends into the valley."

Father Hope got off the road and stood on the narrow strip of grass which was all between the road and sheer space.

Foster looked over and shuddered. "It's dangerous to stand there," he said, turning away. He lit a cigarette and looked for a moment at the sinking sun. The sky was ablaze with a riot of colour. Half of the sun was already shining on another part of the world.

"By the way, Andrews is coming up later. He should be here any minute now. He said he might have some good news." Foster turned as he spoke, ready to walk on.

Father Hope had disappeared.

For a while Foster looked around, puzzled, wondering if he had walked back, expecting him to materialise somewhere in his range of vision. And then his heart began beating like a hammer, and a cold wave of fear swept over him, setting him trembling. He thought he was going to faint and he got down on his knees and put his head between his legs. He got up and peered over the cliff.

"Father Hope?" he shouted stupidly, and the sound of his voice came back faintly from the hills. When he looked down all he could see was the deep green of the vegetation, and his head was giddy.

Foster began to run frantically to and fro, looking for a spot where he might attempt to descend. First he ran up the road, then down, then he ran up again and began to scramble through the thick bush in a frenzy. Darkness was swiftly falling and he could hardly see his way as he skidded and tumbled down, grasping anything in his path to check the headlong descent, and they giving way so that he rolled and pitched downward like a rock let loose from the cliff.

Bleeding and panting and hardly knowing what he was doing, he looked around him. In the gathering darkness every object looked like Father Hope to his frightened imagination and he ran from one to the other in a wild hope. He looked up, trying to gauge whether he was near the spot they had been standing, but it was impossible to tell. He took out his cigarette lighter but it cast a feeble light which was useless. He now began to search blindly, until he was exhausted trampling around in the bush. It was hopeless, yet he went on, losing all sense of time.

Time and again he shouted and listened, the sound of his voice giving him a vague comfort. Then he realised that he was lost. He had strayed from the original spot and he had no idea where he was.

His mind as numb as his body, he began to climb up to the road, feeling nothing now, no sensation of life. There were clots of blood on his face, and his shirt was in ribbons. He didn't know what had happened to his jacket.

After an eternity of climbing he got to the road. He was near to the concrete culvert. He sat on it, his body moving like a bellows as he sucked in the cool air.

After some minutes he lit a cigarette with trembling hands. As his mind cleared he felt a physical sickness and he retched. He felt sharp pains all over his body, and when he rubbed his face the cuts and bruises began to bleed again.

Steadying himself he set off down the road to the spot where Father Hope had been standing. One thought was above all the chaos in his mind, and he went directly to the place. He couldn't tell for sure in the dark, but it was a chance he had to take. Afraid to trust his shaking body, he stretched out on the grass and got his foot to the edge of the cliff. He pounded at it with his heel until a piece of the turf broke away.

He was just in time; down the road the headlights of an

approaching car was playing against the side of the hill as the car turned and twisted on the way up. It couldn't be anybody but Andrews, he thought. Let it be nobody else, please God.

He waved his arms wildly as the car came whining up the hill in second gear.

Andrews slowed down carefully and came to a halt.

"Jesus, what's happened to you, boy?" he came out of the car with his hand still pulling up the hand-brake.

The door opened on the other side and Johnson came out. Foster hadn't expected to see Johnson; he had no time to think what to say.

"There's been an accident," he said slowly.

"What happened?" Andrews looked at Foster closely. "Did you fall off the cliff?"

"It was Father Hope. Get help right away, he might still be alive."

"You'd better let me handle this," Johnson said. "What happened exactly?"

"I don't know. We were standing there talking, and he was peering over the edge. I turned away for a minute and when I looked again he wasn't there." His voice became a mumble. "He wasn't there."

"Did he jump off the cliff, you mean?"

"Oh no," Foster said urgently. "Good lord, how could you think a thing like that? It was an accident. Look, you could see the edge of the cliff is broken where he was standing. I told him it was dangerous."

Johnson turned to Andrews. "Have you got a torch in the car?"

"Yes." Andrews got it, and Johnson took it from him and flashed the beam on the ground.

"Is this the spot?"

"Yes. But we're wasting time talking."

"If he fell off here I'm afraid there's no hope that he may be still alive." Johnson directed the beam down the chasm and turned to Foster. "Didn't you hear him cry out or make a sound?"

"Yes—I did. That's why I turned around. He must have slipped. I went down and had a look around, but I couldn't see anything. We must organise a search party. It happened so suddenly. I can't believe it."

"You're in pretty bad condition yourself. We had better let the local police handle this. Any phone near here, Andrews?"

"No. We'll have to go back to the main road. But a search party could be gathered in the village."

"Good. Foster, you come back with me, you'll have to get attention. Mind if I use your car, Andrews?"

"No. Of course not."

"Then you go on to the village and see if you could organise a search. I'll phone the police and return."

"I'm all right now," Foster said. "Just shaken a bit. Don't worry about me. I'll go with Andrews."

"Sure you're all right?"

"Yes. I'll get something to drink in the village and patch up a bit."

Johnson got into the car. "This is a tragic accident," he said, starting the engine. "I wasn't going to take Father Hope away, after all."

Johnson had to drive on to a place where the road curved and widened a bit to turn. He drove back and waved to them as he went down the hill.

"You ought to have gone with him," Andrews said. "You look in bad shape, old man. How did it happen?"

"I'll be all right." Foster tried to order his thoughts but he felt so wretched and there was an overwhelming dread weighing him down. "What did Johnson mean when he said he wasn't going to take Father Hope away?"

Andrews put his arm around Foster's shoulder to help him along. "He changed his mind about everything. He said it was such a long time ago, and he knew all the circumstances of the case. He was prepared to forget he had ever met Father Hope in Trinidad."

"He wasn't even going to leave it to the local police?"

"No. Why, what's the matter? You're crying!"

"Don't be a fool," Foster sobbed, "I'm not crying. Oh God, why did this have to happen?"

The road swam before his eyes and the trees and the bushes on the hillside toppled down on him. He was glad that that happened, he made no effort to recover himself and when the blackness came he slipped out of Andrews's hold and fell flat.

Two weeks later Andrews drove him to Veronica. They stopped at the scene of the accident and got out. The authorities had erected a flimsy wooden fencing about ten yards long. The press had taken up the matter of the perilous road and a warning sign had been put up near the main road.

It was a warm morning and Foster wore no jacket. It was silent up there on the hill except for the birds singing in the bush and the rustle of leaves. Poui trees were in bloom, wearing a mournful mauve.

"Up to now," Andrews was saying, "I can't get over the tragedy that has happened. What was Father Hope doing out here on the road?"

"I told you. He said he was taking a walk."

"You're not hiding anything from me, are you? I think it was strange for him to have ventured so far." Andrews looked straight at Foster. "Tell me the truth, boy. Did he jump off the cliff?"

"I don't know. I wish to God I knew."

"What were you talking about?"

"Death."

"Did you notice anything unusual about him?"

"You were at the inquest, weren't you? Look, I'm sorry. It's just that I'm feeling sick inside me. As if nothing matters any more. Dreams, ideals, destinations, everything."

"You've got to pull yourself together, you know. You've got to face reality."

"Yes, I know." But he was thinking, I wonder why I burden myself so much when I have you to talk to? His voice grew vicious. "Why the hell shouldn't I tell you? What does it matter? Why should I hold these doubts alone when you could share them? Listen boy. We were walking out here, and talking about death. He was quite his usual self. He stood there for a moment looking down and I said it was dangerous to stand there, and moved away and lit a cigarette. When I looked back he was gone. There wasn't a sound."

"But you said he cried out."

"He didn't. And that is what is driving me mad. Not a sound, as if he had dissolved into the air. Even the broken turf—I did that myself afterwards."

"You thought he had thrown himself off?"

"I didn't think anything, I was desperate. So now you know. You could suffer my torment too—why shouldn't you, eh? You were more his friend than I was. Why the hell shouldn't I tell you, eh?"

Foster smoked and watched Andrews walk up and down. "Thinking, eh?" he mocked. "Wondering, fighting against uneasy thoughts?"

"I don't think Father Hope was that sort of a man. He would have faced the charge—you know that, don't you? You can't believe he committed suicide?"

"Why the hell shouldn't I believe it? He himself said you could never tell what goes on inside a man."

But the faith he had—all the things he stood for. And do take control of yourself. There's no need to shout."

"Ah yes, faith." Foster sat down on the running-board of the car and braced his face with his hands dejectedly. His voice was low now. "I never had the chance to tell him I wasn't going to carry on. All the time he acted as if I would, putting me off when I wanted to speak, as if he were afraid to hear me say no." He raised his voice again unconsciously. "And what sort of bitter irony it is, that you were bringing him the news that he was a free man? What a fool you are, Andrews. You went to all that trouble with Johnson for nothing. Do you think Father Hope would have accepted his freedom at the price of Johnson's conscience?"

"If shouting helps you, then by all means shout."

"Ah, what matter if I shout?" Foster mumbled. "Two and two makes four, the sun is shining, in New York a man rapes a woman, in London the leaders of the world meet to discuss the international situation, God knows what they are doing in China and Timbuctoo. What does anything at all matter, really? Now Father Hope will find out what happened to all the people in the world who died. I wish he would come back and tell me about it. In a dream or a vision or as a ghost or something."

They drove on to the house after Andrews gave up talking to Foster while he was in such a foul mood.

Father Hope had left a letter which the police found bequeathing all his possessions to Foster, and they were going to have a look and decide what was to be done. The accident had received due notice and comment in the press and had been quickly forgotten. Even in Veronica life seemed to be going on as usual, though in their hearts the villagers mourned the loss of the priest who had brought so much comfort and courage into their lives.

Foster was searching the drawers in the room where he and

Father Hope had talked.

"What are you looking for, a suicide note?" Some of Foster's bitterness had transferred to Andrews and he couldn't help getting back at him.

The point had, in fact, occurred to Foster. Perhaps there was some piece of paper which the police had overlooked, some writing which might make sense only to Andrews or himself. It was for his own peace of mind that he wanted to find it, to satisfy himself and put his doubts at rest.

But there was nothing like what he looked for.

"Look at all this balls Father Hope spent his time writing," Foster forced himself to say, lifting sheets of paper and piling them on the table. "A thesis on religion," he said. "All about a universal religion, a common ground. Here, have a read." He shoved a sheet at Andrews.

Andrews read it silently. "It sounds like you, doesn't it?"

"Like me! I don't think any of that stupidness again, boy. I know some answers now. And he thought I was going to continue writing it for him!"

"Well, ain't you?"

"Why, I—I don't know." Foster bent his head to hide the flush on his face.

"You needn't live here, you know," Andrews went on, "but please don't sell the place. Not that anyone would care to have it. It would be nice to come here on weekends, or whenever you wanted peace and quiet. You could use it as a sort of retreat."

"I suppose so." They walked around, looking at the rooms. "It isn't such a bad place. I'll keep it until some other holy man comes to take Father Hope's place."

"No one could take his place. I regret now that I didn't spend more time with him. He was always willing to impart what he knew, and he knew a lot."

They went outside and stood by the church. The villagers had gathered masses of wild flowers and strewn them in the doorway. The flowers were withered and a sickly-sweet smell was in the air. Andrews said, "What with all this business I forgot to tell you that we're having a purge. A royal commission is coming to investigate the administration of the island. We needed this for a long time, and I am pleased to say I had something to do with it. Already there are hints of resignation and signs of alarm, all the rats are scurrying for cover. This will be the best thing that ever happened, I can tell you. With honest, selfless leaders we can go a long way."

Foster didn't hear a word. His thoughts were far away; the smell of the flowers made him feel sick.

"Let's go," he said suddenly.

He was very quiet on the journey back.

"You and Jennie must come to see us soon," Andrews said.

"Yes."

"How long are you going to allow yourself to be upset like this?"

"I'm not upset."

"Like hell you're not. Why don't you go away for a holiday, eh? You and Jennie. To Tobago, or Barbados."

"Yes. I'll do that."

They reached the main road and the car turned in the direction of Port of Spain.

Looking through the windscreen, he tried to shake off the despondency he felt. He could see the world spinning ahead of them. It was as if they were going towards it, but it kept its distance, they were never nearer.

Somehow it didn't seem to matter any more.